THE VOICE OF THE SPIRITS

Also by Xavier-Marie Bonnot in English translation

THE FIRST FINGERPRINT (2008)
THE BEAST OF THE CAMARGUE (2009)

Xavier-Marie Bonnot

THE VOICE OF
THE SPIRITS

A COMMANDANT DE PALMA INVESTIGATION

Translated from the French by
Justin Phipps

MACLEHOSE PRESS
QUERCUS · LONDON

First published in Great Britain in 2012 by

MacLehose Press
an imprint of Quercus
55 Baker Street
7th Floor, South Block
London W1U 8EW

First published in French as *Le Pays oublié du temps*
by Actes Sud, Arles, 2010

Copyright © Xavier-Marie Bonnot, 2010

Published by arrangement with
L'Agence littéraire Pierre Astier & Associés

English translation copyright © 2012 by Justin Phipps

This book is supported by the French Ministry of Foreign Affairs
as part of the Burgess Programme run by the Cultural Department
of the French Embassy in London. www.frenchbooknews.com

Liberté · Égalité · Fraternité
RÉPUBLIQUE FRANÇAISE

A CIP catalogue record for this book is available
from the British Library

ISBN (HB) 978 0 85705 077 9
ISBN (TPB) 978 0 85705 078 6

2 4 6 8 10 9 7 5 3 1

Typeset in 11¼/16pt Minion by Patty Rennie
Printed and bound in Great Britain by Clays Ltd, St Ives plc

For Raphaël, my little prince . . .
And for Albane, who is just starting out on his journey

They were not living beings. We thought they must be our ancestors, come back from the land of the dead. At that time we knew nothing of the outside world. We thought we were the only people alive. We believed our ancestors had gone over there, turned white and come back as spirits. That was how we explained the White Man. Our dead had returned.

Account of an indigenous person from New Guinea describing his first encounter with a white man. Extract from the documentary "First Contact" by Bob Connolly and Robin Anderson (Arundel Productions, 1983)

PROLOGUE

Sepik region, New Guinea – 1936

"Almost there now," Kaïngara said.

Robert Ballancourt nodded and let his eyes drift across the surface of the greasy water. The long dugout canoe slid along noiselessly.

"Just a few more minutes, Robert."

The grey, meandering waters of the River Sepik coiled away into the dense, clammy bush. The warm air was thick with the sweet smell of water hyacinth and decaying dead weed. From time to time, the shrill cry of a cockatoo escaped from the great forest.

"The river is dangerous just here. The current's too strong."

Kaïngara knew the channels through the clawed fingers of the mangroves and the clumps of reeds. With each stroke of the paddle his chest grew taut from the steady movement and the hard muscles tensed beneath his copper-coloured skin.

"You see those whirlpools," he said pointing out eddies in the yellow water, "that's where the spirits of the Elders lie."

As a rule Kaïngara spoke little. Instead he had an open smile that revealed his large ivory teeth.

"The spirits of the ancestors?" Ballancourt asked.

"Yes. Those who have not yet found their home. You need to be careful, there are many whirlpools round here. You must never see a spirit or know where its voice comes from."

"Why's that?"

"It means death . . ."

Kaïngara cast a worried glance towards the clay banks. Hidden archers lying in wait might shower them with arrows. In the front Robert Ballancourt kept his hands clenched on the long, slender sides of the boat. His beige, canvas hat was clamped down over his watery blue eyes. His trousers and rough cotton shirt were spattered with mud and starting to rot. For three days he had been sleeping in the depths of the disease-ridden rain forest, under the heavy, canopied sky, with bats for company. The highland region had furrowed his feverish brow.

"Yuarimo's in that direction," Kaïngara exclaimed, straightening up, his eyes alert. "Over there. We'll be there tomorrow."

They had come to the mouth of Yuat River. On the bank of the river, partly concealed by some Betel palm trees, a strangely pointed roof appeared. Beyond lay the Men's House, with its huge tutelary mask above the entrance casting ferocious looks in all directions. Ballancourt had never seen such a beautiful one.

"These villagers have come across white men," Kaïngara said.

His face had softened, he seemed less anxious. Some warriors armed with spears, bows and arrows watched the visitors in silence. They were naked, with *kotekas* – long penis gourds – across their stomachs. One stepped forward, his skin wizened like old hide.

"It seems they were expecting us," Ballancourt said.

"Yes, news travels fast in the bush."

The dugout landed, grounding on a spit of red mud. Children who had been splashing around in the water clambered back on to the bank and ran towards the village houses. The black pigs rooting among the palm trees were sent scuttling.

The man with the wrinkled skin stepped forward.

"That's the Big Man," Kaïngara warned, looking anxious. "He's the one you have to deal with."

The old man had sparse white curls. Beneath his veined forehead his eyes did not miss the smallest detail of the scene being played out before him. A boar's tusk had been driven through the cartilage of his nasal septum, and it drooped downwards like a thick white moustache. The other men all held back. They had rather wild expressions, curious and suspicious at the same time. Their muscular torsos bore numerous battle scars: thin star-shaped wounds left by barbed arrows and long stripes caused by slashing blades.

The Big Man turned to Kaïngara and questioned him. There was a frightening glint in the old man's eyes and he had the commanding voice of a military leader.

"They are happy you have come to buy things. They say they have much to sell."

"Ask them if it's possible to see the Men's House . . ."

Kaïngara paused to reflect before translating. He knew this was a sensitive area. The Men's House was a restricted place; only the initiated could enter. After an interminable wait, the old man signalled to them to follow.

The Men's House was a huge rectangular construction on stilts. The posts were carved like totem poles; one for each clan. A curtain of dried grass hung from the ceiling, closing off the entrance. Inside the house each pillar, beam, or cross-section of the roof structure was decorated with fantastic figures, or intertwined bodies.

The men remained silent. Some of them were sitting on the ground, others on benches. The Big Man detached himself from the group. He held broad green leaves in his left hand and he pointed to a stool. His gaze was fixed on Ballancourt. He wanted to show them something.

"What's that?" the explorer asked.

Hesitantly, Kaïngara translated: "That's the orator's stool. It represents our first ancestor. We use it to discuss problems in the village or to give out clan names. It is very important. An oath made at the stool can never be broken."

The Big Man uttered some words that seemed to be prescribed by ritual. As he modulated his thin, reedy voice it was as though he was reciting verse. From time to time he whipped the seat with a sharp, powerful gesture.

"When the village had to decide whether to declare war on another village, the stool was consulted," Kaingara nodded as he translated, listening to the Big Man's every word.

The Big Man stared at Ballancourt for a moment then placed three leaves on the seat.

"The first ancestor would command us to go headhunting. In the Men's House everyone would rise to their feet and take their spears from the raised benches. There was great excitement. The headhunting could begin."

The carved face on the stool seemed mysteriously closed. Two cowrie shells split across the middle formed small, almond-shaped eyes that peered into the world of the living. On top of the head was a crown made of marsupial fur. The nose and mouth ended in a long beak; the feet were carved in the shape of birds' feet. They represented the body of the first ancestor. The stool itself was also decorated with shells, pigs' teeth, hair and leaves.

With a swipe of his hat Ballancourt dusted off the back of his trousers. The gesture provoked smiles among the men watching.

"Sell me that stool!"

"I cannot do that," the old man replied, "I'm happy to explain what it is used for, but I can't sell it to you. Never."

"I'll give you all these shillings. There's over twenty here."

"No, stranger."

With a flourish Ballancourt produced some large, shiny coins, "That's a lot of money."

The Big Man's expression lit up. A smile hovered over his toothless mouth which then closed in a hostile pout once more. "No."

The Big Man turned his hands, his palms facing the heavens. He avoided looking in Ballancourt's eyes and repeated, "No."

"It's a sacrilege," Kaïngara added in a low voice, "but if you want there are other things."

Since entering the Men's House Ballancourt had noticed some skulls hanging from ritual hooks. The explorer was captivated by the funereal beauty of one of them. The bone was exposed, smooth like varnish. The eye sockets had been filled with a brown paste in which two round, asymmetrical eyes had been fashioned. Coarse features adorned the skull.

"That one is not from this village," Kaïngara added, "it belonged to one of the enemy. A trophy skull, cut off in battle."

The eyes of the explorer must have betrayed his emotions because the Big Man went up and examined him with an attentive smile.

"And this one?" Ballancourt asked pointing to a more elaborate skull.

"That's an ancestral skull," Kaïngara replied, without translating, "it probably belonged to someone important, like the Big Man here. It's much more beautiful."

One eye flowered from a spiral; the other formed a perfectly round hole. Features in blackish paint like fine tattoos ran in large meandering patterns, from the base of the nose and the corners of the lips, to the top of the forehead. Kaïngara explained that these features recalled the whirlpools of the River Sepik, the place where the spirits resided. The back of the skull was adorned with thick, black curly hair.

"I've never seen anything so evocative of the great mystery of Death," said Ballancourt bending his tall frame slightly towards the Big Man. "It's magnificent. How much does he want for it?"

"He says he needs tobacco for the whole village, glasses like the ones you have in your canoe and some iron tools. It's very expensive."

The old man made a gesture that Ballancourt did not understand. He repeated the same word several times, while letting forth a strange sound from the back of his throat.

"He says that for three iron axes, he will give you the other skull as well."

It was a skull with a shiny forehead, decorated with feathers and white shells. On the nose some small red pearls were set in brown resin.

"It's very beautiful. Tell him I agree. I'll be very proud to show it to people back in France. Tell him it's for a great museum . . ."

"A museum?" Kaïngara asked, surprised.

"Yes. It's a bit like a large Men's House, a place where everyone can come to admire the treasures of the world."

Ballancourt frowned. These skulls were supposed to remain in their sacred resting place in the Men's House, watching over the warriors and their harvests. They had been taken out so the explorers might buy them.

"Where is this head from?" he asked.

The Big Man had understood. He looked away.

"From another village. He doesn't want to say where," Kaïngara whispered.

"Why's that?"

"It's difficult to say. It's taboo, you see. The spirits of the ancestors continue to live in those skulls."

Ballancourt took a skull in his hands that a younger man held out to him. As he felt the jaw in his palms, he sensed he was crossing a sacred boundary.

"Tell me how you go headhunting," he said.

Kaïngara smiled at the question then translated straightaway.

The Big Man disappeared for a moment and returned with a long dagger, which he brandished in Ballancourt's direction.

"We used to use bamboo knives," he said in a voice that had suddenly become high-pitched.

He circled round Ballancourt, miming the gestures, "See: I stab you like this, again and again, right round your head. That's how I cut it off."

The Big Man tucked the large knife between his legs and grabbed hold of Ballancourt's head. He shook it from right to left with small, jerky movements then pulled it towards him. The explorer's hair was all out of place. He smiled, a bit disoriented by the amused looks directed at him and the giggling coming from groups of children.

"That's how you cut off a head. It's very easy. Then I hang it round my neck and take it back to the village. For three days we dance and celebrate."

Ballancourt imagined the bloody head hanging from the Big Man's chest. He could hear the furious battle cries; the wailing of women; the whistle of arrows.

"Have you cut off many heads?"

As Kaïngara translated, the Big Man gave a small cry and slapped his knees, "Several dozen."

A murmur of admiration and fear ran through the men who were sitting on the ground, beating themselves with plaited straw in a vain attempt to drive away the flies and voracious mosquitoes. Ballancourt pointed at the ancestral skull.

"Does a head that's been cut off have special powers?"

The Big Man closed his red-rimmed eyes and breathed deeply.

"For them, yes, it does," Kaïngara said. "Because of it the spirit ceases to wander. It regains human form. The Big Man says he will sell it to you because the missionaries forbid us to own these things and they want us to destroy them."

An inquisitive woman came forward. Her little boy had snuggled up against her leg and was staring at Ballancourt with wide eyes. The Big Man was standing in the middle of a group of Elders, a large bow and long reed arrows in his hand. He had stopped smiling. His face was solemn and his tone grave.

"Here," he said, "this belonged to the man whose skull and bows and arrows you have. Everyone here praised his skills as a warrior. He was the best among us. His weapons are for you."

"What was this warrior called?" Ballancourt asked.

The men seemed embarrassed and looked away. In the distance, between the houses raised on skeletal stilts, a strange cry came through the curtain of birdsong. The sound of women wailing. A clan in mourning. An important man had died.

"Should we leave now?"

"Yes," Kaïngara said in a dark voice.

That night two warriors would take over from the women, playing sacred flutes, those long wooden pipes that produce a spell-binding, thin sound. The voice of the spirits.

They left the River Yuat and went off down the Sepik, which was more turbulent. The canoe slipped quickly through the evening shadows. Silhouettes moved along the earth banks, disappearing into the already dark recesses. Faces appeared in the eddies and whirl-pools, before immediately disappearing again into the depths of the river.

On the bank a warrior observed the strangers. His headdress of paradise bird feathers, carmine and gold, fluttered in the breeze. He had painted his face with dazzling yellow and red strokes; the rest of his body was coated in pig fat blackened by smoke. He raised his spear in their direction and hurled curses at them.

"What's he shouting?" Ballancourt asked.

"Who do you mean?" Kaïngara returned the question.

"That man on the bank, between those two large sago palms. He's wearing a big, white cowrie-shell necklace. Can't you hear him?"

"No."

The guide scoured the bank. Nothing could escape his hunter's eyes.

"I don't see anyone."

"Look more carefully. He's running along the bank."

"There's nobody there, Robert. Nobody."

Kaïngara dug his paddle into the dark water and pushed with all his might, as though he wanted to escape.

"Keep your eyes shut, Robert. Great misfortune strikes anyone who sees a spirit."

Ballancourt closed his eyes. In spite of the heat he shuddered.

PART ONE

THE MEN'S HOUSE

·SEVENTY YEARS LATER·

1

A hand jutted out from the jacket sleeve. A clawed, cold hand; slowly wizened by old age.

Shaken, Michel de Palma took two steps back. The man had died in his armchair. A mask made out of vegetable fibres covered his face, shaped in the form of a red heart. The colour had faded. Two fantastic white eyes bulged, open wide and separated by a black septum. White filaments dangled from an oval mouth.

"How do doctors die?" de Palma wondered out loud.

A huge display cabinet spanned the entire length of one wall. A line of other masks: figures drawn with sharp patterns, slanting eyes, narrow as buttonholes. There was now a gap where the mask covering the deceased's face had been. Some weapons; daggers apparently made out of bone; about a dozen statuettes; a round stain in the dust.

"One of the pieces is missing," de Palma told himself.

Facing the corpse, a book lay open on the desk: Sigmund Freud's *Totem and Taboo*.* On page 213 a passage had been underlined:

One day the brothers who had been driven out came together, killed and devoured their father and so made an end to the patriarchal horde. United, they had the courage to do and succeeded in doing what would have been impossible for

---

* Sigmund Freud (1913), *Totem and Taboo* (Routledge Classics 2001).

them individually. (Some cultural advance, perhaps, command over some new weapon, had given them a sense of superior strength.) Cannibal savages as they were, it goes without saying that they devoured their victim as well as killing him. The violent primal father had doubtless been the feared and envied model of each one of the company of brothers: and in the act of devouring him they accomplished their identification with him, and each one of them acquired a portion of his strength. The totem meal, which is perhaps mankind's earliest festival, would thus be a repetition and a commemoration of this memorable and criminal deed, which was the beginning of so many things – of social organization, of moral restrictions and of religion.

The underlining was not recent. The ink, probably from a quill, had turned a sepia colour. It was a 1920 edition.

De Palma replayed the night's events. The duty team on the second floor of Évêché police station in Marseille; a call to the divisional branch.

"I want to speak to the Murder Squad."

The call was from a phone box. A man's voice, with a strong Marseille accent.

"I'm putting you through to the Central Commissariat," the operator replied frostily.

"I don't want that lot! I want the Murder Squad, the C.I.D.! Put me through to the Murder Squad, do you understand?"

The operator hesitated.

"Come on, move it. Pull your finger out, you bitch!"

The telephone played "A Little Night Music", a string of high-pitched notes churned out by a digital horn. With both feet up on his desk, de Palma was finishing a slice of pizza. It was a warm, peaceful night. He was relishing the chance of a quiet shift, his nose in a sailing manual and Mahler's "Kindertotenlieder" in his ears.

In this weather, in this downpour,
I would never have sent the children out.
They have been carried away!
I wasn't able to warn them!

He was between the channel markers, green to starboard, red on the port side. If he was ever going to sail he had to learn all that stuff by heart. He had always dreamed of faraway lands. The brutal ocean, the wind roaring in the rigging.

The squad telephone rang.

"I've got someone on the line. Sounds like it could be something serious."

"O.K., take a note of the number if it comes up."

"I've done that."

Then came the beeping sound of the call being transferred, and a sound of breathing. Every so often, cars raced by. The person must be standing next to a busy road.

"Murder Squad, Commandant de Palma speaking."

"About time, boss," the words came out in a splutter; a fragile tone, denoting panic.

De Palma stood up and reached for a phone pad, "Who are you?"

"Bugger that! Now you listen to me. There's a bloke down his place, and he's all mashed up. Stiff as a poker."

"Hang on, can you give me . . ."

"Rue Notre-Dame-des-Grâces. I've forgotten the number. The gate's open. You can't miss it. It's the big house with green shutters, right at the end, facing the sea."

"Can you say that again?"

"No, I can't! I've had it with you lot. It's got nothing to do with me. Do you understand, the bloke calling you's done nothing. All I done was discover stuff. I'm a robber, not a murderer!"

The voice of the night hung up. De Palma had a nasty feeling. He knew the road that ended by the rocks near a cove. He got up and wanted to have a slow stretch, but he felt jumpy. He had slept for a while in his chair. No dreams or nightmares, just the emptiness of the night. The refrain from "Kindertotenlieder" had been bouncing around in his head.

In this weather, in this storm,
They rest as in their mother's house.
No storm will threaten them,
They are protected by God's hand.

De Palma parked the squad's Renault Clio at the end of rue Notre-Dame-des-Grâces. Death was lurking there, muzzling him in the back. It was all too familiar, so he put off the encounter for a few minutes, his gaze straying across the Anse des Cuivres.

The day had been a warm one. A late autumnal sun; soft as a ball of saffron. The air loaded with sweat from the sea. Down below the lapping of water against the fragmented rocks, a spreading smell of salt and dried seaweed. Beyond the bay it was dark along the coast as far as the faint lights of La Madrague and Les Goudes.

The house had the appearance of a colonial villa. It could not be seen from the road, or from the coastal path. Above a maze of alleyways and secrets; tiny gardens created from local stone; a three-star Michelin restaurant, and villas surrounded by fishermen's huts with walls of sand. This labyrinth of cobbled streets and terraces ran down towards the sea.

De Palma fetched a torch from the boot of his car. The gate of number thirty-eight was open. The brass numbers in the wall glinted softly. De Palma stroked them with the end of his fingers as though to reassure himself. He took out his Bodyguard. His heart pumped the blood faster through his arteries.

"I hope there isn't an alarm," he said to himself, "I can't stand those things."

14

"That burglar of yours has already taken care of it," an inner voice said.

The small grounds surrounding the house looked over the sea. By a kidney-shaped swimming pool an enormous rhododendron gave off a rotting smell of peat. De Palma shone his torch up at the front of the house. The beam lit up a windowpane on the ground floor like two piercing eyes shooting fiery glances. The policeman shuddered, overcome by fear. Normally he dealt with this by reciting his multiplication tables or by singing something lively and combative from "Il Trovatore."

The horrible blaze of that pyre burns . . .

A grey stone flight of steps; a metal and glass double door ajar; and on the right a plaque that shone in the beam of his Maglite torch.

DR FERNAND DELORME

NEUROSURGEON

MEMBER OF

THE INTERNATIONAL SOCIETY FOR NEUROSURGERY

"Rather unusual to hang a plaque inside," de Palma said aloud, in an attempt to convince himself he was not alone.

"It was outside before," the inner voice replied.

"How do you know that? Did you know Dr Delorme?"

"He was a top specialist in epilepsy and a very distinguished man. Respected throughout the world."

The entrance hall was laid with large vermilion hexagonal floor tiles, featuring a rosette pattern in the middle. Two stone staircases met on the floor above, between two sets of banisters and a double door. De Palma cocked the hammer on his weapon and pushed open one of the doors.

A panelled hallway led to a door set between rows of books. De

Palma turned the handle, his hand wrapped in a handkerchief. He felt around for the switch then flooded the room with light. The dead man lay in his office chair, shoulders slumped.

De Palma looked once again at the book by Freud. Was it sheer chance, or had it been stage-managed? The reference to early cannibalism was perhaps not fortuitous. He had had to deal with this sort of thing in the past; such events were extremely rare.

"*Totem and Taboo*," he said.

He tried to work out the significance of those two words. For him the first one conjured up a picture of a mythical being and a guardian spirit, the second denoted something absolutely forbidden. Something sacred.

"Anyone who violates the taboo is punished by death," the small voice said, "You know that."

"Yes, the person or animal that no-one may touch because their power is so great and dangerous."

A deep, very soft, sound like a note only just formed, rose up from nowhere. The mask covering the dead man's head had moved. The figures arranged in the display cabinet had darkened.

A whistling sound broke through the silence once again. De Palma froze. He raised his gun to eye level, left the study, and slowly headed towards the source of the sound.

A large drawing room occupied the left wing of the house. Masks of every size, with large, dark, round eyes ran along walls that were lined with ochre-coloured paper. Three large pictures depicted faces blurred by a thin veil of grey paint. De Palma put down his torch on one of the bookshelves and listened to the night for a long time. Nothing; only the distant sound of waves lashing on the rocks of the Anse des Cuivres.

On a small piece of walnut furniture there was a black-and-white photograph in a silver frame: a schooner, with all sails set, her jibs bellying out.

16

In the grounds the early morning wind rustled in the shrubs. Dead leaves had been piled up against the trunk of a large cedar tree; and then turned back as though someone had wanted to search inside. De Palma was on the point of leaving when once again he heard a strange sound a few steps behind him. Not a noise, but a sound of breathing concealed behind a partition or a piece of furniture. A presence. The smirking, sleeping statues awoke.

Nobody could be there. Nobody. He had been round the entire room.

The breathing became more distinct, like the plaintive timbre of panpipes. The shrill notes seemed to come from higher up, from one of the floors above.

De Palma slowly climbed the stone staircase, keeping his back to the wall, and his revolver pointed at the landing above. The sound of the flute grew louder. It was primal music that whined; thin and repetitive.

At the top of the stairs there was a door immediately on the left. De Palma kicked the door open, and then shone his torch inside. The sound of the flute stopped. A collection of old toys was lying on a long shelf: china dolls with pale faces and die-cast steel cars in garish colours. A teddy bear with glassy eyes stared at the ceiling.

"No-one can have slept in this room since the 1930s," de Palma said aloud.

The tune began again, faster this time, as though the player were panting down a long pipe. De Palma moved towards the second door and slowly turned the handle. The music stopped abruptly.

In his head he tried to imagine where he was in relation to the garden. This room overlooked the large cedar; its main branch passed a few inches from the window. The last sound he had heard came from inside the room, he was almost sure of it. He opened the door sharply. The tiny room was empty. A window shutter banged in the wind. The windowpane had been smashed and splinters were strewn across the floor. De Palma ran over and leaned outside. Even an exceptionally agile man would not have been able to vanish in such a short space of time. Through the branches of the cedar it was possible to make out the islands and the lights along the coast.

The music had moved further away. The notes now came from lower down; the drawing room, or perhaps from the office where the corpse lay.

"It must be the wind blowing down one of the pipes in this dump!" de Palma yelled in an effort to keep up his spirits.

The flute stopped dead, but the presence could still be felt, as though it were hiding in some remote part of the house.

De Palma rushed down the stairs, through the garden, and dived into the unmarked squad car.

"Time to call in the cavalry," he whispered, switching on the side-lights. The handset was in the glove compartment.

"Pétanque, this is Solex."

Silence. Then the handset coughed and spluttered into life.

"Pétanque receiving, over."

"De Palma, Murder Squad."

Out at sea, with her sails drawing well, a schooner was moving towards the Planier lighthouse: gateway to the world. The captain was running before the wind on the starboard tack. A plume of white foam washed against the stem. A young sailor had climbed to the top and was frantically waving his cap above his head in a last farewell, as though dedicating his impending voyage to the entire bay.

2

"You alright, Baron?" Jean-Louis Maistre asked, calling his friend by his nickname.

De Palma looked pale and his face was crumpled. "About as right as you can be when you've just discovered a corpse in the middle of the night."

In the dull light Maistre looked as though he had put on weight again. His full cheeks accentuated his chubby face and grey, laughing eyes.

"No sign of a wound," he said. "I reckon it's on the head."

"We'll see about that later," the Baron said.

"I've left my phone in the car."

Maistre went out. De Palma remained sitting in the room for a long while. He forced himself to think of all the possible explanations for this crime. The quote from Freud perhaps pointed to a former patient. "Possible, but a bit too straightforward," the Baron said to himself.

On entering the office once again, Maistre hitched up the holster that dangled down his hip, "Tell me about this call," he mumbled.

"Young voice. Shaky," de Palma replied, reaching for his first Gitane of the day.

"Probably a wino or a junkie . . . they always get the shakes when they're speaking. Could be a burglar who decided he was going to play the responsible citizen and told himself it might be a good idea to report what he's discovered."

"Unless he wanted to put himself in the clear . . ."

"You always see evil everywhere."

"By now I've got good reason to."

"Why did he phone the squad?

"Because he's a con and he knows we're not as dumb as the others."

"That's flattering . . ."

Then there was the crime scene, the origin of the mask itself. In the bookcase there were books on Papuan art. Dr Delorme was evidently a collector of works of art from New Guinea.

Something didn't add up.

"Why steal a single piece from the display cabinet?" Maistre asked.

"You're right. Why not nick the rest?"

"The ways of killers are hard to fathom."

Apart from that one detail there was nothing very specific to go on. A bluish glow spread through the office. It was getting light and the squat peak of Mount Marseilleveyre stood out on the other side of the bay. Maistre called in the forensics team.

In the bookcase some books had recently been disturbed, then put back in spaces that were definitely not the ones assigned to them by Dr Delorme. Alphabetical continuity had been broken in several places. In the bottom row a volume was sticking out: a large Octavo fully bound in leather. De Palma opened it. Vigorous, fine writing covered the edges of the yellowed sheets. Printed on the first page:

Captain Fortuné Meyssonnier
Ship's Log of The Marie-Jeanne
– Two hundred tonne schooner from Paimpol, Brittany

The text started by describing the *Marie-Jeanne:*

She's a stout ship our *Marie-Jeanne*. She's done big fishing in
Iceland in winds as strong as any I've ever known. A ship owner
from Paimpol bought her back before selling her on to Monsieur
Ballancourt. She measures one hundred feet from stem to
stern, and like most boats of her type has only one topsail.

She's a magnificent sailing ship. The owner has given her a
face-lift. She has a red and white hull and painted imitation
gun ports that make her look like a pirate ship.

. . .

All being well we sail within the week. Yesterday we tried
out the whole of the sail locker in a force six gale. I've rarely
seen a sailing ship as easy to handle as our *Marie-Jeanne*. Out
by the Planier lighthouse I had three men hoist the topsail. It
only took us four minutes. It augurs well for the breezes of the
South Pacific.

The crew is excellent, all clean and polite. The Petty Officer,
like me, was formerly in the Messageries Maritimes. He has
already done the long voyage down to the Antipodes. I know
that I can rely on him. He has recruited two more sailors, both
Corsicans like himself, who come from the same village in Cap
Corse.

There is much excitement in the harbour. Children from
the Quartier Saint-Laurent come to pinch oranges that have
fallen from the harbour craft. The temperature is already
warm. At the end of the day the Vierge de la Garde becomes
wrapped in thick mist rising from the bay. At sunset her gold
dress is barely visible any longer, so shrouded is it in cloud.
Even the dilapidated old buildings by the quay and the rented
houses on the Colline des Accoules seem unreal . . .

De Palma shut the logbook once more, crouched down and
looked more closely at the traces of dust and the marks between the
leather bindings.

"Someone has touched this book recently," he said, as he heard Maistre coming into the study.

"Are you sure?"

"Positive. Make a note please . . . Seal number four."

"You think there's a connection with this murder?"

"I think that I don't believe in coincidences."

Maistre looked down, a taste of bile in his mouth. "I need to get a coffee and a croissant."

"There's a bar up the Corniche that opens early. Let's go there."

"Too late, here come the bosses."

The head of the Murder Squad, Commissaire Eric Legendre, burst in with Lieutenant Bessour at his side.

"Morning, Baron."

De Palma greeted the two men with a nod.

"Quite a weird sort of ritual, boss. Not your everyday crime scene. Take a look."

Legendre got his breath back. His jacket was too tight for him, making his short round silhouette bulge even further. Karim Bessour was his exact opposite: he had the physique of a sprinter, a sharp profile and frantic look; threadbare jeans, sports anorak and a Tuareg ring on his right hand. He stepped aside nimbly to let the police forensic technicians pass as they lugged a stretcher.

"You look like death warmed up, boss!" Maistre said, eyeing the Commissaire's red tie which had come adrift on his check shirt. "I reckon there's something moody going on. Have you seen the director?"

"Yes. It seems he never sleeps and he has ears everywhere. He's just phoned to remind me that Delorme was friends with half the town, and enemies with the other half."

"Nobody knows for sure that it's Delorme."

"Maybe not, but we're in his house so the director has got his eyes on us. He reminded me that results-wise we've been up shit creek for some time. His words, not mine."

"Nice!"

Legendre adjusted the knot on his tie.

"Has to be said we've had some really tough cases since the beginning of this year," Bessour put in as he scratched the ground with the tip of his trainer.

The small police forensics van manoeuvred in the grounds to let the ambulance pass. The first few faces appeared at the windows. A dozy-looking woman in a dressing gown leaned over her balcony.

"We're going to remove that thing he's got over his head," said a brigadier from the criminal records office. "You coming?"

Two technicians positioned themselves either side of the corpse and slowly raised the mask. The face appeared, an open mouth revealing decayed teeth. The eyes seemed to retain a glimmer of life. De Palma glanced away on seeing the tiny hole that had pierced the forehead right between the eyes.

"The frontal bone has been perforated," the brigadier said laconically.

"Probably a .22, given the size of the entry point. They leave reliable traces in the skull. The bullet hasn't re-emerged, which you'd expect with a .22. No trace of any gunpowder."

Maistre pointed at a black-and-white photograph in the display cabinet: the portrait of a man of about fifty, with a high forehead, sparse hair and a shrewd look behind his small, round, metal glasses. The puckered lips formed a discreet smile. No doubt about it, the corpse in the armchair was definitely that of Dr Delorme.

"I was scared just now," de Palma said, pulling Maistre aside.

"What of?"

"I don't know. There's something in this house. A presence . . . Like a ghost."

Maistre's eyebrows arched above his watchful eyes. "Sure you're O.K., Baron?"

De Palma glanced around to make sure that no-one was

eavesdropping. "Listen, I heard the sound of a flute. It disappeared, then came back again."

"You mean someone was trying to play the flute while you were here?"

"Yes, I searched all over but I couldn't find anyone."

"I see . . ."

"Don't take the mick, mate. I know what I heard."

Maistre didn't dare look his friend in the eyes for fear of offending him, but it was too late.

De Palma withdrew to the garden. Confused, he thought of the quotation from Freud that he had just placed under seal. It went back to the Oedipus myth and to the birth of mankind.

A sea wind was starting to blow.

*

There were no spaces in the car park at La Timone teaching hospital. The Medico-Legal Institute was situated at the other end, in one of the wings of the infirmary. De Palma parked on the central reservation. Maistre put a Ministry of the Interior card on the dashboard.

"Come on, let's go up."

The body was already lying on the stainless-steel table, naked and skeletal; knees raised.

"The bullet hasn't emerged," Dr Mattei said, turning to the policemen. "I think we should find it in good condition. I'm waiting for the X-rays," he mumbled.

The neon light of the post-mortem room gave a ghostly sheen to his greying mane. He always kept it swept back and smoothed down with a discreet gel. His damp, domed forehead shone almost as much as the surgical instruments lying on the stainless steel trolley.

"Tell me, Dr Death," de Palma said, indicating the corpse laid out on the marble, "what do you think about this hole? Looks tiny to me . . ."

Mattei placed his index finger, which was covered in a latex glove,

24

on the edge of the small orifice. The blood had dried in a brown corolla. "Could be a .22," he remarked, blinking his eyes, "unless it's one of those vicious military weapons that goes deep into the body and spins like a top once inside. The hole is tiny, but the wounds are terrible; and always fatal."

The thin sound of a surgical saw came through the partition. Mattei retied the knot of his apron around his ample paunch. "Little ones O.K., Jean-Louis?"

The doctor always asked this type of incongruous question right in the middle of a post-mortem.

"They're grown up now," Maistre replied with a weak smile. "They've flown the nest and can stand on their own two feet."

"Yeah, you get there in the end. I heard they did very well with their studies . . ."

Maistre was going to reply when a beanpole of an assistant, oval glasses on a set-square nose, pushed open the double door and held out a set of X-rays. "It doesn't make sense!"

With his gnarled hands, the assistant attached the negatives to a luminous panel. There were four shots of the skull: three taken head on and one in profile. "There's no tip to the projectile," he said.

"What do you mean?" Mattei asked in surprise, glancing at the two policemen.

The assistant shook his head and pulled a felt-tip pen from the pocket of his white coat. He pointed at the projectile's point of entry, "There's no exit point," he said, tracing an imaginary trajectory. "One can see that the frontal lobe has been damaged and there are clear traces of haemorrhaging here."

Mattei moved closer, silent. His sharp eyes darting constantly from one negative to the other, then back again, "I've never seen anything like it!" he declared after examining them for a few seconds. His eyes settled on a profile shot of the cranium, "What is that thing?" he said, raising his voice.

The assistant drew a circle around what looked like a thin needle about ten centimetres long that had pierced the cerebral matter. De Palma and Maistre glanced over the shoulders of the two forensic scientists.

"Right, let's not argue about it," Mattei broke off. "Let's open it up and see." He caught hold of the instrument trolley and slid it over so that it was level with the shoulders of the corpse.

"I imagine you'll want to know what's what straightaway," he said turning to the detectives.

"Yes," de Palma said.

The scalpel made a crescent-shaped gash in the scalp. Mattei removed the skin and exposed the cranial bone. The saw started up. De Palma turned away so as not to see.

The forensic scientist again looked over towards the luminous panel and examined the X-ray. Two anxious lines ran across his forehead. Minutes passed, interspersed from time to time with the clinking of the pincers, blades and scissors that Mattei placed on the steel tray.

"I'd say it's a splinter," he said suddenly, placing a thin, blood-stained needle in a small steel dish. He went over to a tiled table and put the dish beside a microscope. De Palma and Maistre stood on either side of the doctor.

"It looks like wood," Mattei added, placing the needle under the lens of the microscope. Beads of sweat stood out on his brow, following the line of his wrinkles. He screwed up his eyes several times as he rested them on the eyepieces, "Wood," he murmured after a few seconds. "Could be bamboo, or something like that."

"Bamboo!" Maistre exclaimed.

Mattei stood up straight again, looking doubtful, "It's the only wood I know that produces splinters as long and fine as that. But I'm not an expert. Far from it . . ."

The assistant took several photographs of the needle. In two of them, which had been taken after the needle had been cleaned, the wood fibres were clearly visible.

26

"We'll have a little look and see what he's got in his stomach," Mattei said. "Any other questions, gentlemen?"

Maistre shook his head and put his notebook back in his yellowish-brown leather briefcase. "No."

The assistant had thrown a blue cloth over the back of Dr Delorme's head. With its thin smile and smooth skin the face seemed unreal.

The last rays of sunlight broke through the clouds as de Palma and Maistre arrived at the car park. Maistre was thinking of his children. Life without them wasn't easy. He often phoned them, but each time he did so he felt they were drifting away from him a little bit more.

"I'm going to put on some music," the Baron said.

"No opera, please."

"What do you want then?"

"You know what . . ."

"You can't be serious! Not the Clash! Can you see us zigzagging between the cars with our siren on and the flashing light, playing 'I Fought the Law' at full blast?"

"And why not?" Maistre sighed.

"Opera's best for civil servants like us. Policemen are lone wolves. We need a bit of poetry in our lives. I'm sure there'd be less blunders if the Minister insisted on having the great arias playing in the vans."

"Nice idea, but no Wagner!"

"Especially when the riot squad wades in . . ."

The Baron lowered the shade marked "Police" and stuck the blue flashing light on the roof.

"Drop me on avenue de la Capelette," he said. "I'll do the last bit on foot."

"You going back home?"

"Yep."

"I wanted to ask you round for the pastis ritual."

"Sorry about that, you'll have to say Mass without me. I'm going to try and get some kip."

There was a peppery smell in avenue de la Capelette. A crawling line of cars stretched back as far as the Pont-de-Vivaux district and the large Saint-Loup dormitory estates at the foot of the Massif de l'Étoile.

De Palma walked slowly, so he could savour the area where he had grown up. Striding along through these streets lined with houses that had never been renovated gave him a sensation of time standing still; a reassuring slowness. Finding once more the familiar chalk graffiti: a heart with an arrow, sets of initials; promises of everlasting love.

Behind l'église Saint-Jean, mechanical diggers were in the process of demolishing the high stone walls surrounding the workshops and factories. It was a linear, dreary world, the sunshine notwithstanding. In the 1960s Michel used to go there looking for nuggets of sulphur that had fallen from the scoops. He would then quietly swap these for marbles in the school playground in rue Laugier, convinced that such clandestine transactions would be forbidden by the teacher in the grey blouse.

The door to the boulangerie-pâtisserie Louis XV was open; a smell of warm bread titillating the nostrils of passers-by. Eva, the new assistant, was a childhood friend of the Baron's, and five years his junior. She was talking hairstyles with a woman who sported an enormous silk butterfly across her brown chest. The Baron paused, frozen for a moment amongst the smells of flour and chocolate as he tried to recapture images from his childhood.

"Michel, how are you?" Eva asked, closing the till drawer.

"Fine and you?"

She shot him a teasing look and offered him her cheek.

"So you're working in the bakery now?" the Baron said.

"Yes . . ."

She rested a hand on her hip. Her long chestnut hair tied in a bandanna gave a mischievous look to the little Madonna's face. Two firm, imposing breasts stuck out under a mohair jumper that was flecked with flour. Time didn't seem to have left its mark on Eva. She had put on a bit of weight. That was all.

"I'm about to get divorced, you know!"

"No, I didn't know," de Palma said.

She had highlighted the green of her soft eyes with two thin black lines.

"Which is why I need to work."

"That's good to hear."

"That I'm working?"

"No, that you're free . . ."

She roared with laughter, lips pursed over her small teeth. De Palma was over six feet tall and he looked down at her with the attentiveness of an older brother.

He pined at the school gate, leaning against the enormous trunk of a plane tree. The wind had blown off the dead leaves which rustled underfoot. At five in the afternoon the chemical factory siren emitted a long, doleful blast into the silent streets. The school clock also rang out, its tone more shrill. Eva was the last to emerge, wearing a pink T-shirt. Her girlfriends sniggered on seeing her meeting Michel; the biggest one was chewing gum and flashing her front teeth.

"You been waiting for me?" Eva asked in a tiny voice.

"Yeah. I'm here. Are you pleased?"

She did not reply. He offered her a cigarette which she rejected. His attempts at being a lad were awkward. He knew that girls liked him, but he disguised his shyness, growing his hair long in an attempt to look like Jim Morrison.

"Come on. My friends won't stop staring at us and it's getting on my nerves."

De Palma took her hand. It was the first time and it gave him a funny feeling to hold her thin, manicured fingers in the palm of his hand. They went off in the direction of the Huveaune, a trickle of a

river that ended right in the middle of the Prado beach; along a dead-
end street where stolen vehicles rotted away. Near the water, a bench
had survived.

"Let's go somewhere else," Michel said. He didn't want to kiss her in
the middle of this tip.

Eva's hand was moist, "Where then?"

"In the park at the convent. I know a way in."

Eva was walking on air.

"Are you daydreaming?"

"No, just some old memories from the past," de Palma said.

"What memories?"

"I can't tell you . . ."

She pouted her lips, as if to say: "I've got you sussed."

"What can I get you?"

"I'll have two portions of pizza and an anchovy loaf."

Eva had retained a sweet charm. A few wrinkles ran across her long face and there were crow's feet at the corners of her sparkling eyes.

"Your divorce going alright?" the Baron asked, getting out his wallet.

"We're grown-ups now," she said wearily.

"Or so we like to think."

"You divorced too?"

"Yep."

They looked at one another, lost for words. His divorce had caused an upheaval in his life and he was still feeling the shockwaves. He felt awkward in the presence of this woman who was still confident in her own beauty; and looked at him searchingly.

"See you . . ."

"See you . . ."

One day a woman brought forth into the world two magnificent eagles. These two lords of the air grew up under their mother's protection. When they were quite strong, they started to attack other members of their family, then others close to them and finally the people from their village. Everywhere, they sowed the seeds of desolation and destroyed the harmony in that peaceful society. Several times they killed and ate their victims.

Their mother taught them first to respect the life of their own. She denied them everything that a mother can give her children. Seeing that was not sufficient she ordered them to attack the neighbouring villages and to bring back the heads of the vanquished as trophies.

So the eagles stopped killing those close to them and that is how the tradition of headhunting was born.

Headhunting origin myth among the
Iatmul of Papua New Guinea

3

The visitor entered the auction rooms at the last minute, holding a rolled-up catalogue. The air was heavy with expectation that had been building up since early morning. No hubbub, not a murmur, just the creaking of the floorboards and the panelling on the high walls; furtive, curious glances; discreet consultations. The visitor didn't feel at ease. It was too confined; he was afraid of being recognized.

And yet it would have taken an incredible coincidence for the man he sought to notice him. So many years had passed. The visitor's hatred might have stayed with him, but his physical appearance had changed. However, you could never be too careful, he reminded himself, adjusting the glasses on his nose which was beaded with sweat.

No doubt it was stupid to think so, but he had the distinct impression that he stood out among these connoisseurs and people from the art world. For the most part they were middle-aged men, bimbos and agents with avaricious smiles. Some of them broke with the prevailing monotony of dark suits and austere ties, in an attempt to look like laid-back artists.

The visitor spotted the person he was looking for in the second row and muttered the man's name several times between his teeth: Grégory Voirnec. With wild grey hair and a Trobriand Island bracelet round his wrist, he had aged quite a bit since the visitor had last come across him. Although his chin sagged more and the small wrinkles on his forehead had grown a little deeper, the man's very fresh, almost naïve expession had not changed.

"Lot number 8718. A trophy skull from the Monteil private collection."

It was the piece the visitor had been waiting for. He stood on tiptoe to get a better view. The auctioneer glanced around the room over his half-moons. His round face shone. He had rested his elbows on the rostrum to give himself more height.

"This is a rare piece from New Guinea, dating from the beginning of the last century. An over-modelled skull in the purest Upper Sepik tradition."

An assistant in white gloves and black jacket lifted up the modelled head and moved it before his eyes like a priest displaying a monstrance to the congregation. Scrolled patterns covered the dead face. Braided, black hair hung from the back and a beard of white shells emphasized the chin. The visitor had not been mistaken; it was the head he was looking for. Voirnec had led him straight to it.

"A magnificent piece," added the auctioneer. "Going for 5,000 euros."

A plump man made a discreet gesture with his pen.

"5,500 to my left, 6,000 . . . 500 . . ."

Voirnec raised his finger.

"7,000."

A man in his eighties raised his arm, his face flushed from the heat. The bidding went up to 50,000 euros. The visitor noted each bid and the face of the person making it. He felt giddy. So much money and not one of them knew its real value. After ten minutes, there were only two bidders left: Voirnec and the eighty-year-old. Neither of whom looked at the other.

"60,000 . . . going . . . going . . ."

The old man raised his hand, then it was Voirnec's turn, and so it continued, like a duel without foils. In the audience most purchasers seemed to be losing interest in the bidding, making notes in their catalogues instead.

"90,000 euros . . . going . . . going: sold to the gentleman on my left!"

Voirnec was the winner. His neighbour congratulated him with a ferocious smile. As usual he showed no emotion, pinning his pen in the inside pocket of his jacket and closing his catalogue. The visitor left swiftly, waiting for him outside on the pavement opposite the auction rooms.

Clouds hung from the zinc roofs of Paris. After about ten minutes Voirnec appeared, empty-handed, through the door of the auction rooms. The visitor had assumed that purchasers would leave the auction with the piece they had just acquired under their arm, but he must have been wrong about that. He pursed his lips. That would have been too good to be true.

He followed Voirnec along the banks of the River Seine towards the Institute. The antiques dealer walked at a brisk pace, his hands stuffed in his pockets, indifferent to everything going on around him. Past the Académie, he went under the porch that led directly on to the rue de Seine. Outside the Roger-Viollet photographic agency Voirnec briefly said "hello" to a passer-by, then took the first turning on the left. The visitor did not stop for fear he might be discovered. He spent a good ten minutes dawdling outside the picture galleries on the rue de Seine, and then retraced his steps.

Voirnec had gone back to the galerie Rigodon. He was talking to a rather pretty young lady with chestnut hair, who must be his secretary. From the shop window, statuettes from the New Hebrides stared out into the road, indifferent to the passers-by who stopped to look at them from time to time. Negroid masks on shiny metal display stands sported mysterious smiles.

The visitor glanced at the brass plaque.

GRÉGORY VOIRNEC — ANTIQUES

OPENING HOURS — TUESDAY—SATURDAY 10.00—19.00 HRS

He turned and went back to the rue de Seine. In a few hours it would be nightfall. "Time to return," he said to himself.

*

He had a room in a cheap hotel on rue Ernestine in northern Paris. A scrap-iron bed, with grubby sheets; wallpaper with large flowers eaten away by time. The window overhung the railway lines that ran in long curvy lines towards the suburbs. The tracks looked like silver threads snaking through the black and red ballast. The tower blocks on a council estate stood out through the crosspieces of a bridge; engulfed in the mist. He turned away from the view and took a long shower to get rid of the unpleasant city smells. The hot water calmed him a little. He thought of his mother and of the baths that she used to give him, pouring the water over his tiny child's shoulders. He could feel the vibrations, then the echo, of her voice like honey. His mother's lips were dreamy and her eyes glinted like mica when she smiled at him.

His father's face was always disordered in his memory; it was complex and endless like an unfinished jigsaw puzzle. The face was smooth, regular, almost emaciated. First he had admired, and then hated, that mysterious expression. Hated that haughty, aquiline nose, those bushy eyebrows, those triumphant eyes, and the fine marks of old age that spoke of a history that was out of the ordinary.

For a time this face had no bearing on him, only the anger behind it. He knew how to tell the difference. Over the years he had ended up realizing that his father had also been a victim, just like his mother.

He opened his wallet and looked at the photograph of his sweetheart. The gentle curves of her cheeks; her velvety skin and wavy hair that fell across her shoulders; that smile which resembled his mother's. A miracle in his life. But this woman still spurned him. She belonged to him in another world, another life. In any case it would all happen far too late. Now was a time for hatred, for the cold anger that would make him strong which would not allow his arm to fail.

He remained naked for a good while, standing upright in the centre of the room.

The photograph in the auction rooms' catalogue had come out very well. The modelled head was perfectly lit and a touch mysterious, set against the black background. The sculptor had known how to depict the dead man's nobility; his regular features and high forehead; the slightly flat nose and raised cheekbones. He had painted a kind of domino mask around the eyes with complex whirls running from the base of the nose to the forehead. The eyes were formed of round spiral holes that penetrated deep into the soul of any onlooker.

He waited.

First came the long lament, the meaning of which no-one understood. Secret words that even the initiated did not know.

A sacred flute breathed his name into the long wooden pipe, once initially, then again and again, until it kept being repeated between two breaths.

The rain beat at the windowpanes. The visitor got dressed and swiftly went out. The hotel caretaker, who was sitting in front of a crackling television programme in Arabic, did not even notice him.

4

There was a smell of rusty metal in the air. It was hot under the creeping vine that had reddened in the sun. Large bunches of purplish grapes were already ripe. The Sunday meal was coming to an end. Michel's father was smoking a Gitane Maïs as he read the communist rag La Marseillaise. *He was filling in time working the Corsican ferries as he waited for his retirement. Thirty years at sea had etched deep lines on his brow and around his eyes.*

His mother was bent over the stone sink in the kitchen, cleaning the plates with a slow graceful gesture. She was wearing an apron with small flowers, and her hair was loose. White streaks had appeared a few weeks previously. Michel didn't like these marks of the passage of time. He wanted her to remain his queen forever. Under her apron she wore a rather tight-fitting suit that she only put on for Mass on Sundays, and the brooch that her father had brought back from Pondicherry when he worked for the Messageries Maritimes. She was beautiful in the way Italian women are. Brown skin, proud breasts and dark, heavy-lidded, powerful eyes; her hands still fine despite all those hours of housework.

"I'm going out."

"Where are you off to?" his mother asked.

"The pictures."

Late in the afternoon, de Palma met Eva near L'Escale cinema at Pont-de-Vivaux. It only showed spaghetti westerns: the entire "Trinity" series with Bud Spencer and Terence Hill. Garish posters framed the door of the auditorium. A group of posers from Saint-Loup eyed up Eva, Gauloises Bleues hanging from the corner of their mouths. She was wearing flared trousers that hugged her figure tight and a roll-neck sweater that enhanced her breasts.

"What are you doing?" he asked.

"I'm going home," she said, looking away.

"Do you want me to come with you?"

"No, Richard's offered to take me back."

Richard already had a car. He had a job at the Nestlé factory in Saint-Marcel where his dad was a supervisor; he'd made use of his connections. Michel backed away. Eva wanted to make him stay, but he was hurt.

By nine o'clock a lawyer was already waiting in the corridor at the Murder Squad; a middle-aged man in a dark suit with a domed forehead and relaxed manners. He was sending a text on his gleaming Blackberry when de Palma strolled by, his head still dizzy with the night's events.

"Monsieur de Palma?" the lawyer said getting up.

"Yes."

"Maître Blanchard, from the Paris Bar. I represent Bérénice Delorme, Dr Delorme's granddaughter."

De Palma gripped the hand extended by the lawyer, giving it a hearty shake, "This is the first time in my career that a lawyer has come to talk to me about a case that's still in progress. I'll have you know I don't much like it."

Blanchard broke into his sales rep smile, "Your frankness does you credit. Dr Delorme wasn't an ordinary man . . ."

"Well you're usually supposed to contact the Examining Magistrate," de Palma interrupted, stopping at the entrance to his office. "Melville has been appointed."

"I have a meeting with him at the end of the morning."

"In that case go and see my Commissaire," the Baron grumbled, ready to slam the door in the lawyer's face.

"It was he who sent me to you," Blanchard persisted.

De Palma remained silent long enough to curse the head of the Squad. He cast a sidelong glance towards Legendre's office. The door was shut, a sure sign that he wasn't on the premises.

"Alright then, come in and make yourself at home. My colleagues haven't arrived yet. Your client isn't here?"

"She was abroad when I gave her the sad news. She was shattered by it. She's caught the first plane and should be here soon."

De Palma threw his jacket on the back of the chair and switched on his computer. Then he took out his weapon, tipped up the barrel to remove the bullets and put it away in his drawer. He hated lawyers as much as the Director of the C.I.D. or, for that matter, soggy chips. Some bitter experiences in the Criminal Court had taught him to be wary of defence lawyers. In their presence he had the unpleasant feeling of being thrown against the ropes and forced on to the attack to prevent himself from being floored.

"Can I offer you a coffee, Maître?"

"No, no thank you," Blanchard said, recalling the dishwater he had seen dribbling from the squad percolator a few minutes earlier.

The Baron's office was covered in folders which were stuffed with notes and photographs. Lifting a pile of papers, he came across a Maria Callas compilation that he had been looking for the night before.

"What do you want to know, Maître?" he asked, stuffing the C.D. in his jacket pocket.

"How did Dr Delorme die?"

"A single projectile in the middle of his forehead."

"A projectile?"

"Sorry, Maître, I can't tell you any more at the moment . . ."

The lawyer appeared unsurprised, "Murdered at home, I assume . . ."

"Yes," the Baron replied, "You got any other questions?"

"Not at the moment. In fact I really came to throw some light on Dr Delorme's character."

The lawyer had a lifeless face and smelled of expensive aftershave.

He was wearing black silk socks and preppy moccasins, everything the Baron really hated.

"I'm listening. But you need to know there's no special favours in this office. Just because Delorme received every kind of honour in his life doesn't mean I'm going to neglect files that need sorting out. There are other dead people who need justice too."

Blanchard had rested his briefcase against his chair leg. The end of his red tie formed a small curve over his mean belly. His dull face started to give off a subtle glow like a smouldering fire.

"Are you turning down my offer of help, Commandant?"

"Of course not!" de Palma said grabbing a paperknife marked with the badge of the Berlin Murder Squad.

Blanchard jibbed, his expression defiant.

"Dr Delorme had an unblemished scientific career: head of his department, then professor of medicine. He narrowly missed out on the Nobel Prize and he received several honorary degrees from British and American universities."

"What was his special area of research?"

"Epileptology and Electroencephalography. Some of the techniques developed by his team have enabled progress in the treatment of epilepsy. You will be aware that one of the hospitals in Marseille has borne his name for several years."

"I can find out that sort of thing for myself," de Palma said.

Blanchard did not react, "The doctor was a very prominent figure in Marseille life. He was also an internationally recognized collector of early art. He only had one heir, his granddaughter Bérénice, who shared his name and lived in Paris. She inherited her grandfather's passion and took up his trade. She's a match for any of the big dealers or museums anywhere in the world."

De Palma turned the paperknife in his fingers. A first ray of sunlight penetrated the office and came to rest on the grey cupboard doors. Karim Bessour had taped up two photographs of a village nestling in the Upper Atlas mountains: his father's birthplace.

"Something's been stolen from the doctor's office," de Palma said. "Probably a piece of early art. Do you have you any idea what it was?"

"Not really. I think his granddaughter could tell you more."

"Do you think theft could be the motive?

"That's for you to tell me."

"I'm just asking your opinion, Maître."

"In addition to his various other works the doctor was an unparallelled collector of early art. It was his only real passion apart from medicine. He collected just one type of object from all over the world: human skulls, whether modelled, shrunken, or mummified."

"Human skulls!"

"He had in his collection some of the rarest ones in the world. On several occasions, the Met in New York offered him a fortune for a mummified 'trophy skull' from the Mundurucu Amazonian Indians. He always refused to give it up and finally sold a good part of his collection for a pittance to the anthropological museum in Marseille."

"That's just round the corner," the Baron said.

The barrister opened his briefcase and took out a folder containing some photographs. "This is the famous Mundurucu head," he said, holding out the photographs.

De Palma had never seen a more perfect portrayal of death. He couldn't say why, but in a single expression it captured what he had read in dozens of lifeless faces. The Mundurucu head had long hair. The eye-sockets had been filled with brown paste and two slanted lines replaced the eyes. Thin cords dangled from its mouth, giving it a chilling appearance. It was a trophy skull captured in a raid from days gone by, when hunting spread over the course of several rainy seasons. During the first season the skull was prepared, the eye-sockets blocked up and the eyes re-formed with two tapirs' teeth, then it was given feather pendants. Wearing such a trophy conferred great prestige on its owner and assured him abundant game during the great community hunts in subsequent rainy seasons.

42

"Delorme had a rather secretive life," Blanchard said. "He travelled a lot . . ."

"What do you mean by that?"

"Not everyone was his friend . . . especially in the art world."

The Baron put down the photograph in front of him and stared at it for a long while. The lawyer was shilly-shallying. He didn't like that. He associated intellectual prevarication and mental retreats with a lack of sincerity.

"O.K., let's get to the point, Maître. Did he have enemies capable of killing him?"

"Keep this to yourself, but a few years ago he contacted me because he had received some threats."

"What sort of threats?"

"He was under pressure to sell some of his remaining pieces."

"Some kind of extortion racket?"

"Yes. Repeated phone calls. Barely concealed threats."

"Who was involved? The mob? Art traffickers?

Blanchard collected his thoughts. "I don't know. I understood it was people who were very familiar with the early art trade."

"Why didn't he report it?"

"That's what I advised him to do, but he didn't."

"Any idea why?"

"Not really. I sometimes had the impression he knew the people threatening him and wasn't necessarily afraid of them."

"Would his granddaughter know a bit more about it?"

"No. I never told her about the threats. She was very close to her grandfather. She wouldn't have been able to bear seeing him go through that sort of thing."

"You told me Bérénice Delorme was involved in the art world. It seems to me people in that world aren't as naïve as you portray them. Am I wrong about that?"

Blanchard snapped shut the flap of his briefcase.

"What exactly do you mean?"

"As far as I know early art is a real Eldorado. You pay peanuts for a statue or mask then sell it on for a fortune to some nicely brought up, middle-class people. Those types who get worked up about the fate of the wretched of the earth."

Blanchard stiffened, an exasperated look on his face.

"You don't know Bérénice Delorme . . . Anyway, I've done what I came to do."

De Palma stared at the lawyer, "I don't like briefs coming round my manor telling me where to look. We've all got our own jobs to do, Maître."

The mistral had started to blow at sunrise. Dusty gusts sent plastic bags flying along the walls of the police station.

"I'm going to have to talk to Bérénice Delorme," the Baron said, "the sooner the better."

"She's coming to Marseille as quickly as she can. She'll probably be here this evening if she manages to catch the last TGV train; or if not by tomorrow morning at the latest."

"Could she call me as soon as she gets here? I'd rather not play cops and robbers and issue a summons."

"She will appreciate your concern."

"I'm sorry I was frosty, Maître. Cops tend to get defensive when lawyers are around."

Blanchard responded with a perfunctory smile and went out. The main bell of La Major Cathedral struck half past nine. Its heavy tolling resounded through the old streets of the Quartier du Panier. The light shot towards the Château d'If in specks of brightness.

Maistre and Bessour burst into the office.

"I just passed a brief," Maistre said. "Was it us he wanted?"

"In this specific case, I'd say it was me he was after. Bunch of cowards . . ."

"Legendre had a word with me about it."

"Seems Delorme received threats from some art traffickers."

"Could be interesting?"

De Palma made a vague gesture, but did not reply. He had pinned up some navigational diagrams behind his desk. Below them, in his vigorous handwriting, he had written: "Remember, the rhumb line is in fact a curve!" Although he had not fully grasped the profound meaning of this reality, he had not given up hope. The lines of longitude not being parallel, the rhumb line becomes concave towards the poles. Strange geometry.

He took out his gun from the drawer, loaded it and stuffed it in its holster. "I'm going out to the yard for a smoke. Come and get me in a quarter of an hour. We need to get this visit to Delorme's house sorted."

*

At the age of ninety-six the doctor rarely went out any more. Just a short stroll by the sea, along the coastal path which was half-eroded by the spray. When he got to the low wall overlooking the little port of Malmousque, facing the islands, he stopped to make the most of the spectacular view.

Karim Bessour interviewed the housekeeper who cared for Delorme during the day. A Portuguese woman called Victoria Texeira, who gently rolled her "r"s when she spoke and showered her "s"s. She lived in a tall, thin building on the Heights of Endoume. On learning of the doctor's death she had cried for a long time.

"He didn't do anything special that day. I arrived at nine as usual. He had his nap. At the end of the afternoon we walked along the coastal path as he wanted to see the Planier lighthouse. He always used to tell me it was the gateway to the world. He'd tell me stories about the times when he had sailed off to the faraway islands."

"The faraway islands?"

"Oh, don't ask me their names! I can never remember them."

Karim crossed out something he had written on his dog-eared notepad. As a student he had been meticulous, noting everything down, from the slightest detail to the most eloquent turn of phrase.

"Did he receive a visit from anyone, or a phone call?"

"No, nobody. You can imagine. He never saw anyone. At that age you're of no interest to people."

"What time did you leave?"

"Seven o'clock; the usual time. I got him his glass of port and made him a bit of supper."

Victoria's eyes were heavy with sadness. She gripped the gold crucifix hanging round her neck beween her stubby fingers. She didn't look at the detective. Karim fiddled with his notepad in an attempt to appear composed.

"The doctor," she sobbed, "he was one of those men you never want to die."

Karim held out his notes to the Baron.

"Thanks, son. Methodical as ever, I see."

The key words were underlined, each proper name printed in block letters. The young lieutenant always left a margin on the left-hand side so that he could annotate his work. Often he would list some physical characteristics of the people questioned. In Victoria's case he had written in small letters: dark eyes, face still pretty, snub nose, a beauty spot at the right-hand corner of her lips, man's hands and centre-forward's legs.

"This whole thing has really got me down," Karim said.

"That's all we need!" de Palma grumbled as he read the notes.

Maistre was out on the pavement, standing in front of the grey sea, "He went through the gate."

"Can't be sure about that," the Baron replied. "It's not certain anyone let him in. The alarm system was off as Delorme was inside the house."

"But when you arrived, the gate was open!"

"Because this door is one you lock. You can't open it. Not unless he went and got the keys inside the house, if he could find them that is. So he used the electric gate control to get out."

"And risked being seen . . ." Bessour observed, retrieving his notepad.

"You're right, son," de Palma answered, taking a puff on his second Gitane of the day.

"Which means he isn't too bothered about being recognized," Karim added, shaking his head.

"You're too quick for me," the Baron acknowledged.

The Anse des Cuivres was sheltered from the mistral. A breath of sweet air rose from the bay and shook the sharp spikes of the palm trees outside a neighbouring house. De Palma followed the very high, perfectly smooth perimeter wall surrounding the Delorme house, which was fringed with shards of broken bottles. Suddenly, he stopped. A chunk of rendering had fallen on the ground.

"Here's where he got up. Must be a bloody good athlete!"

A Chrysler with tinted windows came to a halt outside number twenty-seven. The gate opened slowly and slammed back against the pillars.

"Take a look at the cameras," Bessour said staring at the front of the house.

The sun beat down on the white walls.

"If we're in luck the one on the side might have caught something – either the murderer or the burglar."

"Or both. Let's take a look."

"Do you honestly think a climber would have missed those cameras?" Maistre observed.

"How many times have you seen dumb things like that?" de Palma retorted.

"That's true," Maistre said. "Fortunately sometimes they're dumb enough not to notice they're on camera."

The three policemen crossed the street.

"That's the private residence of the United States Consul," Bessour said. "They wouldn't answer any of my questions yesterday."

"We'll see about that!" Maistre rang the bell.

Two minutes later, a man of medium height with pale blond hair and a gaunt face stood in the doorway; legs wide apart.

"And what can I do for you two gentlemen?" he asked with a strong American accent, removing his small, square glasses to reveal blue eyes.

"We're conducting an investigation into the death of your neighbour," Maistre said.

"We didn't know him. How can I help you?"

"Do you record the pictures taken by your security cameras?"

"I'm the head of security. You don't get it do you? You're standing outside the Consul's residence, which means . . ."

Maistre took him by the arm and led him out into the street. "Come here, I'd like to show you something." Maistre walked back a few metres and pointed out the camera. The minder followed him.

"There you are. We just want to know if the camera on the north wall of your compound filmed a man going through the gate, or maybe climbing over your neighbour's wall. I think you can help us."

The American hesitated. He wanted to go back to the residence but Maistre intervened with both hands raised.

"I think the Consul would be very disappointed to find his security team are refusing to cooperate with a criminal investigation, and the guy in charge is in the nick."

"O.K., give me the precise time and I'll go check it out."

"We'll go with you."

"You'll need a warrant."

De Palma put his hand on the American's shoulder. "You may have warrants in the land of the free, in your movies. But we don't do warrants here . . . You see this isn't really a democracy. We do what we feel like."

"So I see," the American said, screwing up his eyes.

"So do I."

The control room was in a hut to the left of the back door.

"I'll have to do a report for the Consul. You need to know I can't accept any responsibility for anything you may find on the recorded material and . . ."

"The judge'll decide that," de Palma interrupted. "We're just the sword of justice, if you get me." He made a slashing gesture with his hand, cutting down an imaginary enemy. The security chief shook his head.

A main screen was surrounded by ten or so monitors each dedicated to the surveillance cameras placed around the consular residence, inside and out. With the help of a lever it was possible to shift from one camera to another and to move it in all directions.

"What day and what time?" the American asked, sounding irritated.

De Palma opened his notebook. "From six o'clock on the evening of the twenty-second, then later that night between one and three in the morning."

The security chief entered the date and the number of the camera. Heavily grained black-and-white pictures passed across the screen. They had been recorded on a hard disc. In the background the top of Dr Delorme's wall stood out, as well as part of the pavement in the street. On the gate security camera, the back entrance of the doctor's house could clearly be seen. At a few minutes past seven a woman came out of the house. Walking briskly, she headed down to the bottom of the cul-de-sac.

"That's Victoria," Bessour said, "bang on time."

At eight o'clock someone appeared coming up from the seashore.

"There he is," shouted Maistre pointing at the camera which was directed towards the wall.

The tall man walked nonchalantly along the pavement. He had no bag; none of the usual burglar's kit. Arriving at the gate he turned the handle, making no attempt to establish whether he was being watched. The gate was shut; the door likewise. He went back to the top of the road and looked at the wall.

The security chief zoomed in. The picture was too blurred to be able to identify a face. "He's black," the American suddenly said.

Maistre and de Palma looked at each other, taken aback.

"You seem to know all about it!"

The American turned round. The C.C.T.V. screens made the little blue squares stand out on the lenses of his glasses. "Yeah," he said, "I'm telling you, that's a black man. I can tell by his hair as he's got that bushy, frizzy kind." He leaned over his desk and fast-forwarded the tape.

"There," Maistre said, "he's climbing over the wall."

For a few seconds the man appeared face-on to the camera, just as he toppled over the other side of the wall.

"We need to send that to the lab," Maistre exclaimed. "They can do wonders."

The shots became strangely fixed. From time to time the headlights of a car passing along the top of the road could be made out. Nothing else.

"The death took place at ten o'clock," de Palma said. "We can forward it to then."

Between ten and eleven o'clock nothing happened. The street was empty. The neighbourhood lights went out one after the other. The policemen checked the other cameras without anything coming up. The film was forwarded to midnight. No-one came out of Delorme's house.

"Good," de Palma said, "let's carry on."

At 1.30 a.m. a Ford Fiesta parked in the road. The driver stayed behind the wheel. Someone got out of the passenger side and headed straight for the gate.

"That's our climber," Bessour said, "he's got a bunch of keys on him. Now he'll open it up, no problem."

"Have you taken the number plate?" de Palma asked, turning to Karim.

"Yes, I'm going to send it over straightaway. With a bit of luck, he's dumb enough to use his own wheels!"

The burglar shut the door behind him. The car went off, turned around and stopped a few metres from the entrance; its lights out. Less than ten minutes later the electric gate opened. The burglar had come out again, empty-handed and visibly shaken.

"He hasn't nicked anything," de Palma observed. "We know the rest. He finds a phone box and calls me because he doesn't want to become a suspect."

"We're going to seize those pictures," Maistre said.

The American hesitated.

"I'm ordering you not to touch your hard disc. If any of these pictures get wiped in any way, I'm going to hold you responsible."

The security chief nodded.

By the time the three policemen came out, large clouds had gathered to the south.

"Which way did he go?" mumbled de Palma, who was thinking about the sound of the flute.

They followed the coastal path to the end of the wall enclosing the doctor's house. The masonry rested on the rocks; there was one spot where the wall was lower. An agile man could easily lean on a protruding bit of stone and jump over.

"This is the only place," Bessour said. "If you jumped over any-where else you'd break your legs . . . After that he must have walked to Malmousque port. He had no choice. Otherwise he'd have had to come back to rue Nôtre-Dame-des-Grâces and get caught on camera again."

"Yes, but why jump over here?" Maistre asked. "He wasn't afraid of being filmed when he went into the house."

Karim shrugged and turned on his mobile. De Palma had turned towards the sea. Around Planier lighthouse the shadows of the clouds traced dark patches over the silvery surface of the water.

"He fled while I was there," the Baron grumbled.

"Or perhaps when he heard the burglar?"

"The flute, Jean-Louis: I didn't make it up."

Maistre shook his head, hands on his hips. "We didn't come here for nothing," he said. "We'll go over the rest of the house with a fine-toothed comb."

"I've just had the vehicle registration service on to me," Bessour said. "The vehicle was stolen on 3 September."

"So they're not as dumb as we imagined . . ." A curtain of rain swept towards the centre of town. "If he left after me, he spent many hours in this house," the Baron thought.

*

Olympique de Marseille were playing Chelsea that night, in a tense quarter-final tie. At the bar du Pont Claude, the proprietor – an ageing Romeo and a bit of a pimp – had put up a giant screen and hired an overhead projector.

His wife, Sylvie, was kitted out in a tracksuit in the club colours. She was in the back room getting out kebabs and *merguez* sausages for half-time. Claude had laid out on the counter some nicely salted home-made olives to go with the pastis, together with small slices of anchovy pizza; enough to dry the hardiest throat.

"Not staying for the match, Michel?"

"No, football doesn't really do it for me. I've never understood the off-side rule . . ."

"Yeah but this is a big match! It's the European Cup!"

"Maybe I'll take a look at home."

Claude grabbed two packets of Gitanes and slammed them down on the counter. "There you go, mate."

De Palma paid up and went out. It was dark. Under the black arch of the railway bridge, a police car had stopped two youngsters on a dodgy scooter without a helmet. De Palma walked to the boulangerie-pâtisserie.

"I had a dream about you last night."

"You don't say!" Eva exclaimed looking mischievous.

"Do you remember that day when Richard gave you a lift back from L'Escale cinema?"

She pouted and stroked the top of the cash till with her finger, "He had a car . . ."

"Yeah, a punter's car. A blue Renault 12 with two white lines on the bonnet."

She leaned her head on his shoulder. "You were jealous, I remember."

"You're telling me!"

"You didn't talk to me for months."

He was about to say that he had never understood how a woman could go out with a jerk, when the baker's boy put his head through the hatch, wearing a white cap spattered with chocolate powder.

"Closing time, Eva."

She nodded.

"Right, I'm going to leave you," de Palma said.

"Not until you've told me about your dream," she said staring deep into his eyes.

"Er . . . not now."

"Some other time then, promise?"

"O.K."

He bought a baguette and two eclairs and went out into the avenue. Supporters were beginning to gather in front of the bar du Pont. He went back to his Alfa Romeo Giulietta and sped along the dreary road running alongside the railway track. As he went through the automatic gate of 102 boulevard Mireille-Lauze, the concierge, Luciano Paronti, caught sight of him.

"There's a parcel for you!"

"Oh great, I was desperate for that to come."

Luciano Paronti still spoke with an Italian accent and rolled his "r"s like a snare drum. A smile lit up his pockmarked face.

"I'll go and get it for you."

Paronti disappeared into his lodge, his back hunched. The sound of pans clattering came through the kitchen window; a smell of basil and hot tomatoes wafted through the air.

"There you go," the concierge said, handing a parcel through the open window of the Giulietta.

"It's just some books," de Palma declared; he was well aware of Paronti's insatiable curiosity.

Once home, he got himself a beer and unwrapped his parcel. A manual of seamanship: 526 pages covering loxodromy, goniometry, not to mention magnetic compasses. De Palma didn't understand the first thing about it all, but he had sworn to work his way through the handbook before discussing it with Maistre who was a whiz at maths. He stretched out on the sofa and flipped through the pages, thinking of his life ahead. His father, who did not waste words, had often said to him: "Try to realize your dreams."

This thought took him back to Eva and he told himself that he belonged to a generation which didn't know how to grow old. He pictured himself on the ocean with Eva, travelling to some distant, unknown destination in the Pacific. In the evenings he would map out their route on navigational charts, having taken moon and star sights by sextant, and then worked his way through the complex calculations. Eva at the tiller; wind in the sails and water slipping under the belly of the ship.

He shut the book and took a swig of beer. The image of Dr Delorme stuck in his mind. He tried to dismiss it, but it clung to him. Then the image of the mummified head imposed itself. And finally the sound of the flute he had heard at the doctor's house.

"You've flirted with death too often," a voice said to him. "Your nightmares are becoming a reality."

"Nightmares have always inspired me, you should know that."

De Palma only very rarely used logic, and this was true of the investigations that he carried out. He waited for a thought to emerge; an impression to surface. Sometimes ideas swarmed in his head and he had to sort through them like a fisherman emptying his catch on the shining deck of the boat. The fish jumped in all directions. But sooner or later the catch would be a good one.

5

The lock on the door clanked. De Palma took a few steps down the gravel alley and stopped. A deckchair had been put out on the terrace outside the Delorme house. The wind beat at the tops of the trees which cast shimmering shadows across the sparse lawn. Dead leaves decayed on the surface of the swimming pool.

On the first floor, a window was illuminated; a shadow passed across it. He knocked at the front door and waited. Someone was watching him; his instincts were never wrong. After a few seconds Bérénice Delorme appeared. She was wearing a very austere, black suit that accentuated the delicate paleness of her complexion and stiffened her long silhouette. A few grey strands set off the locks of her dark hair.

"Hello," she said with a wan smile.

Her bright red mouth formed a sad heart. Two grey bags had formed under her pure green eyes. She held out a frail hand.

"I'm so sorry," de Palma said, "Your grandfather was highly regarded and well known to the people of Marseille."

She nodded modestly and let her eyes wander over the garden. She gave the impression of being alone in life; of moving in a world where de Palma would never feel comfortable.

"I went to see Grandpa this morning. He seemed so peaceful. I asked them to dress him in his black suit; the one I gave him as a present to wear at the reception to honour his entry into the

Académie de Médecine . . . It was the most natural thing in the world to die at his age," Bérénice said. "Ninety-six! But to be murdered . . . I can't come to terms with that. It's no use. I've thought about it over the last two days, but it doesn't make sense."

She struggled to master her emotions and seemed in need of a friend. A strange piece of jewellery adorned her wrist. Made from antique engraved silver, it was out of keeping with the austerity of her suit. She had pleasant manners: a subtle mix of simplicity and formal politeness.

"Let's go inside," she said, "This wind's getting to me."

She took several steps into the hall, and then turned round.

"How did he die? I need to know."

"I'm afraid I can't tell you. He was wounded by a missile that we haven't been able to clearly identify yet."

She shut her eyes. "Do you know if he suffered much?"

"No. Death was instantaneous, that's for sure."

They went into the drawing room, a museum in itself.

"It's always been strange for me coming to this place. It was here I learnt that my mother had died giving birth to me. It was here I took my first steps. My father was sitting over there in that armchair and Grandpa was on this sofa . . . " she brushed its back and continued, "Nothing has changed. Everything is so mysterious . . . All the dramas of my life took place here. Every single one of them. This room has great charm, don't you think?"

"It's certainly very unusual."

"I requested that Grandpa's body should lie here for his last night. His soul is here. You can feel that, can't you?"

On the left-hand wall a collection of African masks stared out at the visitor. One of them was white, with two vertical slits for eyes.

"It's Dogon," Bérénice said, as though to change the subject and dispel the shock. "It's a mask worn in a dance."

In a display cabinet there was a collection of flints of many different sizes, shaped like willow leaves. Above were some very long, lateral wooden flutes.

"Those come from the Sepik region of New Guinea. They're the most mysterious objects. Very common too."

"Flutes!" de Palma almost shouted, "What sort of sound do they produce?"

"It's a bit like someone breathing; soft and deep at the same time. It's quite spellbinding."

The wood was carved with fantastic figures with bird-like heads.

"Can you play this instrument?" de Palma asked.

Bérénice was thrown by his request. "I'm not an expert . . . To tell the truth it's really just the men who play them." She took the long wooden tube and supported it on a raised elbow. "You have to hold it like this. It's quite heavy." She pursed her lips as though to whistle and blew into the mouthpiece; not a sound was heard. "It's really difficult."

"What are these flutes used for?"

"They're important instruments in the life of Papuans. They're used for a whole load of festivities, but also in initiation rites. Some of them are the voice of the spirits."

"The voice of the spirits?"

"Yes, they're not supposed to be heard by non-believers. Those who haven't been initiated are not supposed to know where the voice of the spirits comes from."

"And what if they ever find out?"

"They must die," Bérénice put the flute back on its display stand. "This instrument is male, but there are also female ones. You can tell them apart by the stopper. This one here is a male figure. That one there is made from animal horn, which is quite rare. It comes from the Yuat river region, not far from the Sepik."

She pointed out another flute, which was slightly larger than the previous one, "Here's a female one. Look at the outline of the eyes of the crocodile spirit carved on the stopper. It's magnificent."

"It is," de Palma said, bending over the piece. "Do you know anyone who can play these instruments?"

Bérénice looked at him in surprise. A wrinkle ran down the middle of her forehead, "Why are you so interested in these flutes?"

"Music's a great passion of mine."

"Oh, I see . . . unfortunately, I don't know anyone. Grandpa didn't know how to play them. It's only in New Guinea that you find musicians who can get a note out of them. I mean sounds that have some meaning whether for initiation rites or festivities."

"Do these rituals still exist?"

"Yes and no. It's difficult to say; it depends on the society and the degree to which they have become Christian. I think they still do in the highlands. Near the coast these rituals are just a memory, or for tourists. But you have to be careful . . ."

A ray of sunlight filtered through the old lace curtains.

"Here's a bone knife used in ritual murders and a headhunter's horn," Bérénice said, without even noticing the Baron's discomfiture.

The objects whispered snatches of a distant history; secrets whose importance the policeman could appreciate, but which he was, as yet, unable to understand.

"Please take a seat, Monsieur de Palma," Bérénice said, indicating a low table and two armchairs.

On the other wall there was a line of recent paintings, all very dark and of the same size. They featured Aboriginal faces from Australia. There was a silence. Bérénice put her hands together. Her fingers were grazed from manual labour. De Palma assumed that she must do sculpture.

"It's an impressive collection!" he said to ease the atmosphere.

She responded with a polite smile, "He just fell in love with them. He was a great enthusiast. There is over seventy years of research here."

"And those paintings?"

"They're by a contemporary Aboriginal artist who lives in Arnhem Land in the Northern Territory."

"I have to say, the eyes of those men make me uneasy."

"Yes, these pictures describe the wretchedness of a people who are being murdered little by little, day by day. The artist wanted to depict faces that are fading into the mists of history. My grandfather felt a great affinity for them."

"I had a strange feeling yesterday when I came across the Mundurucu head."

"You went to the museum in Marseille?"

"Yes, your lawyer talked to me about that head, so I went down there. I really wanted to see it."

"Splendid! It was really part of a collection. My grandfather had a particular talent for choosing the finest things. He gave nearly eighty skulls to the museum. I've always wondered where he got his passion for collecting things." She raised her eyes towards a mask from British Columbia, with a drawn-down mouth and ferocious eyes, "It's the sheer strength of these objects. Look at the power of that face. The eyes are looking in different directions, as if the person had a sight defect. You can't stop staring at it."

"It's true," de Palma said. "Even keeping your eye on it is difficult."

"Two years ago I went to the Marquesas Islands. On a few occasions I came across some sacred objects; real things, not the imitations you increasingly get. At one point I felt faint, and I thought I would be sick. Something I had never experienced before. I understood why the people of those islands are always afraid of these objects. You can't explain the energy they give out, but it's real."

With the end of her finger she stroked a statuette that had been placed on a pedestal table. "In the end what is more powerful than to be loved by a woman? To understand each other and recognize one another in the depths of her gaze? Don't you agree, Monsieur de Palma?"

The policeman was embarrassed. "Er . . . yes." He fiddled with the file he had brought.

"My passionate relationship with early art is like that. There is something narcissistic about it for sure. André Breton said: 'Nothing prevents my declaring that this last object has never told me about anything other than myself, bringing me back always to the living centre of my life.' In short, trying to find oneself through objects . . ."*

"I can see that," de Palma said, "I got a glimpse of that when I was looking at the Mundurucu skull."

She opened a blood-red Chinese lacquered cupboard. "We're going to pay our respects to my grandfather in the best way possible. Every evening, behind Victoria's back, he would have an Islay whisky. He would have liked to have joined us in a toast. You can be sure of that."

"Let's have an Islay then," de Palma said.

She poured the alcohol into some cut glasses. They remained silent for a moment in the company of the hollow eyes watching over them.

"We have very little information to go on," de Palma said, clearing his throat. "A piece was stolen from your grandfather's office. Do you know what it was?"

"I spent hours in my grandfather's office. When your colleagues asked me to look over the place, I immediately noticed that a very beautiful trophy skull had been stolen. It used to be on the right of the heart-shaped mask."

"Are you quite sure about that?"

She did not hesitate, "I know every single piece in that study."

"I've put a book under seal. A logbook from the *Marie-Jeanne* schooner. I haven't read it. Do you know what it contains?"

Bérénice's face became tense. She clearly hadn't been expecting this question, "Where was the book?"

"In the bookcase in his study. Left-hand side, on the bottom shelf."

He opened his notepad and looked through his notes. "It was next to an old catalogue of a collection . . ." he added, "the Pinard collection, which focuses on masks from the Aleutian Islands."

He undid a hardback folder containing photographs of the crime

* André Breton (1937), *Mad Love* (University of Nebraska Press 1987).

scene and handed her a shot of the bookcase, "Does that mean anything to you?"

"Yes."

"Can you say anything more?"

She concentrated, her expression frozen. "In 1936 a French expedition sailed from Marseille on a voyage across the Pacific Ocean to New Guinea." She pointed to a photograph, in a silver frame, of an elegant schooner with all sails set. De Palma recognized the Château d'If in the background.

"A friend of my grandfather's bought this old schooner. It was called the *Marie-Jeanne* and had been refurbished for the journey. It had a large hold that could carry all the objects and works of art that the expedition would buy on behalf of the *musée d'Ethnographie* in Paris. There were also personal purchases . . . private ones you might say. In all, almost two thousand five hundred . . ." She fixed her eyes on a large oval mask with a white perimeter and a strange, dark, asymmetric expression that drilled into the soul of anyone who looked at it. "This friend was called Robert Ballancourt. He went on the voyage, of course. He was very young at the time."

"What did your grandfather's friend do on that expedition?"

"They don't make men like Ballancourt any more. He was fabulously wealthy; passionate about art; an adventurer . . . He was fascinated by the Papuans because of their supposed closeness to an early stage of humanity. He wanted to uncover certain customs such as cannibalism, or headhunting. When you're interested in Papuans, or the arts of the Pacific, the spectre of cannibalism is never far away. Remember Margaret Mead and her tales of travel among cannibal tribes? Ballancourt had a secret desire to discover Stone Age people who had never had any contact with white men."

Bérénice Delorme had the gift of being able to enthuse her audience. Each of her words seemed loaded with intensity. De Palma did not understand the references to writers like Mead whom he knew nothing about.

"We found another book on his desk, Freud's *Totem and Taboo*."

"Was it open when you found it?" she asked.

"Yes. A passage was underlined."

"Which one?"

De Palma handed her a photocopy of the extract. She read it in a serious voice:

"One day the brothers who had been driven out came together, killed and devoured their father and so made an end to the patriarchal horde. United, they had the courage to do and succeeded in doing what would have been impossible for them individually."

She stopped and stared at de Palma who picked up where she left off, staring into her eyes:

"The violent primal father had doubtless been the feared and envied model of each one of the company of brothers: and in the act of devouring him they accomplished their identification with him, and each one of them acquired a portion of his strength."

He pronounced the last words slowly.

She looked surprised, "It's the first time I've met someone who's able to quote Freud in the original," she said with a smile, "Impressive!"

"I think that might hold the key to the mystery of your grandfather's death."

"In that book Freud says something that has always seemed terrible to me. But it closely matches the view which they held at the beginning of the last century about our origins."

"The savagery of early man . . ." de Palma said. "He talks about the Aborigines, among others."

"Yes. These peoples are so far removed from us and yet at the same time so close."

"How come you know this text so well?"

She became defensive, "We often discussed it with my grand-father . . ."

"Why was that?"

"As a young man he was very taken with Freud's theories. In the 1930s it was all very revolutionary. And Freud was still alive! Grandfather knew that period. And then over time his views evolved . . . Until eventually he lost all interest in those theories. It's quite complex . . ." she had lowered her voice.

De Palma felt there was something artificial about her friend-liness, a way of disguising her vanity; the pride she felt in her origins. "Can you tell me about this head which has been stolen?"

"It's a modelled head," she said.

The Baron's expression hardened. "Can you be more precise?"

"My grandfather possessed another one . . . He was very fond of it because he obtained it during the celebrated voyage of the *Marie-Jeanne*. So it had a particular power. I am very disturbed by the thought of it being in the hands of a thief."

She coughed into her closed hand.

"Do you have any photographs of this sculpture?" de Palma asked.

"Yes, several. It was even included in a publication."

"Can I see them?"

Bérénice Delorme's face softened. She got up and moved to the bookcase that occupied the entire length of a wall. Unhesitatingly, she pulled out a large volume from the last shelf, returned, and sat down on the sofa. "There," she said opening the book. "Come and look."

He felt slightly awkward sitting down beside her. She moved away a little as she turned a page.

An over-modelled face, fully covered in clay. Ochre paint flowed from the bridge of the nose and surrounded the hollow, round eyes with a thick line, rising in curved patterns and in tracery as far as the temples, the forehead and the back of the skull. The mouth was thin, practically without lips, and revealed worn teeth.

"Can you tell me the significance of this sculpture?"

"Er . . . yes. In some Papuan societies these sculptures have to do with the immortality of the soul, life after death, that sort of thing. Some think that the soul must continue to wander until the skull regains human form. I mean it's basically to do with remarkable people who have died; people who have left their aura on the tribe. In Papua, in many places, they are called Big Men. The name means exactly what it says.

"Headhunting also existed. A sophisticated business! Managing to kill your enemy and capture his head was glorious, a source of pride. In 1924 the colonial authorities outlawed this custom . . . To us Westerners headhunting seems completely barbaric . . . But for the Iatmul it was a civilized practice that had its justification in their myth of origin. Just imagine, the authorities forbade this ritual, while at the same time white men like my grandfather were willing to buy skulls . . ."

"Can a link be made between this head and the quotation from Freud?"

She thought for a few seconds, her eyes on the photograph. "Not really, I can't see any." Her hand trembled slightly. She touched the photograph lightly with the tip of her index finger.

"Tell me about the other members of the expedition."

"I only know about one of them and that was Robert Ballancourt. I've already mentioned him to you."

"Can you tell me anything more?"

"He was an heir of the Ballancourt family that used to dominate the textile industry."

The Ballancourts had hit the headlines for months on end. The name symbolized the end of an era, the passing of old-style capitalism and the ranks of unemployed that it produced.

"My grandfather was very close to him, as a collector and also as a friend. They took part in other expeditions, more discreet ones if I may call them that. Ballancourt frequently used to go to New Guinea in the years after the war."

"For what purpose?"

"To save what could still be saved."

"What do you mean?"

"I'm talking of the Protestant clergy who . . . evangelized the Papuans. It was carried out through the systematic destruction of a great many pieces, like these skulls for example. In the 1960s Ballancourt often had problems with the Indonesian armed forces, who occupied half the island and are still destroying everything: men and works of art alike."

"To general indifference."

"Yes, Monsieur de Palma. We still don't give a damn about the massacre of our brothers and sisters; our Elders in the history of humanity."

A clock chimed five o'clock. De Palma got up and closed his hardback folder.

"I'm going to get up to date with the latest reports from forensics. Will you be staying in Marseille for some time?"

"Yes. I've got a whole load of problems to sort out with the estate."

"Do you have a mobile number?"

"Of course."

She took out a visitor's card from a silver case that was lying on a small table.

"I'll wait to hear from you, Monsieur de Palma."

He held out his hand and she shook it briefly.

"I feel an idiot, all of a sudden . . ." she said in a thin voice.

"Why do you say that?"

"I forgot to tell you another piece was missing from the study."

He stared at her, "Why didn't you mention that to the technicians earlier?"

"I didn't think it was important."

"Everything's important. What was it?"

"A bow that my grandfather brought back from the Upper Sepik at the time of the 1936 expedition. An old warrior's bow and arrows. That's what was missing." She breathed in and gripped de Palma's forearm, "How did he die? Tell me!"

"I'm afraid I can't," the Baron replied, looking towards the door.

*

That evening the boulangerie-pâtisserie curtains were already drawn across the window, but the door was open. De Palma put on the brakes and glanced inside. The owner of the shop was by the till, cashing up, together with her husband. She was enormous in her mauve apron, and his sleeveless vest revealed hairy arms. No sign of Eva. Disappointed, the Baron sped off.

Once home, he put Elgar's Violin Concerto into the C.D. player and sat down on his sofa, with Captain Meyssonnier's log in his hands.

Marseille – 6 June 1934

We are a ten-man crew, myself included. In addition there are Robert Ballancourt, Fernand Delorme and his young wife Lisette. That makes thirteen. I am not superstitious, but for this sort of expedition, I would prefer to make up the numbers to fourteen. A ship's apprentice is due to arrive early this afternoon. He was introduced to me by an old man from the navy who frequents the bar des Galères. I shall set him to work in the kitchen and looking after the cabins.

I've also taken on board a black cat, which has been given the name Bébert. It's lucky to have a mascot on a ship.

. . .

Fine weather. The anticyclone still prevails. There are reasonable grounds for hoping it will continue until we reach

Gibraltar. After that, we will see. The *Marie-Jeanne* is a fine schooner and the crew is reasonably accustomed to this kind of crossing. We will not experience any problems.

I am keen to set sail, as all the visits from journalists are starting to bother me. Ballancourt and Delorme say that this publicity is important for the expedition.

Marseille – 7 June

I asked the *Curé des Accoules* to come and bless the *Marie-Jeanne*. Ballancourt couldn't find anything better to do than arrange for a visit by a photographer to immortalize the event. The priest arrived with great pomp, a little after ten o'clock, accompanied by two choirboys. He waved his censer over the deck, from stern to stem.

It is very hot today. A sea mist has risen. It is scarcely possible to make out Notre-Dame de la Garde. The quay in front of the town hall is littered with casks from Algeria. Dockers doze on a mountain of coffee sacks. It seems that a Three-master from the Transatlantic Company has been placed in quarantine. The port authorities told me that this was for public health reasons.

De Palma imagined the port before the war, before the Germans and the Vichy authorities had gutted the city and blown up its heart. Some sad-looking tall blocks of flats jutted out over the old port; alleyways like dark carotids feeding the heart of the city. The murmur of the *mare nostrum* coiled through the sacred hills of the old quarters. In rue Bouterie, the seediest of all, prostitutes in silk stockings gave the come-on to sailors, soldiers from the Colonial Army and blue-eyed members of the Foreign Legion. The boldest ones snatched the hats of gentlemen who ventured there, only returning them after a spot of loitering and canoodling. The last great sailing ships docked at the quai des Belges, rubbing decks with already rusting steamboats. In this well-worn harbour, among the old clippers and trading ships furrowed by the oceans, the *Marie-Jeanne* cut a figure like a little girl at sea; an upstart daring to steal the show.

We cast off just as the bells of Saint-Victor were ringing the evening Angelus. When I gave the order to lift the gangway, excitement on the quay reached fever pitch. Ballancourt flitted back and forth among the journalists. One of them, who had no doubt come down from Paris, made a little speech: "Your voyage of discovery is probably the last of its kind. You shall save some of the most authentic works of art in the world. The whole of France is watching you."

Sometimes I think of the *Marie-Jeanne*'s dimensions and wonder if she will be able to hold everything that Ballancourt and Delorme plan to collect during this voyage. We could always offload some of it at Noumea before we go to New Guinea. The works of art can be sent to France on a cargo steamer.

. . .

We passed Planier lighthouse at sunset. The sight of the sun sinking softly below the horizon was truly amazing; a huge red ball slowly melting into the sea. The *Marie-Jeanne* was making fifteen knots, with a light, easterly swell. The wind whistled between the jibs. And to think that this is probably my last sailing voyage!

The *Marie-Jeanne* had sailed through the Gulf of Lion with the Captain simply recording details of her course and speed. Until Gibraltar the sea had been calm, or with only a slight swell. Out in the Atlantic a storm had arisen. A force seven wind had shaken the young explorers for the first time.

Ballancourt is often seasick. I wonder if he will make it through this voyage. What can be done about it? Force him to disembark? That's out of the question. Without him the expedition would no longer have any purpose. Anyway Delorme cannot replace him, even though I sense he would not be averse to taking such a role. During my watch yesterday I came across Delorme and his wife Lisette engaged in private conversation. On catching sight of me they immediately changed the subject, which does not bode well.

Lost in thought, de Palma put down the notebook. The clock showed eight o'clock.

We put in at Fort-de-France. Endless heavy rain. Impossible to go ashore without getting soaked. On place de la Savane, facing the sea, colonial troops are on patrol. Riots have broken out across Martinique. The Gendarmes had to open fire. According to the reports I have received there were four deaths: agricultural workers demanding a pay rise. La Savane is immense, a real tropical garden. I very much like walking there.

Yesterday I authorized the ship's apprentice to take shore leave. He returned completely inebriated and I had to have him confined for two days. He is a Corsican, by the name of Ange Filippi. He is sixteen years old, but already has the physique of a man. I think he will make a good sailor.

The Delormes and Robert Ballancourt dined with the Governor. When they returned on board a little after midnight, I smoked a cigarette, while looking at Les Trois-Îlets and the *rade de Fort-de-France*. The Delormes barely acknowledged me. Ballancourt came to keep me company and we talked about this and that. He is a fascinating fellow. At first I took him for a boy from a well-to-do family doing his world tour, but I must admit there is more to him than meets the eye.

A page had been carefully torn out. Probably with a razor blade, or Stanley knife, but the tear was not a recent one. The narrative resumed at the point when the *Marie-Jeanne* was in sight of the entrance to the Panama Canal. Meyssonnier had recorded all the administrative problems in his dealings with the Canal authorities. Nothing else. So what had happened in Martinique, or in the days following the schooner's departure? De Palma told himself that he would never find out unless he could trace one of those who'd been present. He made a note of Ange Filippi's name in his notebook – the only person he had reason to suppose might still be alive.

The Pacific is unmistakable. It has a much greater swell. Every time I get the impression of a vast expanse of nothingness surrounding us. From here to Australia, or the Chinese coast, there is nothing but sea and tiny islands. Archipelagos like specks of mountain dust. I think of the Polynesians who colonized these lost pebbles in the middle of the ocean, using boats far smaller than our *Marie-Jeanne* (and she isn't that large!). I can't help admiring them. Ballancourt agrees with me. He greatly loves the art of the southern hemisphere; of Tahiti and the Leeward islands. Yesterday when we were out on the open sea and the ship was running well, the waves hissing beneath us, we talked a lot about the history of the Polynesians. They were once people with few morals and barbaric customs such as cannibalism . . . Ballancourt told me not to pass judgement on the inhabitants of these islands. He thinks that we are no better than they are, but I do not share this opinion.

. . .

Robert Ballancourt is very anxious for us to put in at the Easter Islands. Delorme is of the same opinion.

It was three in the morning. De Palma shut the book once more, his eyes growing heavy. The night was filled with a thousand and one small noises. He quickly nodded off.

Several hours later: a nightmare. He was alone, sitting at a table during the middle watch, holding a cup, his attention lost on the panelling. The wind chanted mysterious words in the rigging. Steps could be heard on the upper deck. He climbed the ladder leading up to the bridge. The helmsman was hunched against the tiller. A white light made the sea shine like pewter.

"We're making six knots," a sharp voice said coming from nowhere. "Course 140°; on the port tack. Easterly wind, force six."

The sea was building. The *Marie-Jeanne* was sailing under the mainsail, foresail, jibs and topsail.

"We're waiting for the wind to veer so we can make a course to windward. What do you think?" The Captain was standing in front of him, with his back to him. A wave struck the bow.

"You are . . ."

The sailor turned round. His eyes were hollow. The bone of his forehead was waxen in the moonlight. A plume of red feathers adorned the back of the skull. Clay that split into a multitude of tiny diamond shapes formed the hard dry mouth. Two white shells were sunk into the resin eyebrows.

De Palma awoke with a start, his forehead damp. He felt a presence beside him. He went to the bathroom and splashed himself with cold water. The presence had not gone away. It followed his every movement. He went through all the rooms. Nothing. He only managed to get back to sleep at daybreak, gun in hand.

It was considered necessary that every Tchambuli boy should in childhood kill a victim, and for this purpose live victims, usually infants or young children, were purchased from other tribes. Or a captive in war, or a criminal from another Tchambuli hamlet sufficed. The small boy's spear-hand was held by his father, and the child, repelled and horrified, was initiated into the cult of headhunting. The blood of the victim was splashed on the foot of the upright stones that stand in the little clearing outside the ceremonial house, and if the victim was a child, the body was buried beneath one of the house posts. The head, like the heads of enemies killed in warfare, was built up in clay modelling on the original skull, and painted in fantastic patterns of black and white, with shell eyes and glued-on curls . . .

Margaret Mead (1935), Sex and Temperament in Three Primitive Societies *(HarperCollins, 2001)*

6

"You need to draw a distinction between trophy skulls and ancestral skulls," Voirnec said, pointing to the gallery ceiling.

The man standing in front of the antiques dealer wore thick corduroy trousers and a Barbour jacket that was still wet from the rain. His jaw jutted out and his bulging grey eyes were filled with a strange glow.

"Trophy skulls are less rare and less beautiful. They were considered to be less significant."

"What about ancestral skulls?"

"Some are absolutely magnificent and are extremely rare. It all depends on which collection they come from."

"I saw some in the *Musée des Arts Premiers* on quai Branly. I find them very impressive."

"The collection at quai Branly is quite exceptional."

Voirnec wondered whether the man before him was a buyer, or just someone who was curious. He had many such people dropping in. It didn't bother him. The man didn't look like a cop. He looked at the clock at the back of the *galerie Rigodon*.

Almost closing time.

"I dare say you have some of those skulls."

"I don't have any at present," Voirnec replied.

A passer-by stopped for a few seconds in front of the gallery window. Voirnec looked up; he seemed to know the face. The person stared for a few moments at an orator's stool on a platform, and then disappeared. Somewhere in Paris a bell rang the Angelus.

"I'll leave you my card. If you ever find one of those ancestral skulls, be sure to call me. I'm a serious buyer. You can check me out."

Voirnec examined the card: a double-barrelled name and address, a château in one of Britanny's *départements*. "I might be able to offer you something."

"What sort of price would it fetch?"

Voirnec was surprised by the question. Normally, clients looking for this type of work were familiar with the prices.

"It can go from 4,000 euros for what you might call a routine trophy skull, to twenty times that amount if the piece is exceptional and comes from a prestigious collection."

"Give me a call, whatever the price."

"I'll be sure to do that," the antique dealer said with a fawning smile.

The curious man went out. Voirnec accompanied him to the door and watched him for a moment as he disappeared into the distance. The street was calm, with few passers-by; curtains were drawn across windows. Bulging facades weighed down the perspective of buildings with four or five floors. Voirnec glanced once more at the business card and went back into the gallery. No, he wasn't a cop from the O.C.B.C.*

The back room was littered with packing cases. Plastic bubble wrap had been thrown over wooden crates that still bore the blue and red stamps of the Australian customs. Voirnec pulled a white panel which concealed a safe. He manoeuvred the wheels and opened the reinforced door.

On the last shelf, next to jewellery and precious stones that flickered in the cold light, there was a cube-shaped wooden box. About

---

* L'Office Central pour la répression du trafic des Biens Culturels: The Central Agency for Combating Traffic in Cultural Property.

fifty centimetres across, it was somewhat battered and bore a large red and white label, saying "Handle with Care".

Voirnec took the box and put it in a nylon bag. "Good," he said.

He shut the safe door and reset the combination. At that moment he heard the indistinct, wavering sound. He went deathly pale. The voice, muffled as though coming down a long tube, was familiar. He knew its secret and magical significance. Gradually the notes harmonized and an undulating, pulsing sound filled the space.

No-one should know where the voice comes from. Nobody.

"Just a load of old beliefs," he mused aloud to give himself courage, "Primitive superstitions. Just a bunch of savages!"

The melody picked up speed. He had the impression it was coming from the depths of his being. His eyes strayed across the chaos of packaging and shelving where statuettes from Oceania dozed, indifferent to the strange sounds. Voracious smiles spread over their wooden faces.

"Death!" the antiquarian cried huddling in a corner, "I must never see your face. Never!"

7

Early in the morning, Commissaire Legendre stopped de Palma in the corridor as he headed for his office, his mind lost in the mist like a ghost ship at sea in search of its captain.

"The lab called. They've got news on the bit of wood found in the doctor's brain." The Commissaire fell silent giving a faint smile. "It's certainly an arrow, or something like that." He passed his hand over his wrinkled face. He had probably only had a few hours sleep. His work absorbed him completely, allowing him to forget that other calamity in his life: his wife. "I must admit I don't understand any of it," he muttered, rolling his sad eyes which matched his shirt and trousers. "Who uses reed arrows? Normally they're synthetic, or made of wood. I've checked out all the arrows you can find on the market and there aren't any reed ones."

"Bérénice Delorme told me there was a bow missing from her grandfather's study."

"I see," the Commissaire said. "Something to go on, at last. Look into it, will you?" He picked up his post and went through the door into his office, murmuring snide comments as he looked through his mail.

De Palma slipped out. Bessour had already arrived and was sitting comfortably in his chair.

"Morning," the Baron said weakly.

"Hi," Bessour replied, "Have you heard the news?"

"I just passed Legendre."

"So you know: it was an arrow."

"Delorme had a bow in his office. It's gone. Very likely on the night of the murder."

Bessour raised his head in surprise. "You think the killer would have used that?"

"It's possible," de Palma replied, "but if Delorme had a bow, it must be an ancient thing he brought back from one of his expeditions. I get the impression that type of weapon wears out pretty quickly. Especially the bow string . . ."

"You could be right. It might be a coincidence. A crossbow could equally well have been used. Nothing is more silent and effective than that."

The reed splinter had been moved from the medico-legal institute to the safe at the Murder Squad. It was in a transparent plastic tube. The wax on the seal had dripped down the string of the cardboard label, leaving a long red trace.

"Let's assume it was an arrow," de Palma said. "He kills the doctor with a single projectile, and then removes it. He aims, taking his time."

"That's what I was thinking. And when he removes it, a splinter is left in the brain."

Death must have been instantaneous, but the scene revealed lengthy preparations. Did he put out the book by Freud before or after the murder? Did he compel Delorme to read the passage where the father of psychoanalysis talks of the murder of the primal father?

"Can you kill someone with a bow at point-blank range?" de Palma asked.

"Of course you can," Karim replied, glancing over the computer screen, "if your arrowhead is very sharp. You need to stand at least two metres away to have the necessary impact."

"All the same, to penetrate the bone on the forehead!"

"Believe me, Baron, it's possible. You don't know the power of some of those bows. Even commandos use crossbows."

"You seem to know all about it."

"When I was a kid we did archery at the community centre on the estate, just to get us into something different from footie or martial arts. I wasn't bad."

"One thing puzzles me."

"What's that?"

"When you remove an arrow, you make the hole larger . . . because the tip is thicker than the stem."

"I thought of that, but there are a whole load of arrows with a point hardly wider than the wood."

De Palma wondered out loud, "Delorme sees his killer. He looks him in the face: a nutter. Right there in front of him. He begs him. No. He tries to reason with him. The man has put Freud's book on the desk. He knows this book because the passage has been under-lined for a long time."

"Delorme never dealt with madness," Bessour added. "He wasn't a psychiatrist or a psychoanalyst. His only area of work was epilepsy."

"Epilepsy," de Palma repeated. "In some far-off civilizations a person who suffers from epileptic fits is treated with great respect because he is thought to be wiser than other people."

With his left hand Bessour picked up some notes he had made in his careful script on a loose sheet of paper. De Palma watched him for a few seconds. He had always thought that left-handed people were more intelligent than other people; or at least that they had a different way of approaching things from the mass of right-handers.

"I've had a look at some specialist archery sites on the net," the lieutenant said chewing the end of his biro, "None of them sell arrows like that. Not even the sites flogging gear to people who're into wildlife, or the Middle Ages."

"So it's home-made then," de Palma said, putting his weapon away in the drawer of his desk, "Perhaps he used arrows from the doctor's house?"

"Is that what you think?"

"Let's just say that's my feeling."

"We can scour the local archery clubs. Perhaps they'll have noticed a nutter practising with some reed arrows."

"That would be straightforward. But too simple."

"Worth a try, no? There are archery events and then there is the hunting fraternity. You never know."

"O.K., if you want, but your job, not mine!"

The Baron mulled over the quotation from Freud. For the moment he favoured the idea of a former patient returning for some reason to murder Dr Delorme. A man who had undergone E.C.T.

"You're wasting your time, Karim," he said, emerging from his thoughts, "You won't get anywhere with archery clubs. It's too easy for a bloke who's that organized."

Bessour looked up anxiously. He knew all about the Baron's long career. "You think he'll do it again?"

"Yes and no. If it's a former patient looking for revenge, my hunch is no."

"A former patient?" Bessour asked.

"Given the type of treatment the doctor offered, there's good reason to think that way."

"And otherwise?"

"A headcase who wants to prove something to the world."

"Do you have any idea what sort of message he wants to get across?"

The Baron took a deep breath. He would have loved to have answered that question straightaway, but it was impossible. The Freud text led him back to the origins of the main taboos and the Oedipus complex. "The 'primal horde' . . ." he said, "the murder of the father."

Bessour was watching him closely. His expression still betrayed the emotions of a green young lieutenant. For him psychopaths represented dangerous unknown territory.

"I'm not keen on easy conclusions," de Palma said. "A crime of this sort is never straightforward. He took his time, waiting for the right moment. He prepared his weapon, selected his arrow . . . Unless he did it out of anger. He sees the bow, takes it and fires . . ."

He sighed as if an additional load had just been added to his thoughts. "And then there are things the lawyer told us . . ."

"Do you believe them, Baron?"

"We can't overlook anything. Art traffickers could be behind all of this. From now on we need to analyse every little detail," the Baron's face clouded over. "Perhaps he's made a mistake, Karim."

"What kind of mistake?"

"Why did he remove the arrow?"

Frowning, Bessour thought for a few seconds before answering, "So he could put the mask over the doctor's head."

"Well spotted, but maybe there's something else. Why not leave the arrow beside the body – as his signature?" de Palma bit his upper lip and paused.

"Because they're rare. Precious even," Bessour said, "And he had trouble getting hold of them."

"Yes, son. You've just spotted the first flaw. He's using arrows that are very rare. And perhaps they're the ones he finds at Delorme's house. If there's no doubt the bow can't be used, the arrows can be."

*

As he went down to the port area that evening de Palma was humming the great aria from "Madam Butterfly":

Un bel dì, vedremo
Levarsi un fil di fumo
Sull'estremo confin del mare.

He was pursuing a vague idea. Something was telling him not to think like a policeman any more, but he couldn't put his finger on it.

80

E poi la nave appare.
Poi la nave bianca
Entra nel porto,
Romba il suo saluto.

The coastal motorway ran alongside the shipyards that had been dismantled in the 1970s, and the factories that had provided deck fittings to the merchant navy. Drawing shadows from the cranes, the sunset made the port seem motionless and cold.

Maistre had invited him to dinner to share his first *bouillabaisse*. At the mini-market in L'Estaque he bought two bottles of Cassis white wine. The woman on the till had something of Maria Callas about her, with her crooked nose, thin neck and huge, fragile eyes. De Palma paid with a large-denomination note, just for the sheer pleasure of watching the girl's brown fingers with their long varnished nails putting down the change on the black conveyor belt.

E come sarà giunto
Che dirà? Che dirà?
Chiamerà Butterfly dalla lontana.

No-one had ever sung Madam Butterfly better than Maria Callas. De Palma went back to his Giulietta. He had parked the car straddling the pavement in front of the doughnut-seller's kiosk. Away from the metropolis that seemed like one endless building site, L'Estaque didn't change. In the bars on the seafront, the regulars with leathery faces were solemnly discussing tired old ideas. The majority had been sailors, dockers, or rust-pickers on huge hulls. All had experienced the death throes of the great port and the industries that had grown up around it.

When he rang at the wrought-iron gate enclosing the terraced garden, the sound of pans came across the empty road. Maistre was in the kitchen cooking, "Come and help me, Baron, I can't manage on my own!"

De Palma climbed the stairs leading to the house and took off his jacket, "What are you up to?"

"I don't know what to do with the small fish!" Jean-Louis was bent over the sink, the stubborn smell of fresh fish spreading all around him.

"No, Jean-Louis, you don't gut the small fish."

Maistre had got out an enormous saucepan that he had bought in the city centre for his first *bouillabaisse*. He had put on a navy-blue apron that reached down to his knees and was knotted over his round stomach.

"We're going to marinate it for a good hour or so with an onion, some carrots and a leek. And salt, pepper, garlic, fennel, olive oil, a bouquet garni and some orange peel."

"That's not in the recipe."

"Bugger the recipe! That's how my mum used to make it."

From Maistre's kitchen, through the sheets of rain, it was possible to make out the Frioul archipelago which was laid out like a large boat on the grey sea; and further away the shadow of the Maïre and Tiboulen rocks cordoning off the bay.

"Shall I put your marinade in the fridge, or leave it beside the cooker?"

"Leave it by the cooker."

De Palma glanced into the pot and gave the motley mixture a stir with a wooden spoon.

"We'll make the *rouille* and the aioli just before we eat. Have you thought about the croutons?"

"The baker gave me some."

Maistre's living room was stuck in a time warp. For years he had taken his meals facing the bay. His wife always sat with her back to the city; his elder son, Christophe, on his left; and the youngest, Sylvain, on his right. Now the kids had grown up; the older one was at university studying engineering somewhere near Paris, and the younger one was doing medicine. Maistre didn't see them as much any more, especially the older one for whom he had always had a soft spot, because of his poor health. Maistre was proud of his children. His wife was away more and more, on the pretext of being near to her elderly parents. Her absence wore him down. On the mantelpiece he had put a photograph of his mother in a silver frame, taken when he was about fifteen. Her name was Juliette. From time to time the old policeman would look at her, now anxiously, now with a tender eye. He had never known his father.

"Hey Jean-Louis, are you worried or something?"

"No, Baron. It'll work out and then I'm happy enough. I was right to come back to the squad."

"Can you follow what's going on?"

"I was here before you, remember. We meet again at last!"

"Yeah. By the corpse of a doctor who used to fry his patients' brains. Partytime tonight!"

"We've got the Bandol to drink!"

Maistre undid his apron and ran his hand through his black hair while glancing at the portrait of his mother, "I'm a bit embarrassed to tell you this, but you know . . . with Brigitte and me, there's nothing between us anymore. You see we're no longer in love. She's gone. For good."

De Palma gave him a shove on the shoulder that possibly meant "Welcome to the singles club". He had never thought much of Maistre's wife. "In that case you need to get yourself on a diet and get back your waistline! Then we'll see what you can find . . . "

"Nothing left for us except the dregs!"

"Rubbish. Some of the girls here are really fit. No mutton in our meat wagons!"

"Love in navy-blue!"

Maistre opened the door. A gust of fresh air reached him as he stood on the threshold. In the terraced garden running down to the road he had planted some olive trees, which he kept closely pruned. Between the white rocks emerging from the soil, he had planted clumps of herbs and lavender bushes.

Western Europe may have produced anthropologists precisely because it was prey to strong feelings of remorse, which forced it to compare its image with those of different societies in the hope that they would should show the same defects or would help to explain how its own defects had developed within it.

Claude Levi-Strauss, Tristes tropiques
(Jonathan Cape, 1973)

8

The visitor stopped for a few moments on the Debilly footbridge. From there, in the morning light, the dark outline of the Eiffel Tower could clearly be seen. The Seine was swollen from the downpour that had battered the capital for two days now. A barge was hard at work, its belly full of cement, churning up the dark water on its way towards the Île de la Cité.

Along quai Branly, car wheels hissed on the wet tarmac. The visitor walked over the road away from the pedestrian crossing and went inside the perimeter of the *Musée des Arts Premiers*. The building resembled an enormous ocean liner on stilts.

"Can I have a ticket for the exhibition, please?"

A group of children added to the chaos as they burst in, clustering around the white doors. He went past them into a huge room with a broad, white spiral staircase winding round display cases filled with drums, flutes and other instruments arranged against a black background. He went through the turnstile and up the spiral leading to the exhibition. He was overcome by anxiety. At the top, the long dark corridor came to an end by a Djennenke sculpture over two metres high.

He paused. He could hear the voices of the Elders! The sound of the sacred flutes rose up through the racket made by the visitors. How could that be?

He opened his wallet and studied the photograph of the girl he loved. With the tip of his finger he stroked her face and lips, and remained looking at the enigmatic expression peering out at him from the photograph.

"None of this exists for you any longer," he said to himself.

The Papuan art section was a few metres away. Sculptures that used to be placed on the top of the men's house roofs; carved ladders; a great horizontal drum and a pillar adorned with secret patterns. Illuminated by the lights in the display cases, the great hunters' weapons were displayed in all their rough nobility. It was then that he understood. A small loudspeaker was broadcasting the shrill sound of the huge flutes of the initiates. Here, right in the middle of this faceless crowd of people impatient to see art they knew nothing about. A feeling of disgust turned his stomach. This crowd of curious people suddenly seemed to him to be coarse, dirty and stupid. In a way he hated himself for having come this far.

"But I must do this," he thought.

The skulls were nearby. The first one was split in two lengthways. A wooden bar was fixed inside, widthways, so the person wearing the mask could grab it with his teeth. The face had been over-modelled with clay, and decorated with a black ruff and a rather wide nose.

A television screen was showing a scene of an ancestral skull being modelled among the Iatmul on the banks of the River Sepik. Another one presented an excerpt from "Dead Birds," featuring a war scene in the highlands. The warriors were firing long reed arrows and one of them was waving a large white feather.

The person he was looking for stood there, a few metres away, by a set of statuettes. He hadn't expected to come across him so easily. A pure coincidence was forcing him to change his strategy. He watched for a long time feeling both fearful and curious. The man was wearing crumpled jeans, shoes with worn-down heels and a rather coarse woollen jumper.

The visitor needed to think. Everything was moving too fast. He went round the collection, walking between the Melanesian display cabinets and stopping in front of the Dream Time paintings that covered one of the walls in the Australian section. He hadn't let the man he sought out of his sight, not for one moment. The man's name was Lescure, and he had hardly changed, in spite of the fifty or so years that had elapsed. The visitor had known him when he was much younger; when he was a lean and hungry doctoral student.

A girl, probably a student, followed Lescure, taking notes in a large ring binder. The visitor turned back. For a few seconds his eyes met Lescure's and he felt sure that he had been spotted. But that was impossible.

A pack of disenchanted primary school children went past, following their teacher. One of them pulled a face at an ancestral skull. Lescure had put on some white gloves. He opened a display case and put down an object that the girl had held out to him. The visitor moved closer, his eyes riveted on the ritual dagger that had just been put back in the collection.

"Now is the time," he said to himself. "A good moment to start a discussion."

"Excuse me," the visitor said, going up to Lescure, "but do you mind me asking if you're responsible for this collection?"

"Yes, that's right," Lescure replied looking at him with curiosity.

"And those skulls?" the visitor asked.

Lescure replied with a nod of his head as he removed his gloves. He hurriedly double-locked the display case.

"I'm also in charge of the skulls," Lescure said. "These ones and the others in the *Musée de L'Homme.*"

The visitor hesitated to pursue his questioning any further. Too much inquisitiveness might arouse Lescure's suspicions, "Where are these pieces from?" he asked, staring at the severed heads.

"From the *Marie-Jeanne* collection created in 1936."

"The *Marie-Jeanne*?"

"Some young adventurers who chartered a ship to go round the world and buy works of art."

"Must have been a tough journey."

The anthropologist moved aside to let another stream of children pass. The girl tucked her pencil behind her ear.

"It's a strange meeting of two worlds," she said, "I'm not sure they really understood each other."

The visitor gave an odd smile, then his face suddenly became solemn.

"Did the skulls that you are studying at the *Musée de L'Homme* come from the same collection?"

"Yes. That's the subject of my thesis," the student said, "I'm concentrating on that exhibition."

"I went to the museum, but I didn't see them."

"They've been withdrawn from the exhibition," Lescure said, "They've been put in the Malinowski room."

"Why's that?"

"Everything is upside down at the *Musée de L'Homme* at the moment. This way the students can study them in peace and quiet."

The visitor gave the student an urgent look. His deep dark eyes had a metallic glint that made the girl feel uneasy.

"How about you, how do you like the museum?" she asked in order to change the subject.

"Yes, I like it a lot."

"Why?"

"I came to find out the truth about our world!"

She laughed, "And did you find it?"

"Almost."

The girl looked at his strange necklace. A very old piece. She could have sworn it was a wild boar's tusk.

"Do you know Oceania?" the visitor asked.

"No, not yet. Do you?"

"I've travelled quite a lot in the Northern Territory in Australia. From Newcastle Waters to Darwin and the Gulf of Carpentaria . . ."

"Did you meet any of the Aboriginal population?" Lescure asked. He had taken a sudden interest in the conversation.

"The last hunter-gatherers. Yes, in the Arnhem Land region, and also on the islands. The Lardil used to hunt for ducks, lizards and sea turtles."

"Did you go hunting with them?"

"Oh, no. I was a foreigner and they did not trust me. To go hunting you need to be accepted in their society and that takes a huge amount of time. But I saw quite a lot of things, such as circumcision rites. It was very moving. I went as far as Melville and Bathurst islands. There are just a few settlements at Snake Bay and Garden point . . ."

"I dream about doing that," the student exclaimed.

"Yes, but it's not an easy journey. The Tiwi living on those islands only encountered the white man a century ago. I attended one of their funeral ceremonies. They carve and paint totems. The Elders paint their faces white."

"Is it long since you went down there?" Lescure asked.

"Ages. Yes, it seems ages to me. More than twenty years. Twenty-five perhaps? Things must have changed since then. I was lucky enough to meet the Elders. Today they're all dead and the rest will have been destroyed by the modern world."

"Things change quickly in Australia," Lescure said.

"Very quickly. Of course I went to New Guinea too. Same picture there."

"What were you doing in New Guinea?" Lescure asked.

The visitor's eyes flashed as he stared at a statuette, "I was looking for the truth about the origins of humanity. On those kinds of trips you're always looking to find yourself a bit, don't you think?"

Lescure smiled, "I get the feeling I might have met you somewhere before. Your face is familiar."

"Perhaps we met in New Guinea."

"It's odd, I can't remember."

It was nearly closing time.

"Do you think I might be able to see the works in the *Musée de L'Homme* collection?" the visitor persisted.

"Of course," Lescure said. "Then we can try and work out where we met."

"Where can I contact you?"

"At the museum, I'm here every day. Just ask for me."

"Thanks. I'll make sure I do that."

The visitor waited while the girl moved away.

"I'm a collector and a buyer," he said in a low voice.

"There's some good stuff on the market at the minute."

"Modelled skulls?"

Lescure looked around him. The student was coming back with another piece wrapped in a white fabric. "Here's my card. That's my home address."

The visitor stuffed the card in his pocket without a glance and disappeared behind the totems from the Leeward Islands.

9

Gérard Marlin, the Customs Inspector, trained his binoculars on quai aux Charbons, "What the hell are those two up to?"

Two men were sitting on the cold stone of the quayside, their legs dangling over the water. Two fishing rods pointed towards the centre of the inner harbour, their taut, slanting lines scarcely visible. One of the two fishermen took a bottle from his creel and passed it to his neighbour who declined with a gesture of his hand.

"Two more lads after the bass," Marlin thought as he turned to look towards the dry dock and the warehouses.

Stacks of red and blue containers lay waiting for the *Aldébaran*, a cargo ship belonging to the Messageries Maritimes which was due into port that evening. Towards the Mourepiane terminal there was an incessant to and froing of loaders, creating a din of metal and roaring diesel engines. On pier D a tug positioned itself in front of the *Ville de Tunis*. Marlin adjusted his binoculars. A sailor was waving an arm in the direction of the pilot. The casting-off procedure was getting under way. Marlin lowered his glasses. He wouldn't find out any more today. He noted the ferry's departure time in his notebook and stuffed it in his jacket pocket. For two days he had been hiding in an old tub that served as a training vessel for marine firemen, spying on two guards working for a private security company. He had been watching their movements around a container, which he knew was stuffed with contraband cigarettes. The Virginia tobacco cigarettes came from La Goulette, a port on the Tunisian coast, and were routed via Marseille before going up to northern Europe.

"Good," he said to himself, looking at his watch. "It's midday, let's go back."

He left his hideout and made his way along the charred corridors of the boat. The marine firemen regularly poured litres of petrol over the rusty metal for training sessions in the midst of a blaze and smoke bombs.

The two fishermen hadn't shifted. They looked up simultaneously at Marlin as he appeared on the quay. The younger-looking one had taken out a sandwich wrapped in silver foil and bitten deep into it. Marlin stopped beside them.

"Are they taking?"

"No, not really. Nothing at all."

"But it's a good spot."

"Yeah," the older one said putting his hands together. He had a sharp profile, three days' stubble and hollow cheeks; a mop of black hair looped down over his forehead.

Marlin glanced at the bait box: a plastic container with maggots that squirmed in the damp sawdust, and two large American earthworms. "What are you after?" the customs inspector asked.

"Sea bass."

"Good luck then."

"Thanks, guv."

Marlin went back to his car and started it up. Old bass fisherman that he was, he knew you didn't catch that type of predator with maggots, or American earthworms.

"Let's lay into them," he said to himself. "No time like the present."

*

About a hundred people had gathered in front of La Major Cathedral and were slowly entering the nave. Bérénice Delorme, wearing a long black dress and flecked tulle veil over her eyes, was standing at the top of the steps; an elderly lady by her side. An octogenarian who sported a host of decorations sewn on the back of his grey jacket held out a frail hand to Dr Delorme's granddaughter. They exchanged just a few words. The big shots from the *Académie de Provence* arrived, with their grave faces. A Minister had made the journey.

Clouds had massed on the horizon, towards the great Planier lighthouse. De Palma was thinking about the departure of the *Marie-Jeanne*. He could see the young doctor on the bridge of the schooner, fascinated by the movements of the sails, the taut halyards and the jibs filled with a good sailing breeze.

An imposing vehicle with tinted windows came to a stop. The driver got out and opened the rear door. The mayor emerged, his face in mourning, and began shaking hands with everyone. He stopped in front of Bérénice and embraced her, assuring her of the council's condolences.

The Préfet followed behind along with the Regional Director of the C.I.D., with expressions to match the occasion.

"You'd think that they learn to be sad in those schools of theirs," Bessour said. "They all look identical."

De Palma scrutinized each face in his field of vision. Maistre was at the other end of the esplanade with his back to the sea, discreetly taking photographs of the crowd.

"Let's take a run down to the cemetery," de Palma said.

"You think he might show up?"

"It's not impossible. There's something solemn about death that sometimes attracts them."

The Baron pointed his chin towards the gathering on the church square, "Quite a spectacle."

"Not many young ones," Bessour said.

"Yes. Given the age of the victim, that seems pretty logical to me."

They found the squad car and raced down to Saint-Pierre cemetery on the eastern side of the city.

A cold wind blew between the mausoleums and the rangy yew trees. De Palma watched each of the figures he could see among the stone crosses and the curves of the Cypress trees.

"Let's go a bit higher," he said, pointing to an incline. "We can keep an eye on things from there."

"So do you think we look like the fuzz, Baron?"

"No way. Surely not!"

They stopped at a point where four paths crossed and looked around. A cemetery employee was nonchalantly sweeping the dusty aisles with his broom. From time to time, he deftly shovelled up small heaps of pine needles he had stacked in a corner. The world of the dead stretched away over a seemingly endless expanse of marble slabs, mausoleums in the style of operatic temples, broken columns, and crosses, some lavish and others more modest. The Delorme family vault was situated in a narrow aisle paved with small round stones. Sitting on a green metal bench, with his hands in his pockets, de Palma did not take his eyes off it. Bessour had knelt down between two graves and had taken a pair of binoculars out of his bag. He was watching the area around the vault, and then widened his field of vision taking some remarkable gravestones as his reference point.

After an hour no-one suspicious had turned up in this chaotic setting. The funeral procession arrived. Bérénice walked in front, followed by members of the family and some dignitaries from the world of scientific research. Four cemetery employees stood to the right of the vault. They looked rigidly formal in their black suits.

A man suddenly appeared in an adjacent aisle. He was walking quite fast and looped back up towards the gravediggers. Karim turned his glasses on him.

"Something up?" de Palma asked.

"There's a bloke who looks a bit out of place. Fiftyish, dressed in jeans and a grey jacket."

"So?"

"I guess because apart from me, he's the only Arab around here!"

"Let's see," de Palma had to refocus several times in order to adjust the eyepieces to his vision. The man had approached the gravestone and was looking round in all directions. "Inquisitive, that bloke."

"Must be a gravedigger . . ."

"Well he's not wearing mourning gear."

The individual went up to the cemetery employees and held out a piece of paper to the smallest one, who stuffed it in his jacket pocket.

"Let's move closer, but keep it low-profile," the Baron said.

As they went through the aisle of crosses concealing them, the man spotted them. He stopped for a second and looked at the procession that was now only a few metres away from the grave. Then he swivelled away in the opposite direction to the two policemen.

"There's something moody about that bloke," Bessour said.

"Could be. You go down below. I'm going to try and cut him off in the wide aisle if he does a runner."

The two policemen went their different ways. De Palma walked quickly when he was out of sight. The undertakers were lowering Dr Delorme's coffin and placing wreaths on the marble tombstone. Bérénice Delorme's head was bowed. She stared at the gaping hole formed by the entrance to the sepulchre. The priest stood beside her and read a passage from the gospel.

The stranger was going down the main aisle. Bessour, who was in a parallel row, quickened his pace to get level with him. Suddenly, the suspect started running. Bessour raced after him. He leapt over two tombstones and zigzagged between some flowerpots lying on the gravel.

"Police!" he shouted, drawing his weapon.

The fugitive ran like the clappers. Karim felt as though his legs were moving in a vacuum. De Palma had realized what was happening. He was running towards the cemetery gate and would reach it in a few seconds. The fugitive was cornered. He stopped suddenly and raised his hands in the air.

"Don't move!" Karim yelled, completely out of breath.

The man began to snivel. He looked from one policeman to the other, completely terrified, "Please . . . Please!"

He had a strong eastern European accent. De Palma realized they were dealing with one of the gypsies who hung round the Saint Pierre cemetery to sell religious souvenirs or flowers that had been nicked from the market in the centre of town. Unceremoniously he put handcuffs on him and made him sit down on a bench.

"What did you give the gravedigger?"

"Piece of paper."

"Why?"

"Big gentleman outside . . . he give me ten euros to take piece of paper . . ."

"What was he like, this gentleman?"

"Big like him," he said, pointing at Bessour. "Dark eyes. Fair skin. Wearing hat and glasses . . ."

"Keep an eye on him," de Palma said, "I'm going to see the gravedigger."

The priest had finished the reading from the gospel. The Baron made his way between the groups of people that had formed. He avoided Bérénice Delorme, who was receiving condolences from decrepit bigwigs, and gestured to the gravedigger to follow him to one side.

"Police," he said producing his card. "A man just gave you a piece of paper, do you still have it?"

The gravedigger rummaged in his pockets and pulled out a small envelope. "I haven't opened it. The man told me to give it to the lady," he said with a nod towards Delorme's granddaughter.

"Thank you," de Palma said, "Don't mention this to anyone."

"Right you are, sir." The gravedigger swayed from one foot to the other, his hands together in front of him. De Palma went back to Bessour.

"So?"

"Let him go."

The gypsy massaged his wrists, not daring to look the policemen in the face.

"You're free to go," de Palma said.

De Palma opened the small envelope carefully and took out a card.

"You are going up the Sepik River, where the people are fierce, where they eat men. Go carefully. Do not be misled by your experience among us. We are another kind. They are another kind. So you will find it."

*

"Margaret Mead wrote that in *Sex and Temperament in Three Primitive Societies*," Bérénice said, returning the card to de Palma. "I don't remember where any longer, but it could easily be found."

The air in the salon was heavy. She must have burned some incense. Specks of dust circled in the rays of copper light filtering through the curtains.

"Come on," she said, "let's go out. I sometimes feel as though this house is watching me. I can't breathe. Last night I dreamt all these statues and masks were asking me to take them back to where they were born. When I woke up I saw eyes without pupils watching me."

They went down rue Notre-Dame-des-Grâces as far as the coastal path. The mistral had eased in the middle of the afternoon. The white fringes on the breakers rolled over the cobalt-blue back of the sea.

"I love the wind," Bérénice said squinting. "My grandfather loved it too."

She took several steps over the rocks and stopped by a barbary fig tree that had grown through a crack.

"I love those who yearn for the impossible," she shouted into the salty breeze. "It's something Goethe wrote. Grandpa always used to say it to me. It was the only thought in his life to which he was really attached. Like a buoy in a storm. He would tell me that life is just the sum of the dreams we have in childhood. What do you think of that?"

"Well in that case, I'm a failure."

"You didn't want to become a detective then?"

"Not really. Let's just say I didn't know what I wanted to do and you don't always do what you want. Particularly when you're lazy and not that well off."

"Lazy?"

"Yes, because there are always other paths you can take."

The wind whipped at her hair. She had got some colour in her cheeks and was looking at him with amusement.

"Don't play the reluctant cop with me. My lawyer told me you are one of the best in the Murder Squad."

"That's what he says . . ."

"Well, I believe it's true."

"I always do things thoroughly; I get that from my dad. When he was on strike with his comrades, he could blank out everything else. For up to a month, if that's what it took. They stopped everything coming in to the port. At home we managed. A little more, a little less, what difference did it make?"

"You often think about your father, don't you?"

"He taught me a lot, without me realizing it. I refused to see him while he was alive and now he's gone to the Big Sleep, I'm trying to go back to the things he taught me."

"Like what?"

"Sayings used by proles at sea. You might laugh at them, but they keep you strong when things are going badly . . ."

They had walked near the Fausse-Monnaie bridge; its stone arches were wet from the waves. In the cove, the hulls of the boats flashed every kind of colour.

"You spoke about Margaret Mead," the Baron said, "I don't know anything about her."

Bérénice stood facing the sea and pulled her jacket across her chest. "She was a great American anthropologist. A feminist too. She wrote a very famous book that caused a real stir in the States in the 1930s: *Coming of Age in Samoa*. It's fascinating."

Her voice suddenly sounded terse. She stared at the bay churned up by the mistral.

"You told me the quote which I read to you came from another book . . ."

"Yes. The two texts are often combined in a single edition."

"Do you see any connection with Freud?"

"No, I can't. I'd need to read the book again. As I remember it, she analyses the customs of three Papuan societies. That's all very controversial nowadays. Certain specialists in the field even claim that quite a lot of what she wrote was rubbish. She went in search of western stereotypes on the banks of the River Sepik and of course she found them . . . One always ends up projecting one's own fantasies on to these civilizations. It's the same with early art: people often find significance in works which are far removed from their original meaning."

The Baron lit a cigarette. The acrid smoke of the tobacco made him cough, "Margaret worked along the River Sepik?"

"Yes," Bérénice replied in a flat voice, "in the area where the Iatmul live."

"What year was that?"

"The beginning of the 1930s . . ."

She stared at the Baron. Something had changed in her expression. There was a glint of mistrust.

"Did your grandfather know these works by Margaret Mead?"

A lock of hair hid her right cheek and her lips. She hesitated for a few seconds before replying, "Yes. Grandpa knew Margaret Mead's work."

"Can you tell me any more?"

"I don't think it would help your investigation," she replied as she resumed her walk.

"Quite the opposite. That message was intended for you and it makes explicit reference to Margaret Mead. If it turns out that Mead worked in the region your grandfather explored in 1936, then I think the man who sent you this message meant to say something very precise. Even if we don't yet know what to make of it . . ."

As she walked she stared down at her feet. A bigger wave than the rest splashed drops of spray on the cement that covered the coastal path in places.

"Mead studied the Arapesh, the Mundugumor and the Tchambuli. Three ethnic groups living not far from the River Sepik. The passengers on the *Marie-Jeanne* bought pieces that came from that region. That's all I know."

"Where did the head which was stolen from your grandfather come from?"

"It was a skull that belonged to my father's friend, Robert Ballancourt. It's made of clay, shells and hair."

"Let me repeat my question," de Palma said, chucking his cigarette into a hole in the rock. "Do you know why your grandfather attached such importance to it?"

"That skull came from a Mundugumor man from the village of Kenakatem near the River Yuat, which is a tributary of the Sepik. I don't know who killed that man or why. It was probably during a tribal war."

The Baron no longer knew whether the woman opposite him was trying to manipulate him, or not. He remembered the words of her lawyer who had given him the art traffickers' lead. An idea emerged from the jumble of his thoughts, "Tell me about your father."

Bérénice didn't seem bothered by the question. "He had the same profession as me. I followed in his footsteps. He died in a road accident," she spoke in a monotone, "in 1983."

She gave the impression that she was hiding a great rupture in her life; a sad childhood despite all the money and despite her grandfather's affection. An unhappy love affair perhaps. What de Palma had initially taken for pride now came across as reserve. She rarely smiled and when she did it followed polite convention. Had she ever loved anyone? Had she been scorned by a man?

*

"Hi Michel!" Eva said, putting her long fingers on the marble counter. "Are you well?"

"How about you, gorgeous?"

"You're the only one to call me that," she said, shooting him a saucy wink.

"Tell me, Eva, what's happened to your hair? Got left in the oven did it?"

"You mean you don't like it?"

Every couple of months Eva changed colour. Most recently, she had gone a sort of anthracite-black tinge which darkened her sallow complexion.

"I think the new style suits you."

She adjusted a lock of hair on her cheek, "How long have we known each other?"

"Since primary school."

Eva wore an impish, short-sleeved, brown silk blouse and a flowery skirt that bobbed up and down every time she moved, "Would you like a baguette?"

"Yes, and four cream eclairs."

In the shop window, two slices of pizza had been waiting patiently since morning.

"You can put those two in as well."

"You got people tonight?"

De Palma looked down at his wallet, "No I haven't. I'll be thinking of you as I eat the other one."

She took the note from him, pursing her lips together, "Sometimes I say to myself that maybe the two of us missed out on something. Don't you think?"

"Who knows, Eva? There are times when you have to grab what's there and not think of the consequences . . ."

She winked at him, "You're still dead handsome! There's a few of my girlfriends who go on about you."

"You should give them my number."

"No way. I'm jealous, me."

"They ain't got nothing on you."

Eva gave him a knowing smile. As he went through the door of the boulangerie-pâtisserie, he turned round, "Give me a call, if you've got time. I'm not too bothered about your girlfriends."

"I don't have your number."

"But you know my address . . ."

After the earth was created, the trees were made. Then came the Word. And after that our ancestors.

Our ancestors created the first man. The bible came afterwards. The bible didn't create man. My ancestors did that, a long, long time ago.

A very long time ago our ancestors predicted the arrival of the white man. They advised us never to listen to them.

One of my ancestors had three sons. He preferred to ask one of his sons to slit his throat than listen to the white man. That man was my father.

Testimony of a Huli warrior in "The Gospel according to the Papuans," a documentary directed by Thomas Balmès (Les Films d'Ici, 1999)

10

Number 120 boulevard Diderot was a building made of dressed stone very near place de la Nation in the east of Paris. As he passed the lodge, Lescure greeted the concierge who handed him his mail: bills of no interest, a letter from the museum and a copy of the *Anthropological Review*.

His flat was on the second floor. He trudged up the steps, tearing open the envelope containing the *Review*. His article, "Sepik Art Rediscovered", was on the front page. Over the next week he would receive congratulations from most of his colleagues and criticism from his enemies. And in that confined circle of anthropologists he did have enemies.

Anthropological magazines and piles of student dissertations littered the dark corridor of his flat. For months he had been saying that he should sort through this jumble of papers, but he could find neither the time nor the courage.

The hubbub of Paris came through the living-room windows. He turned on a light, hung his coat over a threadbare armchair, and went to the fridge to fetch a beer. The kitchen window was ajar. He cursed himself for having left it open like that on a cold day.

His huge desk was covered with clutter and research files piled high. A very confined space had been cleared in this chaos of paper to make room for his laptop. At the moment a trophy skull occupied that space: a beautiful piece from a village not far from Lake

Chambri, in the Sepik highlands. Lescure was going to sell it to a collector whom he had met recently and who was paying 10,000 dollars for it. A good price for a piece like that. As he waited he allowed himself the rare indulgence of looking at it on his desk. An enigmatic object, it had mesmerizing, hollow eyes.

"At least you won't end up in a museum basement," the scholar said. "You will shine in a beautiful window. And that is probably for the best ... Deep down you wanted immortality and that's what I'm giving you back ..."

The answerphone indicated three messages. He listened to them. Nothing of much interest. He continued reading his article as he rinsed his throat with little sips of Spaten beer, as he did every time he returned home. The *Review* had scrupulously respected his article. It was a study of the craze for Oceanian art, the price of which was reaching giddy heights in sales rooms as prestigious as Sotheby's, or Christie's.

He moved the old, stainless-steel desk lamp towards the skull. He had kept the lamp since his days in student halls of residence. Geometric patterns decorated the skull's forehead and cheeks. The left cheekbone had been slightly fractured, perhaps during battle. The top of one of the eye sockets bore the marks of blows, as did the right temporal bone. The skull told a story of a distant world; one of violence.

He thought of the tidy sum he was going to make and felt a twinge of sadness. Something told him that he had betrayed many of the promises he had made as a novice researcher and that art trafficking was intolerable. How his soul had shrunk ...

"When you're young, you're so naïve."

Suddenly, came the sound of a breath down a pipe; then a short, musical note. Lescure cocked his ear. A second note came up the corridor, followed by another. The anthropologist froze in terror. He did not dare turn round to look and see who was making this music: he knew only too well.

"I must not know," he cried, staring at the trophy skull. "I must not know. Go away."

He couldn't take his eyes off the severed head. His fingers trembled. He couldn't stop them.

"Go away, I beg you."

The rhythm of the music speeded up. Panting quavers.

Lescure held out a hand in front of him and shook it. "I don't want to see. I don't want to know."

His words hung in the air. The trophy had a disdainful smile. The harshness of its expression was terrifying. Death – which it had so often embodied – could be seen in it.

"That's enough!" shouted Lescure, "Enough."

He squeezed his legs together and blocked his ears. Panic seized him. It was impossible to confront it. The shrill, sickly sound of the flute bounced off the walls.

"Go away!"

The mantra suddenly stopped. Lescure breathed out, as though to rid himself of the pain inside him. He searched in his jacket pocket and found the purchaser's business card. He picked up the phone.

"The sooner the better," he said. "I'm going to get rid of you."

The long arrow struck him in the temple.

11

Paul Brissone, aka "Paulo", had fallen. His body lay on the asphalt of a narrow, steep coastal road by the old Solvay factory, the bald buildings overlooking the bay of Marseille.

De Palma pictured a police detention, at dawn one December day, in the Évêché cells. Brissone tense and silent, ready to cooperate, his gnarled body hunched up, his mug covered in bumps; some old, others more recent.

"Let's go, Paulo, we're going up!" de Palma had said.

Paulo had sized up the Baron for a long time. They had spoken of the past, got in some bottles of beer from the police canteen. Paulo had grassed. Before the court appearance de Palma had sanitized the "godfather's" statement reducing the serious offences to minor ones. In any case, in these gangland crimes evil was never where you thought you'd find it. For more than fifteen years Brissone had given de Palma tip-offs in quite a few cases. A supergrass! Less than a year off retirement de Palma thought he was playing a bad joke on him.

"Crooks are a miserable lot," Paulo often used to say, "despair, that's all they know."

Beyond the centre of L'Estaque the road zigzagged upwards, full of potholes made by passing lorries, to the dead end of an industrial world in tatters. Factories with blocked-up windows still smelled of chemicals and salt, and workers' estates with their white stone, bricks and rusting roofs huddled on the side.

The view stretched over the entire bay of Marseille, still warm from the sun.

"Park here, Baron. Our colleagues from forensics won't be long."

Maistre wore a blue shirt and black jeans held up by a large belt.

"Hi there," de Palma said, tapping him on the shoulder.

He kissed him on the cheek while avoiding looking him in the face. Maistre watched his friend for a few moments and suddenly spotted the anger in him: an edginess to his walk, a swaying of the shoulders, violence in the depths of his dark eyes. The wind pushed his hair back over his temples.

"Where is he?"

"Over there."

Maistre and de Palma didn't need words to communicate: they had known each other for almost thirty years. They went through the police barrier tape. The ground was littered with old tins, rubbish bags and empty bottles. An old television had been used as target practice by the local kids, the smashed-in screen spewing forth cables and transistors.

"Do you want to see him, Baron?"

"Yes."

Paulo lay curled up, dressed in a dark Lacoste shirt, grey cotton trousers and deck moccasins; his head rested on a low, white stone wall. His strong hands had scraped at the soil before he died. The marksmen hadn't disfigured him as they often did. They had aimed at his stomach and chest.

De Palma put one knee on the ground and rested his hand on Paulo's shoulder. The body was already as stiff as wood. Death spread its smell of cold wax and rotting matter. A memory came back to him. Paulo, with his hangdog look, banging his gold signet ring on the counter of his bar.

"Let's have another," he shouted, *signalling to the drunks behind the bar that it was his round.*

Brissone drinks as much pastis as he serves to the customers, "Make room! Hey, Baron, your glass is still full!

"I don't like pastis."

"Go on, just for my sake . . ."

Behind his huge smile and streetfighter's wonky teeth, Paulo could not disguise his longing to put an end to his life of fear and shady goings-on. The underworld had dealt him his final blow. He must have suffered terribly: wounds to the stomach are the worst possible kind.

De Palma got up again, with an absent expression. A roll-on roll-off ship that was belting along towards Africa gave a blast of its siren as it passed the Château d'If.

"You got any clues, Jean-Louis?"

"No, none at all. What do you want me to say? Settling of scores. No witnesses. No evidence."

The wind lifted the pages of a magazine that was hanging on a clump of salicornia.

"At any rate," the Baron sighed, "he knew it would end like this."

Maistre scratched his head, "We're going to have to tell his mum."

"If you like I'll deal with that. I think he was on his way to see her. She lives just round the corner."

The two friends stared at each other.

"I know," said Maistre, who had guessed what the Baron was thinking. "Very few people knew that Paulo had a mother around here . . ."

"Who reported it?"

"A worker from the firm cleaning up the site: Mourad Kelbir. He doesn't speak good French. Karim's with him."

"What time was it?"

"Just past three. The court phoned us at four."

"Lucky the seagulls haven't eaten him."

Nearby there was a barrier fencing off the old chemical factory established by Rio Tinto in Braque and Cezanne's time. Stone arcades still supported the terraces that backed on to the uniformly white rocky areas and heaps of earth stuffed with arsenic and asbestos. A worn sign hung from the rectangular wire mesh saying: INDUSTRIAL SITE – NO ENTRY.

The Baron kneeled one last time by the body and said a few words like a prayer. Then he got up again.

"There's nothing more to say, Jean-Louis. They followed him from the bar and struck here. The only spot where he was a child."

"They haven't found his gun."

"What about his motor?"

"It's vanished."

"That's odd."

"Yeah. Why take the car?"

A blast of a siren came from the road down below.

"I'm going to see his mum."

"Want me to come?"

"No thanks, Jean-Louis. I have to tear myself away before those bright sparks from forensics show up."

Maistre nodded, his face sad.

"It's funny," de Palma said, "just as I'm about to quit the police, Paulo gets snuffed. I was going to meet him for a pizza at Les Goudes." He shrugged and lit a Gitane. "Eating with the Bill! That was his idea of a normal life. He told me: 'I've got something important for you.'"

"Any idea what it was?"

"No. He wanted to do me a favour. He said to me: 'I know stuff that'll help you.'"

"Do you think he knew the blokes that put him here?"

De Palma exhaled a little smoke through his nose and removed a wisp of tobacco that had stuck to his lower lip. "Of course," he said, turning to look east, "the mob aren't difficult to understand. You and I both know who might decide to hit."

"Keep your cool. Don't do anything stupid."

By the time the small, grey police forensics van arrived on the scene, the Baron was already at the entrance to the Penarroya estate. The house where Paulo had been born was only twenty or thirty yards away. A rusty old bike had been chucked against a small bank strewn with dry grasses. An old gypsy with a pockmarked face was cleaning his battered Renault Safrane with great sweeps of a chamois leather.

"Hello, I'm looking for Madame Brissone."

"Jeannette?" the old man replied in a falsetto voice. "First house, boss. After the big fig tree."

"Yeah, I know that. What I really wanted to know was if she's in at the moment."

"Well I think so. She hardly goes out any more. My daughter runs errands for her."

"How is she?"

The gypsy raised his dark eyes towards the crime scene, "Bad news?"

"The worst she'll ever hear."

The old man bowed his head towards a hand heavy with rings. His chamois leather glistened. He gave it a sharp flick and started polishing the wing of his car once more.

Brisone's birthplace nestled in what seemed like a miner's terraced house between a breezeblock garage covered with corrugated iron and a gaunt pergola. De Palma pushed at the little wire mesh gate and went through to the cement terrace. Two chipped pots held barbary figs that were weary from the sun. Jeannette was sitting on a worn bench, sorting through a dish full of green beans which she topped and tailed with her fingernails.

She got up with difficulty when de Palma was sufficiently close for her to be able to make him out, "My God, Michel, it's been so long . . ."

She wore a blouse with small pale flowers that stretched across her enormous, matronly bust. Her eyes, although still dark, were slowly dimming and had the same ash-grey tints as her hair.

"I'm almost blind, you know. Come closer son, so I can see you. I'm expecting that rascal Paul this evening, but he's late. I'm going to make him some Pistou soup. He likes it so much."

The rosebushes that Jeannette had planted in the unforgiving ground had produced some subtle mauve Queen Elizabeth roses with a sickly scent.

"There, I think that should be enough," Jeannette said, tossing the beans into a casserole.

De Palma was so overcome with emotion he felt he could barely speak. He put a hand on Jeannette's forearm. "*Maman*, I've come to give you some bad news. He won't be coming back tonight," he said with a knot in his throat.

Jeannette looked at him through a veil of cataracts, "You mean . . ."

He gripped her frail hands that were deformed by rheumatism.

"My poor boy," she whispered, keeping her head bowed for several minutes. Jeannette was a strong, proud woman; she would keep her tears and her despair for when she was alone.

"Oh he was no angel! He did some stupid things . . . But he was a good lad. Believe me." She looked around her at the pathetic setting. A strip of rusty metal hanging from the pergola swayed in the wind. "All his life he struggled to survive. But what can you do? He never had a father . . . that man was a real monster. May the devil take him and all of his kind! If you knew how many times I had to come between him and his dad, to protect him. It was me who took it, but I was used to that. Poor Paulo and poor me . . ."

De Palma clenched his fists. Jeannette stood upright, her hands open on her frayed apron. Her mind was elsewhere now, far away in the back room of her memory.

"While he was in prison I used to do his ironing for him and I always put a sprig of lavender inside. He always wanted me to put one in for him, picked from one of the bushes in front of the house.

Each time the screws would take it off him and chuck it away. There's no God in those prisons of theirs."

The sinking sun was coming through the clouds setting the Frioul Archipelago ablaze. A light breeze carried the sounds of the coastline and the murmurs of the city.

"I want to see my boy," she whispered, wiping her pale eyes.

"I'll drive you there."

She peered at the horizon with her failing eyes, "You'll find the ones who did it? Paulo always told me you were the best detective he knew."

"He said that?"

"Oh yes. So I'll carry on living until you catch them. After that I'll be on my way. He was all I had, you know. Nothing's any use now."

The siren of the marine fire brigade wove through the traffic in L'Estaque.

"Paulo called me just this morning. Do you know why he wanted to speak to me?"

"He never told me his business. Nothing at all. The one thing I can tell you is that he'd been jumpy for a few days."

"No-one came to see you over the last couple of days? I mean people you didn't know."

Jeannette thought for a few seconds. "There were two men at the beginning of the week. They claimed to be Paul's friends. They wanted to see him."

"Did they give you their names?"

"No, not at all . . . Or maybe I just don't remember . . . And then I can't recall their faces. I think they were about your age."

De Palma was almost angry with himself at having to question an old lady who had just lost her son, but he told himself that a serious lead might emerge from Jeannette's recollections.

"What did they want, these two men?"

"That evening when Paul came home I told him about them. He

116

knew them and told me not to worry, but I could tell by the tone of his voice something was wrong."

"He didn't say anything more?"

"No, son. Just that he was going to call you. He had to talk to you about it."

Jeannette leant both elbows on the table and buried her face in her hands. A neighbour passing along the chemin du Littoral stopped. De Palma gestured to her to come in. She was an old woman, her skin like leather from the sun, and she had a scarf over her silvery hair.

"Do you know her?" the Baron whispered.

"Of course I do!"

"Take care of her. Paul's just died."

"Holy Mary, Mother of God!" the neighbour exclaimed.

The cranes at Mourepiane terminal had switched on their flood-lights for the night's unloading. Facing them, the harbour and the Frioul archipelago were melting into shades of grey. At the far end, alone in specks of sunlight, stood the Planier lighthouse: gateway to the world.

12

Paul Brissone had kept a bar in the Traverse de l'Équateur in the outlying district of la Blancarde. Le Beau bar was flanked by low houses and huge plane trees that blotted out the sky. Paulo had felt secure in his joint, standing behind the counter covered in red formica. In a dark corner, a tired pinball machine started up of its own accord shouting: "A million! A million!"

As he pushed open the door, de Palma noticed the waiter dipping his hand under the counter, "Hey, François, you can leave your sawn-off shotgun in the drawer. I'm a friend."

"Sorry, boss! Didn't recognize you."

When François spoke as if he had beans in his mouth, trying not to lisp, it was invariably a sign that he'd been at the pastis more than normal. He was decked out in a Che Guevara T-shirt and blue, striped trousers that made him look like a dull character from a T.V. sitcom.

"You can't spot cops anymore?"

The waiter pursed his lips and cast a ferocious glance through the window. "It's not that, boss. You know how it is these days . . ."

As a token of respect, François had placed a photograph of Paulo in front of some bottles of cordial that were never used. The crook was smiling broadly at the photographer, with a fag hanging from the corner of his mouth, his emaciated face half eclipsed by the flash. Nearby, tied to a magnum of Abbey beer, his boxing gloves hung by their laces. At the age of twenty Paulo had begun his small-time career in the rings of Provence before getting knocked down in a fight by a southpaw from Nice.

"I've come as a friend to ask you a question," de Palma said, "You know I won't be in the police much longer."

"Yeah, Paulo told me. Good to hear that, boss."

"Did Paulo tell you why he wanted to see me so urgently?"

The waiter frowned and put both hands flat on the counter. A heavy gold signet ring with a diamond sat on the little finger on his left hand. "The only thing I remember is when he left here on the evening he died. We had a pastis together, nice and peaceful like. And then just before leaving he went like this: 'I've got to see Gilbert!'"

"Gilbert?"

"The Bishop."

Gilbert Maglia was known as "the Bishop" because of his "ecclesiastical" appearance. His enemies called him "Gigi", or sometimes "The Godmother". De Palma knew him for his burglaries, which were always organized in a masterly manner. He was an artist who did everything with great sensitivity.

"Why did he talk about the Bishop?"

François rubbed his two forefingers together. "They were good mates. Gilbert, he was coming out of prison. So Paulo was happy and helped him out a bit. What you'd expect." He grabbed a bottle of Pastis 51 and served de Palma, "That's all I know."

"Do you know where I can find the Bishop? I don't want to have to hang about waiting for him to report to the police station."

François snatched a notepad that was lying on the bar and in faltering handwriting scrawled down an address and phone number. With the tips of his fingers he pushed the paper towards the Baron.

"Thanks, François."

"That's O.K., boss."

"You'll need to wait a bit before you close the bar. My colleagues are coming to carry out a search. Got anything you want to show me before they come charging in?"

"Nothing, boss."

Hand on his heart, the barman refused to accept the five-euro note offered by de Palma.

*

In this classic gangland scenario of settling scores, there was only one grey area: a bullet from a .38 Special was found thirty metres away from the corpse. Lucky, or what? Maistre had asked them to run the metal detector over a pretty wide patch.

"Paulo didn't have a .38," de Palma said, tapping a Gitane on the blue cardboard packet.

"You sure about that?"

"Sure as my name's de Palma."

"There could be two killers."

In the place where they had found the body, there was a brown stain and chalk markings.

"Judging by the direction of the bullet, they fired from here."

"So it was Paulo, or someone with him."

The Baron turned towards the bay to think. At the end of the port at L'Estaque an old boat was slowly rotting away, its hull studded with big round rivets. The gangway portholes formed two large dark eyes and the door a toothless mouth.

"He wasn't on his own, Jean-Louis."

"That's just what I was telling you."

"Any news on the motor?"

"No."

"We'll find out about it eventually."

"I"m surprised they didn't torch it."

"Maybe it's lying at the bottom of the sea."

A train passed over the thin piers of the bridge spanning the limestone shoulders and disappeared whistling into the belly of the hill.

"Did the technicians find any other bloodstains?"

"I don't know anything about it," Maistre replied. "I'm waiting for the report, but it's taking a long time."

The death of a gangster always ranked below other homicides, with little hope of it ever getting resolved. The clear up rate for score settling was close to zero. The figures were mind-boggling: several hundred thugs died and not a single investigation was resolved.

"We'll need to come back and question the workers at the site," Maistre said.

A scooter went up the hill covered in factories and disappeared sputtering between the corrugated iron walls that separated the demolition site from the potholed road.

"Where have they got to with the search of Le Beau bar?" de Palma asked.

Maistre flipped open his phone, exchanged a few words with Bessour who was in Paulo's café, then hung up again.

"Nothing much, just some pastis that fell off the back of a lorry . . ."

"Are they still on the spot?"

"No, why?"

"We should go back and take a last look round. I think he stashed a notebook away under the counter."

"We can go down there whenever you want."

"Let's go right away . . ."

*

A quarter of an hour later they went into Le Beau bar through the back door. A smell of aniseed and stale tobacco clung to the walls.

"I've often seen him put a notebook here," the Baron said ducking down to cast an eye under the till, "Shit, nothing there!"

"Our lot have gone over everything with a fine-toothed comb."

"And what about the place where he used to put the gun? Did they look there?"

Maistre shrugged, "I don't know where he used to keep his weapon."

"Second drawer on the left. In the place where he used to sit."

Maistre went round the counter and opened the drawer. "Nothing there."

"Oh, shit. Did you check the numbers on his mobile?"

"We didn't find any mobile."

"He had two."

"Or maybe three? Like all cons."

Brissone kept a small black notebook in the drawer where he put his pistol. Only a few regulars, or the waiter, could know this notebook existed since it never left Le Beau bar.

"Do you know where the barman is?"

"François? He lives just round the corner."

De Palma shut the drawer and headed for the door, "Let's go and see him."

*

François lived in a small two-storey house just near La Blancarde station. Maistre had to knock on his door several times before he appeared, his face crumpled and headphones plugged in his ears.

"Oh, it's you."

"Hiya," de Palma said.

"We've come for Paulo's notebook," Maistre added, giving the door a shove with his foot.

"But . . ."

"Come on, we know it's you who's got it," the Baron said, "Hand it over and cut the crap."

The flat smelled of sweat and stale cannabis. On flowered wallpaper that looked as if it dated back to the 1970s, François had pinned up photographs of the stars he worshipped: Johnny Halliday and Michel Sardou.

"How can you listen to shit like that?" de Palma asked glancing at the mini hi-fi system.

"I like it."

"Well Johnny's still alright, but Sardou? Only cops listen to that stuff!"

"Not everyone is an opera lover like you," Maistre exclaimed; he was growing impatient.

François shrugged and disappeared into a second room that had to be his bedroom.

De Palma followed him. "No messing, eh, François?"

"No problem, boss."

The mattress on the floor was covered by a duvet printed with a scene from a Western: Monument Valley with an eagle spreading its wings. An old P38 pistol peeked out from behind the pillow.

"Nice weapon!" de Palma exclaimed. "A legend. My dad had one when he was in the Resistance. What are you doing with that?"

François was trembling. He had crossed his hands in front of his crotch.

"Behave yourself, François!"

De Palma emptied the magazine and put the P38 back on a clapped-out chest of drawers.

"I'm scared, boss."

"Me too . . ."

"How do you mean? I don't understand."

"I'm scared you'll get yourself into trouble."

"No boss."

"The notebook."

François thrust his hand into the chest of drawers, moved aside two pairs of briefs and took out a small black notebook.

"I didn't want the police to find that. You never know."

"You're right. You never know with the police . . ."

De Palma checked that no pages were missing and then stuffed it into his pocket. "Thanks, François."

"No problem, boss."

De Palma tapped him on the shoulder.

13

Bessour's silhouette cast a thin shadow on the shiny tiled floor.

"We've got news, son."

"About Delorme?"

"No, about Brissone. We need your help."

"O.K., on my way . . . Be with you in two minutes."

De Palma gave the coffee machine a kick to get the coin to take, and then pressed the "Espresso with sugar" button. The corridor was dimly lit by a barred window overlooking La Major Cathedral and the inner harbours of La Joliette. On the rota board the unions had pinned up a list of candidates for the next shop steward elections.

"Shall we go?"

Most of the numbers in Paulo's notebook were mobile numbers. Some of them did not have a name attached. Either they were no longer valid or had never existed. Sometimes the police called people who had never seen or heard of Paul Brissone in their lives.

"The numbers without a name are in code," de Palma said, chucking his plastic cup in the basket.

"Not very wise," Maistre replied.

"We're going to have to use our little grey cells. It can't be too complicated. Paulo never went to a top university – let alone a top telecom engineering school . . ."

"Could take time then. Who are we to talk?"

"Too right. We'll start with the numbers written last in the notebook."

They took down about thirty of them and copied them on to a whiteboard. Bessour rushed in wearing a grey tracksuit. He strained his jet-black eyes to look at the board, which was covered in figures, letters and arrows.

"We're stuck, Karim!"

Bessour took off his jacket and puffed out his chest as though preparing for a scrap.

"You'd need to ask our colleagues in Counter Intelligence. They know all about deciphering these bloody codes."

"Yeah, but unfortunately they're keeping their bloody mouths shut," Maistre replied. "You might as well phone the talking clock."

Bessour took a step back. His sharp eyes slowly scanned each of the numbers. "Simple, lads," he said after five minutes.

Maistre and de Palma looked at one another without saying a word.

Karim was renowned throughout the force for being the king of crosswords and mind games, "01 after 06, you can't have that . . ." he pointed with his finger at the third row of figures, "01 isn't a prefix for mobiles. He moves around two groups of digits."

Bessour went up to the board. "We've still got to find out which group of digits is being swapped round."

"Swap the first for the last," de Palma said.

"Why do you say that?" Bessour asked.

"Because that's just like Paulo."

"Maybe he only switches one digit," Maistre suggested, "or maybe a group of three."

De Palma leant on his desk and scrawled some combinations in his exercise book. Maistre and Bessour dialled some numbers. They reached a plumber and a secretary working for the Messageries Maritimes. Two other numbers were unobtainable.

"You're right, Jean-Louis," Bessour suddenly shouted. "The last three digits become the first three."

"That's what we've just tried," Maistre said.

"Yeah, except he reverses the order of the three, one at a time. The second becomes the first and the third becomes the second. Do you get me?"

Maistre started chewing his biro.

"So how did you work it out?" the Baron asked.

"Er . . . complete luck . . . I was trying out a combination and I found your mobile number."

Maistre gave a deep breath and undid the collar of his shirt, which was soaked in sweat. "Baron, I hope you realize what it would mean if a judge or a colleague who had it in for us got hold of that?"

"Yes, but we've got the notebook!"

Maistre shook his head and headed towards the door. "Can you do us a report on these phone numbers, Karim?" he asked as he opened the door. "A detailed, precise report. None of your de Palma stuff, understand?"

"Understood, Commandant," Bessour said. He had begun to put up some new numbers on the board.

*

The next day, the providers supplied the names of their subscribers. There were quite a lot of women, which was standard practice for hoods, who always had two or three phones, sometimes more, using fictitious names.

In order to have a tap put on these mobiles the two policemen needed to apply through the proper channels. In this type of case there was a risk of long delays occurring. They decided to go for a different approach. On one list, de Palma wrote down the "female" telephone numbers, on another, Maistre noted the names of people on police files. There were just three of them. Then on a list they nicknamed the V.I.P. list they wrote down the names that didn't match either of the former criteria.

"If we call the people on the "female" list or the "previous" list, we'll get nowhere, and in two days' time there won't be any subscribers left."

"You're right, Karim. We've got two names in the V.I.P. list."

"Carry on."

"Stéphane Martini and Frédéric Faure."

Maistre wrote down the two names on the board.

De Palma immediately started tapping away in the central police database. "Nothing on Martini. Not even a minor offence to put our minds at rest. A respectable citizen."

"That's just what bothers me," Maistre said.

"You suspect everyone."

Karim repeated the procedure for Faure, "I've got a Faure here, on boulevard Baille." Karim massaged his forehead. Ever since he got up that morning, he had felt as though an electric drill was running through his head. "Shit," he said suddenly.

"What have you found, the Virgin Mary?"

"He's a lieutenant in the Border Police here in Marseille."

"So what do we do?" Maistre asked.

"We do nothing," de Palma replied. "We're going to quietly keep tabs on Faure. I imagine Paulo didn't have his mobile number by accident. So either he's cheating on me, or he had something going with this bloke."

The main bell of La Major Cathedral struck four round, low notes, which were lost in the thin streets of the old town. They were followed by the blast of a siren.

"The *El Djezaïr* is on its way," de Palma said.

"On time for once."

The office smelled rancid. Karim opened the window. The rectangular courtyard at the Évêché station was calm. The early night shift would soon be coming on duty.

"Let's question the lads at the L'Estaque site," de Palma said. "I've a feeling they've still got stuff to tell us."

*

They walked back up the hill for about twenty metres and caught sight of a large man in high boots and grey dungarees. Bessour got out his police I.D. card.

"We're carrying out an investigation into the murder which took place down below. I'd like to see Mourad Kelbir."

The man pushed his blue plastic helmet to the back of his skull, revealing leathery skin burnt by the sun. "Mourad's up there, by the tractor."

The foreman pursed his lips together and whistled, "Hey, Mourad, come here. Gentleman wants to see you."

A great beanpole of a man, his arms swinging like a puppet on a string, came down the path that had appeared on a pile of rubble.

"Salaam," Bessour greeted him, holding out his hand. "Sorry to disturb you again."

"Salaam . . ."

Mourad held his hand to his heart. "No problem," he said in a strong North African accent. He had sharp features and piercing, dark eyes beneath thick, bushy eyebrows.

"When you found the body, where were you exactly?"

"Right here. I was talking to Adama . . . And then suddenly I saw this man lying there and I said to myself there was something wrong. That's it."

"Nothing else?"

"No, nothing."

"You didn't see any cars passing a while before that?"

"No."

Bessour turned back towards the crime scene. A few rays of sunlight were coming at an angle through the large clouds above the sea. De Palma had gone a bit lower down and was watching the road.

"I'd like to speak with Adama," Bessour said, staring at the foreman.

"I don't know where he is."

Mourad lowered his eyes and looked at his boots which were covered in a thick layer of white dust.

"What's the matter?" Bessour insisted. "Do you want me to summon him down the station?"

"No, sir," Mourad replied.

Bessour frowned and assumed a stern expression. "He's got no papers, is that it?"

Mourad looked shifty and rubbed his rough hands together.

"Go and fetch Adama for me," he commanded in a deep voice. "Tell him I don't care if he hasn't got any papers."

The foreman went off and returned a few minutes later with a thin man of average height, wearing a yellow helmet on his head. He had a faded checked shirt, with sleeves rolled up to reveal cracked arms.

"This is Adama."

Adama took off his helmet and shook Karim's hand. Small tufts of white hair were beginning to appear at the top of his temples. His eyes were reddened from the unhealthy air of the building site, and on either side were fine wrinkles that spread all over his face.

"I'm here about the bloke found at the bottom of the road. Did you see anything?"

Adama shifted from one foot to the other, holding his helmet in his fingers. "I didn't see anything."

Bessour went up to him. "You see I think it's the other way round. You saw everything, but as you haven't got any papers, you wanted Mourad to be the witness."

Adama gave a smile.

"When I came to see the body," Bessour continued, "I noticed some blokes working in the place where we are now. That wasn't you, was it?"

The African nodded several times.

"What you tell me, I'll record it as anonymous, see? You won't have to go to the police."

"Talk," said Mourad. "The gentleman doesn't give a shit about your papers."

Adama remained silent for a long while, his gaze drifting across the surface of the sea. "There were two cars," he finally said timidly. "A white one and a blue, I think . . . The white one was parked across the road. When the blue car stopped, I didn't understand what was going on. The driver, he got out to see what was happening. There wasn't any driver inside the white one. Suddenly the driver of the blue one fell. Then the passenger, his colleague, he got out. There was the sound of a shot and that was it. I saw a man coming out from behind the embankment just nearby. As he left he was walking backwards."

"Can you describe these men for me?"

"They were white, but it was too far away to see their faces."

"And the cars?"

Adama thought for a few seconds, his eyelids closed, as though he were replaying the film of what had happened. He had seen a man die right before his eyes, without really taking it in. The discovery of this murder and the body must have produced a shock that wiped out some of the details engraved in his memory.

"There was a white car, a very common make. It was small . . . Might have been a Renault Clio. Yes, it was a Clio like yours." He pointed towards the unmarked car belonging to the Murder Squad.

"And the other car?"

"Now that was a posh one. Blue, maybe black. Four-wheel drive."

"That it?"

Adama raised his right hand with the palm towards Karim.

"That's it."

"Just one shot?"

"Yeah, just one, boss."

Bessour didn't press him. He shook Adama's hand and held out his card. "If anything happens, get in touch straightaway."

Adama took the card and screwed up his eyes to see what was written on it. Bessour went back to the crime scene.

Behind him, driven by the sea wind, a curtain of rain left a light patch on the surface of the sea.

"Anything new?" de Palma said.

"Yeah, I've got some news. There were three of them. Two in Paulo's car and one lying in wait. He'd put his motor across the road to stop them."

"Which means he wasn't there long before them. I'd always told Paulo he had to keep an eye on his rear, but also on what lay in front . . ."

"He should have listened to you. But there's a major problem."

"What's that?"

"Just one shot. That's the first time I've seen a gangland boss snuff it from a single gunshot. Normally they use a full round of bullets."

"You're right," de Palma grumbled. "A single shot means he was killed elsewhere and then brought here."

"Or else Paulo was only wounded. He asked someone to take him to his mum. Then there was the roadblock."

"The driver managed to get away, but meanwhile Paulo had got out of the motor and crawled to the place where he was found."

"That's what I think."

Bessour kicked a can of skimmed milk, sending it bouncing across the tufts of grass growing through the tarmac.

"Good," de Palma said. "I'm going to see Gilbert Maglia."

"Who's he?"

"Paulo's barman gave me his name."

"You don't want to arrest him?" Bessour asked.

"Not yet. If we put him in the nick, he might not tell us much. Best try something else."

The first drops of rain beat down on the white pier in L'Estaque. A crane that must have dated back to the days of the Rove canal tunnel perched its clawed fingers above the pleasure boats nibbling away at the jagged coastline.

14

"The Bishop" lived in the Quartier des Abattoirs at 45 boulevard Bernabo. The four-storey building was a short distance away from the huge sugar silos of the Port Autonome and the Bassin du Président-Wilson.

The shutters were drawn; the place looked uninhabited. The narrow dark stairwell reeked of lavender; the concierge must have recently washed the floor. On the second floor, he pressed his ear to the door of the flat on the right. Inside a television droned. The Baron rang the bell. The voice stopped dead. He rang again. Nothing.

After three further attempts, the door opened, held by a security chain. A woman's face appeared, still pretty, thin and worn out, thick mascara lining her eyes. "What do you want?"

"Gilbert. The Baron wants to speak to him on Paulo's behalf."

The face looked him up and down, an amused grin on its lips. "Don't know a Gilbert, let alone a Paulo! Nor the Baron for that matter."

The woman's voice was rough. She'd outlined her wrinkled lips thickly for emphasis.

"That's O.K.," de Palma said; he had just realized the Bishop was standing behind the door, very likely with a gun in his hands, "I'm a friend of Paulo's. I was supposed to see him tonight, if he hadn't been hit."

"Yeah, but I still don't know who this Gilbert is."

The Baron raised his voice. "Tell me Bishop, I know you're in there and can hear me. Either you open up, or I come in and get you. Because I'm a friend of Paulo's and I'm also a bit of a cop. Do you understand, or do you want me to give you a more colourful explanation?"

The woman stared at him for a moment, then stepped back and released the chain.

The living room was plunged into semi-darkness and smelled of sweat and the sweetish scent of a deodorant. Slanting shafts of light came through the shutters. In his bare feet and with a T.V. remote control in his hand, Gilbert Maglia went to sit down on a French Regency sofa of ancient brown leather. He was wearing a vest that revealed the sparse hair on his chest.

De Palma realized that he had landed in the middle of a bit of leg-over. Maglia's salt and pepper hair was still damp from the exertion. He had a round face, the manner of a crafty priest, two deep lines started on either side of his flat nose and ran down to his chin. He hadn't shaved for at least two days.

"What can I do for you?" he said fiddling with the gold cross that hung round his thin neck.

"Before Paulo passed away he wanted to tell me something important. Do you have any idea what it was about?"

The Bishop rubbed his hands. On the left one he was wearing a wedding ring that was too big for his finger. "Don't think so. He didn't say anything to me. I don't know who you are." He remained silent for a moment.

"What was Paulo up to before he passed away?"

The woman appeared in the kitchen doorway. She had tied back her hair and lit a cigarette. "Can I get you a coffee?"

Maglia waved at her to indicate that she should make herself scarce, and then hesitated. His gaze was fixed on a dot that only he could see.

"You can say what you like," he said in a low voice, "but Paulo was alright. Yeah, maybe he was a headcase, but he had guts."

134

"I know that."

"He wanted to settle down. He was that age . . . God rest his soul."

Maglia spoke in a small, husky voice, using his hand to emphasize each sentence. "He wanted to bow out after one last job. He wanted to know if I was up for it. I said no. Stands to reason. I'm through with all that."

The Baron nodded to show he agreed, even though he didn't believe a word.

"What sort of job?"

"I've no idea. Paulo wasn't the sort to rabbit on."

Maglia got up and snatched a packet of Marlboro from the round table that had pride of place in the middle of the living room. As he moved, the barrel of a revolver peeked out from between the cushions on the sofa.

"Alright Gilbert, we're going up a gear now. If Paulo wanted to talk to me, it wasn't about taking early retirement. Something was bugging him and I'd like to know what. You're going to have to help me before I lose my cool."

"I've got nothing to tell you."

"Well at least you can explain to me what you're doing wandering round with a gun. Got something on your conscience?"

Maglia fidgeted on the sofa, "Not everyone likes me, you know."

"Me neither, but I reckon you've still got stuff to tell me. Hand over the gun, barrel first."

The Bishop produced a Smith & Wesson .44.

"That's some weapon," de Palma whistled. "Don't skimp on the firepower, do we sir?"

Their looks met. The Baron emptied the barrel and stuffed the bullets into his pocket.

"It felt dodgy," Maglia said, looking at his weapon in the detective's hands, "seriously dodgy. I don't know why, but Paulo was scared of something."

"Tell me more."

"He wanted me to go up to Paris with him to sort out a job."

"Nothing else?"

"No, nothing."

"And what was your role in it?"

"I just went with him, that's all. He was in touch with a fence and then the shit hit the fan."

"A fence?"

"Poor old Paulo didn't have time to tell me any more. If I knew something, I'd give it to you, boss. He told me you were on the level."

De Palma got up. The Bishop remained seated, his hands flat on his knees.

"O.K., so you were playing the strong man. Waving your gun around just to impress the fence. But why did the Paulo business go wrong?"

"I'm not a grass, boss."

"Here we are, big drama, straightaway. I'm not asking you to grass, I'm just asking you to tell me what a friend was doing before he died."

"Yeah, but even so."

"As I'm talking to you now, I'm not with the police. I've got what you might call a debt to Paulo. So if I come and see you again, you'll be talking to me personally, not to the fuzz. In your case the second option might have worked better. Do you understand?"

The Bishop shook his head several times and turned up the sound on the television. The woman had gone to the door and attached the safety chain once more. De Palma suddenly remembered her face: a girl who was sometimes on the game in the Quartier de l'Opéra, weekends only. He would know where to find her if he needed to.

"Nice other line," de Palma said.

"How do you mean?"

"Possession of an offensive weapon and living off immoral earnings."

Maglia knew the law and sentencing policy. If he reoffended he would get ten years, "I've had it. I'm too old now. If I go back inside, I'll never come out. I've had enough."

"Two men paid Paulo's mum a visit some time before he died. Mean anything to you?"

Maglia fiddled with the remote. The television was grinding out some grotesque game show. Bursts of laughter mingled with the sound of buzzers being pressed.

"It was because it all went pear-shaped, that's why he wanted to see you. The doctor that died."

De Palma didn't bat an eyelid. "I am in charge of that investigation. What's the connection?"

"Two blokes were supposed to nick some stuff and they came back empty-handed. I was there that evening when they came back. Paulo said they should call you so the police wouldn't think it was them that killed the doctor."

"And that was why he wanted to talk to me?"

Maglia rested his elbows on his knees and held his head between his hands.

"Who killed Paulo?" de Palma asked.

"I don't bloody know! Maybe the bloke from Paris reckoned he'd been double-crossed."

No, it's people from around here, thought the Baron. Thugs from a rival gang.

"I need the names of the two burglars, Gilbert."

"Gilles Berry," the Bishop blurted out. "I only know one of them."

Berry's name didn't mean anything to the Baron. He wasn't high enough in the hierarchy. He must be one of the local wideboys who had decided to supplement his benefits by fleecing the city's bourgeoisie.

"Berry," repeated Maglia, "but remember I haven't told you anything."

"We"ll forget about the immoral earnings and the firearm," de Palma said. "Where can I find him?"

"In Coquet bar," he whispered so the woman wouldn't hear, "on the chemin du Littoral."

"Thanks, your Excellency."

De Palma put down the Smith and Wesson on the table, helped himself to Maglia's mobile which was lying there, and took out the SIM card.

"What are you doing?" Maglia exclaimed.

De Palma bent the S.I.M. card in two and chucked it on the fitted carpet. "I'll give you back your shooter, but I'm going to cut your talk time for a bit. Just in case you get the urge to sound the retreat."

*

Some dumper trucks loaded with rubble tore down towards the scabby, deserted districts by the old docks. Each day by the Porte d'Arenc, a huge tower rose a little higher into the sky. It was to house the headquarters of G.C.M., the maritime freight giant.

De Palma dialled Maistre's number on his mobile. "Maglia's given us a name and address: Gilles Berry, Coquet bar. Mean anything to you?"

Maistre thought for a few seconds. "No, I don't think so."

"Doesn't matter. Meet me over there as soon as you can."

The door of Coquet bar creaked on its hinges as it opened. The place dated back to the 1950s. Originally, it had been a modest house serving as a brothel for sailors stopping off on their way to the Bassin du Président-Roosevelt. The walls were built with planks, later reinforced with bits of stone nicked from the sheds at the naval repair yards. Above the door, a Stella Artois sign wrecked by the mistral and the sun was still hanging on by three ancient rusty screws. In the window there was a circular red, white and blue Routier restaurant sticker.

"Count your trumps, it's not difficult!"

Four elderly sailors, their faces marked with fine wrinkles around the eyes, were playing cards on a red Formica table, jeering every time one of the players didn't trump correctly.

"Who cares. I've got two suits . . . Bugger your trumps."

The Baron went up to the wood-panelled counter. A matronly woman made up to the nines jumped up from her high stool and gave the bar a dust. She had undone the top three buttons of her black nylon blouse; it seemed like an open invitation to have it off with her behind the spare beer crates.

"What can I get you?" she said, wiggling her bum in her tight-fitting leather trousers.

"I'll have a half. I'm looking for a friend of mine: Gilles Berry. Do you know him?"

"Depends who wants to see him . . ."

De Palma shot her a saucy look. "I dare say, if I had the time in this nice weather I might invite you to take a stroll somewhere near Carry-le-Rouet."

"Make my day," she said adjusting the strap on her bra.

"Sadly . . ."

She looked at him in amusement. Her head was rather small, and she had dyed, straw-coloured hair with a black parting right through the middle. When she smiled, her grey eyes lit up, and there was something endearing about her face. "Gilles went out just now. Said he'd be back in a few minutes. You a copper, then?"

"What makes you say that?"

She eyed suspiciously the bulge of the Baron's Bodyguard against his hip.

"I come as a friend," the Baron added. "Bearer of good tidings."

She clicked her tongue against her palate.

"You'll just have to wait."

One of the card players got up to go for a slash, his nose ravaged by all those rounds of pastis. "Another round, Gisèle," he said decisively as he passed the barmaid.

Gisèle crossed the room and picked up four beer glasses, which she rinsed before filling them with a pale, flat, watery liquid.

"Bar doing alright?" de Palma asked.

"No, there aren't any customers any more. Those days are gone. It was my dad who started the business, when there were loads of sailors. Now when the boats come in, the unloading's all done at night. Then in the morning they're off again and you don't see anyone. It's a real disaster. I don't know how I'm going to stick it out till I retire."

The sun beat down on the windows of Coquet bar. On the other side of the Chemin du Littoral stacks of red and blue terminal containers could be seen. The *Napoli* had docked. Grey smoke from its forecastle chimney evaporated into the azure sky.

"You're getting me down," de Palma said.

"You don't say!" Gisèle gave a coarse, resounding, laugh.

"Don't laugh. My dad was a sailor and so was my granddad. To see all that disappear, it really gets me down."

The Baron dipped his lips in the gnat's piss that Gisèle had poured out for him. Berry pushed open the door. Catching sight of the cop, he paused then very nearly turned tail.

"Gentleman to see you," the landlady said, indicating de Palma with her chin.

Berry went over to the bar. He must have been in his thirties. He wore baggy jeans that came half way down his bum. A large gold chain hung over his shiny chest. A poser from a generation that was alien to de Palma.

"What do you want from me?" Berry said with a trace of exasperation in his voice.

De Palma took out the photograph of Paulo and put it on the bar. "He's fallen on the battlefield, a desperado killed in action. Take a good look at his face and tell me when you start to remember."

Berry glanced in the mirror opposite. Between the bottles of pastis the three old men could be seen totting up the scores after their umpteenth round of cards. None of them had looked up.

"Well?"

"Don't know him. Never seen him."

"You sure about that?"

"I'm telling you, I don't know him!"

"Doesn't mean a thing, eh?"

"Give us a break. You're pissing me off with all your questions."

In a flash de Palma had Berry by the shirt collar and with a sharp movement pinned his head down on the bar. Gisèle immediately vanished into the back room.

"Do you know who I am, you moron?"

"Leave it out!" Berry said, trying to wriggle free.

"I'm the detective you phoned after you went to Dr Delorme's house."

De Palma tightened his grip. Berry's nose was red, a thin trickle of blood coming from his lips.

"I suggest you get your memory back and pretty quick too."

"O.K., boss."

The Baron gave him a shove. A beer glass smashed on the floor.

"Hey, it's kicking off!" one of the old men shouted.

"Stay where you are, grandad," Maistre said. He had just appeared in the doorway, his police armband and weapon clearly visible, "Watch those trumps, or you won't have any when you need them."

De Palma looked pointedly at the clock behind the bar. "Did you come on foot, Jean-Louis?"

"No, in the back-up car."

Gisèle reappeared.

"Don't get involved, love," she said to the old sailor with the purple face who had got to his feet.

Berry was leaning on the counter trying to pull himself together.

De Palma thrust the photograph in his face once more. "Take a good look. This man died a few days after you visited his mother. Coming back now, is it?"

Berry frowned.

"Right," de Palma said, putting the photograph back in his inside jacket pocket. "The three of us are going to take a little walk."

"Where are you taking me?"

"Don't worry," Maistre said, "we're not going to the National Police torture chambers. You get the special treatment."

De Palma chucked a five-euro note on the bar and winked at Gisèle. She looked back at him contemptuously. He took Berry by the arm and led him out. "Come on pal, we're going to take a stroll down towards Saumaty. The sea air'll do you good."

Some articulated lorries loaded with containers were passing through the gate of the Mourepiane terminal, heading up towards L'Estaque.

"Tell us about your visit to the doctor's house," said Maistre. "We want to know everything."

"He was supposed to be asleep. We went in, took the stuff and left."

"What stuff?"

"Skulls and masks . . ."

"And then?"

"I went through into this sort of office and I saw a dead man with this thingy on his head. I realized straightaway what was going on, so I left without taking anything. That's all."

"Who was driving the car?"

"You've just shown me his photograph."

"Paulo?"

Berry nodded in response.

"Who was the bloke who went with you to Paulo's mum's house?"

Berry clenched his fists. "You know everything don't you!"

"Too right," Maistre replied. "That's how it is. We know everything!"

"He'd come down from Paris. He was desperate to see Paulo. So I went with him to Le Beau bar. The barman told me Paulo was at his mum's house. So I drove him there. Because that bloke, he didn't know Marseille at all."

"What did he want?" de Palma asked.

Berry kept hiding behind the two policemen, watching every car that passed along the Chemin du Littoral. A siren blast broke through the hubbub of the city.

"There's the *Napoli* on its way," the Baron said to relax the atmosphere.

Berry looked at him in surprise.

"Let's start again, Gilles. Who was this bloke?"

"That's what I've been asking myself."

"And you've never managed to find the answer . . . Bloody hell, Gilles! Do you think we're dumb or something?"

"No."

A lorry screeched to a halt at a red light. Between the huge, rectangular containers the massive, red hull of the *Napoli* was slowly manoeuvring away from the quay.

"The problem with blokes like you," Maistre said, "is that sooner or later you want to belt them to get them to talk. Looks like you're asking for it."

They had got to the squad car. Maistre unlocked the Clio and brandished his handcuffs, "Come on, let's take him down."

"No," de Palma said.

He took out the photograph of Paulo once again and shoved it in Berry's face.

"Paulo was my friend, got it? The guy's name, the one you went with?"

"You don't have a choice," Maistre added. "There are two crimes involved: there's the doctor and then there's Paulo. At the moment you're just a witness and we're not here to pick on you. But if you won't open your trap, we'll have to get you up before the judge. Then you'll be a suspect and you'll spend tomorrow night in Les Baumettes gaol with your file marked 'I killed Paulo'. Do you get the picture? Otherwise you could go back to that little pastis ritual in Coquet bar and this meeting never took place."

Berry bit his lower lip, "There was something dodgy about that job."

"How come?"

"I don't know. Just a feeling." He bowed his head and kicked a tar-spattered pebble.

"Who put you in touch with this bloke? Paulo?"

"No, Castella."

"Nono Castella!"

"Yeah. But it was just a favour. He said to me: 'Take this bloke to Paulo's place.' That was it."

Maistre couldn't suppress a smile of satisfaction. "Don't get stressed, we won't say anything to him. What did you talk about with this stranger?"

"Not much. This and that."

"I see. Describe him for me."

"He wasn't a con, that's for sure. A well-dressed bloke who talked posh. Medium height, glasses . . ."

"What did they talk about with Paulo's mum?"

"Nothing. It was him he wanted to see."

De Palma rested his hands on the roof of the unmarked car, his shoulders hunched. "What you don't seem to get, you jerk, is that if we take you down the nick, it's not going to be party time for you. Give me the cuffs, Jean-Louis, I've left mine at home."

Maistre held out his handcuffs. "Hands behind your back and no funny stuff."

Berry gave a beseeching look. Maistre drew his weapon.

"Wait a minute, I haven't told you everything. I know the guy's nickname."

"Out with it!" de Palma shouted.

"The Antique Dealer."

"How do you know?"

Berry dug his hands in his pockets, "I heard Castella talking about 'the Antique Dealer.'"

"Why? Is he an antique dealer?"

"Yep. That's what I understood."

144

"Does he handle stolen goods?"

Berry nodded in agreement.

Maistre persisted, "And what does he handle?"

"I don't know. I swear."

"Give Gisèle a kiss from me," the Baron said. "You can go."

De Palma got into the car. "That takes the biscuit," he grumbled. "Paulo, the art trafficker. With Castella pulling the strings."

"We need to tread carefully with Castella," Maistre said. "He's in another league."

Noel Castella had only been nicked once, for armed robbery. A youthful error that cost him eight years of his life in prison. Saint-Martin-de-Ré, then Clairvaux, time enough to compile a complete address book of the underworld. No-one really knew how he made his living. He was said to be merciless and vicious as a pit bull. A right bastard. He had links with the police and local politicians.

"Tomorrow we'll start from scratch on the Delorme file," de Palma said. "I'm going to contact a shrink at the Court of Appeal. He's an old hand, an expert I've come across a couple of times."

"Why a shrink?"

"I want to clear up this business of totems and taboos. Can you and Karim have a go at the art trafficking? We need to see things more clearly."

As Berry strode along he tripped on a plastic bottle, sending water squirting across the muddy pavement.

"Hop it," de Palma said. "I've got an important meeting this evening."

"Who with?"

"None of your business."

After a hundred metres, Berry turned into an alleyway and went up some large, white shining stone steps, past a great wall of small houses that had seen better days; terraces shaded by gaunt fig trees with grey trunks; wire pergolas; and dirty vines. He disappeared into his world of small pleasures with its view over the inner harbours, just above the dismal Chemin du Littoral and the huge container parks.

*

That evening, at just past eight o'clock, Eva rang at the Baron's door; a bottle of champagne in her hand. "I told my future ex-husband I was going to see a girlfriend of mine. He didn't believe me of course, but he doesn't care. He's watching the match on the telly."

Her sweet scent pervaded the flat. She was wearing a frilly skirt that fluttered around her. She still had that mole at the edge of her lips which Michel found so irresistible. He kissed her tenderly on both cheeks.

"I think I'm going to do something stupid," she said.

She went through to the living room. A pair of jeans was lying on the back of an armchair. De Palma picked them up and threw them into the corridor leading to the second bedroom.

Her manners were direct, with a trace of masculinity in her character that aroused the Baron. Her eyes ran over the bookshelves, "You're a bit of a bookworm!" She stopped in front of the C.D. collection. "Impressive!"

"You know me . . ."

"I didn't know you had so much music at your place!" she frowned. "It's nothing but opera!"

"There's the Stones and the Clash too," the Baron was apologetic, "even the Ramones!"

"It's all ancient stuff!" She had a mischievous look. The uproar from boulevard Mireille-Lauze beat at the windowpanes. "Play me something I haven't heard. I don't know any of it."

He suddenly remembered that when his wife had asked him the same question, he had introduced her to the final scene from "Tristan and Isolde" – with limited success.

"Let's listen to a really beautiful aria." He took out out an old

146

recording of "Tosca" with Renata Tebaldi and inserted it in the tray of the C.D. player.

Vissi d'arte, vissi d'amore,
Non feci mai male ad anima viva!
Con man furtiva

"I lived for art, I lived for love . . ." he said.
"It's beautiful," she replied, "but sad too."
"It's a tragedy."

Perchè, signore,
Perchè me ne rimuneri così?

"Who's singing?"
"Renata Tebaldi. She's the greatest."
"She's got a fantastic voice. Will you take me to the opera one day?"
"Yes."
He felt slightly awkward sitting on the end of his sofa. "I'm glad we've met up again," he said in a barely audible voice.
She gave him a playful push. "Don't just sit there, turn down that light and go and get two glasses. We're going to make a toast."
He searched in his kitchen cupboard and found the last two champagne flute glasses remaining from his marriage. He hadn't used them in years. When he returned to the living room, Eva had got up. De Palma took the bottle from her hands and sought out her lips.
"Don't be in such a hurry," she said, putting her hand on his chest, "I think we've got a few chapters to catch up on."

15

"I found this in the attic." Bérénice Delorme's face was calmer. She was wearing trousers that tapered down her long legs and a beige silk blouse. She was holding a round box little more than five centimetres thick, made out of rusty steel.

"A reel of film!" de Palma said.

"There are four just like this one. Would you like to see them?"

She had called to tell him she had discovered something important. De Palma had dashed across the city, his siren on, jumping the red lights without ever asking himself what it might be about. When confronted by the old reel he hid his disappointment.

"I've found a 16mm projector," she said, "in perfect condition. If you want I can show you these reels."

"Certainly."

"Come on then."

She led him to a musty room on the first floor, lined with ancient flowered wallpaper. Children's toys were lined up on shelves: a strange collection of dolls with glass eyes, die-cast steel electric trains, robots from another era. In the middle of the room there was a Heurtier projector on a stool. Bérénice loaded the spool and laced up the leader.

"You seem to know what you're doing," de Palma said.

She depressed the starter and let a metre-and-a-half of leader wind through the gate. "Could you put up that detachable screen in front of you?"

He unpacked the tripod and set up the equipment.

"Very good. Now turn off the light and come and sit down beside me."

Their two seats were close together. He moved away a bit. She started the film and settled back in her armchair.

The first images were blurred shots of some trees beyond a river. "That's the Sepik," Bérénice explained. "A large river that flows into the Bismarck Sea in the north of New Guinea. You can follow it up quite a long way into the interior. It was there that the *Marie-Jeanne* arrived in 1936. She went up the Sepik and then ran aground on a sandbank. Several members of the expedition continued in canoes, or on foot."

A few seconds later the focus became sharper. The camera was on a boat and was approaching the riverbank.

"Yuarimo," Bérénice said; she had suddenly become agitated.

"Do you know it?"

She didn't reply, her expression frantic as though consumed by the unfurling images. Some children were playing in the water and seemed to take flight at the sight of the camera. An old man with wrinkled skin made gestures at the boat. A group of women had hidden behind what looked like banana leaves. In the next frame some younger-looking warriors were surrounding the old man.

"That's probably what they call a Big Man. An individual respected for his powers of speech, his courage in battle and his generosity. The Big Man spent his wealth lavishly for the benefit of the community. We'd do well to follow their example."

Bérénice had leaned forwards in her armchair, as though she wanted to examine each of these images in greater depth. "What you're seeing is very rare. It was probably the first time anyone had ever filmed that world."

A large house. A huge mask hanging from a gable just above the entrance: a terrifying face made up with whirls and spirals. A laughing crescent-shaped mouth revealing pointed teeth. A white man appeared in the camera's field of vision. A tall man with an ascetic face, eyes sunk deep in their sockets and a protruding Adam's apple. He was wearing a canvas hat and trousers with large side-pockets. His dress suggested several days spent in the bush.

"Robert Ballancourt!" Bérénice exclaimed.

Her eyes scrutinized the picture. "I can't see Grandpa . . ."

She was visibly very disappointed not to catch a glimpse of her grandfather in the images that flitted across the screen, to the staccato whirring of the projector.

Two stills and then several wide shots slowly revealed the interior of the Men's House. Everywhere there were very long, narrow masks; strange faces with large, bulging eyes open wide that conveyed anxiety and sometimes anger. Skulls hung from broad, stylized hooks.

"Those are 'trophy skulls'," Bérénice explained, "enemy heads captured in raids on neighbouring villages."

A close-up of a modelled face with a frightening expression. De Palma couldn't help crying out in surprise. The head was the one he had seen in his nightmare.

"Is something wrong, Monsieur de Palma?"

"No, just a pain in my stomach. I get it sometimes . . ."

The image vanished, numbers and stripes danced across the screen. Bérénice got up and switched on the light. "What do you think, Monsieur de Palma?"

"It's sad to see those pictures."

She studied the Baron's face, "Why's that?"

"Because that world has disappeared. I imagine the grand-children of those men and women are now wearing T-shirts, eating crisps and drinking Coke."

"You're not wrong about that."

"It's sad because they've been robbed. I imagine those heads you see in the film are now in museums or private collections."

"Yes," she said, "they go for a fortune."

"Who could have stolen that skull of your grandfather's?"

"I don't know."

Her face clouded over. She pointed towards a battered cardboard box. "There are other reels I'd like to show you." She loaded another one and started the projector with a sharp gesture that made her blink. "It was filmed in the same place, at Yuarimo."

The pictures were in poor condition: long, wide-angle shots showed the village scattered among betel palm trees, rectangular houses on stilts.

"Everything you see no longer exists. They have to rebuild everything roughly every ten years."

"Why's that?"

"Because of the climate and the insects. Look at the side of the Men's House, the old posts are rotting away."

"That house doesn't exist today?"

"Well, yes and no, because they rebuild it just the same."

"Have you been to Yuarimo?"

The question embarrassed her. "Yes."

Some men were plaiting long wicker baskets and attaching vegetable fibres to them.

"They're making ceremonial masks. They must have done that to honour the explorers."

On a large lawn facing the Men's House two huge figures appeared, borne by some dancers.

"That's magnificent," de Palma said.

"It is, isn't it."

Bérénice seemed wary of each shot on this latest reel of film. It was as though she feared she might uncover some unknown truth about her grandfather's life. The tone of her comments was colder and more distant.

"What's the meaning of this dance?"

"It takes place in front of the Men's House. At Yuarimo it's a dance for welcoming visitors. It shows they were very well received."

Her eyes flitted swiftly across the screen, looking for the tiniest details. "What do you think?"

"It's fascinating," de Palma replied blinking. "On the other hand, I don't know where it gets us."

"I just wanted you to understand the background to the skulls in Grandpa's office and the environment in which he lived. Part of his life was well known, particularly his life here in Marseille, but this part much less so. It was almost a secret. You'd probably have to see the other reels to understand it a bit more."

He had a feeling that she was flagging up a path towards a destination she had chosen for some reason. Otherwise why the insistence on showing him these images from so long ago? He thought of the ship's log of the *Marie-Jeanne*. The old manuscript also took him back into the past.

Bérénice shook the box of films. "Would you like to see them?"

"Yes, but not here. I have to respect procedure and show them to my colleagues. I'm going to have to seize them." He waited for her reaction, but none came.

"No problem," she said indifferently. "I'm available if you need any further information."

"Of course. I'll call you tomorrow."

He stacked the reels and stuffed them into his bag.

She held out a frail hand. "So, see you tomorrow."

He looked at her intensely. "You haven't asked me how the investigation is going . . . Aren't you interested?"

She pushed back a lock of hair and gave a weak smile. "I don't want to interfere in your work. That's all."

He went out without saying anything further. The walls were wet from the slanting streaks of rain and he was forced to take cover under the cedar tree in the garden. Long, dark-green plaits of ivy ran up the facade of the house to the roof tiles. On the first floor there was a light on. A silhouette moved across . . . De Palma shoved his notepad under his jacket to protect it from the rain and prepared to run to the gate.

A curtain moved. He pretended to look up at the sky while keeping one eye on the front of the house. The curtain shut once more and the light went out.

*

Ever since leaving Évêché police station Bessour had been humming the same song:

J'aime les filles qu'on voit dans Elle,
J'aime les filles des magazines . . .

De Palma was sitting on his right. Maistre was slumped on the back seat, watching the plush facades of the city centre go by. The mood was gloomy. The idea of watching some old films to find a murderer was not to everyone's taste.

Si vous êtes comme ça, téléphonez-moi,
Si vous êtes comme ci, téléphonez-me!

"How about changing the C.D.?" Maistre grumbled.

"I'm trying to improve the mood."

"I've got something really cool to play you," the Baron said, suddenly rummaging in his jacket pocket. "It's a pirate copy of 'La Bohème' at the Fenice in 1973 that one of my opera mates gave me. Renata Tebaldi . . . Sublime."

"Spare us, Baron. We're here now."

The black foyer walls of Le Breteuil cinema were lined with worn posters from Antonioni's "Blow Up" and Ford's "Prisoner of the Desert".

"That's going back some!" Karim whistled.

"They're good films," Maistre said.

"Next you'll be telling me they don't make films like that any more!"

"Too right. It was a golden age."

Bessour smiled doubtfully. He preferred literature to the cinema. He read one or two books every week and dutifully did his Arabic course so he could immerse himself in the great classical writers. He felt that while it might take him a lifetime, one day he would be able to read Ibn Khaldun, Ibn Sina and Taha Hussein.

The side door opened. The projectionist appeared in the doorway, "Come through, we'll go this way. The other person is already in the cinema."

A long, sloping corridor with a tired, red fitted carpet led to the different screens. A crumpled poster for "Monsieur Hulot's Holiday" hung above Screen Four.

"Are arthouse movies still popular then?" Maistre asked.

"No. We're closing down in two or three months' time."

"That's a shame. I often used to come here."

"Not enough audience. No grants any more. People take the car and go to the multiplex in the suburbs."

"What's going to become of it?"

"I don't know. Maybe a minimarket, or a boutique. Who knows?"

"As long as they don't turn it into an old people's home!"

The projectionist pushed open the double doors leading to the Jean-Vigo screen. Bérénice was sitting in the second row. On catching sight of the three policemen she got up. De Palma did the introductions.

"Have a seat," the projectionist said, "I'll put on the first reel. If you want me to stop at any point, just raise your arm."

They sat down in the front row. Bérénice went back to her seat behind them.

"Ready to start?" the projectionist shouted from his booth.

De Palma nodded and twiddled his pen over a fresh page of his notepad. Maistre put on his glasses. The projectionist loaded the reel into the projector and laced up the leader.

"From what it says on the label on the box," Bérénice said, "this reel was shot in 1961 during an expedition my grandfather took part in."

"Does it give any names?"

"No, there aren't any. All it says is that it was shot in New Guinea, in the mountains."

The lights went down. A strip of white film appeared, streaked with lines and pencil marks. Silent, colour images, wide shots depicting a craggy landscape. Some of the peaks emerging from the mist were festooned with snow. The sides of the mountains were covered in dense jungle.

"Do you recognize this?" de Palma asked.

"No," Bérénice said, her eyes fixed intently on the screen.

After a few seconds a village appeared: round houses with roofs made of large leaves, surrounded by a rudimentary enclosure of large twisted branches. Some inhabitants passed in front of the camera lens without taking any notice.

"The members of the expedition must have been a familiar sight in the area," Bérénice whispered. "Normally the indigenous people were very wary."

The cameraman had taken several shots of the expedition team going through a pass high up in the mountains. About twenty porters were following behind three white men, with guns slung over their shoulders. They walked through the tall grasses swaying in the wind.

"Beautiful," Bessour said.

"It's the first time I've seen these pictures," Bérénice replied in a voice overcome with emotion.

The camera suddenly jerked and moved away. Over a ridge covered in dried grasses, at a distance of at least a hundred metres, some heads appeared, shrouded by the yellow tips of the waving grass. The camera immediately moved back onto Delorme who had grabbed his gun and was holding it at the ready. The porters had crouched down – terrified. Some of them hid behind the crates they had thrown on the ground.

The cameraman panned rapidly on to the men lying in wait behind the ridge. One of them had stood up. He bent his bow and aimed it towards the line of explorers. His hair was like a lion's mane and he was wearing a large white collar.

De Palma quickly scanned every part of the screen in search of the smallest detail. Intuitively he sensed that something was unfolding that would give him a new lead.

A new shot, the image jumped, now following Delorme who had moved away from the group of porters and approached a group of warriors with staring eyes. He held some white shells in his hands and opened his arms in a gesture of peace. The warriors stepped back, each trying to hide behind the others' shoulders. The expression in their shifting eyes oscillated between terror and aggression. The tallest one, who had the muscles of an athlete, approached to within a few metres of Delorme brandishing a spear. He stepped up and down on the spot as though performing a dance.

Other sequences had been shot in different places. Women hid themselves, usually behind a curtain of naked men. Most of them wore a long veil of roughly woven cloth reminiscent of a fishing net.

"It seems to me we've just witnessed the encounter of two worlds," said Bérénice, her eyes damp. "Two worlds that knew absolutely nothing about each other. It's quite extraordinary."

As the film continued, the expressions softened and the faces relaxed. Sometimes a smile was caught on camera. Clearly the two explorers had succeeded in being accepted by the group of human beings they had stumbled upon.

A length of leader flooded the screen with white, and then scrawls appeared, followed by other images that had clearly been shot later. Delorme was sitting in the middle of a circle of men and he seemed to be completely accepted by everyone. They exchanged words and gestures, sometimes laughing at what Delorme said. Then the camera paused on the faces of some young girls, who smiled into the lens. One of them had clearly caught the interest of the cameraman.

"What a beautiful face!" Bessour exclaimed.

"Yes, very fine features," Bérénice said.

The face was that of a girl who had barely emerged from puberty. Her nose was slightly flat, her lips soft and sensuous, her eyes almond shaped. Her two small firm breasts jutted out beneath her white shell necklaces. She smiled listlessly as she stared at the camera lens. Delorme suddenly came into shot and put his two hands on the young girl's shoulders, which provoked hilarity among her young companions.

The reel had finished. The projectionist's face appeared in the booth window. "Do you want to see them again?"

"Yes," Maistre replied, "but not today. Could we get them put on a disk?"

"I know a specialist who can do that . . ."

"You don't want to put it through our lab?" Bessour asked.

"No, that'll take too long."

"I can let you have the films on D.V.D. by the end of the week. Is that O.K. for you?"

"Perfect," de Palma replied, turning towards Bérénice Delorme. "I'm sorry, but I'm going to have to keep these films. We'll take great care of them."

"I'm going to have another look in the house," she replied. "I think that there's more stuff. Photos especially."

"Anything that might be of use needs to be examined," Bessour said.

Bérénice couldn't hide her confusion. De Palma wondered if she had just discovered some truth in these pictures that had completely overwhelmed her.

"I don't see where it's taking us," Maistre grumbled.

Bérénice stuffed her notebook and pen in her bag. In her hurry to do so she dropped a mirror. Karim picked it up and handed it back to her.

"Thank you," she said in a small voice.

"Why do you think your grandfather never showed you these films?" Bessour asked.

She hesitated for a moment as if answering this question might force her to confront a reality she feared, "I don't know," Bérénice replied, putting on her coat.

"I know that you were very close," Karim persisted, glancing at his two colleagues who were standing a bit behind.

"It's true we were close, but he didn't tell me everything about his past life. Particularly those chapters . . ."

"Why?"

"I don't know . . ."

"Men like to have their little secrets!" put in de Palma.

She slung the strap of her bag over her shoulder.

"We won't keep you any longer," de Palma said.

Bessour watched her going off down rue Breteuil. Her hair bobbed up and down on her shoulders.

"Strange woman," Maistre said.

"Very attractive," Bessour added, "A right little liar."

"You think that too?" de Palma asked.

"Yeah," Karim said. "I watched her during the film. I'm sure she was pretending to see that stuff for the first time."

"I think so too," Maistre said.

De Palma looked at his watch and winked at Maistre, "Right. Got to go."

"And where might that be?"

"It's just an idea. I'm going in search of a ghost. Who knows, maybe it really exists."

*

He got into the stream of cars heading towards the Quartier de la Joliette. A digger was making holes in the road, causing the air to vibrate. It was single-lane traffic as far as the ring road which ran over the Arenc docks and the rusty rail junctions for freight trains.

He turned off into boulevard des Dames and nearly bumped into an overloaded Peugeot 405 estate that was leaving for Algeria. The *Napoleon Bonaparte* had docked, a thin plume of smoke coming from its chimney.

The bar des Colonies was situated at the corner of a dusty road whose facades must never have been cleaned up. Washing hung from the windows. The glass door of the bar was decorated with a map of Corsica and a Moor's head.

"Hello," de Palma said casually, catching sight of the boss who came out from the back of the bar.

"What can I get you?"

"Just a half. Heineken."

The landlord's eyes sat on the edge of his skull. He had puffy eyelids and a thin, mean mouth. He placed a glass under the spout and put his large, hairy hand on the chrome tap handle.

The walls were yellowed by smoke and decorated with signed pictures of football stars from *Olympique de Marseille*. Above the billiard table there was a black-and-white photograph in a flashy frame: Josip Skoblar, black hair falling down across his forehead and grinning broadly as though he'd just scored a penalty.

"I'm looking for some old sailors," de Palma said. "Men who would have been at sea before the war."

"You a cop?"

"My grandad often used to come and have a drink here."

"What was your grandad called?"

"Henri de Palma."

The boss's face lit up, "Monsieur Henri! I remember him, but that's going back a long way . . ."

"Over thirty years."

"That was when my poor old dad ran the bar. I know because the old men used to tell stories about sailors. Of the times they went to

Singapore or Sydney . . . When you're a kid, those things make you dream!"

"Even when you're an adult too . . ."

The landlord, who answered to the name of Jean-Marc, placed a cardboard beer mat on the bar and put the foaming half on top. "I think I can still picture your grandad," he said, staring at an empty table. "A tall, respectable man, always well dressed, with completely white hair. He used to sit in that place and talk with his old mates. I'd listen to them. Once he told me about Cape Horn. Stories like that stick in your mind."

"He'd sailed round it in about 1910, just before the Great War."

"How old was he?"

"He was born in 1882."

Jean-Marc whistled. Henri de Palma like many sailors had married late in life. He had his first and only son at the age of forty-five.

"So he can't have been that young when he used to come here for his pastis."

"He died a few days short of his birthday. He would have been ninety-eight."

"I hope we get there ourselves," Jean-Marc said, putting away some glasses that were sitting in the dishwasher tray.

A man of about fifty was absorbed in his game of bingo. His signet ring tapped on the chrome-plated slot machine.

"You're looking for old sailors?" the boss said.

"Yes, men who would have been on the sailing ships," de Palma added.

The boss gave another whistle, "I don't know any myself," he said, "There can't be any left."

"Can't be sure about that," de Palma said. "The last sailing ships were laid up at the end of the 1930s. Some carried on sailing until the end of the war. A man born in the 1920s might have known them. At that time you could go to sea very young."

160

The landlord glanced over towards the bingo player. "He's the President of the Cape Corse Association of Former Sailors. We'll ask him. Tell me, Richard, do you know anyone who would have sailed before the war?"

Richard looked up, "There's still a few of them left," he said in a flat voice.

"I'm looking for a sailor who would have sailed on a ship that left Marseille in 1936. According to the ship's log there was an apprentice, called Ange Filippi."

Richard frowned. "I know a few people called Filippi. The first name rings a bell. I'll have to find out."

De Palma wrote his mobile number on a bit of paper and handed it to Richard.

"I'll call you when I get any information."

"The sailing ship was called the *Marie-Jeanne*. It was built for a voyage of exploration, collecting works of art in the Pacific."

The Association President frowned, "Your story rings a bell. I think one of our old fellas might know a bit about it. Every now and then I hold these evenings in memory of old sailors. I get them to talk a bit and my lad's there to film it. You don't want it all to get lost."

"You're quite right, Richard," Jean-Marc said.

Richard leant his elbow on the counter. "What was the Captain's name?" he asked.

"Meyssonnier. Fortuné Meyssonnier."

"I did know him in a way. As President of the Association I went to his funeral. He died not so long ago. In the 1980s."

"Did he live in Marseille?"

"In the Quartier Saint-Laurent, like a lot of them do."

"Did he have any next of kin?"

"Not that I know of . . . When they buried him in the Saint-Pierre cemetery there were just people from the Association. That's where I first heard about the *Marie-Jeanne* because some big noise gave a

161

talk about it. It seems like they travelled round the world and collected a whole load of rare objects."

"Do you remember anyone else who paid their respects to Captain Meyssonnier? A scholar or someone well known in the field?"

Richard was lost in the few memories he had retained of the little farewell ceremony for an old sailor. "No," he said, "I don't remember. I can still see Commandant Joubert reading a long speech, but no-one else. It was more than twenty years ago . . ."

"He was buried in the Saint-Pierre cemetery?"

"No, but that's where he was cremated. His ashes were scattered out at sea by Planier lighthouse. It was moving."

"Were you there?"

"Yes, I can remember it like it was yesterday."

Richard raised his head again and stared at de Palma, "There was an Ange Filippi! I'm so stupid. That's how I knew Ange Filippi."

"He was an apprentice on board the *Marie-Jeanne* . . . Do you know if he's still alive?"

Richard nodded several times. "Of course I do," he said after a few seconds. "He lives in the Quartier Saint-Laurent too."

"Do you think I could see him?"

"His son looks after him a lot. He lives on place de Lenche. He's easy to find."

De Palma paid for another round, engaged in some small talk about the uncertain future of the port, and then said his goodbyes. The street was deserted. The door and window of the bar des Colonies formed two rectangles of light in the night: openings through which sea-farers' memories flooded out. The topmen smiling from high up on the yard. Men furling the mainsail, shouting words that were snatched away by the wind. The Pacific having another of its mad moments that made the white waves roar. Sailors, some thinking of the hostesses they had left behind in rue Bouterie, others of the plump women in the Papeete brothels. Then the weather calming on the approach to the Leeward Islands. The air becoming heavy. In the warm breeze the voices of the ghosts of the *Marie-Jeanne* were coming out from the long night of oblivion.

*

At the bar du Pont de Palma bought two packs of Gitanes. Claude the boss held out a heavy paw. "Hey, Michel, we never see you! What's happened to you? Fallen in love?"

"Er . . . Not yet!"

"Will you have a pastis?"

"No, thanks. Must dash, bye!"

He went out and crossed avenue de la Capelette, deciding that for once he would feed himself properly. He stopped at the butchers, Chez Dédé.

"Hello, son. You alright?"

"Yeah, I'm flying!"

Lina Baldini, an elderly lady whom he had known from birth turned round and looked him up and down. "My God, it's Michel de Palma!"

He held out his arms and placed a discreet kiss on both Lina's hollow cheeks. Since the death of her husband, she was always dressed in black, some large, gold jewellery being her only concession to vanity.

"I'm so pleased to see you, son!"

"Me too, Lina."

Lina shook his arm. Her eyes had a strange glazed look. "I think about you a lot at the moment, you know," she said, "you poor thing!"

"Well yes . . . It's going to be the anniversary in ten days."

"Poor Pierre! Are you going to have Mass said for him?"

The Baron jangled the keys in his hand. "Of course, Lina. Next Tuesday at five o'clock. The priest can't make it any earlier."

"You're a good lad. Your mum always said you were a heathen, but you're a good lad."

The butcher held out a package across his refrigerated glass display case, his eyes following it, "Here you are, Madame Baldini."

Her thin hands caught hold of the plastic bag. "Off you go, son! And look after yourself!"

"I'm going to the opera soon."

"Oh, what are you going to see?"

"'Ernani'."

"Oh that's beautiful! I saw it with my poor dead husband. My God, that was a long time ago."

"I'll be thinking of you."

She frowned, "Tell me, you're not going out with that girl from the boulangerie-pâtisserie are you?"

"Er, yes I am . . ."

"Lucky boy! Alright then, see you on Tuesday."

Lina went out of the shop, clutching her stick with one hand.

Lina's small house at number 20 rue Laugier smelled of old paint and fish soup with saffron. Pietro her husband used to lecture the local youth in his tenor voice. He made his "r"s roll as if they were on wheels and his "u"s sound as though he'd come from across the English Channel.

When he got home de Palma opened a beer and threw himself into reading the ship's log of the *Marie-Jeanne*.

We're going to stay in the New Hebrides for some time. Ballancourt and the Delormes have been invited to the French Ambassador's residence. It's become something of a custom. I have the impression that news of our arrival precedes us at each port of call. It's like having a guiding spirit, like the gods of the ancient Polynesians. The indigenous people we meet are generally very welcoming.

. . .

The holds of the *Marie-Jeanne* are almost full. We have decided to put in at Noumea and stay there for about one month. From there I will dispatch the great bulk of the cargo by steamboat to France.

Ballancourt and Delorme spend like it's going out of fashion. It has to be said that they do not pay much for the works of art they purchase. Most commonly these are masks and totems, some pretty sizable, as we need several men to hoist them aboard.

. . .

Some of the masks have been put in my cabin. It appears they come from a cannibal tribe in the centre of the island. I have to say that the wooden faces with their dark, empty eyes disturb me. I slept badly last night, so I think I will move them to another cabin. These masks have been collected in rather a suspect manner. According to Delorme they had to take risks to obtain them. One part of the tribe refused to let them go. They had to enter into lengthy negotiations. Ballancourt had to give many iron objects and sticks of tobacco in exchange. He will have to stock up on this currency when we stop off in Noumea.

. . .

Yesterday, as we were casting off, some savages appeared out of nowhere! They threatened us. I am happy to be leaving the New Hebrides and heading for Noumea.

I have put the terrifying masks at the bottom of the hold. I will dispatch them to France as a matter of urgency.

From the New Hebrides the *Marie-Jeanne* sailed southwest to New Caledonia. Captain Meyssonnier said little about their time in Noumea. The crew spent three weeks there. Large numbers of Kanak works of art were purchased, both in the north and on the Loyalty Islands.

For the first time the Captain had drawn up an inventory of pieces acquired since the beginning of the voyage: 212 in total! Maori totems, which were tied to the main mast, statues of every size and masks by the dozen. A fair number of weapons and domestic objects. The relics of a disappearing world had been loaded onto the schooner. In the list of weapons were no bows or arrows, just spears and bone daggers.

The *Marie-Jeanne* had left New Caledonia in September 1936.

We are going to sail in a north-easterly direction taking a course parallel to the Australian coast. Delorme wants to stop off for a few days in the Trobriand archipelago. He knows a lot about the indigenous people who live there. Yesterday evening he talked about them with some passion. Each time he lost his temper his wife would put her hand on his arm, asking him to calm down. This simple gesture often pacifies him. His expression is so elated I sometimes feel he must have contracted a fever.

Today Delorme proposed that we make a detour via Bougainville Island and perhaps also New Ireland, which is bigger and more savage still. Ballancourt objected that we should not over extend ourselves, maintaining that the goal of the voyage was to conduct a detailed exploration of the River Sepik and highland New Guinea. For my part I reminded them that we needed to carry out certain administrative formalities at each stage. The French are not always welcome in these archipelagos at the end of the world. The Australians and the Dutch see themselves as masters round here. Not to mention the British and the Americans. Sometimes we are even taken for spies.

. . .

On the Trobriand Islands we encountered an anthropologist who is studying the local populations: a Pole by the name of Bronislaw Malinowski. He has lived a lot in the United States. We had a long conversation with him, but my English is too poor for me to be able to enter into a real dialogue with this amazing man. Delorme and Ballancourt both speak the language of Shakespeare to perfection. They had read one of Malinowski's books: *Argonauts of the Western Pacific*.

Malinowski explained to us the difficulty of detaching oneself from one's own personal opinions and prejudices when one studies populations that are so far removed from us. It is true he seems particularly interested in the sexuality of the inhabitants of the Trobriand Islands . . . I wondered to what extent he has completely immersed himself in indigenous society. He has almost no contact with foreigners except when a boat such as ours puts into port.

The archipelago is quite stunning. One really feels that one is discovering a new world here. People wear heavily decorated jewellery, quite similar to what I've already seen along the coast of Port Moresby in New Guinea. The colours are very bright and contrast strongly with the very dark skin of the inhabitants. The people are so similar to Papuans, it's hard to tell them apart. They are in fact from the same family. We are now very close to the coast of New Guinea.

De Palma put down the book. In the light of the moon the wind pushed the clouds eastwards. For the offices and the factories that had survived the crisis it was going-home time. The city was bustling in one last surge of energy before it fell asleep.

We are going to avoid Port Moresby after all and instead sail directly to the mouth of the Sepik River. At that point we will then drop anchor sufficiently far from the coast to avoid possible attacks. Ballancourt and Delorme will go up the river in a canoe. They have obtained the name of a guide living in a village at the mouth of the Sepik. A man who has already worked with previous French expeditions here.

. . .

A good steady wind. I like to see the jibs and the mainsail drawing well. I like feeling the *Marie-Jeanne* quiver with each breath of the wind. Soon these boats won't exist any more and that's a real pity. The way they creak and shudder in the waves makes them seem alive. They grip the water like nothing else. Especially at good speeds.

Ballancourt is in a real hurry to get there. I often find him on the deck watching the dark coast passing ahead of us on the port side. He smokes the small clay pipe that he bought in Tahiti.

In two, or perhaps three, days' time we will reach the mouth of the Sepik. The start of a new adventure. We are going to stay there for some weeks: "For as long as it takes," Ballancourt exclaimed at dinner.

The first village they plan to visit is called Palembei. There are others further downstream, but they have already been explored extensively by other missions like our own. This part of the world is no longer virgin territory as it was thirty years ago.

. . .

Yuarimo – 3 August 1936

The village isn't very far from the river. One can easily see the houses on stilts with their twin sloping roofs covered in coarse thatch; and the rickety ladders that allow access to the first and only floor. Smoke emerges from the windows. The women must be cooking.

Some children are playing in the water. One of them, it seems, is pretending to be a dragon, emerging from the water to attack the bathers. Our arrival has stirred the flight of a cloud of pink birds: rapidly beating their wings, they skim the water before settling on another bank a little further upstream.

The Men's House is in the centre of the village, in the ceremonial square. Delorme has explained to me that the facade symbolizes a woman's face and the house itself her body. Everything that belongs exclusively to men is thus found in a woman's body, as though the opposition between masculine and feminine has been erased.

A gigantic mask is hung above the entrance proper. The mouth in the shape of a crescent with pointed teeth. On the temples and cheeks, on either side of the nose, run black and white lines, which trace complex swirls.

This house is reserved for men that have been initiated. On the ground floor each post is carved with totemic symbols. Before arriving in the village Delorme told us that each clan has its own space and hearth. There are long slit drums. I've never seen anything like them. They are huge. Some must be more than two metres high. They are cut from tree trunks and decorated with sculptures and paintings.

. . .

We were invited to enter the Men's House. We paused for a moment on the threshold. Everyone was very moved. The old man who received us had a pleasant face and his large eyes were always alert. He watched us constantly.

The door of the house was formed of a curtain of red liana. We went in; Delorme first. It is difficult to describe what I felt, but it was without doubt one of the strongest emotions of my life. No white man, no foreigner, had ever set foot there before.

The room in which we found ourselves was lit only by minimal openings, which let through a soft, diffuse light. Each beam was decorated with paintings or sculptures. The walls were painted. The same swirling patterns and intertwined bodies everywhere. Astounding masks hung from finely carved and painted hooks. The majority resembled birds' heads.

Delorme said nothing. He took photographs while Ballancourt made sketches. On the ceiling and along the walls there were masks with frozen expressions conveying terror or anger . . . But there is an intense passion in their expressions, as though they are alive. It's one of the aspects of the art of these primitive peoples that touches and overwhelms me. It has the ability to address the unknown part of ourselves that lies deep within us. You cannot remain insensitive to the secret music that emanates from these drawn, or carved, expressions.

More disturbing, even terrifying, are the heads of the ancestors and the enemy skulls, which are kept in the house. I have noticed that the men don't look at them, nor do they reply to Kaïngara's questions. They make negative gestures as if a taboo protects these horrifying objects.

. . .

I have gone through the Men's House. Here too each clan has its corner. At the end of the only room an opening over-looks a terrace. The view from there is splendid. One can see the village gardens extending either side of the river. Tiny fields have been demarcated in a precise and sinuous layout. Mountains sit on the horizon, beyond a green line. This is the domain of the impenetrable forest inhabited by countless spirits.

Tomorrow we go up to the high plateau. Very few foreigners have ventured into these lands. Kaïngara has told me that the men of this region are completely unaware of our existence and cannibalism is still practised there. I have spoken to Ballancourt and Delorme about it, but they laughed in my face. They say I am too romantic and probably too credulous.

16

Dr Bernheim was one of the leading psychiatric experts at the Aix-en-Provence Court of Appeal. When he caught sight of de Palma he adjusted the silvery glasses on his pinched nose and gave a friendly wave. The doctor was a beanpole: tall and austere with arms too big for his shoulders. He walked like a preying mantis with a crew cut. He had a nice face, a conciliatory expression and sensuous lips.

"Michel de Palma, I presume?"

"You presume right!" the Baron said smiling at him. "We've met before . . ."

"Yes. In the witness box of this court. Come on. They've given me enough grief for today."

"A case of infanticide, is that right?"

"Yes. His lawyer is an idiot. He wanted to make me to say his client is mad. What can one say?"

"It's a question of responsibility, not madness."

"You are correct, Monsieur de Palma. But you know lawyers . . ."

A clerk dressed in a black gown crossed the waiting hall with a large file under his arm. Some journalists were chattering with knowing looks. Bernheim and de Palma went out.

"Let's go and have a drink at the bar Roi René."

A market was taking place in the square, opposite the stern columns and grey pediment of the old courthouse. They sat down at a table.

"Here's Freud's *Totem and Taboo*," Bernheim said, putting a cheap paperback edition in front of the Baron. "That's what you've been agonizing over. When you called me yesterday I decided to look out my copy. It was in my cellar. I've found the passage."

One of the pages was marked with a blue Post-it.

"Is that the one you were talking to me about?"

"Yes."

The psychiatrist sized up the Baron with a sharp look, "*Totem and Taboo* is a book that aroused huge controversy in its time," he said with a dandyish expression. "Basically, the question being asked back then was how universal are the premises of psychoanalysis. The Oedipus complex may make sense to us, but for Africans, Chinese people, or for Amazonian Indians, it's a different kettle of fish!"

"Freud speaks of a 'primal horde'. What exactly does that mean?" de Palma asked.

Bernheim leant his elbows on the table and collected his thoughts. "An imaginary human grouping placed under the authority of an omnipotent father, the only one who could have it off with the women of the horde." For a moment he stared at his index finger resting on the table and drew what looked like an imaginary circle. "The sons are jealous of the father. They want to possess the women. They rebel and kill off the father."

"And eat him too?"

"Yes, that's what's called the totemic meal."

"What does that mean?"

"Well . . . Having eaten the father the sons feel some remorse. So, to honour their father, and above all fearing his revenge, they make a totem in his image. And as is always the case they establish rules."

"What kind of rules?"

Bernheim put his hands together in front of his mouth. "The two main taboos: incest and parricide. The prohibition on fornication with the women of the same totem and the prohibition on murder."

The waiter arrived: a curt man with his sleeves rolled up and a blasé air. Bernheim ordered a coffee, de Palma mineral water.

"Freud wondered about this," Bernheim continued. "He wondered why the taboos against murder and incest are so important."

"Parricide has a special place in the penal code."

"Quite so."

The psychiatrist gathered his thoughts for a few seconds. "What has to be understood is that Freud wishes to draw parallels between childhood and culture. And between culture and psychopathology. For him the primitive world, the savage horde, is the dawn of humanity. He claims that it is a bit like that for the child, with regard to all the stages he had set out. The incest taboo is similar to the father's prohibition on access to the mother. The taboo against murder is the prohibition on killing the father to gain the mother."

"What is the punishment?"

"If you kill the father, you are left all alone. For a child there is nothing more terrible, because it can't survive physically or mentally."

"Which makes the child give up its mother."

Bernheim responded with a smile. "To put it crudely, Freud is saying that primitive people, or savages as he called them, are still at the anal stage of development, and we, civilized people, are at the phallic stage."

"Great compliment to the primitive people!"

Bernheim gave a resounding laugh. "Father Freud's 'primal horde' never existed."

"Which means everything he said is worth sod all?"

"No, it's not just that . . . He also shows that culture has its origins in guilt. Which amounts to saying that culture is born under the aegis of murder and incest. It's almost as though it offered us a defence against our instincts and allowed us to give them up."

"If I understand right," the Baron said, "primitive societies are humanity stuck at the childhood stage and we are more advanced beings."

"Yes. He talks about that in connection to the transition from totemism, and from polytheism to monotheism."

"God the Father," de Palma said; he had just remembered that Delorme had been a practising Catholic.

"Yes," Bernheim said. "The search for the father murdered by the 'primal horde'. Today that theory has been knocked to pieces, as the myth that is the cornerstone of *Totem and Taboo* has been demolished by the scientific community."

The psychiatrist shook his head, his eyes glued on Freud's book with its dog-eared, dark-blue cover. "One has to view this text in its time: 1913. Do you realize what that means? They still knew very little about these primitive peoples and they looked at them through colonial eyes. At that time the West was the centre of the world."

"Our values are universal, so the Oedipus complex is universal," de Palma said.

"There's something in that."

De Palma had not explained to Bernheim why he was questioning him about Freud. The psychiatrist had respected the detective's wish for secrecy.

"Did you know Dr Delorme?" the Baron asked.

"Very well," Bernheim replied with an amused expression. "Why do you ask?"

"*Totem and Taboo* was found by his body. Open at the page where Freud talks about the 'primal horde'."

The psychiatrist frowned. "I can see where your question is coming from, but I don't have any answers. Why Freud? I don't know. Dr Delorme didn't really believe in psychoanalysis. To be honest he wasn't a friend of psychiatrists either. He was a researcher, a doctor steeped in precise science. Freud's theories must have seemed decidedly woolly to him."

"That was what I thought, too. But the fact remains, *Totem and Taboo* was lying open in front of him."

174

The waiter arrived with the drinks. On the square some crest-fallen traders were starting to dismantle their stalls.

"Last question," de Palma said. "Freud and the Papuans: does that mean anything to you?"

Bernheim opened his eyes wide. "That's a funny sort of question," he said.

"That's probably the reason I'm asking it . . ."

He thought for a long time before answering. "I'm not an anthropologist, but I know Malinowski rejected Freud's theory. Malinowski had worked in the Trobriand Islands, which isn't far from Papua. In the Trobriand Islands the child 'belongs' to the maternal line and the maternal uncle is more important than the biological father. That buggers up Freud's theory about the universality of the Oedipus complex."

"What date was that?"

"The 1920s I think. Freud had tried working with another anthropologist to show the opposite. I don't know much more about it. The problem with Freud's theory is that he goes on about primitive people without ever having met one. It's a nice theory, but a bit far-fetched."

"And what do you think about it yourself?"

"In my field of expertise and in my own clinical practice I have sometimes seen people who come from so-called primitive societies. Most of the time their family relationships are much more complex and sophisticated than our own. So in a way they are more modern than us."

The sun was breaking through the grey, daubing the city in gold. Bernheim glanced at his watch. "The hearing starts again at two o'clock," he said, getting up. "I have to have lunch with a friend before. I hope I've been helpful."

"I think so," de Palma replied, "but I still have trouble working out how."

Bernheim squinted at the Baron's notebook, "It will be interesting to analyse this, if you let me have it sometime."

"Yes, I think so."

The Baron closed his notes. His phone buzzed inside his pocket. He answered it.

Maistre sounded furious. "I"ve been searching for you for the last two hours!"

"Did you have a look in your drawer?"

"Hilarious . . ."

"I keep my phone on when I'm in a meeting. What's up? Have you just met Joe Strummer's ghost?"

"Sadly not. Just a call from the Customs. You've got a meeting with them this afternoon. They've found some skulls."

"Where?"

"On one of the quays at the port. I don't know any more about it. Seems it's in the papers."

"I don't read the press."

"Me neither."

When he left the café the Baron bought a paper from the nearest kiosk. The front sheet was covered with news of Olympique Marseille's latest defeat. Three goals conceded at home and a headline that screamed: **DoooOMsday!** Michel scanned through the paper to find the "News in Brief" section. A short article recounted the discovery of some skulls on one of the quays at the Port Autonome. That was all. He scrumpled up the paper and chucked it in the first bin he came across.

Going down Cours Mirabeau he found a university bookshop. He went inside and asked for a copy of *Sex and Temperament in Three Primitive Societies* by Margaret Mead.

"It's over here," the bespectacled sales assistant said, her face like a blank sheet of paper, "on the ethnographic shelf . . ."

De Palma paid for the cheap paperback and left.

*

The message they had intercepted at Dr Delorme's funeral was about

Mundugumor society. It came from chapter nine of Mead's book, entitled *The Pace of Life in a Cannibal Tribe*. In it, the American anthropologist compares the mentality of the Mundugumor with that of the Arapesh, whom she had studied in the preceding chapters and described as peace-loving:

> The violence and the strange reactions of this cheerful, tough, and arrogant people came as a shock to us, as we were not prepared for it.

Mead then described the course of the River Yuat, along which Mundugumor communities were established. She spoke of fertile riverbanks, of virgin lands left deserted:

> The Mundugumor inspire such terror that no other tribe ventures to occupy these banks . . .

At the time of the *Marie-Jeanne*'s voyage, the Mundugumor numbered only about a thousand people and Mead characterized them as headhunters fearing neither God nor man. A people where brothers were wary of brothers, and fathers trusted their sons no more than their traditional enemies. Engravings illustrated the text: a mask resting on the back of an orator's stool; the Men's House at Kanduanum, Middle Sepik.

The aim of the *Marie-Jeanne*'s voyage had been to explore along the River Sepik. The Mundugumor lived at a confluence a few dozen kilometres from the zones explored by Delorme and Ballancourt. What exactly did that mean?

The headquarters of the Port Customs and Excise Authority was situated close by. De Palma had a meeting in an hour's time. Passing the Turkish restaurant on boulevard des Dames, he bought some chips and a kebab which he filled with a liberal dollop of *tsatsiki*. He devoured it behind the wheel of his car, as he watched the secretaries in their suits, and the office workers silently passing by in front of the renovated buildings of the docks.

*

The underground car park at the customs house smelled of rubber and cold oil. Inspector Marlin plodded along slowly, searching through his bunch of keys. "There," he said, getting his breath back.

With a sharp movement he inserted a flat key into the electric lock and turned it. The metal storehouse door squealed as it rolled up on its rusty runners.

"We put the stuff here because we haven't room anywhere else," Marlin said, standing erect on his short legs. "You know how it is, we're chocker in the customs house."

Marlin was sweating in spite of the cold. He passed the time scratching the end of his turned-up nose. A lock of hair was combed carefully across his bald, shining skull. Two bulging eyes protruded from his moon face. In spite of appearances he was a first-rate sleuth: capable of sniffing out a car stuffed with goods in the queues stretching over several kilometres, in the sweltering heat in the African departures waiting area. He could spot that momentary emptiness in the smugglers' eyes.

"Was it you that set this up?" de Palma asked.

"Yeah. For a while now there's been something dodgy going on down by the quai aux Charbons. A few too many blokes fishing for bass in the Bassin Mirabe."

"Seems there are some though."

"Bass? Of course there are. I once caught one that weighed three kilos . . . But these blokes," he went on, "never caught anything. So we moved in, quiet like. Just as they did the deal . . ."

"Did you question them?"

"No, unfortunately they split. The Border Police refused to lend a hand."

The metal roller door slammed on the retaining bar.

"It's over there," Marlin said.

The Customs Officers stored some of their seizures in a basement in the Regional Office, not far from the *gare Maritime*: a huge room lit by neon lights, it was like a contraband museum. An enormous copper sculpture still had pride of place, among the stuffed animals, snake skins and old wood African statues.

"Over there at the back," Marlin said, slamming shut the cover of a box filled with Real Madrid shirts.

In a second room, shelves piled high with cartons of Marlboro manufactured in China rose up to the ceiling. A container bound for London had been opened up near the Bassin Mirabe: ten tonnes of Virginia tobacco cigarettes.

"We've seized a lot of art at the moment," the Customs Officer said, "but the main office in Paris deal with that. Down here we don't have the brains for that sort of thing."

He pointed to two reinforced metal cupboards. They bore the name of a cargo ship, the *Pass of Melford* and its port of registry, Panama, marked in large red letters on a yellow adhesive strip.

"There are some Mesopotamian antiquities in there. We're waiting for an expert to come, someone's due from head office . . . But you're not interested in that. The loot was destined for Holland. Nice stuff."

"It wasn't going to Marseille?"

"No, no. Just a stopover. It came from Iraq, probably looted from the Baghdad museum, via Belgium and Rotterdam on its way to the States. We don't have the rich people here able to fork out for that sort of stuff.

The Customs Officer opened a third store. The door made a strange mewing sound like a spirit escaping from its iron prison.

"In here, on the other hand, this might interest you . . ."

"Four small wooden crates about thirty centimetres high had been placed on a shelf.

"According to our sources* these parcels were due to go up to Paris. We seized them last week hidden behind a container ship lying alongside the *Melbourne*. The ship is registered in Singapore and had come from Indonesia. She'd stopped over here on her way to Spain."

"Where were the boxes?"

"Behind the container ship."

"You told me the blokes split . . ."

"We were watching through our glasses from a lookout post we've got near the sea wall. We saw this guy coming down the *Melbourne*'s gangway. On his way to chat to the two bogus fishermen we were watching. We saw them disappearing behind this container. We said to ourselves the deal was going to happen and we moved in . . ."

"And the birds have flown."

"Got it in one."

"And the bloke from the *Melbourne*?"

"Never saw him again. He must have gone back on board, but we haven't been able to identify him. We searched the ship. But found nothing."

The Customs Officer put a small crate on a table cluttered with leopard and panther skins. Carefully, he took out what at first looked like a large cloth ball, and one by one he undid the white swaddling layers.

"Magnificent, don't you think?"

It was a skull. The polished, smooth bone shone like varnish. The front teeth were missing. The back of the head was adorned with white cock feathers and shells. The flat nose had been remodelled in a brownish paste encrusted with red seeds.

"According to the expert, this is an ancestral skull. Papuan art. An incredibly rare piece probably stolen from a private collection."

* A customs informant. In France, the Customs and Excise authorities, unlike the police, can remunerate informants for tip-offs.

The second box contained another skull, adorned with vegetable fibres. The face had been completely remodelled. Ochre paint flowed from the nasal bones, circled the round, hollow eyes in a heavy line, and rose in curved patterns and in tracery as far as the temples, the forehead and the back of the skull. The thin mouth with practically no lips revealed some worn teeth.

"I can't show you the third one, it's with the experts."

"Do you have any photos?"

"I'll let you have the file, but . . . keep it to yourself."

"Thank you."

Marlin put the two heads back in their wooden boxes and locked the cupboard with the fastidiousness of a deacon closing the reliquary of the Blessed Sacrament after bringing it out on Sunday.

"Does that sort of piece fetch a good price?"

"Depends a lot on how rare it is. The expert told us one of these heads was recently sold at Christie's for around 90,000 euros. But it can go up to 200,000 . . . It all depends on the quality and rarity. Those ones there are extremely rare . . . and also very beautiful."

De Palma whistled, "The previous owner would have bought them for just a couple of shells from an old Papuan chief. How's that for appreciation, eh?"

"Outrageous."

The underworld had been engaging in this sort of clandestine trade for a long time. When it came to the art market, no-one could tell the exact size of the cake, but there was a lot of money circulating. And the fashion was for primitive art.

"You still got the *Melbourne* under obs?"

"No, we can't spare the men. At the moment we've got hundreds of kilos of shit arriving."

"That's where the money is!"

"That's right, Baron. We're just like anyone else: we have to make a living. No-one gives a fuck about works of art. Unless it's the big names."

Marlin inserted his key in the electric lock. The roller door slowly descended.

"The *Melbourne* has been impounded at the quai du Maroc," Marlin added. "The captain should be on board. He's an Australian called Shane Mulligan. Officially we've got nothing on him, but it wouldn't surprise me if there's some more dodgy stuff there."

"Thanks, mate."

*

At about ten o'clock at night, de Palma parked his car by the entrance to quai Wilson. The line of the long dock ended in the green light of the lighthouse. Only the darkness of the sea lay beyond. Harsh lights illuminated the container terminal. De Palma climbed up on the Grand Large sea wall, a rod in his hand and a creel slung over his shoulder, looking every inch the sea bass fisherman. And there were quite a few bass in those waters.

The sea wind had whipped up a heavy swell that lashed against sections of the pier. The Baron lit a cigarette and glanced in the direction of the *Melbourne*. Two hundred metres separated him from the ship. Enough to keep an eye on things, without being noticed by the sailors on watch. He had brought his old pair of Zeiss binoculars.

Along the quay the street lights were bright enough for him to be able to watch the comings and goings around the ship. The gangway of the *Melbourne* had been raised three metres. An old Audi, registered in the Bouches-du-Rhône, was parked by the mooring bollard. Michel had noted down the number as he passed and called Maistre on his walkie-talkie so he could pass on the number to the police central database. Nothing to report. The Audi's owner didn't have a record; the central police database didn't even show a minor offence.

The port was at a standstill. From time to time there was the sound of a siren racing towards the northern hospital, or Évêché police station. Beyond the inner harbours and the deserted piers,

Marseille throbbed deep in its dozy veins. Faraway, some stars lingered in the sky above the Château d'If, perched on rock and surrounded by inky sea.

De Palma attached some bait to the end of his hook and flung it out as far as he could, then he wedged the fishing rod in a hole in the concrete. A bigger wave churned the sea in front and whipped the air between the rocky breechblocks of the sea wall. He fixed his glasses on the *Melbourne*. The forecastle was lit up. Two Chinese men were chatting on the poop flicking overboard the ash from their fags. The lights of the ship scored their faces with golden glints and shadows.

Almost an hour passed. De Palma thought of his own father's departures on the roll-on roll-off ferries of the Messageries Maritimes. Those sinking heart farewells at Cap Janet pier and the coming home again which meant presents by the dozen. Pearls from around the world brought back by his old man for the family.

"Have you got us anything, Dad?" his brother Pierre would invariably ask, looking up at their father admiringly.

"Have you been good?"

He ran his hand through his hair under the fond gaze of their mother, who would say nothing of the thousand and one stupid things that the two brothers had done during the weeks that he had been away at sea.

"One day I'm going to be a skipper," Michel said to himself. "Five gold stripes." And then after a few days the dream would evaporate. His father's rages returned. He could not tolerate children shouting, or their tantrums, particularly when he was drinking apéritifs with his mates from the Party cell. The engineering petty officer had big ideas. Ideas that were going to make the world a better place, but which always ended up back where they had started, in that huge realm of carnivorous dreams.

At eleven fifteen the sound of metal roused the Baron from his torpor. He hadn't noticed the time going by. The *Melbourne*'s gangway was being lowered.

He put away his rod and rushed to the car. The lifting bridge spanning the harbour had been raised. It was time to get on the radio to Maistre.

"The Audi's on its way, mate."

"Be with you in two minutes. Porte d'Arenc, the others are closed."

"O.K. Keep in touch."

A man was coming down the gangway of the *Melbourne*. De Palma started up the engine and waited.

"I'm just getting to Arenc, Baron. I'll nab him and you join us. If there's any aggro I can ask one of the crime squads to control them."

"Forget it. He's on foot."

The man passed in front of the Audi and made his way towards the bridge. The bridge started to come down. De Palma waited for him to cross before accelerating and keeping him in his sights at a distance of two hundred metres. He left his lights out and took care to ensure he kept out of range, in the line of a warehouse or piles of containers.

"I've got him in front of me," Maistre shouted. "He's going through the Porte d'Arenc. One metre eighty, maybe a bit more . . . Forty to fifty years old. Dark hair. He's white. Nothing else to report. This is beginning to look like a complete waste of time."

"Follow him all the same."

The man walked up towards the passenger terminal, hugging the walls of La Joliette dock. De Palma parked between two sheds on the site, got out of his car and sat down like a tramp in the doorway of a Hi-Tech company. A silhouette could be seen in the yellow beams of the streetlamps. It made its way through the shadows of the concrete pylons along the dual carriageway. From time to time white headlights wiped across the grimy walls of the old buildings. Some articulated lorries charging towards the North African terminal set the tarmac spine of the slip road quivering.

184

The man avoided the harsh lights of place de la Joliette and continued his way between the dark facades and poster-covered palisades hiding the earthworks. Boulevard des Dames was cluttered with diggers and skips. Huge overloaded cars were parked, waiting to embark for Algeria. The owners raised their eyes swollen with sleep as the solitary walker passed by. At the intersection with avenue de la République, he stopped by a betting office bar that cast a greenish light on the pavement.

"He's looking at a map," the Baron said. "I'm going to continue on foot."

"Alright mate. I'll pick you up when you give the signal."

The man quickened his pace and turned into avenue de la République. De Palma stopped by a cash machine and made as if to withdraw some notes. Road works divided the main road in two. An enormous crane stretched its powerful frame over a hole illuminated by spotlights. Workmen in shiny helmets were fixing a pipe over a muddy conduit. The man stayed close to the walls, without giving a thought to what was behind him. He walked at the same pace until he reached the quai des Belges and stopped in front of the Frioul launch departure point. A blue banner with a white background read: OLD PORT FESTIVAL. The walker looked at the surrounding scenery. De Palma hid himself behind the bay window of the Samaritaine brasserie and waited. The man took out a map once more from his pocket and consulted it for a long time.

"I'm going to nick him and see what he's got to say," the Baron whispered into his phone.

"Don't take the bait. It's better to do a follow on him and assess the situation."

The stranger crossed the quai des Belges and went along the deserted terraces of the nightclubs. The Quartier de l'Opéra was just a step away.

"I get the feeling we're tailing a sailor who's taking his nuts out for a bit of exercise," de Palma said.

"Not very nice, Baron!"

The stranger turned into rue Glandèves. The pavement was littered with greasy paper; he knocked against a rubbish bag. De Palma let him continue for a few seconds, and then quickened his pace. As he turned into the same street a working girl threw him a mocking smile. De Palma scoured the red interiors of the private clubs. He saw only blasé faces and legs as lengthy as promises. The man had disappeared. Most of the windows had gone dark. On the second floor of a flaking facade an eiderdown was hanging from the wrought-iron balcony guardrail.

"I've lost him."

"We'll wait and see if he comes out again. Doesn't take long to get your leg over."

They waited for an hour, but the man didn't re-emerge.

"I'm ravenous, Baron. With all this adrenalin I think my stomach has run away with me."

"How about a kebab at the Turkish place on place de la République. Or a pizza?"

"Yeah, yeah . . . I'm not eating any of that junk food you eat. Come round to my place."

*

Maistre had put on his usual housewife's apron, which made him look like a fireman. He put a dish of lasagne in the oven and opened a bottle of Bandol wine.

"You know you don't need to dress up like my Nan just to put some frozen food in the oven."

"I'm a new man!" Maistre said, giving the Baron a withering look. "Not a scally like you who spends all day stuffing himself with kebab and chips!"

The Baron looked for two plates in the dresser. "It's been a long time since I felt such a twat," he grumbled. "Fancy doing a follow on a sailor who's getting his end away."

Maistre poured out two glasses of the Bandol. "I enjoyed our little jaunt, didn't you?"

"No," de Palma said, wetting his lips in the wine, "I don't like doing a follow for no reason."

The oven buzzer sounded twice. The lasagne was ready. Maistre put on a large oven glove and took hold of the dish. "Wait till you taste this! Even a wop like you won't know the difference. This is four-star frozen."

"It's even got 'Cordon Bleu' on the box. Dish it out and we'll see . . ."

Maistre put down the oven dish on the table, "I've been thinking about the quote from Freud that was found by Delorme's body."

"Me too. I must admit it keeps going round in my head. I know it off by heart," de Palma said.

A silence ensued. Maistre ate fast, his face solemn, his denim shirt stretched over his powerful shoulders and chubby chest.

"You know I never knew my dad," he said, without taking his eyes off his plate.

"I know," de Palma said; he was always uneasy when his friend confided in him.

"When I was a kid, I often used to try to imagine what my dad was like. The only thing I knew about him was that he was a good-looking man who seduced my mum at a dance on 14 July. A fucking fireman's ball, in a fucking fire station, in the fourteenth arrondissement in Paris. So I thought he was one of those everyday heroes who make life so wonderful."

Maistre put his knife and fork together on his plate and stared at the photograph of his mother on the mantelpiece. "She never told me who he was and I've always tried to find out. It's the only investigation really worth doing. I went back to that fire station in the fourteenth arrondissement. I checked out the mugs of the firemen and not one of them looked like me. But maybe it was just some bloke passing through. Don't you think? A bloke who falls in love for the night and then vanishes into the blue." His face hardened. "I've always wondered if I've been a good father myself."

"Of course you are!" de Palma said, quietly taking a Gitane out of its packet.

"In that case why is this house empty tonight?"

"Because the youngsters have grown up. That's all. Can you see them now, wanting to share some frozen lasagne with a couple of old cops?"

Maistre got up and took a few steps across the living room, dragging his Doc Martens. He slipped an old Patty Smith disc in the C.D. player. He had idolized her in his youth.

Every Sunday I will go down to the bar
And leave him the guitar . . .

"I'm sorry Baron," Maistre said, clearing the table, "it's not opera."
"You need to know how to stay young."

Say you dream of me
Dream of my brother . . .

Maistre slumped on his sofa. "Do you believe in that theory of Freud's?" he asked, staring at the end of his shoes.

The Baron tapped his cigarette on the packet. "I did sometimes hate my dad," he said after a pause. "But not to the point of eating him . . . "

"That's just a metaphor."

"I think that's the way things are. And now he's not here any longer, I'm angry with myself for having such dumb thoughts, though I have to accept I did have them. He was a hard man on those he loved. I realize my mum went through hell with him. Especially after my brother's death. He was a hard father, but fair."

"You're like him . . ."

The roads of the city glimmered in the distance between the disturbing silhouettes of the hills. Maistre cleared the table and poured out two glasses of wine.

Oh the stars shine so suspiciously for we three
You said when you were with me that nothing made you high.

De Palma opened the window and leaned out to light his cigarette. "Tomorrow we're going on board the *Melbourne.*"

"Karim's off tomorrow. He's booked a day's leave to take care of his mum. She's going into hospital," Maistre said.

"Anything serious?"

"I don't know. When it comes to personal things, he just clams up."

"It isn't easy for him. You don't find many second-generation North Africans in the C.I.D. He must think everyone's watching his every move."

The port stretched away in long dark lines. In the distance the white hulls of the Corsica ferries formed two bright dots. De Palma pictured once again the silhouette of the lone sailor they had followed: a frail figure in the huge expanse of docks and empty streets of the city. He stubbed out his cigarette in a *coquille Saint-Jacques* that was lying on the window ledge.

You say you pray for me
Pray for my brother . . .
Oh, the way that I see!

17

The Porte d'Arenc led across to the Port Autonome. Over towards the African departures point there were lines of secondhand agricultural equipment: battered tractors, trailers loaded with ploughs and harrows. On the right, facing the *City of Macao*, which had raised her huge stem above the cobalt waters, there were some wooden crates marked with mysterious ideograms and numbers. The dockers' forklift trucks waited, their claws pointing up into the sky.

As de Palma approached the gate he held out his tricolour card to the guard, who was wearing a white shirt and sunglasses.

"Right you are, boss."

He went along the quai du Maroc, the deserted piers huddled against the azure sea. A blue-and-white cargo ship belonging to the Société Nationale Corse-Méditerranée dozed in the dry dock. In front of the Arenc detention centre, two policemen from the Border Police were frogmarching an illegal immigrant: handcuffs on his wrists. De Palma hated that image. He sped off. The lifting bridge leading to the sea wall and the quai Wilson was lowered. At the end he turned left, went along the Bassin de la Pinède and parked behind a rather rusty shed. He went the rest of the way on foot so as not to arouse the suspicion of the *Melbourne* crew.

About a hundred metres from the ship, he caught sight of the old container behind which the customs officers had seized the skulls.

He took out his phone and called Maistre. The sun was hammering down on the white flags of the quay. It was hard to believe winter was approaching.

The *Melbourne* was a pot-bellied old ship, three hundred feet long; red and black with a white superstructure. Fraying, blue moorings ran down from its beautifully curved bow. The hull was spotted with rust that had nibbled the raised waterline.

A sailor appeared at the top of the gangway. The Baron waved at him. "I'm looking for Shane Mulligan."

Gesticulating, the sailor invited him on board. The gangway was composed of two right-angled sections that rose to about ten metres above the cold stones of the quay.

Mulligan appeared on the first level of the forecastle, "*Vous . . . cherchez . . . moi*?" he said in a singsong accent.

"C.I.D., Captain. Can I have a word?"

"O.K. No problem."

Mulligan was a big strapping lad with heavy hands and a freckled face. His lively, small blue eyes seemed to dart out from his heavily wrinkled face.

"Sit down please," he said to de Palma, indicating a stool beside the card table in the wheelhouse. "*Que pouis-je faire pour vous, Monsieur?*"

He pulled a face as he tried his best to deliver the few words of French that he knew.

"I've come about the works of art that were seized near your ship."

The question didn't seem to take the sailor by surprise. He pawed the air with his two hands, "*Oh . . . Il faut . . . le traduction.*"

He picked up the phone tucked between two radar screens and gabbled some incomprehensible words. Two minutes later a small man appeared on the wing of the bridge and entered the wheelhouse.

"Hi."

"Do you speak French?" the Baron asked, having made up his mind to conceal his basic knowledge of English.

"Yes. I'm from Pondicherry. I'm the helmsman."

He had a small, nasal voice and threw timid glances in the captain's direction.

"Right," de Palma said, staring at Mulligan. "I'm conducting a criminal investigation. A man has been murdered and it's possible there is a link with this art-trafficking business. I think it would be best for you if you tell me everything you know. Do you understand?"

The helmsman translated into English. The captain massaged his mop of blond hair and put one hand on the small steering wheel that took the place of a tiller. He addressed the helmsman in a staccato manner.

"Captain Mulligan says he is not responsible for what is found on the quays," translated the helmsman. "He is very sorry. The captain can't check what his sailors are doing. It is impossible. He has already said this to Customs."

De Palma raised his hand to indicate that he understood and was not accusing anybody.

"Can you show me the crew list?"

"No problem," the captain replied in English. He had understood the question. He gestured to the helmsman who disappeared fast. Through the broad portholes could be seen the long line of the sea wall, the navy-blue inner harbours and the white lines of the quays around the Bassin Wilson. Some sailors on deck were painting an engine room ventilation shaft emerald green.

A man was watching the gangway. Forty, maybe fifty, tall and with black hair. De Palma immediately thought of the person he had followed the day before. There was an obvious resemblance. The man turned his head away and pretended to mingle with the painters. The helmsman re-entered the wheel-house with a notebook in his hand.

"What is that man called?" the Baron asked, pointing at the sailor.

"Leacock," the helmsman replied. "He's the head chef."

On the deck Leacock left the painters and approached the gangway glancing in the direction of the bridge.

De Palma went out on the wing of the bridge and called him, "Hey you, stop! Stay here!"

Leacock paused for a moment then quickened his pace, bumping into an old cardboard box lying on the deck. De Palma charged down from the bridge and tore down the ladder to the first level. The chef had disappeared. The Baron raced down a second ladder, ran over to the ship's rail and leaned overboard. Leacock was already fleeing across the quay in the direction of the lifting bridge, turning round every now and then to estimate the distance that separated him from his pursuer. De Palma drew his gun and raced after him. The sailor was running fast. By the time he arrived at the unmarked squad car the policeman was completely out of breath.

At that same moment the two arms of the lifting-bridge started to move. The Baron switched on the engine and did a U-turn making his tyres screech on the rough cobbles of the quai des Anglais. Three hundred metres away, Leacock scaled one arm of the bridge. Accelerating like a maniac, de Palma just managed to avoid a small van belonging to the Compagnie Générale de Navigation. As he arrived at the bridge there were only three metres separating the two iron arms.

The Baron hurled himself out of the car and pointed his gun at the chef. "Police. Don't move!" He kept his sights trained on Leacock's thigh, "No messing, move towards me."

The sailor turned his head to size up the distance separating him from the other arm of the bridge: about two metres. De Palma fired into the air. Leacock crouched down and shouted something incomprehensible. The Baron slowly moved forward, hands clenched on the grip of his revolver. A car appeared at the entrance to the bridge. Leacock took advantage of this distraction, stood up again abruptly and leapt onto the other arm of the bridge. De Palma wanted to follow him, but jumping over the dark sea scared him. He shot once more into the air. The head chef disappeared behind a pile of containers.

The two jaws of the lifting bridge came together in a colossal grinding of iron. An acidic smell of cordite hung in the damp air. De Palma dialled the Border Police number and gave them a description of Leacock.

"We'll cordon off the area and we'll patrol," the duty policeman replied.

"I'm going back onto the *Melbourne*. Speak soon."

Captain Mulligan was waiting on the wing of the bridge, his forearms resting on the parapet. He was following the cop with his eyes and drawing on a fag. The helmsman appeared at his side as de Palma raced up the ladder.

"Take me to Leacock's cabin," he ordered.

"No problem."

They went along the poop deck leading to the stern. Leacock's cabin was next to the petty officers' mess. The door was locked.

"I'll go and get the key. Wait for me here."

The handrail was blistered with rust. On the aft deck two sailors were busy working at the foot of a derrick.

"Here," the helmsman said, shaking a big bunch of keys.

"Keep behind me!"

The cabin smelled of spices and ripe fruit. An oilcloth with a map of Oceania covered a tiny table. A coffee machine stood beside an empty ashtray. Leacock had pinned up some photographs on the wall. A view of what looked like Port Moresby several decades ago. Several black-and-white photographs of villages of rectangular huts perched on rocky hillocks above vast jungle valleys. Some naked men with worried looks posed in front of the photographer, long penis gourds across their stomachs, and their hands resting on spears.

"Papuans!" de Palma said.

The helmsman shrugged.

On a fairly old photograph a boy in shirt and shorts was standing rigidly between two old warriors with their bows and arrows held at arm's length.

"Leacock?"

"Yes . . . yes . . ."

Leacock looked very young. The two Papuan warriors by his side smiled proudly with deep wrinkles furrowing their brooding faces.

Under the mattress were hidden wads of Australian dollars and a small statue about thirty centimetres high. A very long, enigmatic, pointed face with slanted, button-hole eyes and a triangular nose that went down just below the chin.

"Do you know what this is?" de Palma asked.

By way of response the helmsman shook his head.

"Must be Papuan art," de Palma told himself; he had seen similar figures elsewhere.

The hard brown wood had a sheen. Dust and grease had accumulated in the cracks. De Palma rolled the statue in some sheets of newspaper that were lying on a shelf.

"Tell me about Leacock," he said. "Where exactly was he from? What was he doing?"

"Er . . . I don't know much. He boarded in Singapore. I didn't know him before that."

"Did the captain know him?"

"No, no. Leacock replaced a cook who was ill. No-one knew him."

The Baron glanced round the cabin for the last time, made some notes and drew up a very precise list of all the objects there. He drew a sketch to mark their exact position. Captain Mulligan appeared in the doorway.

"Don't touch anything after I go," de Palma ordered. "Is that understood?"

"No problem!" Mulligan said, "I'll have the cabin locked, O.K.?"

The Baron stared at him. "How did you meet Leacock?"

Mulligan muttered into his beard. "Through the Port Authority in Singapore," the helmsman interpreted. "One of our cooks was ill."

"What sort of illness?"

"Some sort of liver problem . . . Quite serious apparently."

"What was this cook called?"

The captain didn't blink. "Nguen Van Minh."

"Vietnamese?"

"Yes. From Saigon."

"Leacock hasn't any papers, is that right?"

The helmsman translated in a low voice. "He said he was waiting to get his passport renewed."

"Have you seen his papers?"

The Captain had understood the question. He shook his head. "Er . . . no, you understand . . ." the helmsman answered on his behalf.

"When are you due to leave?"

"I don't know, there's this customs business. We're waiting to get the go ahead from them."

"And if you do?"

"Supposed to be Thursday."

"Where are you heading?"

"Barcelona, in theory," the helmsman said. "Then we stop off in Senegal, but sometimes the owners change things. Do you think we'll be detained because of your investigation?"

"Without a doubt."

De Palma searched the rest of the cabin. He didn't find anything else. The helmsman watched his every movement, giving little smiles whenever he caught his eye.

"Show me where Leacock worked."

"In the kitchen. Come with me."

They hurtled down a series of narrow ladders and rickety

gangplanks into the heart of the ship. The Baron noted how easy it would be to hide something in this maze of pipes, cables and double partitions.

A strong smell of curry rose from a huge pot, simmering away. The heat was stifling.

"This is where he worked, as a chef."

There was a stool by a metal table and some drawers containing order forms for provisions and tedious statements full of figures.

If Leacock had been smuggling works of art, he thought, the captain of the *Melbourne* had lied when he claimed that Leacock had replaced a Vietnamese cook at very short notice. Leacock's journey had been carefully planned, to collect, or deliver works of art.

De Palma asked to go down to the hold. The engine had been running for an hour to carry out some routine checks. An acrid smell of oil and fresh paint caught in his throat. Two mechanics in vests were dismantling a bearing with some huge, flat spanners. They confirmed that they had only got to know Leacock when he first boarded the ship and added that the afternoon of the day before they had twice seen him leaving the ship with some large parcels. The policeman went back up to the upper deck, certain that Leacock was an art smuggler. It wasn't sheer chance that he had appeared on the *Melbourne* as a replacement for a sick sailor.

Captain Mulligan was in his cabin.

"What have you been carrying from Singapore?"

"Coffee from Irian Jaya," the helmsman translated, "and containers of electronic goods we took on board in Singapore."

The sun had gone down. The *Melbourne* had switched on the lights at the top of its loading derrick. White light flooded over the compass bridge and the upper deck. On the mess deck life had slowly resumed. Leacock's name was on everyone's lips.

The Baron questioned several sailors: Malays and Filipinos for the most part. In faltering English, punctuated with vague gestures and facial expressions, their answers were identical: no-one had seen or heard anything at all.

The captain went to the top of the gangway with the policeman. Maistre had just arrived. He was waiting for de Palma at the bottom of an iron ladder, examining the parcel he held under his arm. "You look gloomy, Baron."

"No more than you'd expect for someone who's just let a murderer give him the slip for the second time. You're late!"

"I bumped into some colleagues from the Border Police and gave them a hand. No sign of Leacock. He's vanished."

"Shit."

"You've said it."

Maistre kept his eyes glued on the cobbles of the quai aux Charbons.

"I found a Papuan statue in Leacock's cabin," the Baron said. "A really beautiful piece."

"Papuan?"

"Almost certainly. But we'll need to ask a specialist."

*

There was a ring at the door. De Palma looked at his watch. It was seven in the evening. Eva was wearing a simple short skirt and a jacket of the same colour over a lace blouse. The Baron whistled in admiration.

"You haven't forgotten our date, have you?" she asked, looking sternly at his jeans.

"Er . . . no, not at all. But you know, opera's not as formal as people say."

"Maybe, but it doesn't stop you making an effort for me."

He dashed into his bedroom and searched in the cupboard for his last remaining white shirt. He put on a black jacket and some trousers with front pleats that he hadn't worn for ages.

"Is this O.K. then?"

"I've never seen you so chic!"

The Old Port tunnel was crowded at that time of the day, its tubes of yellow light reflecting on the car bonnets.

"Nothing's going right," de Palma said.

"What's up?"

"I've let a bloke get away. I've been had like a complete novice."

"Is that serious?"

"He's a killer, Eva."

She suddenly realized that the man next to her encountered death and violence on a daily basis. She thought of the other women in his life who had come and gone. In a drawer in his bedside table she had found some photographs that left a lump in her throat. Why had these women left him? Intuitively she knew the answer. There were evenings when Michel reeked of death. You had to take him or leave him.

"Is that the one who killed the doctor?" she asked.

He looked at his watch and sighed, keeping his eye on the traffic. "How did you know?"

"I read the papers, Michel, so I can be a part of your adventures."

"Are the papers talking about it?"

"Yes."

"Well in that case you know everything. Yes, it's him. We had him. It couldn't have been more straightforward."

She let a moment's silence pass. "The other night you started talking in your sleep. You were talking about skulls and saying you had to arrest the sailor. Were you talking about the man you're looking for?"

"Forget it. I must have been having a nightmare."

Through the double doors of the foyer of the Municipal Opera, the high wire circle made you giddy as you looked down, taking in the huge auditorium and the warm, empty space filled with expectation.

Eva took in the lofty ceiling, vast as the heavens, the silver frescoes, the theatrical masks from antiquity with their black eyes fixed on the tiny audience, and the stage frieze depicting the arts engraved in pink marble.

"It's a bit strange for me," she said.

De Palma took her hand.

The Gods and the upper circle were already full. This première of "Ernani" was a Paris Opera production that the local critics had panned. De Palma was waiting to see the great baritone Leo Nucci sing the famous aria of Charles V. He had not heard him for over a decade. Besides, he loved daring productions.

Eva smiled at the usher as she handed over her ticket and walked formally down the velvet steps of the central staircase one by one, taking her time. Their two seats were by the rail on the garden side. De Palma had seat number thirty-five and she was in thirty-four. A woman in her fifties draped in jewels sat waiting in thirty-three, and an opera buff in horn-rimmed glasses occupied number thirty-two, his nose in the programme and his fingers fiddling with the glossy pages. Eva watched them in amusement.

In the orchestra pit the musicians were tuning up. Furious trills bounced off the marble walls of the auditorium. Eva raised her eyes and studied her surroundings. The lights went down. From seat to seat whispers were pursued by the sound of persistent shushing. The conductor entered. The auditorium buzzed.

As the final notes rang out, Eva's head was resting on the Baron's shoulder. For a moment he thought that she had gone to sleep.

"Did you like it?"

"I loved it," she said. "If anyone had told me that dead-handsome boy next door would bring me here one day, I'd never have believed them. But I know that with you anything's possible."

She put her finger on his chest. "So what are you supposed to do after you've been to the opera?"

"We go and have a dinner and talk about the performance."

"And what if you're not that hungry?"

"Then I guess there's no alternative but to head straight home and make love all night."

"You sure about that?"

"That's what the real opera buffs say."

18

Ange Filippi, the former apprentice on the *Marie-Jeanne*, lived in a flat that looked out over the quays from La Joliette towards L'Estaque. His son visited twice a day and brought him what he needed. At the end of the afternoon Ange would go down to place de Lenche and sip two or three pastis, his elixir of longevity. He had sailed the oceans, but he had never ventured higher than La Canebière. His entire life had taken place overseas. His face was deeply wrinkled, from the sun and from old age.

"Why are you so interested in the *Marie-Jeanne*?" he asked, resting his blue eyes on the Baron.

"I'm a detective and I'm investigating the death of Dr Delorme."

Ange coughed. "I read about it in the paper. Not good at all. A bunch of yobs did it, took everything he had . . ."

"Probably. But I want to find out a bit more about his life. You're the last person to have known him as a young man."

"There can't be many of us left. I was thirteen when I first went to sea. The *Marie-Jeanne* was my second trip," he said. "Before that I'd been out to Singapore on the *Cyrnos*. She was a steam launch, as they called them then." Ange rubbed his eyes with bony hands. He had a stiff finger, from an accident in a squall near the Cape of Good Hope when he was changing the bearings on a connecting rod.

"How old were you in 1936?" de Palma asked.

"Not very old at all. Fifteen, almost sixteen!"

"Can you remember it?"

"You're telling me! Like it was only yesterday. It was the only time I ever went on a sailing ship. It was strange. You didn't get the sound of an engine, or all that buzzing. All you could hear was the sea, wood creaking, and the sound of the wind."

Ange was sitting in the middle of his living room in a velvet convertible armchair covered in large fleurs-de-lis; he was facing the television which was switched off. African masks, assegai spears and Thai puppets were hanging on the walls. On the chest of drawers there was a photograph of him with his wife taken on their diamond wedding anniversary.

"We set sail one afternoon, I remember. It was Meyssonnier who took me along. He was a good captain. He really knew how to handle a ship. We stopped off in Martinique; we sailed on to Panama, and then Tahiti . . . without a hitch."

"Do you remember Delorme and Ballancourt?"

Ange strained his ear. De Palma repeated his question more loudly.

"They were the two guys in charge. They were young."

"Did you often talk to them?"

"Not at the beginning. They kept themselves to themselves up on deck. Smoking away and chatting near the mizzenmast. As for us, we had our work to do, we didn't listen to them. Things changed when we got to Tahiti. They started to buy works of art, those totem things. I forget the name. When we got to the New Hebrides and New Caledonia, they bought more of them. We kept this stuff from savages all over the place. Even in the sailors' quarters. We slept with drums and statues. So when we got to Noumea everything was put on a steam launch called the *Ville de Tanger*. I remember that because my late cousin, he was working on board."

"And after Noumea?"

"We went up to the islands further north. I don't remember which ones any more. There are loads of islands up there. Each time we stopped we'd drop anchor in a sheltered cove. We'd lower a rowing boat and go off to buy stuff. Sometimes it took a couple of days."

"Did you go ashore with them?"

Ange's eyes lit up. "Whenever I could. We met these incredible blokes. Women too."

"Do you remember New Guinea?"

"'Course I do! We were supposed to be there for a month. We ended up staying for three. I thought we'd never get out of there."

"Why was that?"

"We went up north following the coast about two miles out, as far as the mouth of a river whose name I forget."

"The Sepik."

"That's the one. It's this great river with jungle everywhere. It was bloody hot. Mosquitoes everywhere."

Ange was thirsty, and with a trembling hand he pointed at a carafe and two glasses on the table. Then he looked towards the bottle of Pastis 51.

"No ice, just a little water. Otherwise it's not good for my stomach."

De Palma filled the two glasses. There was a long silence.

Ange dipped his lips in the aniseed, his face relaxing. "We got into trouble on the Sepik. We hit a sandbank and couldn't get off it. Meyssonnier was furious, but there was no damage. We'd just got stuck on a high bar. Then everyone took it in turns to go ashore. Me a bit more than the rest."

"Why was that?"

Ange gave a mischievous wink. "I made friends with Monsieur Ballancourt. He took a shine to me. So he'd take me with him when he went ashore."

"How about Delorme?"

"He used to come with us, or else he'd go his own way with some of the other sailors."

"Did he tell you where he was going?"

"Maybe he did. I don't remember. It's a long time ago. And I didn't much like that Delorme."

"How come?"

"All high and mighty he was. Always with his wife . . . He didn't talk with the sailors, he only spoke to give orders."

"And Ballancourt?"

"He was a proper gent. Always ready for a chat, asking you stuff about sailing so he could find out himself. And he was uppercrust, you know."

He raised his eyes towards the balcony. A siren rang out. A Maltese cargo ship was emerging from the Passe Sainte-Marie. There was a big red cross below the hawsehole.

"Do you remember your expeditions with Ballancourt?"

"Oh yes," Ange replied, "I couldn't forget them. We went upriver in a canoe, stopping off at villages. As time passed we went further and further upstream. You had to be careful because the tribes were at war with each other."

"Were you armed?"

"Oh yes. The guide was too. Ballancourt had a pistol."

"What did you do when you stopped off somewhere?"

"It was always the same. We'd meet with the local Elders. We'd parley, and then Ballancourt would buy some works of art. Most of the time the people would be waiting for us on the banks and they'd have stuff ready that they wanted to sell. They knew strangers were coming to buy stuff."

"I thought they were savages."

"Yes, higher up they were. One time we went for three days in a canoe and then walked for I don't know how long. Up there they hadn't come across many white people."

De Palma handed Ange the photographs of the modelled skulls. "Do you remember these?"

The old sailor's expression became sombre. He looked for a long while at the skull with painted whorls round the eyes and over the temples. "I remember that one."

"How come?"

"Ballancourt bought it in exchange for some axes we'd taken in the canoe. Because over there they only had stone axes. Prehistoric things, really . . ." Ange took the photograph between his fingers. "I got the feeling the village people wanted to get rid of that skull . . . And it was after that our troubles all started."

"What happened?"

"We were attacked on the way back. Savages fired arrows at us from the bank. I can still see them running with their bows. They were stark naked and they were shouting. We rowed out into the middle of the river. It was wide, so they couldn't reach us. After a bit we fired back at them. Ballancourt was a good shot. I think he killed one of them.

"And then what happened?"

"The water level went down. The *Marie-Jeanne* grounded, tilting slightly to starboard. It was a real disaster. It was impossible to shift her."

"You think that was all because of the skull?"

Ange gave a sigh. His thin fingers were bunched up on the threadbare arms of his chair. The sun had sunk low on the horizon and was now flooding the living room with a soft light. A seagull had settled on the balcony, looking at the two men with a sidelong glance.

"Those savages, they curse you something terrible. Ballancourt believed in all that stuff."

"And Delorme?"

"Delorme – he didn't even believe in the Virgin Mary. All he was interested in was skulls. He didn't give a toss about anything else."

"Anything else?"

"That was another time. But I wasn't there myself. Ballancourt had gone off on his own with the guide. He returned with another skull, but it wasn't as frightening. Two statues too . . . At least I think so . . . And then a bow. Well, Delorme was only interested in the skull . . ."

"There was a bow?"

"Yes, with loads of arrows. This old man from the village had given it to Ballancourt. I remember because we had a laugh shooting at these big rat-like things that used to run along the banks. You needed to be tough to draw that bow, I can tell you. It was hard."

Ange told hundreds of anecdotes about their enforced stay at the mouth of the River Sepik. Not a day passed without some mishap. Until the rains came. The level of the river rose and the *Marie-Jeanne* was able to extricate herself.

"We came back via Singapore, round India, to the Suez Canal."

"You went round the world!"

"Oh, that wasn't the only time."

Ange rose to his feet and picked up his glasses, which were lying on the chest of drawers, "I want to show you something."

He opened his cupboard. In a hardback photograph album there were some pictures of the *Marie-Jeanne*. She was a beautiful ship. A photograph had been taken from the quai des Belges. In the distance the square towers of the Abbey of Saint-Victor were visible and the bastion of the Fort Saint-Nicholas.

"She was 100 feet long," Ange added. "When you were out in the Pacific going at a good speed it felt as if you were flying."

He turned a page. Several small shots showed him on the deck of the schooner, wearing boots and a cap, with a scarf round his neck. "It got freezing after the Azores."

He looked through some of the other pages. Sailors filing past. Bays in the distance. A portrait of a handsome man with beautifully shaped muscles and glossy skin. A name was written in lead pencil on the white border of the photograph: Kaïngara.

"That's the guide we had. He was a wonderful bloke. He spoke loads of languages, so the savages could understand him. Because down there you get as many languages as there are villages."

"Where did you meet him?"

"I don't remember any more. I think it was near the mouth of the river."

Another shot had been taken from the deck of the *Marie-Jeanne*. Coiled rigging could be seen in the foreground.

"There you are," Ange said, "That's me shooting with that bow." He placed a trembling index finger on the photograph with crimped edges, "That's Monsieur Ballancourt. He's dead chuffed because he's just hit the target."

"Did he bring the bow back to France with him?"

"Yes, I think so. Once the level of the river had returned to normal we didn't use it any more. We didn't have time. He must have kept it in his cabin."

The *Marie-Jeanne* passed the Planier lighthouse again at the end of 1937, almost two years after it had first set out. Ange disembarked at Alexandria. He had found a ship that was heading for Saigon. He had a Corsican cousin over there.

"Did you ever hear from Robert Ballancourt after that?"

"I went to his funeral," the sailor paused; "I don't remember the year."

"1984."

"Could be, if you say so. It was Captain Meyssonnier who let me know through the Merchant Navy association."

"How did he die?"

"He had a heart attack. My late wife was still alive. We were sorry to hear about it. There were a lot of people at his funeral."

"Was Delorme there?"

"No, he wasn't. He didn't come."

"Do you know why?"

"No. Those people belonged to a different world from me."

Ange was tired. His fingers trembled as he put the album back in the cupboard and gently closed the door. "At the funeral someone played some strange music."

"Music?"

"I don't really remember what it was. Some sort of flute they have in those countries."

"Did you see the flute player?"

"No, no. I was at the back behind all those important people. Afterwards I left. But it was moving and it brought back memories for me."

"Why was that?"

"Because I had already heard that music down there, in the places where the savages live . . ."

Ange's expression darkened and he froze for a few seconds. His lips quivered. "My son won't be long," he said, raising his eyes to the clock above the television which was adorned with a purple mat.

De Palma was in a thoughtful mood as he got into his Giulietta parked near the Church of Saint-Laurent esplanade. Ange had heard the flautist at Ballancourt's funeral. That was the first lead that needed to be followed up. He wouldn't mention it to Bérénice Delorme. Not until he trusted her.

Captain Meyssonnier had not dwelt on the damage to the *Marie-Jeanne*. He had preferred to describe his travels in the interior. Out of shame, perhaps, de Palma concluded. The captain hadn't wanted to acknowledge he had run his ship aground on a sandbank, just like a novice.

All that remained of the Old Port and the world of Ange Filippi and Captain Meyssonnier were the yachting set and some quays closed off to the public by large, white wooden barriers.

*

"Where were you?"

"In another life. An era that no longer exists."

"That's no answer."

"I was with an old sailor."

Eva had dyed her hair. It had gone from black to chestnut. "That's

209

my natural colour," she said, looking through the door of the Giulietta.

"Can you dye and undye it as you please?" the Baron asked.

"It's women's stuff. You wouldn't understand."

"Maistre used dyes like that when he was in the Drugs Squad. One day it turned bright pink. There must have been something that fouled up with their products."

"So what happened?"

"He was working undercover. When you're mixing with junkies you can show up with pink or green hair. It's no big deal."

"Do you regret leaving the Drugs Squad?"

"No, I hated it."

She lowered the window and looked at him affectionately. In spite of the season the temperature was mild. She let her hand flutter in the breeze. "Do you remember us smoking joints while we listened to Mahler?"

"I do. If you really want to know, I used to put on Mahler because I didn't like the Floyd. And I remember you refused to make love because you thought you were so sophisticated. You used to tell me I didn't understand anything about pop."

"Don't get so worked up."

"There's nothing to understand about the Floyd."

He parked rather casually at the entrance to the small port of Vallon des Auffes, in front of a little boat owned by Roger Minelli who had worked for the Murder Squad in the past.

"Thanks for bringing me," Eva said, slamming the car door. "It's been ages since I came here."

"This was where I did my first drugs bust with Maistre."

"Did he have pink hair?"

"No, that time he was on our side."

The boats bobbed up and down on the lazy water. A seagull drowsed, balancing on the metal sides of a fish tank.

"Still nostalgic, Michel?"

"Seems I live with the past on my mind. You never really belong in the present . . ."

He pushed open the door of the Les Gabians restaurant. Sauveur Paoli came over to greet them.

"Hey, Michel, mate. You've come to see us then? Well, that is really nice." Sauveur looked enquiringly in Eva's direction.

"This is Eva."

"Good morning, Mademoisclle."

Sauveur held out his hand.

"I'm Sauveur . . . I'll introduce myself because if we wait for him to do it we'll be waiting all day."

They sat in front of the large window. Two enormous arches of the Corniche Kennedy straddled the Vallon des Auffes, separating it from the city. Facing them at the cnd of some unassuming alleyways was the dark hill of the Vierge de la Garde; the gold-plated Holy Mother looking out to sea.

"There you are, this'll be nice for you."

Sauveur still had something of the Adonis about him, but he was developing a stoop. The local gangs had nicknamed him "Ciggie", not because he smoked like a chimney, but because he got busted in the Combinatie affair: a low-tonnage ship involved in smuggling cigarettes in the 1950s.

"So, tell me, what's Maistre up to?"

"Well, what do you know? He's come over all mysterious."

"Jean-Louis is an old devil. Lucky he's not here tonight."

"Why's that?"

"Too many pigs round here."

"You don't like pork?"

"I only do fish here."

Eva burst out laughing. Her lips and eyelids were delicately made up. She was wearing some earrings that de Palma had never seen on her before. Sauveur served them two grilled sea bass. He poured a tiny saucepan of warm pastis over them and lit a match. The fish sizzled in the blue flames. They made small talk until the dessert came. De Palma had downed more than two-thirds of the bottle of Bandol wine.

"Can I ask you something indiscreet?" Eva whispered.

"Go ahead."

"A friend of mine who works down the station told me you used to live with a colleague of yours called Anne. Is that right?"

"Yes," de Palma said.

"You don't want to talk about it?"

"Not really. We separated because we didn't have much in common any more. She took the exam to become a commissaire. She passed and that's about it . . ."

Eva did not insist. Behind the counter, Sauveur was setting up the betting for the horse racing the following day. He must be getting some tips, as he often won. Unless he bought winning tickets from time to time so he could launder his ill-gotten gains.

De Palma went over to him. "Tell me, Sauveur, I've heard Castella is involved in art trafficking. Is that cobblers, or is it for real?"

The boss crossed out a horse on the last race. "I don't know. But if I was a serious buyer and wanted something nice, I'd certainly go and pay him a visit. He's a real specialist."

"And Maglia?"

"He's a jerk. A little guy who's got too big for his boots. He's heading for a fall if he carries on like he is."

Sauveur thought for a few moments. "They nearly got nicked by the Belgian fuzz. They route it up that way, they say."

"And what about the port?"

"You hear rumours every now and then that there might be some detectives and security guards around who want to make some dosh and are willing to let stuff go through. I don't know any more than that."

"Thanks, Sauveur."

"That's O.K., son. Don't worry about the bill. It's on me."

By the time they returned home, even the darkest corners of the city were asleep. Eva had rested her cheek on the ledge of the car door. The night wind blew her hair about. He drove slowly, with one arm on the door. The air was light and sweet like nowhere else.

19

Michel went into the cool shade of l'église Saint-Jean and crossed himself. He was early. Lina Baldini was reciting the rosary and staring at the flaking fresco above the altar. She must be praying for the soul of her husband who hadn't always been a saint, and who was doubtless biding his time at the gate of Saint Peter. De Palma gave her a discreet wave. She responded with a serene smile.

Father Joseph came down from the altar. "Hello there, how are you?"

"Like a man coming to see you on the anniversary of his brother's death."

Father Joseph had a hearty handshake. A constant smile lit up his face with its protruding jaw and bright, slightly crazy eyes. "They tell me you're going to quit the police?"

"Yes, I'm getting near to retirement."

"Comes to us all one day. What are you planning to do afterwards?"

"Join the Church . . . that's the civil servant in me."

"You heathen! Don't make me laugh."

"I often thought about it after Pierre's death. I wanted to live on Planet God, but I think maybe he wasn't so keen on me.

Father Joseph's face turned serious. At such moments one never knew whether he was joking or not. "Don't blaspheme, Michel. You're in the house of God . . . God loves you, as you well know."

That God of yours took my brother, and he's never given him back, thought the Baron.

The priest turned towards the squat door of the sacristy. "I can still see you when you were an altar boy. Pierre went first, holding the big missal in his little hands, the one with the leather cover. He used to puff out his chest. And you were so chuffed about the chalices . . . You always had to try and make everyone laugh."

"That's the artist in me."

Father Joseph was a very young priest at a church buried away between the railway track by the big rubbish dump and the factories that struggled on: engineering workshops and plants producing playing cards and colonial hats. Sulphur hung in the air.

La Capelette was a "red" part of town and almost happy. Most parishioners were first-generation Italian immigrants from Naples, or the mountains of Sicily. They feared divine wrath more than the Party edicts, especially on the occasions of baptisms, marriages and funerals. At Mass on Sundays the church was filled with workers in their over-ironed, double-breasted suits. Their hands were all broken from cement, or rough manufacturing, and they wore gold signet rings and patent-leather moccasins that creaked. Their trouser legs were either too short or too long, never quite right; the women were always dressed in mourning, with jewellery on their huge bosoms.

At his brother's funeral the whole district had turned out for the Mass. Somebody's child was everyone's child. The kids from the local Party cell had placed a large white wreath; the pupils from the primary and secondary schools brought drawings. The all-white coffin of Pierre de Palma was decked in flowers.

"Are you expecting someone?"

"Yes, I'm waiting for my friend Jean-Louis. It's not like him to be late."

"Oh, let's wait a while then." Father Joseph looked at his watch. "I've still got two more Masses this evening, one in Pont-de-Vivaux and the other in Saint-Loup. After that I'm off to the hospital chaplaincy. Dashing here, there and everywhere. I'm going to get changed." He paused a moment. "When you dress up in your finery, it encourages the latecomers."

Maistre appeared in the rectangle of white light inside the doorway and crossed himself awkwardly. For more than twenty years he had never missed this occasion.

The priest knelt down in front of the altar. "In the name of the Father, the Son and the Holy Spirit . . . "

De Palma had lost his faith early in his police career and it seemed certain to him that he would never recover it. God had ceased to exist for him one June evening as he stood in front of a dead child, a little girl, in the thirteenth arrondissement of Paris. As for Maistre, he retained some doubt, but he had a belief in something.

In a faltering voice that trailed away at the end of sentences, the priest read from the Beatitudes, the one and only part of the gospel that de Palma had requested over the years.

Blessed are the poor in spirit: for theirs is the Kingdom of God . . .
Blessed are the meek: for they shall inherit the Earth.

Pierre was laid out on the ground. A trickle of blood oozing from his ear. Why had he asked him to come with him? Why did he find himself in this empty road between the high, dry-stone walls of the factories?

The air smelled of electricity. Close by an arc-welding machine crackled in the engineering workshops. There was no-one there to help, and already, Pierre had stopped breathing. It's your fault, his conscience whispered. He wanted to sob, but in that setting at that late hour, all he could do was scream.

The Mass finished without de Palma noticing the time go by. He said his goodbyes to Father Joseph, who was still in a hurry, to the schoolmaster and to the elderly milliner who was suppressing her tears. Lina still had to recite a couple of rosaries.

"Bye, Lina."

"Farewell, son. I've asked the Lord to protect you."

Maistre was waiting near the font, his face crumpled and rings round his eyes.

"Come on, Jean-Louis, let's go for a beer at the Bar du Pont."

"No, I'd rather not. They're all lags there and I can't face drinking that piss."

"As you wish."

On the church square some kids were playing footie with a worn ball on which the Marseille team colours could still be made out. De Palma dribbled round a nipper who had provoked him with a mischievous look, tried to nutmeg him and lost the ball.

"We've got a problem," Maistre said. "A real blow. A Parisian antique dealer by the name of Grégory Voirnec has been murdered. A fortnight ago. An arrow right in the middle of his forehead and another in his shoulder."

De Palma froze. "*What*?"

"Paris are dealing with the investigation. They've found two items at the scene: an arrow that is now with forensics and a card on which someone had written, 'The barbarian is first and foremost the one who believes in barbarism.'"

"Nice quote. Who's it by?"

"Our lot in Paris haven't managed to find that out yet. Assuming they've tried to look . . ."

"About time they let us know. It's outrageous!"

"Keep your cool. They'd have had a job making the link, we've played this one low-key from the beginning."

"That's true. So why did they call us today then?"

"Because they've found a name in the antique dealer's address book: Paul Brissone."

The Baron remained silent.

"They've faxed us a file," Maistre added.

He walked to his car and returned with a blue folder which he handed to the Baron. The crime scene photographs showed a man lying in foetal position, his head back and his face contorted in terror. The forensics team had taken several shots of an arrow.

"I guess it's the antique dealer."

"Yep, but that's not all. A man called Gérard Lescure has been killed at his home in the same way. Lescure was an anthropologist specializing in Papua."

"Any message?"

"No."

They arrived back at the Giulietta. De Palma remained lost in thought for a while.

"Do you think this bloke wants to lead us on a paperchase?" Maistre asked.

"Can't rule it out," the Baron replied vaguely. His mind was elsewhere, remembering the images from the films Bérénice had shown him. Everything still seemed impenetrable.

On the church square the goalie had pushed the ball away for a corner. A tall black kid with shoulders bulging under his yellow-and-green Ronaldo shirt stepped back between two old car bonnets to shoot from an unlikely angle. The ball crashed against the door of God's house. Michel opened his car door and sat behind the steering wheel.

"Did he steal anything from the antique dealer's shop?" he asked.

"No. At least not according to the inventory drawn up by Voirnec's wife. But it's possible he had some pieces from dodgy sources."

The Baron put his hands on the wheel and bit his lips. "So did Voirnec act as a cover for the handlers?"

Maistre rubbed his chin. "Hard to say. I had a long chat with a colleague from the O.C.B.C. He'd come across Voirnec's name. The O.C.B.C. suspected him of doing some under-the-table dealing in early art. The sort of stuff that's easy to deal in and launder. It's very profitable."

"Naturally," de Palma said. "The previous owners aren't exactly going to turn up and complain."

"Then there's the academic," Maistre said. "I don't understand that at all."

"It's the first time there hasn't been a message."

"Maybe he didn't have time."

"We'll discuss all that tomorrow."

Maistre patted the car roof and went back to the squad's Renault Clio. The kids picked up the ball and went their different ways. In the early evening the neglected buildings of rue Saint-Jean looked strangely gloomy. Some passers-by disappeared into the entrance halls. De Palma dialled Bérénice's number.

"I'm expecting you," she said simply.

He postponed his rendezvous with Eva and went up to the fashionable part of town.

*

Bérénice was wearing a dark suit and flat shoes. She had a tormented look and there were deep lines across her forehead. "The barbarian is first and foremost the one who believes in barbarism," she said. "This quote is from Claude Lévi-Strauss. It's very well known."

She was having difficulty recapturing the calm and strength she had displayed up until now. "Claude Lévi-Strauss wrote that in *Race and History*," she paused for a moment, "a very militant book written under the auspices of U.N.E.S.C.O. The aim was to combat racism and intolerance. To demonstrate there is only one race: the human race."

De Palma knew very little about Lévi-Strauss. The only one of his books he knew was *Tristes tropiques* and that celebrated first sentence: "I hate travelling and explorers."

"Do you think that quote from Lévi-Strauss means something, coming after the one from Freud?"

"Of course," Bérénice said. "Claude Lévi-Strauss knocked Freud's theories to pieces. To oversimplify, they were diametrically opposed to one another; although that isn't quite true as Lévi-Strauss respected psychoanalysis. He accepted it had proved that the role of the conscience is self-deception. But he didn't acknowledge the role of instinct and emotion that is so important in Freud. For him all that came under biology."

She fiddled with the string of pearls hanging round her neck, her eyes lingering over the masks hanging on the living-room walls.

"And what about *Totem and Taboo*?" de Palma asked.

"Claude Lévi-Strauss hated it . . . The book made his hair stand on end, because it made the Oedipus myth the starting point for our entire culture. Lévi-Strauss wouldn't stand for that. He demonstrated that the thought systems of savages, which Freud discusses in *Totem and Taboo*, are extremely diverse and complex."

"So . . . a man who wants to dispose of Freud could go and do his shopping *chez* Lévi-Strauss?"

Bérénice couldn't help bursting out laughing. "I guess you could put it like that." The sparkle in her eyes had returned.

De Palma didn't know how to talk to her about the murder of the Parisian antique dealer. For a few seconds he hesitated.

"Is something wrong, Monsieur de Palma?"

He put his hand on his file. "I have some photographs here that might shock you. But I need to show you them."

"What are they?"

"Probably the projectile which killed your grandfather."

She stiffened. "Why didn't you let me see them before? My lawyer told me you hadn't found the crime weapon."

"I'll explain about that later, but it's not the weapon, just the projectile."

His file contained photographs of the arrow that the criminal records office on the quai des Orfèvres had found on the body of the Parisian antique dealer.

"Papuan," she said without hesitation. "It's reed, from the Upper

Sepik region. I've seen similar ones among the Iatmul, but I can't be sure about it. Several societies make those kinds of weapons."

She stood up and turned towards a window. "It's very old," she said with a sob in her voice, "extremely old."

There was a long silence. De Palma cursed the fact he had to be there with his policeman's questions. He hated causing this woman pain, "I'm sorry . . ."

"Grandpa was killed with that arrow. And with the bow that was found in his office."

"It's probable, but I can't be sure."

"Why not?"

"An old bow doesn't have the same power, the bowstring might break . . ."

"Not that one . . ."

"Go on."

"We tried once . . . A long time ago . . . Maybe twenty years ago. Grandpa had changed the cord as the old one had dried up."

"Was anyone else there that day?"

"No."

She took a handkerchief from her pocket and wiped away her tears. "Deep down, it does help to know."

She went to a sideboard, opened a creaky drawer, and took out a packet of cigarettes. De Palma hadn't noticed that she smoked.

"Would you like a cigarette?"

"No thanks," de Palma said.

"Do you have a light?"

He went closer and flipped open his Zippo lighter.

Bérénice did not take her eyes off him. "Where did you find that arrow?" she asked exhaling the smoke.

"In the body of a Parisian antique dealer: Grégory Voirnec. Did you know him?"

She flicked her cigarette with the end of her finger and let some ash drop. "Everyone in the trade knows Grégory Voirnec."

"You don't seem bothered by his death."

"He was a crook!" she said coldly. "A man who brought discredit to our profession."

"Why do you say that?"

She remained silent and stubbed out her cigarette on the bottom of an ashtray, suddenly distant. "That arrow is at least thirty years old . . . It's a long time since guns replaced barbed points in the Upper Sepik region."

"Barbed points?"

"They were basically used in battle. I don't need to tell you the wounds they produce are horrific."

"When we watched that film here, you talked about 'First Contact'," de Palma said.

Bérénice nodded. An exhibition catalogue lay behind her; beside it were her mobile and a notepad on which she had scrawled some figures.

"In that film," he went on, "we saw men who had the same type of arrow as the one used to kill your grandfather. Do you think it all might be linked to a particular event in your grandfather's life?"

"The 'First Contact' was one of those great western fantasies. Particularly during the first half of the twentieth century. Have you heard the story of the Leahy brothers?"

"No," de Palma said; he was starting to lose patience.

"They were Australians who went to New Guinea hunting for gold in the 1920s. They were convinced they could make a fortune in the highlands. They thought no-one lived there. But on the high central plateaux, they found about a million Papuans who'd never set eyes on a white man. There were other 'First Contacts' at different times – always in the same region."

She was staring into space. "In 1961 Robert Ballancourt went back on the road, so to speak. He went a long way up the Yuat River. He wasn't really a young man any more, but he was brave enough to confront a particularly hostile environment and peoples who were not always very peaceable. That's the background.

"Ballancourt would succeed. With his companions, including my grandfather, they marched for days on end before chancing on a people that still lived in ignorance of our 'wonderful' civilization.

"I met Ballancourt several times. He was rather proud of what he had discovered, but at the same time completely shaken. I sometimes felt he had left something behind. He'd left a part of himself in those remote areas of New Guinea."

Bérénice's expression changed. She took off her glasses. A strange light clouded her eyes. "I've gone over the entire house, but I haven't found any other films. Just a book, with photographs of the voyage. Would you like to see them?"

"Of course," de Palma said.

The first picture, in black and white, showed a village resting on a hill covered in bush.

"That's the village Robert Ballancourt visited on 31 October 1961," Bérénice said. "You see the rectangular huts and the small gardens around them. Those tall pillars with the nest-like things on top in the third picture are the huts used by lookouts. They climb up to the top of those poles and keep watch to see if the enemy is in sight. Like everywhere in Papua the tribes are always waging war on each other, following a precise code of vengeance. Each group seeks to avenge the death of one of their own killed in the most recent battle."

De Palma flicked through the photographs one by one: at the beginning they were just stark mountain landscapes, small tracks following twisted paths and basic huts with pigs rooting outside.

"Here's the 'First Contact'," Bérénice said suddenly, placing her finger on a photograph. A terrified man stared into the camera lens. The body leaned forward, a long penis gourd across his stomach, holding out a stone axe.

"I don't need to spell out the effect Ballancourt and his companions had on these men," Bérénice said.

A second shot showed a group of men armed with long thin spears. They all wore penis gourds. The oldest one sported a boar's tusk through his pierced nose.

De Palma was immersed in the photographs. He was looking for a sign, a breakthrough. The expressions did not vary from one photograph to the next: the same terror, the same anxious look in their eyes. The women with wizened breasts, netting on their heads, and grass skirts. Some of them seemed less scared than the men. Children hid behind their legs. One or more fingers on their hands had been amputated. The majority of them were pretty and had pleasing proportions.

The last photograph was a portrait of a young woman – very beautiful, with melancholy eyes. Her breasts were firm and the nipples protruded through her long braided hair. A strange smile suggested that she regretted something; a cleft in her life.

De Palma noticed that the page was turned over. A slight stain marked the right edge of the photograph. The face was familiar. He realized he had seen it in Dr Delorme's film: the last image in the fourth reel.

"Does that face mean anything to you?" he asked.

Bérénice stared sadly at the photograph, and then turned away, "That woman is from another region. She has a history. I can't really remember any more. Grandpa called her Agnès, but he always refused to tell me anything else.

The masks on the walls seemed to snigger at the sight of these two human beings leaning over photographs from another era.

"Give me one of your disgusting cigarettes, Monsieur de Palma. I don't have any left."

As he held out the packet, with a cigarette sticking out, he looked straight into her eyes. "Have you heard of Gérard Lescure?"

"I know him as a scientist."

"He's also been murdered."

She pulled a face as she swallowed a mouthful of brown tobacco,

"Was it an arrow?"

De Palma was disconcerted by the question. "Yes," he said impassively.

She stubbed out her cigarette, which she had hardly touched.

"Did he have links with the antique dealer?"

"I haven't a clue," she replied nervously. "I only knew him by reputation. Same for Voirnec. The gossip was that he topped up his income by selling stuff."

"You mean they were part of a network of traffickers?" He watched for her reaction, but she remained cold, as she gazed up at two statuettes positioned on a piece of furniture.

"The spirits have returned," she said. "They are taking revenge."

"How do you mean?"

"The power of those pieces which I talked to you about the first time we met. The spirits still live within them. The power has never left them."

She lowered her eyes to the photograph of the *Marie-Jeanne* in its silver frame. Her face trembled. There was an anxious expression in her eyes. She handed the book to de Palma. "Take it, you can borrow it."

De Palma realized there were whole chunks of her grandfather's life that she had concealed. Perhaps because she couldn't find the strength to talk about them. Why had she led him to that girl's face?

*

Five naked men sat on the dusty earth, their bodies coated in white paint. The sculptor was sitting on a stool. A pot of resin lay on the ground. The sculptor took a lump of resin in his hand and crammed it where the nose had been, saying, "The nose defines a person. That's what women notice first." Then he fashioned the cheeks and face. Two circles of shell formed the eyes, a tongue of resin, ears. The dead man was coming to life.

The sculptor then attached hair to the back of the skull and made a crown of small white shells. He dipped his paintbrush in a pot of ink and slowly traced the magic swirls, starting at the base of the nose and up to the top of the forehead. The five men watched him, chasing away the flies that plagued them. In a few minutes the skull had become a human face once more. The sculptor said: "The soul that wandered without a home is now finally at rest."

The five men rose to their feet and went back to the Men's House. The skull had returned to the House of the Dead. It would now protect the harvest and the warriors.

2 0

A thread of blue light was coming from the cemetery lodge. The sound of applause broke the silence, followed by a muffled voice. At that time of night the caretaker would be watching trashy programmes on the television. In the distance the hum of the eastern motorway could be heard.

In the rendering of the perimeter wall, the visitor spotted a gap that would allow him to get a hold with his right hand. He pulled with his arm and made it up to a ledge where he could rest the inside of his left foot. A large crack between two stones gave him a second hold for his free hand. He pushed as hard as he could and caught his hand on a protruding shard of glass. It went into the flesh of his thumb and the blood ran down his forearm. With his other hand he undid the sleeves of his jacket and laid it over the wall. A car was coming along the street below. It stopped at the lights at the junction. If he didn't disappear swiftly the driver would be bound to see him. Gritting his teeth he pulled on his wounded hand and managed to hoist himself up onto his jacket.

The tomb was in section six between the crematorium and the small necropolis reserved for the First World War dead. The visitor made his way along the first aisle and quickened his pace.

From what he could remember it was at the end of a row of low tombs. A cat crossed the path, stopping for a moment, its glassy eyes resting on him.

The grave wasn't far off. Nearby was a tall cypress tree. The inscription had not changed:

ROBERT BALLANCOURT
1899–1984

That was all. On the tombstone there was a plaque raised on a tripod:

FORMER PUPILS OF
THE ÉCOLE NATIONALE DES PONTS ET CHAUSSÉES

The visitor moved the plaque aside, put down his bag, and took out two iron bars which he fitted together. A night owl let off a string of dark notes. At the end of the aisle down below he could see the caretaker's lodge. The television cast cold reflections on the living-room windows.

He put the flat part of the bar in a notch in the stone which was used by the gravediggers. His first attempt at levering made the enormous slab of granite move just a centimetre. He tried again, angrier this time, and managed another couple of centimetres. After fifteen minutes he had widened the gap enough to enable him to slip inside the vault. First he pushed his bag inside, and then he switched on his torch and went down.

There was only one coffin, to the left, placed on the ground. The visitor held his breath. No smell of a corpse. The wood had turned black. The front was completely eaten away by worms. He gave it a small blow with his bar and shattered the oak. A black suit collar appeared, half eaten by vermin.

The visitor forced open the planks with small blows of his iron bar. The lid quickly gave way. The skull appeared. A tuft of hair was still hanging from a bit of dried-up, leathery skin. The teeth stuck out. A smell of must, dry leaves and acidic cinders spread through the vault.

He lost no time. With a sharp tug he twisted the head towards him. With a cracking sound the spine immediately gave way. He removed the rags and lifted the skull up to his eyes.

Slowly he put the skull in his bag. Then he turned round. The evil ones were standing at the back of the vault, with ash-white faces.

"Get out!"

The first one turned away and disappeared into the wall of the tomb. The second one continued to stare at the visitor.

"Get out!"

The evil one moved back until its hands were resting against the wall.

"Out! Get out of me!"

The evil one nodded and disappeared.

PART TWO

The Land that Time Forgot

The peaks of the Snow Mountains, on bright mornings, part the dense clouds and soar into the skies of Oceania. Beneath the clouds, like a world submerged, lie the dark rocks which form the great island of New Guinea; climbing abruptly from the Dampier Strait in the East Indies, the range extends eastward fifteen hundred miles, until at land's end in Papua, it sinks once more beneath the ocean.

Peter Matthiessen, Under the Mountain Wall –
A Chronicle of Two Seasons in Stone Age New Guinea
(The Harvill Press, 1995)

21

Yuarimo village – 7 February 1961

Kwenda sat down opposite Ballancourt. Two fingers were missing from her left hand. The stumps formed bumps under her skin which was already worn from toiling in the fields. She had been mutilated as a sign of mourning: for Kaïngara, her father; and for Mawa, her first husband.

"So you are Kaïngara's daughter," Ballancourt said, surprised.

"Yes," Kwenda said, staring at the huge white man in front of her, "I was born just after he died."

There was something brazen in her expression. She did not fear this man who was admired by everyone. In spite of his milky-white skin he was attractive, with lean muscles and an acidic smell. She thought he smelled of death. But it didn't matter; the way he looked affected her.

"Your father was my friend. In the old days he was my guide. He took me up the Sepik to places where people from the West had never been before; to the mountain plateaux of the interior. Your father was a brave man."

Ballancourt's eyes glazed over. He was embarrassed. "The sort of man you don't find any more in this country. I saw him in wartime: he was steadfast in battle. When he gave orders everyone listened, even the old headhunters. He carried a long white feather in his right hand and a spear in his left. He always stopped the battle as soon as the first man was wounded, as he considered that reparation had taken place. It was enough for him that his men and his enemies had displayed bravery."

Kwenda had not known her father. She only knew that the Elders still celebrated his memory and that he still loomed large in the minds of the young men. Once or twice old Wabe had talked to her of the Big Man who had come down the ghost road.

"How did you become my father's friend?" Kwenda asked.

"It was wartime. We had just bought a skull in a village whose name I forget and suddenly in a fast bit of the river some men attacked us. Warriors whom Kaïngara didn't know. Long arrows with pointed barbs rained down. No-one was hit. We rowed to find shelter behind the reeds."

"Those men wanted the skull you took," Kaïngara said to me. "It must belong to one of their Big Men. It is possible the people who sold it to us had stolen it during a raid. It is a great sacrilege to steal a skull."

"I thought it was something that didn't happen. That it was taboo."

"Not since Westerners started to buy them," he said.

"We're going to give it back to them," I replied. I was in a terrible state. I realized the wrong I had done. For a long time your father stared at the skull, which was wrapped in a white cloth.

"No," Kaïngara said. "They would kill us anyway."

At that moment a warrior suddenly appeared out of the reeds. He strung his bow and was about to shoot your father. I raised my gun and shot him.

"You saved Kaïngara's life!"

Ballancourt did not reply. He looked down. He wasn't the sort of man to talk about himself. Reminiscing about Kaïngara threw him into a deep melancholy. "Your father is probably the only real friend I ever had."

Kwenda saw that Monsieur Robert's eyes were moist with tears. She rested her head on Robert's shoulder, took his hand and planted a kiss on it.

"Do you know why I've come back?" Ballancourt asked.

"No."

"I went to buy Kaïngara's skull."

"And did you find it?"

"Yes."

Monsieur Robert fell silent. When night falls it is never quiet under the skies of Oceania. The incessant croaking of frogs swelled and almost drowned the deep breathing of the European. Everywhere tiny insects clashed in the muggy darkness.

"How did your husband die?" Ballancourt asked

"He was killed during a war. They came here and destroyed everything. That was when Mawa was killed."

"When did that happen?"

"Two years ago."

"Did you avenge his death?"

"Yes. In the spring our men went to take a life. Since then there has been no more war. The wrong has been put right."

"But they are still your enemies?"

Kwenda smiled sadly. War would start up again on the slightest pretext. Something in her young life had been shattered. Ballancourt often watched her going barefoot to the fields. She walked like a queen, with a gentle swaying of the hips that made her look like a goddess, in spite of the small mattock on her shoulder and the net full of holes that she used to carry sweet potatoes. She was shunned by the village. The young men didn't want her. She was no longer a virgin and it was said that she brought bad luck. Ballancourt knew that her late spouse Mawa had not been a good husband to her. Even after he had converted to Christianity, he would drink and beat his young wife. He left her neither children, nor property. Kwenda had not been baptized. She still believed in the ancestral spirits, in the spirits of the great forest. After her husband's conversion, Mawa spent everything on the construction of the church. On the day of his first communion he slaughtered lots of pigs and gave a feast for the entire village. If Kaïngara had been alive to see all that he would have killed his daughter's husband. He was magnanimous, a quality that Robert had always sought in a man, but had only discovered in his guide.

At nightfall Kwenda slipped into Robert's bed. He said nothing. She was naked and her seething body gave off a subtle scent of cinnamon. She put her hand on Robert's chest and felt his slow heartbeat. In her mind the hearts of heroes beat slowly. The sounds of the night rose up from the banks of the River Sepik: large insects endlessly chirping; nocturnal birds trilling darkly though the large trees; and everywhere the streaming heat. Robert's gun rested by the head of his bed; its bluish sheen glinting in the weak light.

Kwenda raised her leg and brushed against the great man's penis. It was hard and full of vigour. She sought out Robert's mouth and with a thrust of her pelvis she sat astride him. Her long hair fell down across her face, smelling of ripe fruit and of the forest. Ballancourt had closed his eyes. His heavy breathing became more and more rapid as she gave him what he had desired since he first set eyes on her.

22

For two days the skies had been daubed with the movements of vessels out at sea. Long white skeins scored the azure sky right up to the limestone cliffs surrounding Marseille.

"Hi there, Baron."

Maistre lifted the rope that cordoned off the crime scene. A dark-skinned man was lying spreadeagled on the cold stone of quai Wilson, one hand over his face and his left arm dangling over the sea.

"Must be about forty," Maistre put in. "Can't be much more. The blood hasn't dried yet."

"Settling of scores?"

"Yeah," Maistre said, watching the patrol car from the Northern Unit that had just parked behind the cordon. "I think it's the bloke we followed the other day."

De Palma pushed back the greying fringe that looped over his forehead. He was wearing a tan leather jacket, black trousers and a grey shirt with the sleeves rolled up. He squatted down and looked at the corpse.

"What do you reckon, Baron?"

De Palma rested his finger on the dead man's temple. "Same hole as with Delorme."

"That's what I was thinking."

He lifted the hand covering the man's face. "It's definitely him."

Beside the railway junction the points squeaked as wagons of chemical goods passed over them. The Head of the Murder Squad came charging up with Bessour at his side.

"Hello Baron."

De Palma greeted the two men with a nod. "It's Leacock, boss."

"Shit," Bessour said.

"You're right there, son," de Palma nodded.

The crime scene forensics team had removed the clothes from the corpse and put a white body bag on the ground.

"We need to find witnesses," Legendre said, "and that's not going to be easy. Karim's going up to the *Melbourne*."

The forensics team took the corpse by the wrists and ankles and placed it in the body bag. The zip whistled.

"When we tailed him he vanished into the clubs round L'Opéra," Maistre said, "We could make a start there."

"Excellent," Legendre said. "But I'm wondering why that hasn't been done before?"

"We didn't want to move too fast in case we lost him."

Legendre groaned.

De Palma mentally retraced the route they had taken when they tailed Leacock. He could picture the Quartier de L'Opéra with its seedy bar signs. He had been twenty metres away when Leacock turned into rue Glandèves. He had paused for about ten seconds, not much longer. There were two bars there: the Banana and the Marimba. A tall, brown, long-legged street girl had been standing outside the Marimba. She had propositioned him as he went by. The other clubs in the street, the Sagittaire and the Valparaiso, were much further down. Leacock couldn't have vanished into either of them unless he went like the clappers, and in that case de Palma would have heard him running. He switched on his mobile and dialled the number of a customs inspector in charge of the squad dealing with clubs.

"Hey Christophe, de Palma here."

"The Baron! Well I never! Virgin Mary had a baby boy?"

"Not by me she hasn't. I just need the names of the owners of a couple of clubs down by the Opéra."

"Fire away."

"The Marimba and the Banana."

"That's simple. 'Nono' Castella," the customs officer said. "He's put them in his wife's name."

"Do you know how Castella makes a living?"

"Not really. If you find out any more, give me a call; it's always useful to know these things."

The Baron and Maistre got down to mapping out the underworld. Maglia and Berry worked for Castella. The sailor they had followed from the *Melbourne* to the bars in the Quartier de l'Opéra led them directly into Castella's manor.

"He's one of the big names in this fucking city," Legendre grumbled. "His teams do the posters for most of the local politicians, right or left."

"Model citizen then!" Bessour quipped.

"We could respectfully put a few questions to him," Maistre said.

"You go with Karim, right away." Legendre turned to de Palma. "With blokes like him you have to strike while the iron is hot."

The light was fading. Long blue shadows were settling over the docks, plunging the corners of the warehouses into darkness. A car belonging to the Port Authority parked in front of the police cordon. A spindly man in a blue suit strode towards them.

"Here comes the Deputy Public Prosecutor," Maistre said.

"Must be missing the sea air."

"Afternoon gentlemen," the Prosecutor said, avoiding the corpse.

"Back to square one," Maistre declared, pointing at the body.

"Any idea who it is?"

"Its Leacock, boss."

"That's not good news."

"Is it ever?" de Palma said, jangling his car keys in his hand.

He left the crime scene, while Bessour made a call on the

walkie-talkie. The sea wall receded in a long straight line of white stones, punctuated with rusty mooring bollards and enormous rings. On the other side, the hill of Notre-Dame de la Garde and the buildings that clung to it seemed tiny in the reddish light of the setting sun.

*

They found Castella in his stronghold at the bar des Galères by the junction of rue de la Paix and Cours d'Estienne-d'Orves; at the heart of what had been the arsenal for the Sun King's galley ships.

"You stay outside for a couple of minutes," the Baron said, "In case he tries to give us the slip. I'm going to get the barman out of there and see to anything else. Then you come in and join me."

"Do you want me to call in some backup?"

"No Castella's a heavy number. We need to move carefully."

"You'll do the talking?"

"Yep. This is kid-glove policing. The devil in sheep's clothing."

"They say he's behind half the murders in this town."

"Yes, son, but the underworld don't like a vacuum. When one thug dies, another comes out of the woodwork. The biotope has its needs and he knows that. It's up to us to smoke him out."

"What's your plan then?"

"We don't have to tell him Leacock was killed by a psycho with an arrow. We'll go for a .38, that'll give him something to think about. Have you got any of those bags for seals left?"

"Er . . . yes."

Bessour rummaged in his pockets. "There you go," he said, taking out a small plastic bag.

De Palma put a cartridge case in it and sealed the packet. "I always carry one, just in case."

Bessour looked at him, his face tense.

"I know son, it's dirty policing. But Castella's not exactly the straightest kid in town." He went on, "An ex-con gave me a tip-off.

Apparently there are some blokes in the job topping up their pay packet, covering up the trafficking going on down the port. I'll give my right arm it's the two cops listed in Paulo's address book."

Bessour nodded. The setting sun was dividing the road into two separate areas of light and shade. The first night birds had already begun to settle on the café terraces.

"You sure this is going to work, Baron?"

"Yeah, no problem."

Castella stood at the end of the tropical-wood bar, gazing over the comings and goings on rue de la Paix and the Cours d'Estienne-d'Orves. He didn't turn a hair when he caught sight of the Baron in the doorway.

"Hello," de Palma said.

"Hello," the thug said, looking him in the eye. He was going on fifty. Since coming out of gaol two years previously he had dyed his hair deep black to disguise some grey hairs that were starting to emerge on his temples. A young woman who looked like a model appeared in the kitchen doorway.

"Monsieur Castella, I'd like to talk to you in private."

Castella gave a dark look and ordered the girl to leave.

The Baron settled by the bar and asked for a beer. "Right, you know why I'm here?"

Castella turned to the barman, "Why don't you go take a fag break outside?"

The barman left.

"What do you want to know?"

"I've come as a friend," the Baron said.

Bessour burst into the bar.

"Stay there," de Palma ordered, "and block the door."

"Hang on," Castella said, "What's going on?"

"Just a precaution," Bessour said, gesturing to him to calm down. "We wouldn't want anything to happen to you."

The Baron took another sip and put down his glass. "Monsieur

Castella, we're under orders to remand you in custody for the murder of Jim Leacock."

"Hang on, are you dreaming or something? I'm supposed to have killed this bloke?"

"That's what we have been told by several sources. Do you have anything to say?"

"You've got no proof. I don't even know who he is."

"Maybe, but we have good reason to believe what we've been told. We're going to have to take you down the station . . . I'm sorry about this, Monsieur Castella. But you know the law."

Castella thought for a few seconds, "You told me you'd come as a friend."

"And believe me I'm as good as my word."

"What do you want to know?"

The Baron switched stools and sat a few centimetres from Castella. "The crates from the *Melbourne*. Where were they heading?"

Castella frowned, "I don't know anything about all that."

"Art trafficking in the port."

Castella gave a dubious smile.

"There's a sailor from the *Melbourne* who's dead, and it's not by accident," de Palma said.

"Criminals never die by accident."

"A single bullet in the temple. That's not the way criminals die, is it, eh? What do you say?"

Castella looked back and forth between the inscrutable faces of the two men questioning him. "Probably had it coming, just like all criminals."

De Palma stared at Castella for a long time. "Something very unusual happened this afternoon. Very, very unusual."

He took an olive from a bowl on the bar and swallowed it. "For the first time in ages, we caught two guys as they were taking someone out. We're holding one of them. My colleague, he's a crack shot, he let him have one to calm him down. We're going to patch him up a bit and then we'll have a little chat with him. Tonight, I reckon. Don't want to delay things."

De Palma took another olive. "And I'm telling you he's going to squeal. I promise. These blokes who kill people in cold blood, I can't stand them. It's inhuman what they did. Don't you think?"

"I agree with you."

The Baron's face was just a few centimetres away from Castella's. "So if we ever get to hear your name, what are we going to do about it?"

Castella gave a satisfied smile. "I'm cool. No-one's going to talk about me."

The two men stared at each other defiantly.

"You haven't asked us what happened to the second bloke?"

Castella shrugged. De Palma turned to Karim.

"A colleague blew his head away with a Flash-Ball," Bessour said coldly. "When you get it, it's painful. He's lying at death's door on a stainless-steel bed."

Castella looked worried. His face went pale.

"I think you now appreciate war's broken out and maybe you're next on the list," de Palma said. "We're not short of killers in this wonderful city of ours."

"I don't have enemies."

"Maybe not. But they're clearing up, they're clearing up. The lumberjacks are at work, Monsieur Castella."

De Palma threw the packet with the cartridge case down on the bar. ".38 Special. Have you got a name for me?"

"What do you take me for?"

"For someone who knows exactly where his interests lie, settling scores isn't good from anyone's point of view. Not good for morale, or for business."

Castella had that mean look gangsters wear when they sense they are losing their grip and that a higher force has taken control of their destiny.

"The man killed by that bullet was spotted in one of your places on rue Glandèves. Do you see where this is going, Monsieur Castella? Down at court there's a couple of crusaders who dream of turning Marseille into a paragon of virtue. Just like it was in the good old days."

De Palma looked at Bessour. "Yes, gentlemen. The Roman patricians sent their sons up to Massalia to give them a taste of morality. We were Greek here, Monsieur Castella, and Greek is the language of philosophy. Don't you think?"

"Er . . . yeah. It's true the judges sometimes . . ."

"They're crusaders, I'm telling you. It's not a court any more; it's the Spanish Inquisition."

Castella had rested his arms on the bar, his eyes fixed on the bluish glint of the bottles. "I've heard people talk about trafficking down the port," he replied after a long silence. "Two blokes from the Border Police. I don't know their names."

"What was Leacock doing with them?"

"I dunno . . . well I do. He was bringing the stuff in and your two mates were taking care of the rest."

"Can you describe them?"

"One of them is tall with dark hair and round silver glasses. He's got a scar on his forehead, a bit like yourself. The other one's smaller, greyish. He's fat. Talks with a Paris accent. I only saw them once."

"Have they flogged much art then?"

"I haven't bought anything from them myself. But from what they tell me it was the third time. At least that's what I think, but I'm not sure. These are rumours going round. I'm trying to help you."

"Is this all from the same source?"

"I don't know."

De Palma swallowed another olive and turned to go. "Thank you, Monsieur Castella. You won't be having any more problems with bent coppers."

*

As he left his car in the parking area outside the block of flats, the living-room light was on. He stayed a few seconds watching the rectangle of light on the second floor of Block B. It was years since he had last seen that comforting sight. He raced up the stairs.

Eva was in the shower. She didn't hear him come in. A C.D. was playing "Aïda"'s great aria.

"All you've got is opera," she said, appearing in the doorway, a towel tied round her head.

A hefty sailing manual lay on the sofa.

"You been swotting away then?"

"Yep, I really want to get a boat and do some sailing when I retire."

"Will you take me too?"

"Yes. But first I need to learn everything in this bloody manual. Otherwise we might end up one evening in the Bermuda Triangle in a cyclone."

"That'd be a nice way to go," she said, leaving her bathrobe slightly open and drawing herself up on tiptoe so she could kiss him.

23

Marseille. October 1976.

"So how's young Kaïngara then?"

"He's been unwell," Ballancourt said, shaking Fernand Delorme's hand.

"And how are you, my boy?" the Doctor asked turning to Kaïngara.

Kaïngara smiled shyly. He was already a young man, almost as tall as his father. He already had that feverish gaze that went through everything.

"Come on, Robert," Delorme said, "let's go into my office. Then I'll ask Victoria to make us some nice fish. I've got to go to the hospital this afternoon, but I do have a bit of time."

They went into the office. Kaïngara immediately noticed the scary masks in the bookcase. There was an ancestral skull on which red spirals had been drawn. It had a friendly expression. He had seen a similar skull in the Men's House, but his memories were already distant ones. It was so long since he had played in the shade of the betel palms, or in the still waters of the river. He stared at the floral patterns carved in the wood.

"So you see Fernand, for some weeks now Kaïngara has been having fits. When it happens he can't move, or say a single word. I'm concerned about it."

Fernand Delorme watched the young man for several seconds, "How long does it last for?"

"Just a few minutes, maybe a bit more, but at the time it seems to go on for ever."

"Are his movements sometimes uncoordinated?"

Ballancourt hesitated before replying, "No. Not as far as I know."

The Doctor turned to Kaïngara, "Explain to me what happens."

The boy mumbled a few words then burst into tears.

Delorme, embarrassed, put his hand on the adolescent's shoulder. "It's nothing, nothing at all. Everyone can have fits like that. Sometimes it's just because you're growing faster than expected."

Delorme looked at Ballancourt and then said to Kaïngara, "Go and wait for us in the drawing room. Victoria will get you whatever you want. And you can go and see my granddaughter, Bérénice. I think she's there now. Your father and I need to talk."

Kaïngara went out. He crossed the waiting room and went into the drawing room through a door that seemed very narrow to him.

Victoria was in the kitchen. She had a friendly smile. "Would you like something to drink, love?" she said in a funny accent that reminded him of the men from the highlands with their singsong way of talking.

"It's not serious, Robert," Delorme said, putting his glasses down on his desk. "It's possible that in time these fits will go away."

Delorme stared at his friend for a while. "How long is it since he last went back to Yuarimo?"

Ballancourt looked down. "It's five years now."

"Five years! Can you imagine what that means in a young boy's life? Five years without seeing his mother!"

Robert Ballancourt shook his head. Delorme had never seen him unhappy before. He looked depressed.

"What's happened, Robert?"

"Kwenda won't speak to me any more."

"Does Kaïngara know?"

"No. I haven't had the heart to tell him. He seems so frail."

Delorme rested both forearms on his desk and pressed his fingers together in front of his mouth. He looked pensive.

"How did you find out?"

"It was two months ago . . . She called from the police station. She accused me of having abandoned her. A priest must have turned her against me."

Ballancourt was no longer the intrepid explorer of the past. He looked down at his shoes. His eyes seemed lifeless.

"I think that Kaïngara's fits are due to the separation from his mother," Fernand Delorme said.

"He doesn't show anything though."

"Children often hide these things very well, Robert. But it has an effect inside."

In the garden Kaïngara and Bérénice had sat down by the swimming pool. Ballancourt was proud of his son. He was polite, did very well at school, and was considerate when he needed to be. He had a slender face like his mother and his muscular physique reminded Ballancourt of the boy's grandfather. It was obvious that Bérénice was attracted to him.

"I don't know what to do, Fernand."

"Tell him the truth," Delorme replied with the bluntness that had always clashed with Ballancourt's refined manners.

The explorer shrugged. "The truth is we left part of our souls down the Yuat and Sepik rivers."

"Yes," Delorme said, looking at the photograph of his son, which never left his desk. "I lost more than just part of my soul there."

Shortly after his last expedition, the doctor had lost his wife to a degenerative disease of the central nervous system that no-one had been able to identify. An eminent British specialist consulted by Delorme had thought it might be some tropical disease. Then several years later, Bérénice's father had died in an accident. Delorme had concluded that his family had been struck down by a curse.

"Sometimes a severe psychological trauma can trigger these types of seizures. There's no need to worry about it."

"And what if that's not it?"

"It could of course be epilepsy . . ."

The word shook Ballancourt to the core. He had torn his own son away from his mother and from his people. He had wanted to turn him into a civilized person like himself, and was stung by his failure to do so. "I should never have brought him here," he murmured.

"He has seen a lot of things and learned a huge amount. Now you must let him go back to his ancestral village. He must see his mother again. That's the most important thing."

Ballancourt felt as though, little by little, a rogue spirit was knocking down the wall of certainties that had framed his life.

"Would you like me to do some tests?"

"I don't know."

"Epilepsy can be diagnosed very quickly."

"No. I don't want that. My son isn't mad." It was all that Ballancourt could manage to utter.

"But that's not what I'm talking about. It's not E.C.T.," Dr Delorme said.

Ballancourt looked sullen as he thought deeply about Kwenda. Life was very unjust.

Delorme smiled at him kindly. "Do you remember that book of Freud's we had during our first voyage? I was obsessed with it."

"*Totem and Taboo*?"

"Yes. I read it again, recently. I found it quite horrendous. To label as savages the people we loved so much!"

"Freud knew nothing of the things we learned. Why do you mention *Totem and Taboo*?"

"Because we often used to talk about it. I read it at the beginning of the *Marie-Jeanne* voyage."

"That's true," Ballancourt murmured.

"Because I think we always viewed the people we met from that point of view. We thought of them as savages, even if we didn't dare admit it. I think we were searching for the 'primal horde' without knowing it."

Ballancourt looked gloomy. Once again Fernand Delorme's line of argument made him feel uncomfortable. But he knew that his old friend wasn't totally wrong.

"My family won't let me acknowledge Kaïngara as my son," he said.

"They don't have the right to do that."

"Of course not, but my mother has threatened to disinherit me. She's got lawyers for all that. She won't totally cut me out, but I could lose a lot. She's not young any more and I don't think she has much longer to live."

"Take your son up to the highlands and let him rediscover himself while there's still time. Then you'll see. But first you must tell him the truth."

The two men turned towards their children, who hadn't stirred. Kaïngara seemed happy. As he spoke he had the gestures of a gentleman. Bérénice listened in admiration. She was wearing a pleated kilt and canvas shoes.

"They are all we have left," Delorme said.

Ballancourt did not reply. His mind was far away. He could see himself in the long yellow grasses with Kwenda nearby; and Kaïngara barely visible above the grass. That day he had caught sight of an eagle wheeling above the great forest.

24

"Brigadier Stéphane Martini, fifty-three years old and Lieutenant Frédéric Faure, thirty-eight."

"An officer too!" Legendre exclaimed. "You're doing this on purpose, Baron."

"Yes. Those are the two guys in Paulo's notebook."

Legendre closed his eyes and shook his head, "Bloody hell, we're going to miss you."

"I hope so."

Maistre had found a small knife in the jumble in his desk drawer and was silently sharpening a pencil.

"There's no room for sentiment in this. It's not easy banging up bent cops. Whatever the risk, I'm going to take it. But we need to catch them on the job."

"What about the Police Complaints Authority?"

"Not a good idea. We'll take this forward ourselves and tell them when we know the score."

"We need Judge Melville to issue a warrant," de Palma said. "He won't want to do that without good reason."

"Two cops from the Border Police, what more do you need?" Maistre exclaimed, flinging his pencil in the basket.

"Let me remind you we've got nothing on them," Legendre said. "No proof, no case file. Just the say-so of a con who fell for some bluff."

"I've got an idea," Bessour said. "The *Melbourne*. Let's make them believe the loot is back on board."

"Nice idea, Karim."

"Captain Mulligan will go along with it," Maistre said.

"Why?" Legendre asked.

"Because it's in his interest to cooperate: otherwise he won't be able to sail his boat. So there's no reason why he won't lend a hand."

Each stage in Legendre's inner reasoning was accompanied by little jerks of his head.

"You've got a free hand, Karim. What's your plan?"

"Easy. I ask Mulligan to phone the Border Police. He says he wants to talk to the two rozzers because some crates have been found at the bottom of the hold and he thought they might be interested."

"Perfect. We'll stake out the *Melbourne* till it sails. If there's any argy-bargy, it's bound to be just before they leave. We'll keep our distance. Keep an eye on any comings and goings round the ship. Mulligan can keep a watch on what goes on inside."

De Palma swept a crumb off his desk with the back of his hand. "And I hope we have God on our side."

"So you believe in God now, do you?" Legendre said in surprise.

"Just as much as a Freemason like yourself . . ."

"I am a deist," Legendre protested.

"One day you'll have to explain the big difference to me."

"There is one."

Legendre shot back a knowing smile at Maistre, who had started grinning. The Baron opened his drawer and took out a gun, tipped up the cylinder and rotated it in the palm of his hand.

"So we do a follow on them," Legendre resumed. "I'm thinking about the operation. Yes, Jean-Louis . . ."

Maistre got up, took a felt-tip pen and, in bold outline, drew on the board the sea wall, the quai aux Charbons, and the position of the *Melbourne*.

"Karim's on the sea wall, watching the *Melbourne*," he said drawing a cross. "He'll give the signal. We need to post two blokes here, near the Border Police offices."

"That's you and me," Legendre said.

Maistre drew a second cross at the other end of the dry dock. "What about an escape route?"

De Palma went up to the board and indicated two spots. "Here and here. Port d'Arenc and over towards Mourepiane. O.K. the quay is broad, but not that broad. If they split we can collar them no problem."

"We need reliable blokes in the places Michel has indicated," Legendre said. "We can't ask our Border Police colleagues."

"It'll just be us," de Palma added. "We have to nab them on our own."

"Er . . . yes," grumbled Legendre, "I guess you're right."

The Baron stuffed his Bodyguard in its holster. His movements were rapid and imprecise. He took out his weapon again to set the safety catch. Something in his expression had changed.

"Shall we go?" he asked stiffly.

"Yes, get on with it!" Legendre said. "I'm going by the gun room to pick up some hardware."

De Palma had already put on his jacket and was disappearing down the corridor.

*

A strong swell was whipping up the spray from the waves breaking by the sea wall. Bessour kept his eyes fixed on the *Melbourne*. On top of the forecastle and the cranes the lights had been switched on. The square windows on the bridge cast dazzling white reflections on the hull that looked unreal in the setting sun.

The gangway was drawn up. A crew member posted aloft was watching every movement on the quay. Mulligan's lookout, thought Karim. The captain had been alerted by phone and had assured Legendre of his complete cooperation in return for a smooth departure. The ship was therefore due to leave that evening for Sydney, its final destination. At the last minute the ship's owner, a company in Singapore, had decided to alter the original route. The *Melbourne* had been loaded with containers of car parts and second-hand earth-moving equipment bound for Alexandria. There the ship was due to pick up a cargo of cotton and take it to Singapore, without a stopover. After that was a mystery. The port authorities hadn't been able to say any more. Besides it was not their concern.

A large wave crashed, forming huge puddles. A drop splashed against Bessour's cheek. He wiped it off with the back of his hand and tasted the salt on his skin. The wind intensified. Squawking sea birds hovered over the crests of the waves. De Palma and Legendre were posted in a container a few dozen metres away from the Border Police offices.

Bessour went down to the quai aux Charbons on the other side of the sea wall to shelter from the wind. He moved away from the *Melbourne* so as not to draw attention to himself. After about a hundred metres he stopped by a shed used by workers stripping down an old crane. He sat down on some crosspieces and took out his binoculars. At the back of the *Melbourne* two men were leaning on the ship's rail, chatting while they had a smoke. From time to time gusts of wind carried the rather harsh syllables of their mysterious language. A gate was open on the port side, just over a metre above the water level: the opening used by pilots to get into the boats they steered into the inner harbours and channels of the port. A silhouette appeared in the doorway and bent down. Bessour glanced at the inner harbour. On the quai du Maroc, a cargo ship from the Messageries was loading large earth-moving equipment bound for North Africa.

"Rouge, this is rouge," Karim whispered, grabbing hold of his walkie-talkie. "We've got some movement down here. Over."

"Rouge receiving. Nothing this end. Over and out."

Five minutes went by. The silhouette appeared once more and stood still. Two hundred metres to the left a Zodiac was moving at high speed. As it got close to the *Melbourne* it did a sharp turn and came to a halt a metre from the gate.

"Rouge, this is rouge. A Zodiac has just stopped by the *Melbourne*. It's a Border Police boat."

The silhouette hurled a bulky parcel onto the dinghy and watched as the boat disappeared towards the container terminal.

"Shit. It's going off towards the repair yards."

Karim looked through his binoculars one last time. The Zodiac had just pulled in by the hull of the *Caprice des Mers*, a small, ageless cargo ship.

"*Caprice des Mers*," Bessour whispered into his walkie-talkie. "Pier J."

"Perfect," Legendre said. "The Baron and Maistre are already on their way. They'll make contact in two minutes."

Bessour looked at the Zodiac once more: everything was calm. The gate of the *Melbourne* had just closed. He jotted down the time in his notebook and waited a moment before emerging from his hiding place and returning to the sea wall.

"What do I do now?"

"Go back towards the ship," Legendre said. "We're going in."

De Palma slowly made his way between a row of old lorries bound for Africa. From his vantage point he could see the Caprice des Mers. On the right of the H.G.V.s some pallets with wheels and seats could be used as a lookout point.

Two men were talking on the gangway of the *Caprice des Mers*. He had no difficulty in identifying the Border Police lieutenant. Martini, the older cop, was looking around constantly. De Palma went on another two metres then came to a halt. The two policemen went down the gangway and realized immediately what was happening.

"Police!" Legendre shouted, "Don't do anything stupid."

The two policemen looked at one another.

"What's up with you? We're mates!" Martini shouted, his face haggard.

"I believe you've got something to tell us," Legendre said. "From now on you'll be remanded in custody. Warrant from Judge Melville."

Bessour had just had a long conversation with the captain of the *Melbourne*. He was due to leave Marseille before nightfall.

The superstructures of the ferries glinted in the setting sun. On the City of Macao they were starting up the engines, sending a wash over the cold stone. The Baron had walked a long way along the quay until he was just a tiny silhouette against the gigantic leg of a steel crane.

"Is the Baron O.K?" Legendre asked Maistre.

"Yes. He just needs time to think."

The *City of Macao*'s mooring rope strained through the front hawsehole. A tug belonging to the Port Authority pulled the cargo ship to the middle of the inner harbour and headed it in the direction of the Passe Sainte-Marie. The manoeuvre took just a few minutes. Before going through the channel, a launch from the port authority came up on the port side and the pilot jumped down into it. The bow of the cargo ship threw up a shower of spray as it went over the first wave.

*

The two officers from the Border Police had just been protecting the trafficking in the port organized by Castella's gangs. Castella was acting as a go-between for some international traffickers. The police had raked in commission for allowing the goods to leave the port. It was left to the gangland bosses to transport them to their final destinations. The smuggling had been going on for years: Egyptian antiquities, objects looted from the great museum in Baghdad, African statues . . . In this bric-à-brac of masterpieces there was genuine, authentic stuff as well as fakes, with no difference in the price.

Legendre had passed on the part of the file relating to the works of art to the O.C.B.C. That side of the case logically didn't come within the Murder Squad's brief. Leacock and Paulo's murders remained unsolved. It was going to be a closely fought game and the Baron held very few trump cards.

"You've got to tell me everything now," de Palma said gritting his teeth.

Martini had curly hair, a sad lower lip and charcoal-rimmed eyes. "There's nothing to tell you, mate."

"In the first place I'm not your mate and secondly I'd advise you to talk . . ."

The Baron stared at his computer screen and typed in the initial formalities of the statement.

"What's in it for me?" Martini asked in a thin voice.

"What you get is . . . I go easy on the charge sheet."

Martini nodded several times, "Alright, alright."

De Palma pushed back his computer keyboard and got out his exercise book. "Who's Jim Leacock?"

"A smuggler. That's all. He was bringing in stuff from New Guinea."

"What sort of stuff?"

"Stuff that sells well."

"Skulls for example?"

"Yep."

Martini looked up at the Baron, who ignored him.

"Who killed Leacock?"

"For Chrissake if I knew that I'd tell you! I'm having a bad time of it."

The response shook the Baron. Martini seemed sincere. He removed the photograph of Leacock that he had attached to a page of his notebook with a paper clip.

"Do you recognize him?"

Martini glanced at the photograph. "Sure do. That's him. I only met him once, but I can picture him in my mind."

"Up to now I thought he was the one who'd shot Dr Delorme with a bow."

"I didn't know that. Er . . . I never saw that."

"Well you have now," de Palma said.

He put the photograph back in his notebook and rested his elbows on the desk. "Let's talk a bit about Maglia and Berry."

"Climbers," Martini muttered. "They're not a bad lot. Maglia's my grass."

"What tip-offs has he given you?"

"About trafficking in the port."

"Art?"

"Not just that. We busted quite a lot of gear thanks to him."

Martini sniffed and pulled a face. He seemed relaxed, although he didn't stop fiddling with the cuff that kept him prisoner to the wall. He wasn't a bigshot, just a petty official who dreamed of becoming a bigshot; living the life. At his house Bessour had found luxury furniture, an infinity swimming pool, and two brand-new Harley Davidsons. De Palma allowed ten minutes of silence to elapse, in an effort to unsettle him. Ten minutes can seem like eternity when you're in custody.

"I almost nicked Leacock on board the *Melbourne*," de Palma said. "He slipped through my fingers. I got the impression he ran in your direction. Am I wrong about that?"

Martini couldn't suppress a bitter smile. "I was on patrol over by Cap Pinède and I heard a shot being fired."

De Palma gave a sigh and drummed on his notebook with the end of his pen. "It was me that fired the shot."

"That's what I thought."

"That's not the answer I want. Where was Leacock in the days after he escaped?"

"We kept him on board the *Caprice des Mers*."

"Why protect him?"

"Because he made us believe there was still some loot on board the *Melbourne*. We'd paid up front and we had nothing to show for it, because of Customs."

"What kind of loot?"

"A statue and a skull. So Leacock went back to look for them. And that's when they killed him."

De Palma hit the desk with the palm of his hand. Martini jumped.

"He left the *Caprice des Mers*," the Baron said, raising his voice, "Because he had a meeting down on the quays. It was a set-up. Who was behind it? Who?"

"I don't know."

"Did you know Customs had seized part of the loot?"

"No, not straightaway. Maglia and Berry didn't tell me anything. I only found out when I saw it in the paper."

"Who were you supposed to flog these skulls to?"

"An antique dealer from Paris."

"Grégory Voirnec?"

"Yes."

"You know he's dead?"

Martini crumbled. De Palma sat down again and chucked his pen on the desk. "We need to talk about Paulo."

"It was me who drove his car when we got ambushed."

"I don't understand."

Martini swallowed. "Let's say some people thought he was a grass."

"Why had Voirnec come to see him?"

"To make sure he hadn't been double-crossed."

The Baron felt as though he were on a boat heading for the coast but never managing to reach it. "Do you know what's in these skulls?" he asked suddenly.

"Er . . . no."

"The spirits of the people who inhabited them when they were alive. They're sacred objects, understand? The spirits of the

Elders live inside them; those who were respected by everyone."

"Didn't know that."

"Well I don't think you give a toss. You're just someone that's raking it in. What sacred means to you is getting a swimming pool for your villa, or buying yourself a swanky vintage car, and that really gets on my tits."

"I'm not the only one."

"Clearly not, you moron. There's people like Leacock ready to bring in the skulls of their fellow human beings to the port of Marseille. But you know, I can't help thinking if it wasn't for blokes like you, this trafficking couldn't happen."

The Baron leant over to Martini, his two fists on his desk. "The spirits of the ancestors have got their revenge. You're going down for years. I guess they're going to have to auction off that nice swimming pool and swanky car of yours."

He sent Martini back down to the cells.

Legendre appeared in the doorway. "Finished your statement?"

"Yes, boss."

"Good, we'll take it to the judge."

Legendre turned away. Of all the policemen he had known during his police career, Legendre was one of the few the Baron would miss. He looked at the stainless-steel office clock. It was gone midday. Just time for a snack at the local café.

That afternoon Judge Melville examined Faure and Martini and committed them to Les Baumettes prison. Their convictions: International Trafficking of Works of Art by Organized Gangs; Handling and Aiding and Abetting the Handling of Stolen Goods; and Criminal Conspiracy.

*

Eva was reading by the lamp in the living room. She had taken off her shoes and put up her feet on the sofa. She had slender ankles. A silver chain encircled the right one.

260

"I'm tired, Eva," de Palma said, as he took off his boots.

"Bad day?"

"I got a man sent down. That's never easy." He put his revolver on the pedestal table.

Eva didn't take her eyes off him. Two small, anxious lines ran across her forehead. "Can you put that contraption somewhere I can't see it?"

"Why? Does it scare you?"

"Sure does."

She shut her book. She had done a blitz on the Baron's flat. A smell of lime hung in the air. The bookshelves sparkled.

"What did you do all this for?"

"Let's just say I don't like flats that look like tips. It really gets me."

"I hope you haven't been snooping round everywhere."

He sat down at the table and looked out at the buildings cluttering the view of the Saint-Loup hills. His eyes were burning. His brain felt as if it were full of sand.

"I didn't snoop," Eva said coldly. "I can go if you want. Anyway I must be home by midnight. I'm still married."

She went up to him, wrapped her arms round his chest and rested her chin on his shoulder.

"Thank you," de Palma said. "It hasn't been that clean since . . ."

" . . . your wife left, eh?"

"I'm sorry. I didn't mean to talk about that . . ."

She removed her hands. "Do you remember when we were in the first year at secondary school? You didn't want to come with me. You didn't want to carry my satchel anymore."

"It went down badly with my mates."

"I was thinking about that when you arrived. You've still got that stupid shame thing. The same stubborn pride."

"It's my Italian blood . . ."

She waited for him to say something more, but he said nothing.

He was staring at Eva's book: *Transit Visa*, by Anna Seghers. There was something enticing and mysterious about the title.

"Is that any good?"

"It's set in Marseille in 1940. People losing each other. I really like it. They meet on a balcony facing the old port, over a slice of pizza and a glass of rosé. It's got everything. Veterans from the Spanish Civil War, deserters, Jews, intellectuals and artists. It's as though they're all trying to forget about the war. As though the Mediterranean represented a dream of somewhere else; an oasis of peace."

The gold cross that hung over her white shirt was askew; small, silver-rimmed glasses rested on her nose. He hadn't realized she was a person who read.

Later, after they had made love in the warm room, he left her sweet body and took a long, boiling-hot shower. When he emerged with a towel round his waist, he looked to see where she was. She had gone, leaving a note for him on the fridge door: *There's some pizza in the microwave. I'll call you tomorrow.*

One day one of us was hiding when he caught sight of the white man defecating. "The man who came from the sky has just defecated," he told us.

Once the man had gone, everyone went to have a look. "Their skin may be different," we said, "but their shit smells just the same!"

Extract from the documentary "First Contact",
by Bob Connolly and Robin Anderson
(Arundel Productions, 1983)

25

There were two or three hotels on boulevard Belzunce that rented out rooms to illegal immigrants and old hookers. "That'll do me," the visitor said to himself on seeing Hotel du Globe. Since arriving in Marseille, he had changed accommodation and moved to a different area every couple of days.

The tired-looking manager fleeced him fifty euros for room number thirty-eight on the second floor. A fortune! He paid and went up the steep staircase that stank of urine and detergent.

The room was a quite large. There was a bed with rough, grey sheets, a yellowish blanket and a chamber pot. A smell of sweat and sex clung to the mauve paint. The royal-blue paper blistered around the bed. It was stained with head grease and brown finger marks. A flaking window looked out on rue du Tapis-Vert, with its wholesalers from North Africa, Berber shops and alcohol-free restaurants.

There was no lavatory, just a basin and a large mirror with worn silvering. The visitor looked at himself for a moment: tall, thin and muscular with a quite a lot of scars. He had a hunter's body.

He took off his short-sleeved shirt and flexed the muscles under his taut skin. Then he opened his wallet and looked at his true love for a long time. There was no emotion anymore, no more strange contractions in his stomach. He felt completely empty, the anger giving way to brute force. "They've turned you into a killer," he said to himself. He realized for the first time how straightforward it had all been. All great murderers must have felt the same, he mused.

He went up to the mirror and peered at the reflection. Behind his pupils he could see a great emptiness; an abyss. He needed to be reborn; to return to the origins of everything. Happy and free.

He unpacked his bag and he placed Robert Ballancourt's skull carefully on the table with its oilcloth cover. He had cleaned to perfection the frontal and occipital bones. He only had to knead the resin. The other skulls were in the suitcase.

He rolled a red ball the size of a fist between his fingers and moulded it for a long time to soften it up. Then he separated it into two smaller balls and filled the sockets. *The nose defines a person. That's what women notice first.* He moulded a piece of resin the size of an apple, flattened it and reshaped it into a rough pyramid shape. He looked at the skull for a few seconds then stuck the resin on the nasal bone and modelled it afresh with the ends of his fingers pushing back the soft matter into the cavities. The result wasn't too bad, worthy of the best sculptors of ancient times.

That left the cheeks and the jaw. Often the jawbone was made from a piece of wood as the bone itself was kept for other rituals. It didn't matter. He observed his work for a long while.

Completely covered in resin, the skull already had a strange appearance. The spirit was slowly returning from the world where it had been wandering. It was no longer really a dead person, but it was not yet a living being. The spirit was not yet present. The eyes didn't look right.

He moulded some fine strips from the resin then flattened them out. They would form the cheeks. He stuck them on the bone with his thumbs, taking care to recreate Ballancourt's ascetic side. For him that was the key to Ballancourt's face. Besides the eyes, it was what best revealed his passionate and quick-tempered temperament. For a long time he smoothed the surface of the resin dipping his fingers regularly in the water from the basin.

After two hours the skull had reassumed its human form. He

266

created the eyes. A simple hole for the right one and for the left a spiral of resin, reminiscent of the eddying waters of the Sepik and the Yuat. With a blade he split the lump of resin stopping up the mouth, and with the tips of his fingers he raised the lips. The face began to lose its funereal character and to smile.

The spirit is here. It is prowling around us. Soon it will find its home once more.

He moulded some resin into a crescent shape and attached it like a ruff to the back of the skull directly against the bone. One by one, he sunk in the small white shells, which made a glorious hairband.

There was a rumbling down the street. A delivery van stopped in front of the hotel. The driver opened the two back doors and released some men, probably Indians, who went straight into the grey building opposite.

The visitor massaged his shoulder and lay down. His whole body was aching, from the joints to the smallest bones.

He still had to fix the hair and make up the head. That was the last stage: the most important and the most magical. He would have to wait until the next day, or perhaps longer, for the resin to dry out completely and set.

He closed his eyes, his mind far away. Far, far away, back in his childhood: at Yuarimo, where the Sepik River meets the Yuat.

"Do you hear me, Kaïngara?"

"Yes, mother."

He was facing the wall of the house. Through the loose planks he could see the plots of land and sparse lawns where snuffling pigs rooted around. The church bell rang ten thin notes.

"Today is a great day. The day we will be baptized."

Kaïngara was overcome with sadness. He had difficulty breathing. Perhaps he would have another of those paralysing fits.

"In a few hours you won't be Kaïngara any more, you'll be Christian. That's a good name. The best name for any Christian. My Christian name will be Agnès. It means lamb: Lamb of God."

Kaïngara looked up at his mother. He had difficulty understanding, but he was listening to her. She had always been his guide. He simply could not say no when she had asked him to become a Christian. In any case it wasn't that important, in his heart he would remain the same. The important thing was not to disappoint his mother. She had suffered so much.

He thought about Bérénice. They had written to each other after he left France, and then the letters had become less frequent. He missed her and the absence was like a Seton stitch slowly draining the Westerner's blood still running in his veins.

He could see his father again at last. Tall and awkward, on the day he said goodbye to him at the airport. His words ringing out like a final farewell. He looked like a sailor departing from a quay that he would never see again.

"Here's your nice white shirt and your tie."

The starched collar dug into his neck. He felt that his heart would explode inside his chest. Agnès wanted to knot his tie, but the stubs of her fingers prevented her. Her son gently removed her hands, kissed them, and turned away to tie the silk ribbon. He felt grotesque in this get-up. It was off the peg from Port Moresby, tacky and out of date; cast-offs from Australia. The blue synthetic trousers rubbed against his calfs and thighs, and the nylon shirt made him sweat in the tropical heat.

"Do you remember what the minister said? Have you got your reading?"

"Yes."

"You need to know it by heart when you are immersed in the water. Do you want to recite it to me?"

"No."

Kaïngara leaned his temple against the wooden wall. He wasn't sure what was happening. He felt as if he were watching a puppet show. "None of this is real," he said to himself, "none of it." The pain was intense. He crouched down. Everything went red. The sago palms waved their enormous branches. He wanted to close his eyes, but some force stopped him. He did not want to hear anything, but an evil spirit compelled him to listen.

"It's time," his mother said.

They went out. The church was on the other side of the dirt square. The women had hung bunches of mauve-and-white flowers from the woven walls. Sitting to one side, a little to the left, Wabe was drawing on his pipe. His torso, still strong, was painted in his clan colours. He had put on his finest headgear, the one with cassowary feathers, down and cream-and-red flowers. Kaïngara did not dare to look at Wabe. That would be like an admission of betrayal.

Bérénice had made him promise never to deny his origins. "You are most beautiful when you are just yourself," she had declared one summer's day.

That day, he had thought she was attracted to him. He knew that sometimes she would look longingly at him, especially when they went to the Plage des Catalans and played volleyball.

But today he was alone. His mother held his hand and he wanted to run away. Wabe's intense, fixed expression was unbearable. In his right hand he held his warrior's bow and the long arrows with pointed barbs. Wabe would never become a Christian. Never. He was beautiful.

The sound of a choir rose from the chapel. The singing was out of tune and failed to disguise the discordant sound of the minister's guitar.

"Good morning, Christian," the man of God said, plucking the rusty strings. "Good morning, Agnès. Come in, brothers and sisters. Today is a day of great joy."

Kaïngara stopped in the church entrance and turned around. Wabe had vanished. Two large tree trunks had been thrown into the river to retain the water. A crowd had assembled above the small dam, waiting for the baptism. The women swayed as they chanted psalms.

"You are most beautiful when you are just yourself."

The visitor wiped his eyes and dialled a number on his mobile.

"Air France, bonjour."

"I'd like a ticket to Singapore."

"Yes, and when are you thinking of leaving?"

"As soon as possible."

"We've got a flight leaving the day after tomorrow, on Thursday."

"O.K., that's perfect."

The skulls still had to be smuggled through. That shouldn't be difficult. Traffickers knew how to cross borders. He picked up his mobile and dialled the number of his contact in air freight services at Marignane airport. The formalities would only take a few hours. He would deal with that the next day.

A rectangular box was lying on the bed. He opened it. The last skull was exposed and ready to be modelled. Perfectly clean.

"So, Doctor," he said softly raising the skull to his eyes, "you collected our skulls, didn't you? And now your spirit is mine."

He put down Delorme's skull and started to knead the resin vigorously. Trophy skulls did not require as much care as ancestral ones.

26

20 October 1936

The Marie-Jeanne *is all set to sail. The waters of the Sepik have risen. Robert Ballancourt wants to undertake one last voyage of exploration. Last week we spotted some Mundugumor. Of all the peoples in the region they are the most feared. The Tchambuli are outstanding artists, but the Mundugumor are savages and cannibals. They have only been "civilized" very recently; for about four or five years according to the district officer at Marienberg.*

To reach the land of the Mundugumor you have to go up the Yuat. It is a much faster tributary of the Sepik and, more to the point, rather dangerous. The tribes that live up there have hardly ever come across white men and are not particularly keen on them. Robert Ballancourt insists that I should join the party, but I don't think much of the idea. To tell the truth I'm in a hurry to put out to sea and head for Singapore.

In the end Captain Meyssonnier did not take part in the expedition to the land of the Mundugumor. For three days he had tidied up the *Marie-Jeanne*, checked the sails and taken on stores. Ballancourt spent three days among the Mundugumor. He had stopped at the village of Kenakatem and then spent a whole day in a more remote region.

Robert arrived back late yesterday afternoon. He was not in good shape. The voyage had clearly taken its toll on him, and on Ange Filippi, the sailor who accompanied him. What did they see in the country of the Mundugumor? I have no idea. He was very evasive, just showing me a trophy skull that was even more hideous than the others. He grunted in reply to Delorme's questions. Filippi didn't want to say anything either. I spotted arrow marks on their canoe and I sensed from the young sailor's face that terrible things had happened on this journey. All I could establish was that they had been attacked at the confluence of the Sepik and Yuat rivers.

   . . .

   I didn't sleep during the watch. Someone was playing a flute which woke me up. It must have been a sailor who had bought an instrument from a Papuan and was playing it to while away the time. I went up on deck, but couldn't find the watchman playing. When I wanted to go down to my quarters the flute stopped, but I didn't manage to get back to sleep."

De Palma had laid out the three messages left by Delorme's killer – the extract from *Totem and Taboo*, and the Lévi-Strauss quotation:

The barbarian is first and foremost the one who believes in barbarism.

He was intrigued by the quote from Margaret Mead:

You are going up Sepik River where the people are fierce, where they eat men . . . Go carefully. Do not be misled by your experience among us . . . They are another kind. So you will find it.

Freud and Lévi-Strauss somehow seemed to contradict each other. And for the time being de Palma could not clarify things any further than that. There certainly seemed to be some hidden meaning in the quote from Margaret Mead. On a map of the Sepik region he put crosses in the places where Ballancourt and Delorme had collected artefacts. The map was not very detailed, but the relevant area was mostly Iatmul country. Delorme had gone as far as the Tchambuli, whom Mead had studied and labelled "artists". According to Captain Meyssonnier's log these meetings had taken place without the slightest hitch. The only unknown part was the River Yuat, a region apparently unreached by civilization in 1936. De Palma took his jacket and went out.

Quartier Saint-Laurent was just round the corner from the police station. At the end of the afternoon Ange Filippi must be at home. The Baron climbed the road overlooking Fort Saint-Nicolas, the Passe Sainte-Marie and Planier lighthouse.

"Take a seat," Ange said in a sleepy voice, pointing to a cane chair near the table. The old sailor's living room was in semi-darkness. The television was on, showing "Countdown". Ange fumbled with the buttons on the remote as he tried to switch it off.

"Would you open the window please?" he asked. "I like to watch the sunset. Sometimes I tell myself it could be for the last time. At my age you know when you're going to sleep, but you don't know if you're going to wake up again."

He gave a loud sigh. De Palma folded back the shutter panels. There were some old cardboard boxes on the balcony and a folding chair with large, fading blue-and-white stripes. It was overcast. Over the Château d'If, huge slanting rays broke through the clouds. There was an intense glow; red at the centre and crimson at the fringes.

"We need to wait a bit. It's not like the islands, but our sunsets are still beautiful. In Tahiti or Noumea the whole sky becomes red at night. It looks as if the clouds have caught fire."

De Palma came to sit back down by the sailor.

"What did you want to know?"

"Tell me about your expedition to the Mundugumor. Can you remember it?"

Filippi stiffened; his eyes blank. A ferry had just appeared between the white islands. "That memory is the worst one of my life. It was just Monsieur Robert, me and the guide. I forget his name. They were inseparable." Ange suddenly stopped. He had rested his

273

pale hands flat on his thin thighs. His knees formed right angles through his trousers. His eyes were casting about for images from the past.

"Three of us," he said starting again. "The guide and two puny white blokes up against a bunch of savages. There are no other words to describe them. The first village we came to, there was a right to-do. All the men had painted faces and they were dancing, jumping up and down with their feet together and waving their arms about."

The sailor's lips quivered. He raised his arm and pointed to some spot that only he could see. "A group of warriors was returning from headhunting. Believe it or not, there was a man carrying a skull round his neck. I can still see it now. Just imagine: a totally naked man, his chest caked in human blood, with this head he'd got from God knows where."

De Palma recalled the films he had watched at Bérénice's house. He was sorry he couldn't show them to Ange Filippi. He was convinced Ballancourt had gone back to the Mundugumor to take some pictures and these were the ones that Bérénice had shown.

"How did Monsieur Ballancourt behave when he was with the Mundugumor?"

"He took a lot of photos," Ange replied. "He never stopped! Snap, snap . . . all sorts of stuff. But one of the warriors didn't like it and threw his camera in the river."

The sailor's knees shook. He asked de Palma for a glass of water.

"For two days it was as if we were prisoners," he said, after taking a sip.

"Prisoners?"

"Yes. We had to hand over all the glasses and iron axes that we had."

"Why were you taken prisoner?"

"They accused us of having bought one of their skulls. It was the head of someone important to them. They demanded reparation. In

fact I think they wanted to punish us. We had to give them everything we had in the canoe. We had nothing left and still they asked
for more. They weren't satisfied."

"And then what happened?"

Ange shut his eyes and swayed his head from right to left. "They
killed our guide. Right in front of our eyes. They killed him and cut
off his head. Then they let us leave."

A long silence ensued. Some chattering seabirds circled above
Tour Saint-Jean. The sun had broken through the bank of clouds
setting the harbour ablaze.

"Our guide was called Kaïngara. Now I remember: Kaïngara. It
was all so long ago."

"And what happened after that?"

"We went back down the Yuat, then the Sepik, to the *Marie-
Jeanne*. Ballancourt told me not to say anything to anyone. You're the
first person I've ever told."

"Why did he tell you to say nothing?"

"Oh . . . I think he wasn't too proud of himself. Going all that way,
and death was the price we paid for it."

"Didn't anyone ask you about it?"

Ange shrugged.

"If you'd known Ballancourt . . . He had clout. Everyone feared
and respected him. The Captain would never have dared to question
him."

In the corridor a clock struck six. The sun had gone down. From
the great grey-and-black walls of L'Estaque to the hill of Notre-
Dame de la Garde, the bay was shrouded in a blue, sometimes
purple, light where it met the bone-white land. The hum from the
old port and the roar of the dual carriageways running along beside
the quays rose, roaring in the evening wind. These memories from
another era awakened a feeling of fear in de Palma. His grandfather
had also told him terrible stories of the South Seas. From Wallis to
Noumea via Tuamotu and the tiny archipelagos, the Pacific and its

mysterious peoples had captured his imagination as a child. Ange was giving a glimpse of its most brutal side.

"The next day," the sailor went on, "we went to the village where Kaïngara lived . . . to give the news to his wife. I remember it as if it were only yesterday. She had two boys with her. She didn't cry. She just listened. Monsieur Robert gave her some money and a load of small items. Then she withdrew and we left."

Ange was moved. His Adam's apple bobbed up and down under the tight skin on his neck. "She was a small woman, sturdily built. I did know her name, but I've forgotten it. She wore a net across her body. You could see her big stomach. She was pregnant."

De Palma recalled the face on which Ballancourt's camera had settled for so long. In his mind Kaïngara's wife must have looked like that girl. The same beautiful, sad face. The same hint of a smile. Ange Filippi rose with difficulty and put on the living-room light.

"My son won't be long," he said, peering round as if looking for some ghostly object.

"Goodbye, Monsieur Filippi."

"Goodbye, my boy."

The Baron held the sailor's hand. His eyes were moist.

*

That evening he went to the office to drop off a file and returned home late. Eva was lying on the bed.

"I'm sorry . . . I didn't know you were here."

"I hadn't planned to come. I wanted to give you a surprise."

He took off his jacket and threw his boots in the middle of the room.

"Put your gun away, you old warrior, and come and lie beside me."

When he lay down, she put her hand on his chest, and then moved it down inside his shirt. He stared into the dark. The maritime pines by the block of flats stood motionless, holding out their needle fingers in the starry night.

"I remember the first time I saw you having a fight. It was with the Chenier lad. Do you remember him?"

"Yes."

"He was stronger than you, but you were determined not to lose."

De Palma had only a dim memory of that childhood scrap. He could picture Chenier's ruddy face. He was a stroppy little blond kid who used to cheat at marbles.

"I just remember getting punched and the thrashing my dad gave me afterwards when he found out I'd had a fight in the playground."

She pinched him in the stomach. "You fought him because he'd been taking the mick out of me. You couldn't stand bullies."

"Maybe that's why I've done thirty years in the police."

She undid the buttons of his shirt. "I hope I'll still be around when you leave the police. I prefer you without a pistol on your hip."

Until now I've managed to hide. I've put up a wall round me so I can't hear that Bible of theirs. I've even managed never to see a Bible.

They won't stop telling me I'm all on my own, that I'm the last one left. How can I carry on living here on my own? They're all becoming Christians.

Can I remain alone with the water? With the trees? Alone with the spirits of the forest?

I think I'm going to have to follow them.

Testimony of Wandipe, a Huli warrior.
Extract from "The Gospel according to the Papuans",
a documentary by Thomas Balmès (Les Films d'Ici, 1999)

27

War had broken out with Kenakatem, sparked by a trivial incident over the crafts workshop. A man from Yuarimo had stabbed a youngster from Kenakatem twice because he refused to repay a gambling debt. The enemy had immediately demanded reparation and war had resumed; the same one that had been going on for seventy years.

Christian's house was peaceful, cooled by the breezes flowing through. Lying on the bed in his room, he was thinking of his mother. He seemed to feel her small, velvety breast against his cheek ... That loving gaze, her dark skin and black pupils; that intoxicating cinnamon smell.

His mother had short curly hair. The nape of her neck reminded him of the statues in museums: perfectly formed and unbelievably delicate. He had never seen anything as beautiful.

Christian followed his mother everywhere; he couldn't be parted from her. In the past she had carried him about on her back for hours on end, his face covered with a veil to protect him from the fiery rays of the sun. He let himself be lulled by the movement of her body and the graceful rhythm of her step. And then he had grown too big; too heavy. His mother could no longer carry him.

He didn't like it when she picked him up and planted a kiss on his cheeks. It was the only thing he didn't like in this woman who was sweetness itself. She had lost the middle and little fingers on her right hand. The feel of the hard stumps was repulsive to him. He often asked her how it had happened. And she would reply that he was still too young to understand. In his imagination the devil himself had inflicted these wounds, only too happy to see such beauty fade.

The other day his mother had taught him how to make a basket using branches from a very flexible shrub. He had looked at her mutilated hands and had run away to hide. She had come to console him and he had pressed her to tell him where his father was. By way of response she had given a melancholic smile and just said that he was still too little to understand.

Christian knew that his father wasn't like other men. He was a real hero and he had a thousand tasks to accomplish before returning to see his son.

"Tell me Mamma, what is the Ghost Road?"

"Who told you about that?"

"Old Wabe. He told me that my Dad came down the Ghost Road."

His Mamma slowly stroked his hair. "You shouldn't believe everything Old Wabe says. He's a bit mad."

"He told me, one day, he will show me the secret path."

She seemed far off, her voice barely audible. She was speaking, but he couldn't hear. He strained his ear, his cheek brushing against her cold mouth; those wondrous, fleshy lips that had given him so much. He tried to recall her small velvety breast, but everything was cold; her cold, hard body was like the marble statues in the museums. He shrank away and fled; far, far away. Down to the end of the tunnel, but his legs couldn't seem to move. His body froze. His face blurred. His skin was a different colour to hers. He could pass for white. He was only Kaïngara inside.

His father was not coming back. Old Wabe had said so.

"Why?"

"You must be strong, my boy."

"Dad didn't leave me."

His right leg began to shake. His eyes blurred. The evil ones were at the far end of his bedroom, sniggering at him.

280

"He's not your dad, you little imbecile. You never understand what people say."

"Liars! It's not true."

"No, Christian. We never lie."

They smirked and swapped inaudible jokes.

"I'm going to kill you."

At the beginning of summer he had met Old Wabe, the only man who had not been baptized.

"I'm the only one left now," he said. "Everyone else has been baptised. They believe I'll have to join the priest, but which one? There's the Pentecostals, Adventists, Catholics . . . Some people say at the end of the world the Pope's going to come and kill everyone who's not a Catholic. So I'd rather stay as I am."

"I am Kaïngara," Christian repeated. "I am brave like my mother's father. My own father was a great man." He raised the thick curtain hanging in the window of his room. The square in Yuarimo was deserted. It was night. The moon was in decline. The rustle of the broad leaves of the sago tree mingled with the flowing Yuat and the ceaseless chirping of the insects.

Two days earlier, a few hours after his arrival, his business partner Alis had come to tell Christian that during his absence another person had been killed and the factory was no longer operating. Alis wore that sad look he always had when he was no longer in control of things. The Elders had held talks; the war was spreading. The enemy had already destroyed the coffee harvest, and soon they would set about the crafts factory. He felt responsible for all that.

He had set up the agricultural cooperative and a crafts factory with loans from Port Moresby. The price of coffee had suddenly collapsed. The banks called in their debts. Alis and Christian requested an extension, to allow them time to make some profit on their next harvest. But it was no use, the moneymen would not budge. They treated him like a common peasant, with his savage customs, a Papuan who knew nothing. However much he boasted about his connections and his university degrees, everyone just laughed in his face.

Now his lands were mortgaged and part of Alis' land was under threat. The men and women of the village had toiled in vain. The factory employees noticed that on their sites the art dealers and craft industry charged more than a hundred times the price they'd paid for their work.

They roughed up two collectors who used to come from Australia. Since then no-one had dared to come and buy anything.

Christian knew his own people. When he had left New Guinea for France, war was imminent. Two days before his departure he went to see Old Wabe in his little wooden house on the edge of the village. The old man sat down on the ground and played his three-reed panpipes. He had two black lines painted above his eyes and across his temples and a long line that went down from his forehead to his chin. Christian had always loved the indomitable Wabe. The man who had never accepted the rules of priests and government agents. They had talked about his father and his grandfather.

"They have built a church on the House of the Spirits," Wabe said, "and since then nothing has gone right. They are hypocrites; they carry on stealing and fornicating. Soon there will be war again, mark my word."

"What can I do?" Christian asked.

Wabe paused to think, his eyes dark and piercing. Christian looked at his hands, then at the great bow leaning against the wall of the house, the long reed arrows. Wabe had killed many men in his youth. He was one of the best shots in the village.

"The spirits of the Elders no longer protect us. Your father told me to beware of the priests and anthropologists who come to our lands. I have always followed his advice."

"How can we bring peace again?"

"The Ancestors must return."

Christian thought. He was on the brink of the abyss. Wabe's world no longer existed and would never return. That was the reason he had wanted to set up a factory and a cooperative. So people would not have to live in poverty. But the bankers in Port Moresby were the ones with the power.

"You must believe in magic. Soon I will die. What will become of my head? I think it will rot in the earth. My spirit will wander forever. When I think of that, I tell myself that it would be better to convert, but I don't think that their God exists. In any case they haven't shown him to me and I can't believe any of it."

Christian realized that his life was absurd. The shirt he wore, the trousers that were too tight, the moccasins covered in dust from the track. He wouldn't know how to make a beautiful headdress of feathers and branches like Wube. He would be ashamed to wear a loincloth or penis gourd; to paint himself like the warriors. He wouldn't have the courage to face the enemy's spears and arrows.

He thought of Bérénice. He hadn't seen her in years. She had stopped writing to him. Since his mother had died he no longer had any horizons. He was seeking a way through the remorse, the blurred landmarks of his life. He had thought about going back to France, but he knew that he no longer had any connection with his father's land.

"I'll take care of your head," he said, "your spirit will not wander. You can trust me."

"In that case I need to teach you . . . these days no-one knows how it's done."

Wabe pulled out a long flute from a leather sheath. "Only the initiated can know where the voice of the spirits comes from. Come with me, let's go inside. It is time for you to know."

Christian turned and stared at the suitcase. It contained the skulls of the Elders. He put them on the chest of drawers in his room and stared at them for a long while. Then he glanced out of the window again.

"It's time," he said. He put the skulls in a hessian bag and tiptoed out so as not to wake the old housekeeper, who always slept with one eye open.

In front of the factory two betel palms were growing in opposite directions. They formed a large V shape that rose up into the inky sky. Christian stopped and looked up at the church. In the half-light it seemed squat and ridiculous. Two crossed branches hung above the door.

A dog shuffled past. It stopped, stared at him for a few seconds and then went off again.

28

Victoria sat with her knees pressed together, hanging on to her hand-bag. She listened to the murmur of the police station, occasionally casting anxious looks down the corridor.

"How long did you work for Dr Delorme?" de Palma asked.

"Thirty-two years," she replied, clasping the strap of her bag.

The Baron put Bérénice's album down on his desk. He had inserted a bookmark in the page with the woman's photograph: the one whom Delorme's granddaughter had referred to as Agnès.

"Does this face mean anything to you?"

Victoria hesitated, her eyes shifting from one page to the other. Then she looked up sadly at de Palma, "I know who it is," she said nodding her head and biting her lips. "The doctor talked to me about her a couple of times. He did sometimes confide in me. The first time it was after Monsieur Robert came with his son. He was a bit foreign-looking; curly hair, reddish, suntanned. The doctor explained to me that he was mixed-race and his mother was the woman in that album."

"Did you see Robert Ballancourt's son again?"

"Oh yes, often . . . He really liked me. A nice boy. Sometimes he spent the whole day at the house. His father put him up in a guest-house, I can't remember where. But at the end of the week he often used to drop in and see us."

"So he used to see Bérénice?"

Victoria put her two index fingers together. "They were

inseparable. Joined at the hip, they were. When he wasn't there all Bérénice did was talk about him. She didn't have any other friends, as far as I can remember – girls or boys. So the doctor ended up getting worried . . ."

"How do you mean?"

"Well when they were children it was alright, but later . . . He could see that . . ."

A door slammed in the corridor. Victoria gave a start.

"You mean they loved one another?"

Victoria nodded and fiddled with her large, gold wedding ring. "Dr Delorme didn't take kindly to the relationship."

"Why was that?"

The housekeeper shrugged. "One day I heard him saying to his granddaughter: 'You'll never be happy with him.'"

"And what did she say?"

"It was the first time I heard her answer him back. She had huge respect for him. But she knew his decisions were final. You didn't argue with Dr Delorme."

"So what happened?"

"She shut herself up in her room for the whole weekend and there was a big scene."

"And what happened after that?"

"The doctor wouldn't budge. He was working very hard at the time. Down at the hospital and then he was off abroad, going to conferences. I never really knew."

"Was it you who looked after Bérénice?"

"Yes. But after the summer holidays he packed her off to stay with some cousins near Paris."

"She had no mother, is that right?"

"Yes, that's right. And so she was the focus of all of the doctor's affections."

Karim Bessour appeared in the doorway. De Palma waved him away, discreetly.

"So our Christian went back to his own country," Victoria continued. "I never heard any more. The doctor didn't talk about it."

"And Bérénice?"

"She didn't talk about it either. And I didn't ask her. Sometimes I got the feeling she wanted me to say something, but her grandfather's will was all that mattered. I'm telling you, you didn't cross Dr Delorme."

De Palma closed his exercise book once more. Night had fallen. "Did the Doctor talk to you about the skull in his study?"

"Holy Mother of God, I could never get used to that monstrosity. He told me he was fonder of that one, more than any other piece in his collection."

"Did he tell you why?"

"He told me he knew the man whose skull had been mummified. A great man, he said."

De Palma fell silent. There was a link between the skulls, but what was it?

"Did you know Monsieur Ballancourt?"

"A little," Victoria said. "I never really talked to him. I was just the housekeeper, you know."

De Palma nodded in agreement. He twizzled his pen in his fingers. An idea was developing in his head. Logic made him fear the worst, but there was something he needed to rule out, "Was there a bow in Dr Delorme's office?"

"A bow?"

"Yes: a weapon."

"I never saw one," Victoria replied without hesitation.

De Palma got up. He needed to test out his theory. "Karim'll drive you home," he said to her. "Thank you very much for your cooperation."

He accompanied Victoria into the corridor. Bessour was by the coffee machine, thumping the "espresso" button in an attempt to get his fix of caffeine.

"Karim, will you take Madame Texeira home and meet me in an hour's time at the entrance to the Saint-Pierre cemetery?"

"There . . . tonight?"

"Yes. Stiffs won't do you any harm."

"What do you want to do in the cemetery?"

"Have a look at something on Ballancourt's grave."

"Do you know where it is?"

"Soon will."

*

The street lights cast tawny halos over the high, stone walls enclosing the Saint-Pierre cemetery.

"I live just round the corner," de Palma said, stuffing his Maglite torch in his pocket. "Over there, just beyond the flyover."

Karim looked closely at the surrounding landscape of charmless streets, bounded by dead-end estates, low houses, and a grim flyover, "Odd sort of place, isn't it?"

"I know, but I was born near here," the Baron replied heading towards the entrance to the cemetery.

The caretaker spotted the two policemen and emerged from his white stone cottage. "We're closed!" he shouted raising his arms in the air.

"Police," de Palma said, holding out his card. "We just need to check up on something. A grave that's not far from here."

"Ah, O.K. then."

"Thanks."

They went up the main aisle, which was lined with sumptuous vaults, small mausoleums and shattered pillars. From time to time a sculpture loomed in the twilight. The east wind blew through the tall cypress and clawed pines.

At the end of the aisles there was a crossroads leading to the plots. On the left was the monument to the dead of the First World War. Further on was the crematorium. The noise of the great city was barely audible.

"Nearly there," de Palma whispered.

Bessour had moved closer to him. His eyes shone in the weak light that still reached them from the road.

A branch snapped a few metres away. A silhouette was moving between the gravestones in Plot 8. Bessour was unable to suppress a small cry when he caught sight of the silhouette again moving behind a tomb shaped like a Greek temple, barely twenty metres away.

"There's someone's there, Michel. I'm sure of it."

The Baron pointed his Maglite in the direction Bessour had indicated. For a fraction of a second a head appeared above a gravestone, the gold letters of the names shining in the beam of the torch.

"Seems a pity to spoil the party . . ."

"You think . . ."

"Yes I do. Unless it's Ballancourt's ghost . . ."

"Very droll."

Out of sight a flowerpot tipped over and smashed.

"Aren't you going to do anything?" Karim whispered.

"What do you want me to do? Nick some bare arse for outraging public decency? It won't bother this lot now they're pushing up the daisies."

Karim looked down. "Sorry. Sometimes I ask these dumb questions."

"We've come to pay a visit to the Ballancourt family," de Palma said, "and that's what we're going to do."

The tomb was at the end of the row. It was a simple tombstone with no cross, and one memorial plaque of grey granite. Gold letters and figures, a name, and two dates.

"Looks like the cover's been moved," Bessour said in a low voice.

The Baron lit up the joint of the vault. Some recent scratches were visible at the top.

"They jammed a miner's bar over there and the metal has scratched the stone several times."

"You're right."

"Oh dear," the Baron said. "We'd better go home and call in those bright sparks from forensics."

"Hang on a minute. I think we should check Delorme's tomb."

"Come on then."

Two huge flowerpots concealed the opening to the Delorme family vault. Karim moved them aside. A fetid smell made him back off. The Baron aimed his torch.

"He's used a sledgehammer to smash the lid."

He shone his torch inside.

"And broken into the coffin."

The collar of the jacket worn by the doctor on the day of his funeral appeared through the splintered wood.

"The skull's gone," de Palma said, getting up again.

Karim turned towards the lights of the blocks of flats surrounding the cemetery. "It gives me the creeps. I'm shit scared. Do you know what I mean?"

"Sure do."

*

Next day, the gravediggers at Saint-Pierre cemetery removed the lid from the Ballancourt family vault. The coffin containing the explorer's body had been smashed. The skull had been severed at the third vertebra. The knife used to cleave the head had been left behind in the Delorme family vault. There were no fingerprints that could be used.

"Never seen anything like it," the Deputy Public Prosecutor exclaimed, as Commissaire Legendre burst in. "We've really plumbed the depths this time."

"But it's an old ritual, you know. Something to do with the immortality of the soul."

The Deputy Prosecutor shrugged his shoulders. "How did he manage to break a stone like that?"

"I reckon he just used a sledgehammer," de Palma grumbled.

"Have you questioned the guards, Baron?" Legendre asked.

"Affirmative. Saw nothing. Heard nothing."

"No surprises there, then."

"Seems that after dark this place turns into a right old knocking shop," Bessour said. The quip fell flat.

The Deputy Prosecutor went up to the tomb. "I have to go. I'm due at court." He held out a bony hand and said goodbye to the Baron and Bessour.

"We've messed up on procedure," he said. "I think a member of the family should have been present when the grave was opened. But I'll carry the can. I'll wait to hear from you."

He turned to go and went back down the grey tarmac path leading to the exit. The wind tugged at the strands of hair plastered over his skull, making him look like an eccentric musician.

"He'll be far away by now," the Baron growled, "probably in Papua."

"And we nearly had him."

"I know son," de Palma said, putting the flashing light on the dashboard, "but that's how it goes. Policing isn't an exact science; it's just a dumb way of making a living."

"We'll check out all the flights to Port Moresby over the last fortnight."

The Baron switched on the ignition. "We've only got one lead to go on."

"Which is?"

"That lady who's keeping shtum."

"Bérénice? Are you serious?"

"Absolutely."

De Palma gave a blast on his siren and jumped the lights at the corner of rue Saint-Pierre and boulevard Sakakini.

"I can't imagine him carting skulls in the baggage hold of a plane," Bessour said.

"But they're not skulls he's moving, they're works of art."

"I hadn't thought of that."

Bessour leaned his elbow on the car door. "Normally you need the right documents to move works of art."

"Yes," de Palma said, "and he's got those documents. You can be sure of that."

"Maybe you're right."

De Palma cut through the drab districts of Plombières and Saint-Mauront, the streets grey in the sunshine. Near the wasteland adjoining the docks, on a plot of land bounded by ruined walls, two gypsy caravans were parked on blocks. Behind the railings of the Port Autonome a cargo ship belonging to the Messageries Maritimes had raised its bow doors and opened up its great belly.

29

"By now your grandfather's murderer will certainly be in New Guinea."

Bérénice remained silent, frozen in a timid pose.

"Let's say that's my own personal conclusion," he added, "but of course I can't be sure about anything."

She watched the Baron's impassive face. The palm trees in the garden rustled in the morning breeze. The sound of the backwash could be heard against the rocks in the cove.

"You're going to look for my grandfather's murderer, aren't you?"

"No. It can't be done. We don't have any extradition agreement with New Guinea and the legal system there could take time to respond. If, that is, they decide to deal with this matter."

She screwed up her eyes; her chin sagged. A dry branch had snapped off and hung, hideous, at the end of the silver trunk of a pine tree. "I find it hard to believe they could kill Grandpa and get away with it."

"That's the sad truth, I'm afraid."

"I know, I know. I just can't take it in, that's all. How could anyone be so cold and cruel to an old man?"

"That's a question I often ask myself with these killers."

"So do you have any answers?"

"Yes, on the whole they have all been wounded in some way during their lives. The kind of wound that never heals and makes you lose the best part of you."

She rubbed her shoulders as though she were feeling the cold. "Last night I could sense the spirits. They came to me in my sleep, and they spoke to me."

De Palma remembered the skull he had seen in his nightmare, the sound of the flute and that strange presence he had sometimes felt. He looked down and tried to think straight.

"Let's go in," she said. "I was just making some coffee when you rang."

She went ahead of him to the kitchen with its glazed floor tiles. One of the walls was covered with copper pans. A smell of garlic lingered, bringing back Victoria's robust cooking.

Bérénice stopped short and turned to de Palma, with her dark eyes and pale face. "How did you know?"

"It was the stolen skulls. All these thefts have a meaning. The sculptures share a history. You know that very well. It couldn't be otherwise."

A thin ray of sunlight filtered through the blind covering the window. She went out of the kitchen and headed to the living room. She put a cup of coffee in front of the Baron. Her silk skirt rustled as she sat down.

"I think you are right," she said. "The mystery is what links these heads together."

The masks hanging in the living room looked sad. Their searching eyes had gone pale.

"You know, in the old days, Papuans believed that the spirits of the dead wandered in an unknown world and came back as white men. They returned down the forbidden path, the path that no-one was ever supposed to take: the Ghost Road. In a way the *Marie-Jeanne* explorers were like ghosts . . . It's the sad story of two worlds never meeting and never coming together."

Pale waves of light danced round the centre of the living room, the edges were left in the shade. Bérénice lifted her hair up and closed her eyes, lost in her confused thoughts. Her coffee had gone cold; she had left it untouched. "I'm going back to Paris. I'll wait to hear from you."

"I'd like to ask you a couple more questions," de Palma said.

"Go ahead." She was suddenly defensive.

"Why did your grandfather keep only one of the skulls?"

"I guess it had a particular meaning for him. I must admit I've never really asked myself why."

"Why that one and not another?" de Palma persisted.

"The skull definitely came from the Yuat River region."

"From which village?"

"A village further towards the centre of the country. It is highly likely to have been stolen during one of their wars."

"I thought that kind of thing didn't happen."

"You've got a point, Monsieur de Palma, but lots of things changed with the arrival of the white man. Those skulls fetched a high price. They became a source of income for the people who owned them. And as they claimed to be Christian converts, it no longer seemed like such a sacrilegious act."

"If someone comes all the way here to steal one, there has to be a reason for it."

"If it's a Papuan, then I think he wanted to take it back to the House of the Dead. Perhaps he rejects Christianity and is adopting the old rituals again. The skulls of the ancestors were supposed to protect the warriors and their harvests."

"Why do you think it might be a Papuan?"

She was shaken by the question. "Just an assumption . . . you told me that Grandpa's murderer is now in New Guinea."

"These skulls used to protect the warriors, didn't they?"

"There aren't any wars anymore."

"Who knows?"

She took the handle of her coffee cup delicately between her thumb and index finger, and wet her lips. The tepid, dark liquid made her wince.

"The skull in your grandfather's office was none other than Kaïngara's, the guide who accompanied them on the 1936 expedition. That's why your grandfather was so fond of it."

She didn't seem to take it in. The exotic world of Dr Delorme now seemed like a jumble of guilty consciences revealed by the sunlight.

"I think it's time you told me about Robert Ballancourt's son," de Palma said.

Bérénice's hands trembled. She put down her cup and buried her fingers between her knees. "What do you mean?"

"You know very well. He's come back."

"Christian . . . Kaïngara . . ."

"The man who loved you and has never forgotten you."

"Why didn't he come and see me? It's crazy."

"Only you know the answer to that."

She stammered some inaudible words, then looked up at de Palma. The light had almost gone from her eyes. "Do you know what it's like to live with guilt?"

"No," de Palma replied, "I've never felt like that. Even if I've made mistakes in my life; even if I haven't always made the right choices."

"It's like being trapped in a cage and the bars are your guilty conscience. You tell yourself that life might have been different if you hadn't obeyed all those stupid traditions. My grandfather made me happy. Everyone will tell you that. But you know he also made me unhappy. He stopped me from loving a boy because he wasn't supposed to be right for me. Now my life no longer has any meaning."

The photograph of the *Marie-Jeanne* was on the table beside her. She touched it. "I always knew we were made for each other. Can you understand that?"

De Palma tried hard to remain detached. "Do you know where Christian is?" he asked in a hard voice.

"Don't ask me to tell you. I can't."

He looked her in the eyes and felt sorry for her. She wanted to look away, but chose not to when his expression hardened, as he was about to speak.

"Why did you tell me there was a bow in your grandfather's office?"

She gave a start and clenched her hands so tightly that her finger joints turned white.

"Please forgive me."

The tone of her voice did not ring true. She had lied, but to what extent?

"You know very well what I'm talking about. I think that from the very beginning you knew the truth about your grandfather's murder. Luckily for you I've checked out your movements."

Bérénice didn't demur. Her hair fell across her face.

"Christian knew where that bow was," de Palma added. "It wasn't in the office. Perhaps it was where you found those reels of film. Dr Delorme's secret garden."

"I don't know why, but I wanted to protect him by saying that. In fact, as soon as you told me about the arrow, I knew he'd come back."

She took a handkerchief discreetly from her pocket. "I wanted you to understand. I showed you the films and the photos. I wanted there to be someone who understood."

She looked up. "Don't hurt him. I couldn't bear that. You do understand, don't you?"

De Palma put his hand on her shoulder, "I do understand, but what he has done is unforgivable."

"What do you mean?"

"He desecrated Robert Ballancourt's grave."

There was no reaction. She was overcome by shame, unable any longer to defend the man she still loved. She gripped de Palma's hand. "What about . . . ?"

Her voice caught in her throat.

"Yes, Bérénice. He also desecrated your grandfather's coffin."

She moved away from him and took a few steps across the large living-room where she'd been a child. "He took the skulls . . ." she sobbed.

Besides the window the sharp-angled statues glowed weakly. A Trobriand figurine held out its thin arms like a dying warrior.

"Go to Yuarimo," she said, "not far from Yuat River. That's where you'll find him."

De Palma did not want to look at her one last time. "Good-bye, Bérénice Delorme."

She gave a vague wave and watched as he disappeared down the garden.

30

A fortnight later

Lieutenant Somare raised an arm above his balding head. Heavily built and of medium height, he wore a khaki short-sleeved shirt, grey, cotton trousers and moccasins flecked with red earth.

"Hello, Monsieur de Palma." Somare produced a chrome-plated police badge. "Pleased to meet you." The Papuan detective thrust out his huge, firm hand. He had a forceful, direct look; an emaciated face with two deep scars on his right cheek; and something sad in his eyes that de Palma took as a reflection of past setbacks. With each of his wan smiles the corners of his thick lips wrinkled sourly. "Did you have a good journey?"

"Awful, I travelled cattle class. I feel like my legs have been amputated and my head has been pushed down into my shoulders."

Somare gave a resounding laugh. "You speak excellent English."

"Thank you. I don't think I do too badly for a cop. And a Frenchman at that."

"Most people will understand you, but here people mainly speak Tok Pisin or Hiri Motu. Or one of our eight hundred other languages. In the rural areas you'll need a good interpreter."

They went through the cordon of taxi drivers and porters screening the international arrivals, hailing the white tourists as they emerged.

"My car's outside in the car park," Somare said, pointing down a huge corridor littered with trolleys and souvenir stalls loaded with cheap masks and jewellery. The policeman walked along easily; his arms dangling. From time to time he cast a bored glance at the people he passed. The heat was becoming oppressive. At the far end of the corridor, the airport extension works were visible through two large windows. Outside, the air reeked of kerosene. The heavy white outlines of the planes wavered in the light and the heat.

Somare opened the boot of his Toyota Land Cruiser and chucked the Baron's case inside. "Your hotel is in the centre of town."

For a long while the airport road followed a long, straight, bumpy line. Somare drove erratically, glued to the cars in front, as if he wanted to shunt them. On either side of the hot, red moorland there were small houses planted on stilts.

"Many people come here from the rural areas. People who have been uprooted."

"Are these new neighbourhoods?"

Somare sighed. "You could say they're more like shanty towns."

Children were running along the earth tracks. The two policemen went through a provincial toll gate: a double bend between four red barrels filled with cement, an axle-breaker, and a rusty barrier. An official, dressed in a uniform that was too small for him, handed them a ticket. Further on the road became less crowded. They drove through a burning hot landscape devoid of trees. Somare increased his speed, hooting repeatedly as he overtook the vans used as bush taxis.

"I have some good news for you," he said suddenly. "We've located a mixed-race man in the Sepik region."

Somare frowned. "But there's a problem."

"That's good if there's only one."

"A big problem."

"What do you mean?"

"The police don't have much power in those areas. It's not like it is with you in France. Up here in a lot of cases it's the Big Men who make the law." Somare held out his finger in front of him as though pointing to some imaginary destination. "The state doesn't mean much to them."

Somare was more relaxed now they were entering the suburbs of Port Moresby. They drove through arterial roads that crossed each other at right angles, lined with cube-shaped houses and shops with flashy signs. Some old men were chatting in the shade outside a fish and chip shop, sipping fizzy drinks, one of them a giant, in shorts and sandals.

"New Guinea is still very poor," Somare said halting at a red light. "We have only been independent for a few years now. We still have much to do. It's tough."

"Yes, but independence is the most important thing," de Palma said.

"Easy to say that. Queen Elizabeth is still the head of our state and our island is divided in two."

They went through a neighbourhood of small houses with corrugated iron roofs. Large trees with enormous trunks cast a dense shade over the dirt alleyways. Children on their way home from school taunted some aggressive-looking dogs.

"Not too hot, Monsieur de Palma?"

"No, I'm O.K. I just feel like I've been thrown in a pressure cooker."

Somare gave a hearty laugh.

"You can call me Michel."

The policeman held out his hand once again. "I'm Joseph, as you know."

"Joseph," de Palma repeated.

"That's my Christian name."

"Are you Protestant?"

"Yes, Pentecostalist."

"There aren't many Catholics round here."

"I don't know any."

Somare suddenly changed tack. "The Sepik is in the north-west.

Tomorrow we'll take a small plane, and then a car will take us further up. After that we go by boat."

He glanced in the mirror and indicated to turn right. Thirty metres further on he came to a stop and double-parked. "Here we are," he said violently ratcheting the handbrake, "This is your hotel."

The Park Hotel was a four-star establishment. Its facade had been eroded by the humidity. Under the balconies there were dark semi-circles. Two huge satellite dishes stuck out from the edge of the roof.

"Make yourself at home and get as much sleep as you can. They have a restaurant here too. I'll come round and get you in the morning at about eight." Somare turned and strode back to his car.

*

The hotel bedroom was icy cold. De Palma preferred to switch off the air conditioning and use the huge fan hanging from the ceiling instead. After half an hour the air grew heavy. A musty smell oozed from the red-and-green flowered wallpaper on the blistered walls. The atmosphere reminded de Palma of his bedroom as a young man: the summer sun beating down on the neighbourhood and torpid nights spent sleeping on the floor tiles in the hope of cooling down.

He put the photograph of Kaïngara's skull on the bed and stared at the eyes made of shells and the pupils carved in brown resin. The mystery of these over-modelled heads had troubled him more since he had arrived. He put the photographs back in their folder and went out onto the balcony.

On every floor the air conditioning units were purring away. He lit a cigarette and searched for signs of life in the dead parts of the town. A drunkard was lying at the corner of a three-storey building. His swollen face shone under the white light of the street lamp. There was nothing welcoming about Port Moresby. The harshness of this town, born from the exodus of highland peoples, was palpable, as though it had impregnated its already sickly walls.

302

Nothing was left of the world discovered by Dr Delorme at the end of the 1930s. Nothing at all. The Baron was disorientated by that thought. He suddenly felt out of place in this dilapidated setting; alone and useless, with his staunch determination to establish the truth about a murderer's trail. He told himself that for a man like Somare these murders and this search must mean very little at all.

Delorme had travelled across a territory governed by Australia. A land without a state, where all that existed were the villages and societies that recognized each other through the languages that they spoke and the tiny territories they occupied. Each village was master of its own land and outsiders were forbidden. Every violation of boundaries brought wars that were perfectly regulated by custom. They fought each other until the first man was wounded, or until they considered an equilibrium had been restored between the tribes.

When Delorme returned to New Guinea in the 1960s, he had tried to make contact with tribes that still lived in the Stone Age.

De Palma was certain that some documents existed. Perhaps Bérénice had not revealed everything about her grandfather's papers.

The Papua the doctor had journeyed across in the 1960s was an island divided by a dead-straight line: an arbitrary border that ran right through the middle of a huge virgin forest and mountains that were often over 4,000 metres high. In the east was a region that would soon gain independence. But in the west, probably the more primitive part, the rule of Sukarno's Indonesia took a heavy toll. Massacres were frequent. It was a lawless zone; a mining area where multinationals, American for the most part, carved out and cut up sacred lands as they pleased. Over 10,000 Papuans had paid with their lives for resisting the Indonesian occupation, to the indifference of the rest of the world. Delorme and Ballancourt had lived through all that. To what extent where they involved? Were they happy just to be collectors in a land of Cockaigne for early art lovers?

The Baron's investigations had got him nowhere: while Delorme's life was known about, Ballancourt's remained very hazy. His time as an industrialist in France had revealed nothing. He had lived off his share dividends without troubling himself too much about the companies in which he had invested. His life as an explorer was simply a mystery. His expeditions had lasted for months, sometimes years. Always in New Guinea, in the independent part as well as the part occupied by Indonesia.

A scooter went down the street, its engine leaving a noisy trail in the balmy night. De Palma shut the window and closed the shutters.

*

The flight on the A.T.R. plane was an appalling ordeal. With each air pocket the Baron felt as though an evil genie was tearing out his guts. Somare spent most of the flight asleep. It was after midday when they landed at the small airport at Wewak. A strong, hot wind was blowing in from the Bismarck Sea. In the distance, through the grey air, a range of mountains could be seen, covered in black clouds like knobbly fists.

They took a taxi to the central police station. A chubby officer received them in a room with scurfy walls. He was sweating profusely and wiped his forehead and neck with paper tissues from a pile on his desk that shrank before their eyes. He greeted de Palma with a nod, indicating the empty chair opposite him, and went back to his paperwork.

"You must understand, Monsieur de Palma, that we know almost nothing."

"What does that mean?" the Baron asked; he was starting to get concerned at the turn events were taking.

"Things move slowly here. From what I've heard the man you're looking for is not just anyone."

"I must admit I know very little about him."

"Me neither, but I have contacts in the highlands."

The police sergeant got up and helped himself to a glass of water from the drinking fountain at the end of the office. "Usually my authority goes no further than the door of this place," he said, after downing the plastic cup in one. "What do you say, Somare?"

"I have already explained that to Monsieur de Palma."

The sergeant sat down again and mopped his brow. "There is disturbance in the Yuat region," he said, looking up at the map of New Guinea hanging to his right. "Papuan unrest. Do you understand?"

"I've read one or two things, but in France we know almost nothing about it."

"There are men smuggling weapons through the forest, who make quite a lot of money. We think the man you are looking for is one of them."

"Is it possible he came to Marseille to get supplies?"

"It's possible. Show me the photo of the skull you're looking for."

De Palma spread out the photographs one by one on the desk.

The sergeant's expression suddenly altered. "Those things should have gone for ever!"

"Why do you say that?"

"That's the old world, Monsieur de Palma. The world of Papuan savages; cannibals and cutting off people's heads. That world must be destroyed."

The sergeant handed back the photographs to the Baron. "For me as a Christian all that is a symbol of evil. All those customs we had and which, thank the Lord, we have now lost."

"Those skulls are worth a fortune in the West and in the United States."

"That's what they say, but believe me, we must get rid of them. They represent a time of ignorance and darkness."

De Palma closed his bag.

"Somare can't go with you to Yuarimo. You'll have to manage yourself. That region is not very safe; I don't want any trouble. Is that clear?"

De Palma had not been expecting this. "I thought that . . ."

"No," interrupted the sergeant, "There's nothing more to say. Somare can't join you on your investigation. When you go out of the door of this police station, you are just a tourist. You can look for the owners of these skulls if you feel like it, but don't stir up a revolution. Peace is very fragile in Papua. War is part of our ancient culture."

The sergeant dismissed them. De Palma felt as though heavy doors had just slammed shut behind him.

Somare averted his eyes. "I'm sorry," he said, scrawling a name and phone number on a bit of paper. "There's a French anthropologist working in the Yuarimo region. He'll be able to help you."

Serge Meunier. It was a mobile number.

"He speaks some of the local languages and knows the Elders well." Somare scratched his head. "Don't hesitate to call me, Michel, if anything goes wrong. I have lots of relatives in the Yuat villages. I'll wait to hear from you. 'Bye."

The policeman turned to go. Flashy chrome Yamaha and Suzuki bikes were spluttering away in the middle of the square. Women in garish dresses walked across, trying to avoid the cars, their heavy feet in worn-out sandals that afforded little protection from the soil. Despite the lateness of the hour, a covered market at the end of the square was still packed. A group of white tourists was bargaining for masks with a trader who had spread out his wares on a blue blanket on the ground. As soon as he saw the Baron he hailed him with expansive gestures.

The tourists were Australian. De Palma managed with difficulty to make himself understood. They were returning from the Upper Sepik region like thousands of other visitors. They gave him the address of a local tour operator who arranged cruises up the river. Yuarimo was mentioned twice in the conversation.

"Many people can guide you," added the trader. "If you like you can go by the road. You have to go to Angoram. It's not very far.

From there you can go up the Sepik. There are boats that make the journey."

As de Palma went round the market he came across other merchants. They had spread out their masks, hooks, ritual daggers. and large flutes. The artists were quite skilful at imitating the art of their ancestors. Sometimes next to a statue with an enormous phallus the trader had placed a Sacred Heart, Christ figure or Our Lady of Lourdes. Even back in the 1930s Delorme had seen craft workshops producing artefacts.

De Palma returned to the centre of the square and asked for directions. Some Land Rovers were making the journey to Angoram. For a few kinas he climbed in to the back of a bush taxi and squeezed between two sunburned New Zealanders. The taller of the two reeked of insect repellant.

"We're going to see the dancing on Lake Chambri," he said to de Palma. "Are you going too?"

"No, I'm going to Yuarimo and to some other villages. Do you know the Sepik well?"

The New Zealander nodded. "It's my second time. The last time we went up Mount Hagen. It was really wild. Amazing."

The road cut straight through the great, dank forest. At times it was just a red track where the logging trucks dug huge, sticky potholes. A thick mist hung like a plume from the enormous trees. A heavy downpour had just stopped. The air was so dense de Palma felt he could taste it on the tip of his tongue.

"This is Margaret Mead country," the New Zealander said. "She did a lot of work on this region. It's thanks to her it's so well known today."

"Unfortunately," the Baron said, looking up at the top of the great trees set against the background of grey sky, "wherever the anthropologists go, the missionaries and soldiers are never far behind."

The town of Angoram was smaller than Wewak. Dirt tracks led to houses, mostly raised on stilts. De Palma got caught up in the stream of tourists and found himself in the Men's House. There were a lot of Japanese people milling around the craft stalls. Some artists were working on the ground.

"This house was rebuilt with the help of photographs from a German expedition in the 1950s," explained a guide in broken English. "Because this place was occupied by the Japanese between 1941 and 1945. The war destroyed quite a lot of things. Many people from this region were forcibly conscripted into the Japanese army. You will meet a former combatant later. He still knows some Japanese songs. Over seventy years later, he can still remember them!"

De Palma put away his camera and left. He was thinking about Captain Meyssonnier's log and the explorers from the *Marie-Jeanne*. Their world had gone. In spite of all their good intentions, they had been its gravediggers.

Some youngsters were sitting by the pillars supporting the Men's House. They wore faded short-sleeved shirts. De Palma looked away and headed off towards the Sepik.

The Government has sent me here to tell you about the new laws. If you do not obey these new laws the police will come and find you. The police will come and they will kill all of your pigs. These laws forbid many of your customs. They ban your bows and arrows. They ban your spears and axes. They ban your tribal wars. Tell that to the members of your clan. If you don't respect these new laws, you will have to pay a minimum fine of one hundred kinas. A hundred kinas is the minimum fine. Those of you who have gone to church will definitely have heard of the Ten Commandments. You must understand that from now on that is the only law that counts. Those who do not go to church should find out about the Ten Commandments.

A New Guinea government
official in a Huli village (1999)

31

"Look what you have done. Just look! You're worse than a dog!" Old Païkab was barefoot. On his pointed head he wore a frayed cap that had once borne the badge of the New Zealand rugby team. He had rounded up the entire village. Christian stood to one side near the trunk of a palm tree.

"Look what the half-caste has done! Look what the bastard has done! He has put the skulls of the Elders on the altar in the church. You knew that was sacrilege. You have brought shame on us. You are the fruit of sin."

Païkab held a spear in his hand. He pointed it in Christian's direction, positioning himself in profile as though he were about to fire. "If I wasn't your cousin, I'd have killed you already by now. You don't deserve to live among us. I don't want you in my family any longer. I don't want you as my cousin. My aunt Agnès: she sinned with a white man."

Two young men whom Christian barely knew moved towards him, looking aggressive. One of them had a Colt 45 in his hand, the other a machete, the handle of which was made from a rolled-up strip of leather. They came from a friendly village further up the Yuat.

Christian did not dare to look at the crowd facing him. There were about a hundred men. The women stood apart; they seemed indifferent. Wabe was dead. The only person he could count on now was his old friend Alis. Unless he had already changed sides. Alis wasn't very firm in his convictions. Christian looked for him in the crowd, but couldn't see him.

"When you came back from Port Moresby," Old Païkab continued, "we all believed in you. You promised us money. You said that our sons would thrive and now all that has come to nothing and you commit sacrilege."

Christian remained silent. Two deep lines scored his balding forehead. He looked from face to face. Each of the men in front of him now hated him. Every dark eye glowed with ferocious hatred: the same that had driven him ever since he overheard a conversation between his father and Fernand Delorme: "Christian is Papuan. He will never be one of us!" The sound of Delorme's nasal voice still echoed inside his head. He recalled the doctor's face on the day he died.

"Do you recognize me?" he asked.

The elderly doctor studied the person who had violated his space. "Who are you?"

"Christian: Robert Ballancourt's son."

Delorme took a deep breath. The air whistled as it went through his shrivelled nose. His hands suddenly trembled.

"You have come a long way," he said.

"A very long way. I have come to seek reparation."

"Reparation for what, my boy?"

"For abandoning me."

Delorme's eyelids dropped, as if devoid of life. His cheeks hollowed out a little more. "What could we do? Robert couldn't take you with him. It was impossible, his family would never have accepted it."

Christian studied the books on the shelves. His eyes fell on the spine of Totem and Taboo *by Sigmund Freud. That book belonged to his father.*

"I have come to ask you to adopt me. I want to belong to your people. I don't want to be nobody's son any longer."

"But that's impossible. I cannot accept such a thing. I can't make up for Robert's mistakes."

The words cut him to the quick. "Where are the skulls you took from us?"

"I gave them to a museum."

"What about the one in that case?"

The doctor had a coughing fit that made his whole body shake, "That skull," he said in a husky voice, "belongs to Robert's guide, Kaïngara: your grandfather. He was killed by a tribe on the River Yuat."

Christian's eyes misted over. He no longer dared to look at the skull. He went up to the bookcase. Totem and Taboo was still in the same place. "Why have you got this book? It belonged to my father."

"He gave it to me before he died, along with other mementos. There is a passage in it that he often used to read. I have never really known why. If you open it you'll see."

Christian searched and found the underlined passage:

One day the brothers who had been driven out . . .

"That's it," Delorme said. "We often used to talk about that theory of Freud's. Your father didn't agree with all that . . . But it's an old story."

"Cannibal savages as they were," Christian read in a low voice, "it goes without saying that they devoured their victim as well as killing him. The violent primal father had doubtless been the feared and envied model of each one of the company of brothers . . ."

Christian thought of Wabe and his mother's gentle smile. "We need money. We need to restore peace."

"I don't know what you're talking about."

Christian was confused. How could he explain to an old man that nothing of what he had known existed any longer? He was referring to the crafts factory and the agricultural cooperative.

"I don't have any money. My granddaughter has everything. I don't have anything anymore."

"Liar!" shouted Christian, "You've never stopped lying to us."

He went out of the office. A few minutes later there was the sound of a flute, wavering and growing louder.

"The voice of the spirit," Delorme sighed.

Christian reappeared in the doorway. He had drawn two red marks: one on his forehead, the other under his eyes. The doctor trembled. He understood.

The bow had lost none of its power. Christian took a step back and brought the notch of the arrow up to his eyes. Wabe had taught him to take aim when he was a child. They had often gone hunting together.

"I knew that voyage would bring us nothing but bad luck," the doctor said. "Ballancourt had heard the voice."

There was a short whistling sound, then a noise like a twig snapping. The doctor fell back. Christian removed the reed shaft. He felt nothing, just the emptiness that follows hatred.

"Kill them all," he whispered. "I don't have a choice."

The crowd had moved closer.

"Listen to me," Christian said, "You've worked on the coffee plantations. You worked hard. Then you worked in the crafts factory. And what has it brought you? You've made them rich, those big businessmen from Port Moresby and Australia. They're the ones who set the rates and fix the prices. You never get a say. Today you are poor because the prices have collapsed. Whose fault is that?"

A swelling murmur spread through the crowd. Alis had just appeared at the end of the path leading to the Men's House.

"You've stopped being yourselves. Look at you. All you know how to do is sell sacks of coffee and stupid masks. The youngsters don't even know the meaning of these masks. Your Men's House has become a supermarket for the tourists."

"That's how we make a living," said Alis. "What else do you expect us to do? And now all you bring is conflict."

The crowd growled. Christian raised his hands in an attempt to calm the men. "I haven't betrayed anyone, and the proof is that I'm still here among you. I haven't run away like a thief. I'm really sad about you, Alis, because I thought of you as my brother. But you don't understand that the price of coffee has collapsed and the crafts trade isn't the same as it was two years ago. It's the bankers in Port Moresby and Australia who fix the prices for the things you make. Not you. You're their servants."

A young man emerged from the crowd. He wore a red hat, which he removed angrily and flung on the ground. "I've never been anyone's servant. You're just like the white men. You made us believe we could follow you because you have the same blood, but in your head you think like a white man. Your father came to buy skulls from us. Your father brought disaster on us."

Christian moved towards him, threateningly. "Don't insult my father's name, or I'll kill you. It's his skull that's in the church and next to it, the skulls of my grandfather, Kaïngara, and the great Dr Delorme."

At the mention of these names, Old Païkab went past the young man and stuck his spear in the ground. "I'm going to kill you with my own hands if you don't go away."

Alis intervened. His hands were shaking in panic. "We must respect the law," he said. "We can't be like our fathers, headhunting and eating our enemies. We can't do that. Today we are Christians."

"Exactly: you're Christians. You've destroyed the House of the Spirits to build a church. You've destroyed what has lasted for centuries to replace it with a God whom you don't know. And ever since, you've been in a state of disarray. You, Païkab, how many pigs did you steal before you converted? How many women did you sleep with? How many men did you kill?"

"I'm a Christian now. The life you talk about no longer exists."

"No, Païkab, it's still inside you. Do you think it's so great to work on the coffee plantations? Do you think it's so great to make sculptures for a pittance, which are then sold for a fortune in the West?"

"It's whites like you that buy them," shouted Païkab, "You've no right to lecture us."

"I brought back the spirits of the Elders to give you back your dignity. I wanted to shock you to bring an end to this farce. I left when war broke out. Today you must stop fighting, or else the police will come with soldiers and you'll all be wiped out."

Païkab raised his arms above his head. "We're not afraid of anyone. The enemy has taken a life. We must seek revenge. Their blood must flow too."

Alis positioned himself in front of him, "Listen to me. The enemy have automatic weapons. They'll cut you to pieces."

"We've got them too and we're going to use them."

Christian shook his head, his eyes streaming with tears. He held out a trembling hand towards the church, "That used to be the House of the Spirits. The missionaries made you knock it down to build a church. And what did it achieve? The spirits no longer protect us. It's like we're lost in a fog. We don't know where we're going any longer."

He took another step towards the crowd. "I did all that to impress you. I wanted to shock you. I wanted everyone to live in peace. When war broke out I went to the West to look for those skulls including the one that was the cause of this war. For more than seventy years we've been killing each other because our ancestors sold my father a skull that was captured in a raid on an enemy village. We're going to give it back."

"You're crazy and you're a blasphemer!"

"You've sold out to the white men," someone shouted in the crowd. "Sell-out!"

"Me a sell-out to the white men? But I came to give you back what the white man took from you!"

"Sell-out!" the men shouted again. "Go back where you came from!"

The crowd moved forward. The youngest members jostled to get to the front.

316

Christian moved back. "I'm not afraid of you!"

"You're crying like a girl," a young man replied.

"I'm crying because you've all gone mad. As soon as there's a problem you give up and run away from all your responsibilities."

Christian went towards the church. "I'm telling you once again for the last time. We must live in peace. The spirits of the ancestors will protect the harvests. They are going to protect us. Let's make peace with our enemies. They have gone to war over money, but really they're angry about the collapse in the price of coffee. Everyone wants war because everyone is poor. I'm going to talk to our enemies. They'll listen to me."

"What are you going to promise them? It was your father who brought war on us."

"It's not me that grows cannabis to buy weapons from the Australians. It's you. All you young people think about is fighting."

A spear whistled through the air and struck Christian on the ankle. He let out a cry and retreated several paces. He knew that he had to react and face up to them. But he preferred to turn away, take flight. Distance himself from this world which had never really accepted him. Once more he saw his mother's small face. She was also crying. His car was parked behind the factory. He turned on the ignition and disappeared up the track leading to the River Yuat.

32

The *Spirit of the Sepik* traced a long curve in the grey water of the river. De Palma had put his rucksack by his feet, and watched the riverbank go by. The huge catamaran had three levels with square openings and tinted windows; inside it was fully air-conditioned. It was supposed to resemble a traditional house with its angled roof almost sticking out over her bows. The tourists, Australians and Japanese for the most part, had gathered on the upper decks. When the boat left Angoram some dug-out canoes had gathered round.

In the fields that now spread out on either side of the river, women were following a large orange tractor, occasionally bending down to pick up what looked like large potatoes. In the village of Kambot, the House of the Spirits had a strange-looking roof that almost hung over the water.

As they approached the mouth of the Yuat, men in worn shirts and Bermuda shorts paddled towards the massive boat in long, needle-like canoes. Low clouds weighed down the horizon. The air was saturated with humidity. A radio blasted out pop songs in the local language. The melodies had a strange character that could have done without the quavers of the violins and the rolls of the snare drums. Between the sago palms children waved at the tourists leaning over board. The *Spirit of the Sepik* drew along-side a wooden landing stage, causing yellowish eddies in the dense water. A phone call from Somare had preceded the Baron's arrival. Serge Meunier was waiting a few metres away.

"Hi," Meunier's face was tanned from the sun. His blue eyes were a bit sad. His mouth seemed constantly about to break into a smile. He wore a khaki sun hat, shorts that revealed his hairy calves and faded canvas boots. His brown T-shirt was stained with sweat under the armpits and over his paunch.

"Did you like it?" he asked, pointing to the *Spirit of the Sepik.*

"Very fast and comfortable. Unfortunately . . ."

A group of youngsters appeared. They looked at de Palma in amusement. He looked rather anxious and a bit lost.

"Come on," Meunier said. "Otherwise they'll try and sell you their crafts."

"I get the feeling it's the main industry round here!"

"Crafts and tourism, yes. That's what I'm working on. This society is in the process of becoming alienated."

"If it hasn't already happened."

"You're right Monsieur de Palma. Tourism is never a good thing, but it's unavoidable."

The anthropologist exchanged a few words with the young men who immediately burst out laughing and rolled some marbles in the Baron's direction.

"They're not making fun of you. I just told them that you come from France."

"Is it that funny?"

"It's just that I've told them a load of funny stories about French people. The stories about sex are the ones they like best."

"I can see their point."

"They also love it when I tell them there are women doctors. Here that would be out of the question. Just imagine an old Papuan warrior letting a young woman take care of him."

His glasses hung on the end of a piece of string. His expression suddenly changed. "Somare told me about the photos," he said, looking at the Baron's bag.

"So Somare's told you everything has he?"

"Yes. He also asked me to keep an eye on you."

"Am I in danger?"

"Well, in a way, yes. Like everyone who comes to stir up the ghosts in this country. So let's not waste any time, let's go straight to the Men's House," Meunier said. "I've organized a little meeting with the Elders. But don't be surprised if everyone turns up."

They followed a path fringed with tall grass and banana trees. The ground was littered with plastic bags and beer bottles. The House was at the end. It looked strangely like the one that Delorme and Ballancourt had filmed seventy years earlier. Each pillar had been delicately worked, turned and carved.

"One pillar for each clan," Meunier pointed out. "That's the Orator's stool. It no longer serves much purpose except to impress the tourists."

Some old men, their eyes clouded by cataracts, were watching de Palma. One of them wore a T-shirt decorated with Mickey Mouse. Despite his age, he still had a powerful physique. Meunier did the introductions. Smiles were exchanged; words of English rang out.

"We're going to show the photos to the oldest man. He knew Delorme and Ballancourt very well. His father worked for them."

The old man watched them in amusement. His yellow shirt with tucked up sleeves revealed his lean torso. Two long wrinkles framed his thick mouth. His ears had large pierced holes; and he probably wore earrings occasionally.

De Palma took out a brown envelope from his bag. He had taken care to make several photocopies of each photograph. First of all he handed over the ones he had found in Bérénice's albums.

"I don't know them," the old man said.

He had two teeth missing at the front and when he smiled his large lips revealed a gap that made him look like a naughty child.

"Who is Christian?" de Palma asked.

Meunier interpreted, "He is mixed-race. His mother died long ago. She had a child by Robert Ballancourt."

"Is he here?" de Palma enquired.

The old man shook his head and pointed his arm into the blue.

"No," translated Meunier, "he is higher up."

"How does he know him?"

"Christian often used to come with his father to the villages at the river mouth. For a time he came to do business here. He bought works of art and took them down below. But it's a long time since we've seen him."

"How come?"

Meunier translated. The old man was embarrassed. He shook his head by way of response. He wanted to change the subject and invited the visitors into the Men's House.

The large rectangular building could easily have been mistaken for the one that de Palma had seen in Bérénice Delorme's films. To the side, in a mad tangle of grass, voracious bindweed and dwarf trees, carved pillars slowly rotted: the remains of the former house that had had to be rebuilt before it was destroyed by damp and termites. On one of the pillars there was a naïve drawing of Donald Duck as a masked bandit.

In a corner of the house a tinny radio station was churning out Australian rap. A sculptor was putting the finishing touches to an oval mask with a nose in the form of a bird's beak.

"In the old days they used to work to the sound of sacred flutes," Meunier said.

The old man sat down. He had taken the photographs and was passing them round a committee of Elders that had formed spontaneously. The photographs came back to the Baron.

"They don't want to talk about it much," Meunier said, waving his hand. "I don't know why that is. They won't even tell me where he is."

"Do you know the highlands?"

"Not really. I concentrate on round here. That's more than enough."

De Palma took out the folder with the photographs of the skulls from his bag. As soon as they caught sight of the first skull there was a murmur from the men.

"It's a trophy skull," said Meunier. "Generally they don't much like it when you show them those. They're a bit ashamed."

"Why?"

"You don't know the missionaries out here in New Guinea. Everyone claims to be a Christian here. They find these reminders of the past degrading. Photos of Papuan cannibals or headhunters, you know the kind of stuff."

"The sergeant already talked to me about that."

The photograph passed from hand to hand. The oldest man put it right in front of his eyes to examine it more closely; suddenly he began to shout a string of short sentences.

"They say it comes from a village really far away," Meunier translated.

The two oldest men had started discussing the photograph. They seemed to disagree and were clearly angry.

The anthropologist moved closer to the group of old men. He couldn't understand some of the words. "They don't want to tell me where it came from. I think they must have captured it during a war with a village some distance away. They won't talk about that sort of thing."

De Palma handed them the photograph of the skull that had been stolen from Delorme's house.

"Kaïngara! Kaïngara!" the old man said.

"You know him?" the anthropologist asked.

"I wasn't born when he died; it's a very old story. He was a very well-known guide. He worked with Monsieur Robert."

"Who was he exactly?" Meunier asked.

"A Big Man. A very generous man. He was killed by the man who became the district officer in Marienberg afterwards. The government official."

"You mean the man who did the hiring and firing?"

"Yes."

The old man said a few words, as an aside. Meunier strained to listen. He couldn't understand the Elders' whispering, but finally managed to catch a few words.

"That man was killed in a war?" he asked the Elder. "Is that right?"

"I don't know. My father just told me that the official ambushed him by the Yuat."

"Who was this official?" the Baron asked.

"He won't be missed. I've heard all about him. A Big Man whose job it was to make people work for a pittance."

"Why did he kill the man whose skull we have?"

"Perhaps he had stolen his wife," the old man said laughing.

The Elders invited de Palma to visit the Men's House. They passed through a dried-straw curtain and found themselves in a huge room. De Palma felt as if he'd been there before. A mask with pointed teeth looked at him with ferocious eyes. Some masks, clearly made recently, were spread out on the ground. Everything was for sale.

"In the old days we used to come here to teach the secrets of our clan to the youngsters," the Elder said. "Each clan has its own place in the house."

Two adolescents had sat down on a wooden bench. Shafts of light pierced through the muggy air. Through an opening one could see the fields stretching away towards the meandering waters of the Sepik. Pigs were rooting through the ground by a betel palm tree. In the distance beyond the river a thick fringe of jungle sat on the horizon.

"As I understand it, Christian can be found in a region to the east of here," Meunier said. "The problem is I don't exactly know where."

"They're refusing to tell you?"

"Yes."

"Do you know how far the *Marie-Jeanne* explorers went up the Yuat?"

"From what I've been told they went as far as Kenakatem. The Elders say they might have reached other villages further up, but it's not certain."

"Ask them if they've heard of Bérénice Delorme."

"Of course they know her. She has often come here to buy things."

"Have they seen her recently?"

The old man shook his head. "She passed through last year," he said, "since then we haven't seen her."

"Where was she going?"

Meunier spoke to the Elders. He seemed to be searching for words.

"They don't know."

"I get the impression they don't much like Bérénice Delorme."

"That's right."

"Why?"

"She did business with villages that were their traditional enemies."

"Traditional enemies?"

"Yes. Less than a century ago the men from up there used to come headhunting down here. Then the men from this village would go and take revenge. That's how it was. The old customs have disappeared, but not the bitterness. Many of the Elders can remember those wars. Their parents took part in them. They say the old fella even took part himself."

"He cut off people's heads?"

"Who knows?"

Most of the men were sturdy, with wide torsos and muscular arms. De Palma found them good-looking, despite their ragged appearance and the awful stories surrounding them. Meunier was having difficulty making himself understood. The men's faces betrayed anxiety whenever Ballancourt's name was mentioned. An old man pointed east.

"Mundugumor," he shouted.

"Further up the Yuat."

Meunier seemed sorry not to be able to answer further. "Our questions are starting to annoy them. I think it would be better to come back later. Here, it isn't like France. You have to give things time."

"Unfortunately I have to leave tomorrow if I'm going to make any progress," de Palma said.

"Our sense of time isn't the same as theirs. They feel pressurized by our questions about the past. They know a lot more than you'd think, but their reserve stops them opening up."

"I think I can understand."

The tinny church bell rang the Angelus.

"It's time for us to go."

*

The village wasn't visible from the riverbank. First you had to go up a tributary clogged with dense reeds. The small motor on the water taxi spluttered from time to time, spitting puffs of blue smoke. In the front two bare-chested men had loaded two brightly coloured cockerels imprisoned in cages. Over by the reeds, some fishermen in slender canoes were fixing their nets. Wading birds followed behind at a distance, on the lookout for any fish that might get away. Arms were wet from the heat; clothing stuck to the body.

When he re-read Captain Meyssonnier's log de Palma had made a note of a place further to the south. Ballancourt touched on it in his book, without ever really describing his stay there. His account suddenly seemed reserved and his normal fondness for detail was lacking. He just alluded to some villages and tribal wars, which he had no doubt witnessed when he passed through the area in 1936, and later, at the end of the 1950s.

The first thing we see as we travel round the world is our own filth, thrown into the face of mankind.

Claude Lévi-Strauss, Tristes tropiques,
(*Jonathan Cape, 1973*)

33

"You needn't think I'm going to beg!" Christian shouted.

The three men were agricultural labourers. One of them, the youngest, had pushed a felt pen through his nasal septum. He had small, white flowers in his short, frizzy hair and bulging, red-rimmed eyes. The oldest looking one had a gentler, almost naïve face. He wore cut-off jeans and a faded, baggy T-shirt over his muscular chest. Christian knew the third one: his tall, sturdy cousin whom he had never got on with.

They flung Christian on the ground. His hands were bound behind his back. A knotted creeper shackled his legs. His shirt was torn under the arms and spattered with stains of sweat and blood. In front of him the old Ghost Road opened up. Two large sago palms formed the great gate, and then the track disappeared into the dense forest.

"Do you recognize this place? That's where your father and his people came from."

"And that's where you're going."

The youngest one put his foot on Christian's chest.

"You illiterate bastards. You're just envious and jealous. You'll never have what I've had." Christian tried to free himself, but he received a kick in the side that winded him for a few seconds. Then another kick that made him reel. He buried his head in the mud so as not to cry out.

"Untie him now! Let him go back to his people!"

A machete blade slipped between his ankles and cut the ties.

"Get him up!"

"No. Let him get up by himself!"

Christian crawled a few metres. He gripped onto the trunk of a dried-up palm tree and managed to stand upright on his shaky legs. His muscles had been crushed by the blows he had received.

"Just look at the hero of the Yuat! Look at our saviour! The man they said was going to make a fortune for us poor slaves."

"He looks like a dog that hasn't eaten for days."

Christian moved away from the tree trunk. The pain in his right ankle was agonizing: he could only put his weight on the ball of his foot. The Ghost Road was just a few metres away. It rose away high into the distant hills that overlooked the valley and the great meadow where men had once waged war. A cool wind from the cloud-capped cordillera traced golden waves in the dried grass.

The three men surrounded Christian and circled him, glaring ferociously. He didn't seem to see their macabre dance. He looked at the long grass playing in the wind and thought of Kaïngara, his grandfather. His blood alone now ran through his veins.

"Walk. Come on now, walk," he said to himself, gritting his teeth. Christian took a step forward, then another: sleepwalking towards the Ghost Road.

"Kaïngara," he shouted, "Kaïngara! See how strong I am."

As he passed through the sago palms that formed the huge entrance to the Ghost Road, the first spear struck him on the hip. He fell to his knees and put his hand over the wound. He was bleeding profusely.

"So, great man, you can't walk any more," the three men shouted.

He put one hand on the sago palm and raised himself up, "Kaïngara! Look at me! I'm coming to you."

The pain was intense, but he could still walk. He started down the path. The tall grass came up to his waist. The birds had fallen silent. A spear whistled through the air.

"You missed him!"

"Let me do it . . ."

Christian advanced several metres. A fresh spear landed in the ground.

A distant voice rang out: "Stop! Your spears are powerless against the spirits!"

Two Elders were running across the meadow raising their arms above their heads. "Stop!"

The snapping of a breechblock was the only reply.

Christian closed his eyes, waiting for death. The hail of bullets came, tearing his back apart. He no longer felt anything, not even the need to breathe. With his eyes wide open he could see the rays of sunshine breaking through the tops of the trees casting golden reflections on the soft green shoots. A silhouette slipped between two palm trees. He thought he saw the great Cassowary bird with its unreal blue feathers.

Then a face appeared. A girl with a pale, ivory complexion. She was wearing a kilt and she had long hair that concealed her shy expression. He held out his arms and wanted to run to her.

A second hail of bullets flung Kaïngara's last descendant to the ground.

34

It was a long journey and not very safe.

"What brought a man of Ballancourt's background to such remote areas?" de Palma said to himself. "The kind of pride that pushes a person to experience what no-one else ever has. An encounter with one's origins."

A silhouette was running along the riverbank, and then crouched down behind a pile of abandoned crates. The driver of the water taxi shouted in his direction. A tall man appeared. He was wearing a green polo shirt and his face was painted red. A boar's tooth had been driven through his nasal septum. In his right hand he held an ancient automatic rifle, a Colt MI6, which must have done service in the Vietnam War.

The driver headed for the pontoon that had been thrown across the river. A crowd of men had gathered, all armed with guns. Their faces were covered in fearsome paint. De Palma felt a knot in his stomach. He had never seen war close to, or faced savagery in the eyes of his fellow human beings. He felt he was just a plaything in the hands of these warriors. For the time being no-one seemed to be paying him any attention, but there were fierce exchanges between the men, falling like so many blows from a hatchet.

"You don't need to be afraid," a voice said behind the Baron. He turned round swiftly.

Lieutenant Somare stood right behind him. "Don't be afraid, the war is over."

De Palma looked Somare up and down. "I've never been so pleased to see another cop!"

"Your life is not in danger. This is a tribal war."

De Palma eyed the automatic weapons that the men held dangling.

"In the past they used spears and arrows. These days when they fight it's bursts of automatic weapons."

"And the government does nothing?"

"This type of war has always existed. Sadly . . ."

Somare went up to the group of men and said a few words to the one who appeared to be their leader. The man's bulging eyes were rimmed with red. He couldn't have slept for days. His shoulder had been grazed by a bullet. As he answered Somare, he turned towards a hill overlooking the river, covered in tall grass. Thin, acacia-like trees stood out against the cloudy sky.

"The war is over," Somare said. "They have killed two of the enemy and that is the reparation they were seeking."

"How long did it last?"

"Three months."

"And you let them carry on?"

Somare did not reply. He climbed into his battered old Land Rover and signalled to de Palma to join him. The barefooted driver in shorts seemed an outsider in that setting. A SIG automatic pistol lay on the dashboard. It was a recent model: 9mm calibre.

They drove through the coffee plantations for quite a while. A tractor had gone headfirst down a ravine. Some pallets and an old cart had been thrown across the road to form a barrier, and then pushed back to one side.

"I'm from this area," Somare said, without taking his eyes off the side of the road. "I knew Christian a bit before he went off to France."

"Why didn't you tell me before that you knew him?"

"Because of my bosses. I preferred to follow you."

The children hanging round a red corrugated iron shed watched them go by. One of them climbed on the shaft of a trailer and raised his arms in a sign of victory. Everything seemed to have come to a halt because of the war.

"At first Christian wanted to develop this region; then he changed his mind. He became a sort of politician campaigning for his people's identity and a return to the traditional way of life. He is opposed to tourism and against the exploitation of Papuans."

"But war is also traditional!"

"Christian isn't very clear about that. He told me one day it was a custom that needed to be forgotten about, or perhaps replaced with sport. Another time he told me that in the end it was a good thing because you could never stop men from fighting wars."

Hectares of coffee plantations stretched away in serried rows. At the end of each row of small trees, crates had been put out ready for the harvest.

"There won't be much coffee this year," Somare said, sighing. "Everything has rotted in the ground. The beans have gone black now and it has rained on them."

"Because of the war?"

The policeman nodded without taking his eyes off the fields curving elegantly over the hilly contours. In the distance the peaks were disappearing into the clouds. Mount Hagen wasn't very far away; over 4,000 metres at its peak.

Before reaching the village they came across more armed men; their faces painted in garish colours. Some were barefoot; others wore old trainers. An old man appeared at the entrance to a wooden house. A yellow penis gourd looped down from his wrinkled stomach. Some women had formed a circle in front of a grocer's shop. The driver of the Land Rover drove round the central square, leaving a circular trail in the red earth and almost running over a black pig rooting about in a muddy puddle.

"Christian lives in the house at the end of the square," Somare said, jumping out.

"How long is it since you left this village?" de Palma asked.

"About ten years," Somare replied, "but I often come back."

Christian's house was the nicest one: a bungalow with a flat roof and wide casement windows. It was surrounded by greenery: a lush lawn and bushes with large red and purple flowers. The gate was painted black; the low walls surrounding the garden had been white-washed. A large woman in a sky-blue apron stood in the entrance, near the glass door.

"We would like to see Christian," Somare said.

"Christian has gone," the woman replied.

"Since when?"

She didn't reply.

Somare glanced inside the house. Through the living-room window rattan chairs could be seen, placed around a low table on which stood a mat and an empty flowerpot.

"Where is Christian?"

"He fled because of the war. They were after him. Everyone said he was a troublemaker."

"Why?" de Palma asked.

"It was him that wanted the crafts co-op and all these coffee plantations," Somare said, "and then he stopped looking after things. It was a mess. He promised everyone mountains of gold. He made people think that the coffee would sell, that if things were going to work we needed to make an alliance with our enemies. A lot of people here believed in that . . . And then one day, as I told you, he changed tack and said we needed to do something else."

"Was he the cause of the war?"

"People started fighting because of him and his lot."

"What do you mean?"

335

"When his father came here he brought us more into contact with the outside world. Then he came back in the 1960s, and Christian was born. He's not really one of us. He thought he understood us, but he is mixed-race and he grew up mainly in France and Port Moresby. After he came back from Europe his father used to send him big sums of money, but they never saw each other. When Monsieur Robert died he got these strange ideas in his head."

De Palma noticed a new building at the other end of the square. It had been destroyed by a fire. It had happened fairly recently. Charred beams had collapsed on the ground. Some children were playing in the rubble. One of them was brandishing the remains of a wooden mask.

"That's Christian's co-op," Somare said, pointing at the ruins. "It was burned down by men from around here."

The two policemen crossed the square. A small crowd gathered around them. Their expressions were hostile. De Palma suddenly felt that these men, who had been engaged in a senseless war for weeks, were directing their anger at him. Somare had to calm tempers several times. De Palma stepped into the cooperative. The fire had spared the metal workbenches and some tools that had buckled in the heat.

"They are angry with Christian and with all white people," the Papuan policeman said.

"Why?"

"He did something that shocked everyone. No-one can forgive him for it."

Somare looked around him. The men seemed to understand what he was saying. One of them, a man with muscles taut as straps shouted what seemed like threats. De Palma heard Ballancourt and Christian's names being mentioned.

"He displayed skulls in the church."

"What was he trying to do?"

336

Somare kicked the ashes, wet from the recent rains. "He wanted to avoid all of this. He wanted peace."

Somare lit a cigarette. There was a deep sadness in his expression. "He thought that the presence of these skulls would have a big effect on people. Because the skulls are never supposed to leave the house of the dead and they built their church on the site of that ancient house."

An old Toyota Estate crossed the square. Three men were sitting in the front. A fourth was in the back, with his head down. The barrels of their weapons hung out of the doors. No-one looked at them.

Suddenly an old man came forward, shouting, "Monsieur Robert! Monsieur Robert!"

Somare interpreted what he said. "You came here with your money and your strange ideas. You discovered us and then you abandoned us. Look at our poverty now. Because of the skull my son died in the war."

The group stood back to let the old man through. He had been crying, his leathery cheeks were still wet. He was wearing a rainbow-coloured woolly hat.

"Christian come back this village, my hands kill him!" he shouted in broken English, planting himself in front of de Palma.

De Palma looked away. He did not know what to say. Nothing came to mind. Words were superfluous; utterly useless. All he wanted to do was run away from this devastation.

"A good part of the co-op's money was used to buy weapons. From Australia."

"I saw cannabis plantations too, just before we reached the village," de Palma replied. "I imagine that the money they get from drugs is used for weapons."

"You're right about that. It's the same logic as everywhere else."

The authorities allowed it to happen. Most policemen were bent. The arms trade was profitable and people raked in their commission at every stage. It was in no-one's interest that the tribal wars should come to an end. What was Somare's role in this trade? De Palma believed that he was honest.

"Do you have any idea where Christian might be?"

"No idea at all," replied the policeman. "Perhaps in Port Moresby. He must be trying to escape. Australia?"

The Toyota with the three men in it came hurtling back after an hour and skidded to a halt in the centre of the square. The men got out and opened the back of the pick-up. A bloody head jutted out. The men started shouting.

"What are they saying?"

Somare remained silent for a moment. "It's Christian's body that's in the back of the car. Make sure you don't say anything."

Christian's face was barely recognizable. He must have been dragged along the ground. His lips were torn. His skin was tanned, his reddish hair slightly curly. He was a handsome man who had looked after himself, with blue flannel trousers and an expensive polo shirt. His slender fingers must have scraped along the ground as they dragged him: the nails were bent back. His hands were bunched up and his eyes still open. Christian seemed to be asking for forgiveness. Unspeakable pain was written across his bloodied face.

Somare searched the body. His wallet was in his back pocket. The policeman opened it and found a driving licence and a woman's photograph on the laminated back.

"Do you know her? She's European."

The Baron's heart sunk when he caught sight of the young face. "Her name is Bérénice Delorme."

"The art dealer you spoke about?"

"Yes." He wanted to add that Bérénice had withheld her love from a Papuan and it had driven him mad with rage. He wanted to say that Kaïngara had spared the woman he loved, but the words stayed inside him, left unsaid.

338

Bessour and Maistre had phoned him the day before. Bérénice had disappeared without a trace.

"Your investigation ends here, Monsieur de Palma," Somare said. "Justice has been done."

"Killing the killer has never been justice. Never!"

The Baron looked away and walked back to the charred buildings. In a corner of the workshop one statue had survived the disaster. The flames had eaten part of the wood, giving its mouth a ferocious look. De Palma looked up. Through a collapsed wall he could see the lines of coffee trees. Two men were walking at the end of a row: white men. One of them was tall with a worn-out hat that gave him the look of an old explorer. The other had tied a mud spattered jacket round his waist.

"Who are those men?" de Palma asked, turning back towards Somare. "Those two white men over there . . ."

Somare frowned and scanned the lines of coffee trees. "I can't see anyone," he said, then added, "you shouldn't look."

"Why?"

"Because this is where the Ghost Road ends. Anyone who sees a spirit here is in great danger."

When the sun went behind the high mountains, Kaïngara's body was laid out on his bed. A portrait of his mother stood on the bedside table: Agnès looked at her lifeless son with mournful eyes.

De Palma kept watch over the dead man for a long while, and then left shortly before nightfall. For the first time in a long while he felt a deep sadness, as though a heavy wave had borne him up and was pushing him towards the abyss. He knew nothing about philosophy, or the distant world of the great thinkers. At that moment he hated travelling and explorers. He hated himself.

A single sentence came to mind: the quotation that Kaïngara had written on a card and left on the forehead of that robber of souls, Voirnec.

The barbarian is first and foremost the one who believes in barbarism.

As night fell two men took up position by Kaïngara's body. Their faces were painted in fearsome mourning colours.

"They have been initiated," Somare said.

The two men played the long lament of the sacred flutes until the early hours: the voice of the spirits whose origins may never be known.

No-one ever found the skulls of Robert Ballancourt and Fernand Delorme.

XAVIER-MARIE BONNOT has a PhD in History and Sociology, and two Masters degrees in History and French Literature. He is the author of *The First Fingerprint* and *The Beast of the Camargue*. *The Voice of the Spirits* was the winner of the 2011 Crystal Feather award for crime writing.

JUSTIN PHIPPS is a translator who translates from French and Russian into English. After studying modern languages and social anthropology, he has worked in overseas development and as a solicitor specializing in employment law.

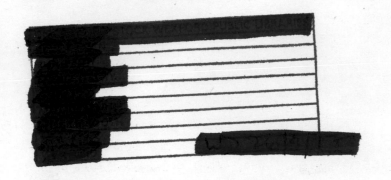